DEMONS

OF

DIVINE

WRATH

A NOVEL

By

EDWARD IZZI

DEMONS OF DIVINE WRATH

Third Edition – July 2020.

ISBN 978-108-414-34-01

AUTHOR'S DISCLAIMER

This book, "Demons of Divine Wrath," is a complete work of fiction. All names, characters, businesses, places, events, references, and incidents are either the products of the author's imagination or are used in a fictitious manner to tell the story. Any references to real-life characters or events are used purely as a false means of reciting a narrative, for enjoyment purposes only.

The author makes no claims of any real-life inferences or actual events, other than to narrate a fabricated story with a fictitious plot. Any resemblance to real persons, living or dead, or actual events is purely coincidental or used for entertainment purposes.

ABOUT THE AUTHOR

Edward Izzi is a native of Detroit, Michigan, and is a Certified Public Accountant, with a successful accounting firm in suburban Chicago, Illinois. He is the father of four grown children, and one incredible granddaughter, Brianna.

He has written many poems and stories over the years, including the fiction thrillers:

Of Bread & Wine (2018)

A Rose from The Executioner (2019)

Demons of Divine Wrath (2019)

Quando Dormo (When I Sleep) (2020)

El Camino Drive (2020)

His novels and writings are available at www.edwardizzi.com.

He currently lives in Chicago, Illinois, far away from the wrath of any demons.

For Gianna, Robby, Matt & Stefano

Watching you all grow up, from the very minute you were born until now, has made me so very proud.

You've all become incredible adults.

Being your father has been an amazing journey.

CHAPTER ONE

The traffic on Michigan Avenue was quite heavy that sunny, December afternoon, as shoppers were bustling everywhere to scurrying through each popular store and retail shops to finish their Christmas shopping. The weather was rather mild for a December day, as the snow had already melted from the last weekend's snowfall. Every shopper was in the Christmas spirit, as the blaring holiday music was playing everywhere along the exclusive, gold-laden sidewalks of Chicago's most elite boulevard. Several carolers were singing 'Deck the Halls' on the corner of Randolph and Michigan Avenues, even though they were being drowned out by the Salvation Army volunteers loudly ringing charity bells on every other street corner.

Don Carlo Marchese was downtown in the Chicago Loop doing some last-minute Christmas shopping on that day, as he knew he wouldn't have time to finish before Christmas Eve in a few days. He usually had his associates finish his last-minute items but needed to visit his friend at his favorite jewelry store over on South Wabash. There was a special gift that he needed to buy for his forty-five-year-old girlfriend, Caroline Tortorici. There was a unique string of pearls that his friend, Ralph Zupo, the owner of Goldstein Jewelers, was holding for him. Of course, Don Carlo had to make sure that this particular gift was the right one. He had just spent over $20,000 in cash for his girlfriend's gift, as they were celebrating their tenth Christmas holiday season together. He was confident that he could bring that kind of currency into his friend's jewelry store without having a problem.

Don Marchese was an older, distinguished gentleman in his early seventies, with slicked-back gray hair and a moderate five-foot, ten-inch frame. He prided on taking excellent care of himself, was an avid walker, and religiously followed a vegan diet. Don Marchese sacrificed and refrained from eating red meat, bread, and especially, his beloved pasta dishes years ago. His blood pressure and prior cardiac problems seemed to be a curse that he had inherited from previous generations of his Roman ancestors. Don Marchese was dressed in a plaid pair of checkered pants, brown leather shoes, and a white shirt, wearing a worn-out, green winter jacket. He was not a flashy, over-the-top Mafioso who 'dressed to the nines.' Quite the opposite. Dressing as a vagabond was his public disguise. He enjoyed staying under the radar, and if anyone ever met him judging by his appearance, they would never guess who he was.

He had already shopped for his wife, Angela, his three daughters, and his five grandchildren, and only had his girlfriend left to shop for. Besides his family's gifts, he would usually fill their stockings with envelopes for those he may have forgotten or neglected to buy gifts for this Christmas. He also made a special 'busta' for all his daughters and grandchildren to put into their holiday stockings as well, usually just a cheap Christmas card with $1,000 in large bills stuffed inside.

His driver picked him up at the corner of Randolph and Michigan Avenue as instructed, as the black, older model Buick pulled up and double-parked in the middle of the busy boulevard. Don Marchese then quickly entered the car. He had a date later with Caroline at the Dei Amore Trattoria on North Hubbard Street, where they had planned to exchange gifts since he would be with his family at Christmas.

"Paolo stop and park at the Blackstone, please. I need to change and drop off a few things," he instructed his chauffeur.

Don Marchese had leased a two thousand square foot luxury suite on the eighteenth floor of the Blackstone Hotel, which he rented and paid for in cash every month. This suite was his 'home away from home' when he wasn't living in his opulent Sauganash, five thousand square foot mansion. The Don spent a considerable amount of time there while he was downtown doing business. He also gave a key to his girlfriend Caroline, where the two of them set up housekeeping whenever they needed privacy. He also conducted his 'family meetings' at the Blackstone, where he was often required to oversee family business matters.

As Paolo dropped off him off in front of the Blackstone Hotel, Don Carlo grabbed several gift bags and items from the trunk of his car and entered the hotel lobby. After exchanging holiday greetings with the hotel doorman and the elevator operator, he opened his hotel suite room 1821, clumsily dropping a few items in the hallway. Don Carlo fumbled with his keys as the Mafioso tried to juggle all his bags and enter his hotel room. He removed his winter jacket after dropping his bags on the floor and quickly used the bathroom. After several minutes, he then went into the bedroom and changed his shirt and pants, as his attire needed to be more fashionable for the Italian restaurant where he was meeting his girlfriend.

As he exited his hotel bedroom, he suddenly heard a deep voice call out his name from behind. He then felt a Beretta pistol being pointed directly up against the back of his head.

"Don Marchese...Happy Holidays," was all the voice said, as another man grabbed his arms from behind and handcuffed his hands. He was quickly blindfolded, gagged, and his ankles were tied.

A twelve-foot rope serving as a noose was fastened around his neck. While he violently struggled, the two men forcefully escorted him over to the eighteenth story window in the bedroom. Don Marchese was trying so desperately to talk and formulate words with the handkerchief gag tightly wrapped around his mouth.

The other end of the rope was securely tied to the foot of the bed, and the bedroom windows were opened wide, exposing the noisy, holiday traffic down below. They knew that the violent jerk of the rope around the Marchese's neck would instantaneously kill him when they quickly pushed him out of the window. The two men planned to casually leave his hotel room and take the stairwell to their getaway car outside. One of the men grabbed a chair and stood behind Don Carlo, holding him steady in front of the window ledge.

The two men then lifted the older Mafioso onto the ledge of the window, standing erectly, facing Michigan Avenue down below. The rope around his neck began to jerk the foot of the king-size bed, abruptly pulling it towards the bedroom wall as Marchese continued to struggle.

Just before pushing Don Marchese out of the eighteenth-floor window of the Blackstone Hotel, one of the men loudly said these final words:

"His Holiness sends his regards."

CHAPTER TWO

The newsroom at the Chicago Sun-Times was especially loud that late afternoon, as everyone was trying to make their news article deadline for the morning addition. My Subway turkey sandwich with extra mayo was still sitting at the corner of my desk, wrapped and untouched. It was getting old and stale, as I was far too busy to even break for lunch that day. For some odd reason, although it had been a slow, newsworthy month of December in our newsroom, I was busy. But I was also fearful that my dear editor was going to pull me off of my downtown beat and have me start answering 'Dear Santa' letters.

Being a veteran reporter with the Chicago Sun-Times for over thirty years, my editor usually gave me my pick of the newsworthy stories that I was interested in covering. Other than the standard south-side gang bangers and the occasional drive-by shootings, nothing exciting was going on in the City of Chicago. It was as though all the thugs and hoodlums were 'good for Santa' for the holidays. I was getting the impression that all the criminals, low-lifes, and mafia 'wanna-be's' were holding off on the homicides and waiting to dump their victim's bodies into Lake Michigan until after the New Year.

I had been working on a Mayoral Election City Hall piece, writing and interviewing all of the enumerate candidates that were running for Chicago Mayor in the coming primary elections. It seemed like everybody was running for mayor in this damn town, with eighteen mayoral candidates in all, and the paper wanted me to do a short biography on every one of them. As unexciting as all of that was, I was preoccupied and in my 'writing zone' when my desk phone rang.

"Crawford here."

"Paulie, you gotta minute?" It was my assistant editor, trying to talk to me with his mouth full, as usual.

"Sure, Mike, I'll be right there."

My assistant editor, Mike Daudelin, was a no-nonsense, pull-no-punches kind of guy who always went to bat for me when I was jammed up on a story. He was a six-foot, five-inch, 310-pound former Michigan State University linebacker, and he was a good man to have on your side. He was always there to push for me and 'pinch-hit' when I needed to get something past the editor when covering a news subject. I had worked for him since the 9-11 terrorist attack story broke in 2001, and we had developed a mutually respectful relationship over the many years of working together.

I walked into his office and noticed the same Subway sandwich bag sitting on the far corner of his desk as well when he asked me to come in and shut the door.

"How was the sandwich?" I asked Mike, who was still picking at his lunch at three-thirty in the afternoon.

"Very stale and dry, like my ex-wife," he responded.

"Too much information, Chief." I smiled as I sat down in front of his disheveled, inordinate desk. It was crowded with papers, files, scattered books, lunch bags, and an empty McDonald's drink cup, probably from yesterday's lunch. It was no wonder he could even find his lunch on his desk, let alone eat it.

"What's up?" I eagerly asked as he was dusting off the breadcrumbs from his black pants and his freshly coffee-stained white shirt.

"I'm pulling you off the City Hall beat, for now, Paul. Something big has come up, and I need you on it."

"Something bigger and more exciting than writing sleepy biographies on every irrelevant candidate running for Mayor of Chicago? Come on, Chief. I was starting to have fun."

Daudelin started to chuckle.

"You *do* wanna answer letters to Santa, don't you?" he joked.

"You're getting me excited here, Chief." I always tried to get under his skin by calling him 'Chief jokingly'.

Daudelin finished wiping his hands on his white shirt and started fidgeting with his computer mouse.

"There's a dead wise-guy dangling out the window over at the Blackstone," he said matter-of-factly.

I looked at him a little confused at first, as there was a five-second delay in my brain-processing.

"A dead wise-guy? Who?" I curiously asked.

Daudelin looked at me directly now, "The eighteenth floor of the Blackstone Hotel; it looks like a mob hit."

At first, I didn't take him seriously, as I only shook my head and laughed at my editor. He was known for his tasteless, practical jokes from time-to-time and made no secret of being a very frustrated comedian. I immediately figured he was pulling my leg and thought Mike was trying hard to push off those "Santa Letters" on me.

"A mob hit? Oh goody, goody," I played along.

It had been a long time since we had a decent mob hit in this town, as I was starting to believe that all the Chicago mobsters were all getting either too old or too soft.

"You're not gonna guess who?" Mike was replying with a smile, although I thought he wasn't serious.

"Well, Tony Accardo and Sam Giancana are already dead, so cross them off," I joked.

A five-second delay, as my editor was having fun with my curiosity.

"Okay, I give up...who is it?" I figured I would play along with his stupid joke, still believing he wasn't serious.

Another five-second delay.

"Carlo Marchese," he finally said with a smile.

13

"You're kidding?" I exclaimed, suddenly realizing he wasn't joking.

"Carlo Marchese? The Capo? The Mafioso from the North Side? Seriously?"

I couldn't believe Don Carlo was dead, as I had just seen him at a charity function at the Palmer House a month ago. He was with another woman that evening, and everybody knew he was there with his much younger girlfriend and not his wife.

Carlo Marchese was a very well-known Chicago mobster and was the head of a large crime family on the Northside of Chicago. He was a low-key, down-to-earth, wise guy who prided himself on staying under the radar. The man boasted that he never spent a night in jail. It had been ages since Don Marchese had said or done anything that made it into the six o'clock news or in the papers. He was usually being driven around town in his black, traditional, four-door Buick. The car was an older model, and it was typically dirty. It was a rare occasion when his chauffer took the Marchese's car to a carwash.

Don Marchese made his millions in the garbage and disposal business, and he did a great job of playing 'nice' with everyone, including the local politicians. I had met him several times. He was very respectful and always a gentleman. From talking with him on the many occasions that I had, I got the impression that he probably didn't have an enemy in the world.

Being an experienced reporter, I had encountered more than my share of Mafia hoods in this town, and Carlo Marchese didn't fit the bill.

He wasn't your typical, flashy, old school wise guy. Marchese never flaunted his money and influence around town and was well known for keeping his variant business affairs on the down-low.

In other words, he was a quiet, cheap, old bastard.

I once saw him coming out of an upscale restaurant on the north side of Chicago and handing over a new, crisp, one-dollar bill to the valet after he brought up his Buick Skylark. He was proudly wearing a pair of white shoes that had gone out of style back in the seventies, and an old, black raincoat that looked like he had stolen from a donation dumpster. If there was a category for 'cheap, unassuming mobsters who 'dressed like shit,' Carlo Marchese was its poster boy. Chicago Crain's had once estimated his net worth at over a billion dollars in business investments and real estate holdings, which probably included every dollar of his first communion money.

He ran very profitable bookmaking and 'juice-loan' business and had most of his full-time Teamsters driving around in garbage trucks making collections. He also had his hands in some illegal offshore betting sites that he oversaw. He was involved in numerous real estate partnerships and developments in and around the city and had intense political connections in Building and Permits Department at City Hall. I was wondering how many of Chicago's aldermen were going to receive 'special Christmas cards' this holiday season.

I had heard through the grapevine that Marchese kept his chauffer around because he didn't know how to drive. When he did get behind the wheel, he would bang into fire-hydrants and garbage cans. His driving skills could give 'Mr. Magoo' a run for his money. I also heard he didn't like carrying around a concealed weapon because he had never fired a gun in his life. Seeing that his chauffer doubled as his gorilla-bodyguard, keeping him around was a good idea.

"What time did this happen?" I eagerly asked.

"About a half-hour ago. I got a call from dispatch on the police blotter. Why don't you run over there and check it out?"

"Got it, Chief," as I quickly got up from his desk, still waiting for the reality of a Chicago mob hit to settle in.

"Take Cunningham with you and get some pictures," referring to the Sun-Times photographer.

"Okay, Chief." I knew my editor loved it when I called him that, as he enjoyed pretending, he was Perry White from the Daily Planet.

I grabbed my suit coat and my backpack, which always included my portable laptop and a couple of small writing tablets. I met Mike Cunningham downstairs in the lobby, and we grabbed a cab from the Sun-Times building over to the Blackstone Hotel.

The whole block of South Michigan Avenue was blocked off by several police cars, from Harrison to Balbo Streets, as we were trying to penetrate through the squad car blockade and get into the Blackstone. As we were walking southbound, I had approached my buddy detective, Tommy Morton, from the Sixteenth District, who was outside talking with another patrolman.

"What do we have, Tommy?"

"Mr. Paul Crawford," as he extended out his hand. "I thought the Sun-Times retired your old ass?" At the ripe old age of 54, I was far from ready for retirement.

"You wish," I smiled, as I watched the detective finish up his cigarette and flick it off in the air.

"How did we get a mob guy to hang himself from the eighteenth floor?" I sarcastically asked.

"No, Paulie, this looks like a mob-hit. All-day long."

"Really?" I replied in a snarky voice, as they were pulling the covered body on a stretcher out of the hotel lobby and placing him in a Cook County Coroners truck.

"Was he dead at the scene?"

"Oh yeah, he was killed instantly. He was dangling from the eighteenth floor, with a rope tied around his neck. It was attached to the bedpost up in Room 1821. Seemed Marchese had a private hotel suite here at the Blackstone. We think the killer or killers originally intended to make this look like a suicide. But the victim's hands and legs were handcuffed, and he was wearing a mouth gag," Morton explained. "He must have put up a fight, so they cuffed and gagged him."

"So why didn't they just throw him off of the ledge and be done with it? Why did they bother hanging him outside of the hotel window?" I asked.

"Good question, Paulie. That's why I think it was a mob hit. They wanted Marchese to suffer, and they probably wanted to hang his body out for display on Michigan Avenue."

"Really?" I was taking down some notes, as Cunningham was taking some pictures of the still open window of the eighteenth floor of the Blackstone.

"Can we go upstairs and get some pictures?" I asked.

"Go ahead, if you can get through all of the top brass hanging out at the lobby."

There had to be two dozen policemen and squad cars parked everywhere on that block of Michigan Avenue. I maneuvered my way through all the coppers and detectives hanging around and made my way out to the elevator. As we got to the eighteenth floor, several more policeman was investigating the crime scene in Room 1821. The Chicago CSI team was also there dusting for prints, and there were a few crime scene photographers taking pictures in the bedroom.

As Detective Morton had stated, there was a rope tied to the foot of the king-size bed, which looked to have been pulled toward the window. Some of the detectives were dusting for prints around the room, and although there was a lot of detail to dust for, there wasn't anything blatantly unusual about the crime scene. I overheard one of the detectives mentioning that the Blackstone Hotel suite was one of the hotel's more private luxury rooms, which was only rented out to exclusive, VIP customers and guests of the hotel. Knowing Marchese's personality of throwing around his quarters like manhole covers, it

17

seemed unusual for me to believe that Marchese would rent out such opulent digs.

I saw another one of my detective buddy's taking notes and interviewing hotel staff in the hallway, and I approached him with a few questions.

"Detective Dorian," I exclaimed as I saw him talking one of the hotel maids.

"What's up, Crawford?" as we shook hands.

"What's your take on this? Think it was a mob hit?" I asked him.

He looked at me rather coldly, not feeling sure about whether he should be volunteering anything to the media. When it came to getting any information from Detective Philip Dorian while doing a news story, he was definitely on the stingy side.

"Not sure," he slowly answered. "This was a hit, alright. But not sure who ordered it. All the crime families in Chicago have been getting along and playing nice these last few years. We haven't had a mob ordered hit in a long time in this town."

'Yeah, I know," as I agreed with Dorian's assessment.

"Any suspects?" I asked him, knowing that I was talking out of turn.

"None that we want you to publish," he answered in a sarcastic voice.

"So, I can assume you'll be hauling down a long list of wise guys over to your district, correct Detective?"

"Look," as he seemed to be getting perturbed. "All we know right now is that we have a homicide. We're not going to have a parade of wise-guys lining up anywhere if that's what you're asking, Crawford," Dorian impatiently replied. "I'm still not sure what this is right now. Dangling a 'family capo' out of the window of a Michigan Avenue hotel room is not the style of any Chicago Mafiosi's that I'm aware of," Dorian said.

"Did you look at the surveillance tapes from the hotel lobby and elevator?"

"We're still researching and reviewing the tapes. We should have more answers once we investigate and review those," he said.

"Thanks, Detective."

I wrote down a few more notes while Cunningham took some more pictures. I figured I had enough for a front-page story and could elaborate that the Chicago P.D. was still suspicious of this murder being anything but a mob hit. I just thought I would make a few more phone calls to some of my 'mobbed up' friends and see if any of them can give me some more information on this homicide.

Little did I know at the time that the murder of Don Carlo Marchese on that warm December day was anything *but* a mob ordered hit.

Far from it.

CHAPTER THREE

THE ART DEALER – CHICAGO, SUMMER 2018

It was a beautiful Saturday afternoon on that last day of June last summer, as Wolfgang Schmidt was closing his storefront art dealership on North Wells Street. He was looking forward to meeting his wife, Dora, and their oldest daughter Lisa, for dinner later that evening at the posh Italian restaurant, Andiamo, located at 1437 North Clark Street. They had been planning and putting together a backyard birthday party for his granddaughter, Emily, at their expansive mansion in Winnetka and needed to meet with the restaurant manager about catering to the party later that summer. This was their only grandchild, and they wanted her first birthday party on July 30th to be an extraordinary one.

Schmidt had an established art dealership, Kunstgeschäft, at 524 North Wells Street. His grandfather, Hans Schmidt, had opened the store back in 1927 and has been an established art dealer of fine art for over ninety years. As an art dealer and international collectibles broker, Schmidt has traveled the world in search of expensive, valuable artwork and invaluable art pieces which he bought and sold to museums across the country and in Europe. His family was well established and world-renowned for their exceptional art expertise.

As an active art and collectibles broker within the art world, Wolfgang Schmidt has participated in almost every major art auction within the United States and Europe, buying and selling expensive artworks from established artists across the globe, spanning from high-priced, art masterpieces from Pablo Picasso's and Henri Matisse's to Edouard Manet's and Vincent Van Gogh's. Wolfgang Schmidt was a significant buyer and seller of fine art within the Midwest and especially in the

Chicagoland area. Every major museum or collector looking for art had Schmidt's store on speed dial.

But the Schmidt Family legacy had some other skeletons in their past that not even Wolfgang chose to talk about, and was not well known to anyone outside of the family. His grandfather, Hans, was a Nazi sympathizer here in the United States and had direct contact with many of the 'Schutzstaffel' or SS officers who were high within the realm of The Fuehrer, Adolf Hitler. His allegiance to The Fuehrer was legendary, as he did everything that he could to assist Nazi Germany in their quest for world domination during the Second World War. When the Nazis began stealing and robbing museums of their priceless artwork, it was Hans Schmidt who assisted the Nazis in storing and keeping some of these expensive art pieces from the rest of the world after the war. Schmidt found buyers and art collectors in Venezuela, Brazil, Argentina, New York, and in Chicago, to keep and hold these expensive pieces on consignment for safekeeping. Many of these temporary owners would hold these stolen masterpieces until the actual fair market values of these valuable excellent artworks could be introduced back into the art world at their appraised fair market value.

Within the last few years, many art galleries throughout Europe have made several requests. They have appealed to the German government to assist them in returning some of the fine art that was stolen from their museums during the Second World War. The German government was neither sympathetic nor useful to these various European museums, as requests related to these thefts and crimes were well past any statute of limitations. They officially had no idea of any of the Nazi crimes committed during the Second World War. But in reality, these valuable pieces of art were directly shipped by the Germans in 1944, to South American destinations like Caracas, Buenos Aries, San Paolo, Rio De Janeiro, Lima, and other far off ports of call.

Throughout his lifetime, Hans Schmidt had overseen the safekeeping and black-market sale of over 1,000 works of art from museums like Paris, Milan, Genoa, Warsaw, and other European art galleries. These stolen cultural artworks now had an estimated value above several billion dollars.

As an art dealer who dealt in fine stolen art for the Nazis from Europe, he sold these valuable European pieces of art to various art collectors around the world after the war. As a result, the Schmidt family made millions, and it is said that the Schmidt family has direct access and knows the whereabouts of over eighty percent of many of the still missing European masterpieces stolen by the Nazi's.

However, the Schmidt family also paid dearly for the exclusive access to those stolen works of art. In 1959, Hans Schmidt was found murdered in the basement of his art store, supposedly for an arms-length transaction gone bad. He was hanging by the neck from the rafters of his stores' basement. He had been stabbed several times, and his body was severely mutilated. Back then, the Chicago Police Department automatically knew that it was a mob hit, as it was rumored that Schmidt had fallen in disfavor with Chicago Mob Boss Salvatore "Momo" Giancana, in an art deal gone south.

His father, Urs Schmidt, narrowly escaped an early death in 1972 when the Cadillac Eldorado he was driving exploded at a Dunkin' Donuts parking lot. It was found that the car bomb had misfired while he had gone inside to get coffee that early morning. It was also rumored that many of these former Nazis had come out of hiding to lay claim to those expensive stolen art pieces, for which only Schmidt knew of their location.

Although the Schmidt family had made a deal with the Nazis that they would only 'hold on consignment' these stolen pieces of Renaissance European art, they also quickly realized that 'possession was ninety percent of the law". The Schmidt family held up their middle finger to these former Nazi's and had no problem reselling these expensive artworks back to these German art collectors for a substantial profit, which also created a lot of dangerous animosities.

It is also believed that deep down within the basement of their North Wells Street art store, belays a large safe which contains a listing of the expansive inventory of stolen European museum artworks, indicating which piece is on consignment, and every stolen art painting's exact location. After his father ran the Chicago art dealership for three decades, he turned the business over to his son Wolfgang, who is now the sole owner and keeper of these stolen art secrets. This now made him a significant person to anyone interested in buying, selling, and dealing with expensive artwork and treasured Nazi stolen masterpieces.

Wolfgang Schmidt was a valuable person indeed.

CHAPTER FOUR

There was a soft, steady drizzle of rain on that summer day last July in Munich, as the drab, gray clouds continued to dampen that dreary Sunday morning. The scattered water puddles continued to make loud, splashing noises as the city traffic passed over the all the unrepaired, potholed streets. There were a significant number of cars bustling through the Bavarian capital on that misty, grey morning.

Hermann Kalkschmidt, an older man in his early eighties, had just arrived home from the Munich Farmer's Market and was struggling with his umbrella as he fumbled with his keys to open the front door of his apartment building. He had just attended morning mass at St. Ludwig Munchen Catholic Church and walked over to the market to pick up some fruit and vegetables for his early afternoon lunch. He lived several blocks away from Ludwigstrabe Street and walked every Sunday morning to eight o'clock mass before going to the nearby town square to do his grocery and produce shopping.

Kalkschmidt was in excellent shape and looked a youthful eighty-one years young. He didn't own a car and walked or took public transportation everywhere. Most everything that he needed was within blocks of his urban Munich apartment. When he needed to go anywhere long distance, he usually took a taxicab or public transportation. He lived alone, had never been married, and always kept to himself.

Except for a few friends from church and a few other acquaintances that knew him around town, he seldom interacted with anyone. He walked to the market, then to the bakery most every morning, and purchased whatever food and grocery items that he needed for that day.

Hermann had a good pension, as he had worked as a government clerk for the waste management department for the City of Munich for forty-five years. He had retired almost fifteen years ago and was able to make ends meet with the money he received from his government pension and investment income each month.

As he climbed up the two flights of stairs to his apartment, he always cursed to himself that he didn't live in an apartment building that had an elevator. He had a difficult time maneuvering his bags of groceries and other items while going up the dark, narrow stairwell. He opened his apartment door, and clumsily placed his grocery items on the kitchen table.

One would believe that with all of his cluttered items crowding his apartment, that Hermann Kalkschmidt was a 'packrat' of sorts. The older man saved nearly everything and only throwing out whatever necessary garbage he incurred. There were papers, books, magazines, and other assorted items strewn everywhere. Old Hermann had a pathway navigated within his two-bedroom apartment where he could negotiate his way around his kitchen, living room, both bedrooms, and his bathroom. The condo had a significant lousy odor, which may have come from the strewn old musty books, documents, and even some unwanted trash that may have gotten lost in his over-packed and littered apartment.

Herr Kalkschmidt was a voracious reader, and spend most of his days reading books, magazines, and newspapers. Although he owned a single television in his living room, he seldom turned it on.

He appreciated the urban silence that his small, cozy apartment offered him there in the middle of the inner-city sprawl of his beloved Munich, a city that he had lived in all his life.

With all of the items packed within his musty old apartment, there was one room that was off-limits to whoever entered or visited him at his home. It was a large bedroom, located in the upstairs attic above his apartment that he kept secured under lock and key. There were three padlocks along with the steel deadbolt that securely fastened the old, solid wooden door, keeping its contents safe from the rest of the world. Kalkschmidt seldom went into the upstairs attic, as he knew the room's valuable items and priceless materials by heart.

These valuable items had been inherited from his father, Klaus, who was once a highly ranked, Nazi German soldier, and had stolen and stashed these precious, priceless objects for the past eighty years. His father was a lieutenant in the Nazi Army and was once the personal secretary and military aide to Heinrich Himmler. Himmler was once the third-ranking highest officer within the Nazi Party, behind Hermann Goring and Adolph Hitler. He was the head of the "Schutzstaffel," or SS Army, Chief of the German police, and Himmler was later named as the Minister of Interior. Himmler was directly responsible and was the 'architect' for the many various concentration camps and oversaw the capturing and transportation of the millions of European Jews that were shipped off to these encampments. He was also very dominant in Nazi Party art acquisitions, or the 'looting' of many of the valuable art pieces and master artworks that were a significant part of the European art galleries and museums of the many countries the Nazis invaded. Herr Klaus Kalkschmidt assisted Himmler and the Nazi Army in hiding and stashing away many of these valuable, priceless works of art to various locations throughout Germany and in South America after the war.

After the end of World War II and the collapse of Nazi Germany, the elder Kalkschmidt immigrated to Argentina for several years until 1953, where he then returned to his family-owned apartment in Munich. In this urban-dwelling, Hermann Kalkschmidt now lives. The younger Kalkschmidt had moved into that apartment to care for his father in 1974. After his death a few years later, he has lived in the old, malodourous apartment ever since.

On that day, Hermann Kalkschmidt had decided to make himself some chicken soup, and he negotiated his way around his overcrowded, overly cluttered kitchen. He chose to stay indoors and finish a book he was reading, rather than go for his usual walk to the Munich public park just seven blocks away. He usually went there on Sunday afternoons when the weather permitted, sat on a park bench and read one of his many books for several hours. The older man spent the afternoon reading his books until almost 9:00 pm. By then, Hermann was exhausted and decided to retire.

Across the street, hiding under a black umbrella, a tall, dark-haired man was keeping watch on Hermann's apartment. He had been following him most of the weekend and had patiently waited for a good time to approach the older adult. It was just after 10:00 pm, and it had stopped raining. The dark, tall stranger had his hand in his pocket, ready to withdraw his Beretta M9 Semi-Automatic 9mm pistol. He had attached the silencer and pushed the safety switch to the on position before approaching the apartment building across the street on that wet, summer evening. The uninvited visitor took out an old plastic credit card and jammed it into the old lock on the apartment building's front door. He then quietly walked up the dark, narrow stairwell, scaling the two flights of stairs, until he encountered the senior citizen's apartment.

The stranger put his ear up against the old, wooden door. He only heard silence, as he took out a pocketknife, and quickly picked the old lock separating Hermann's apartment from the darkened hallway upstairs. He quietly pushed open the front door, as he was sure the squeaky sound of the hinges would alarm the older adult of his presence. But Kalkschmidt was sleeping in his bedroom and didn't hear a sound.

The dark-haired intruder, dressed in a black jacket and black gloves, quietly entered the apartment, holding the gun in his hand. He briefly looked around the living room of the apartment, overwhelmed by the stench and odor of all the mess and clutter.

For some reason, realizing that the old man was probably in his bedroom, the would-be assassin made a decision: The stranger decided to make this 'hit' a very clean, very quiet, and very neat kill. He quietly walked over to the stove, and without lighting the match, he turned the gas knob on high. He then quietly left the apartment, locking the door behind him. The intruder, on his way down the stairs, notices the entrance to the utility room ajar. He thought that this made for a perfect hiding place in case the police immediately were alerted. Looking towards the furnace, he noticed a cheap rubber attachment leading from the main gas line to the building furnace. Taking out his knife, he disconnected the black rubber attachment, allowing the gas to begin escaping from its copper pipes. The intruder then quickly exited the old apartment building.

It was just after 11:30 that evening, and old Hermann briefly got up to go to the bathroom. He was groggy from his brief sleep and was still very tired. After urinating, he negotiated his way back from the bathroom to his overly cluttered bedroom and returned to bed. He couldn't understand why he had such a throbbing headache and did not notice that the gas stove was on. He did not smell the strong gas odor was engulfing his apartment, but like most seniors, Hermann's old age had greatly affected his olfactory senses. As the gas from the stove consumed his apartment, Kalkschmidt did not even bother taking off his bathrobe. He just simply laid back down and closed his eyes.

Wilhelm Guerling, who lived next door to Hermann's apartment, was awakened by a strong, protruding gas smell that very late Sunday evening. Guerling was a lifelong insomniac and usually awakened himself early, often at two or three every morning. He got up and investigated around his apartment, eventually realizing that the strong, 'gasgeruch' was coming from the apartment next door. As he walked out into the hallway, the protruding gas smell was even more potent, coming directly from his neighbor's residence and consuming the entire building. He knocked on Hermann's apartment door several times, loudly banging and pounding on the entranceway, without a response.

Realizing that something was dreadfully wrong, he called the 'Polizei.' Within several minutes, three Munich policemen banged and forcefully opened the apartment front door, finding an open gas stove within the very cluttered, overly packed two-bedroom apartment. They knocked on the doors of the other building tenants and demanded that they immediately leave, as the gas smell was overpowering. The policemen then covered their mouths and noses as they cautiously entered the older man's apartment. After finding their way around the jumbled, excessively littered items strewn everywhere around the 'Wohnung, 'or flat, the officers encountered the old man lying down, lifeless in his bedroom.

29

The 81-year-old Hermann Kalkschmidt was unresponsive, as the officers called an ambulance to assist in reviving him. They placed the older adult on a gurney and rushed him over to the local Munich hospital, where he was later pronounced dead.

Because of how the old man was found in his bedroom sleeping, the 'polizei' ruled his death initially as an accident, not immediately believing that there was any foul play. As the Munich detectives arrived at the apartment to investigate his 'accidental' death, they had a difficult time negotiating their way around the overly littered, cluttered apartment. As they continued to take an assessment of the apartments' contends, they found the closed, securely locked bedroom upstairs in the attic. One of the polizei tried to open it but was reprimanded by one of the detectives that they had to get a court order to pry open the upstairs bedroom door. When the detectives finally got the court order that was needed that morning, they forcefully broke open the three large locks and opened the deadbolt.

As the 'dachgeschoss' or the attic room was opened, the police and detectives could not believe what they had discovered. Within that old musty room, securely locked and hidden away from the rest of the world, were three secured wooden crates stacked from floor to ceiling, stamped with the Italian word '**FIRENZE**' in bold black letters and the Nazi swastika engraved on each box. Each crate had the printed black name and symbol stamped on each wooden container. Upon further investigation, the detectives removed each of the boxes and, with a crowbar, opened each wooden crate.

To their surprise, they soon realized what these were: These were missing stolen art pieces that the Nazis had robbed from the Uffizi Art Gallery in Florence, Italy, back in 1943.

The forty-two priceless oil masterpieces included the works of Raphael, Rembrandt, Donatello, Giotto, Botticelli, Caravaggio, Lippi, and other prominent Renaissance period, artists. Their current, realizable value in today's market was probably in the several millions of euros. The paintings, inside of their wooden crates, were each individually wrapped in dark, plain burlap and stamped with the Nazi symbol. The stacked containers covered up the only shaded window of the attic, prohibiting any light from entering in. They were all neatly set and overwhelming the walls of that attic bedroom, as it took several men to remove these many canvased containers. These priceless crated paintings had not seen the light of day since the Second World War. The musty smell and overwhelming dust protruded over its tarped canvas coverings, making the wooden crates extremely difficult to remove and maneuver. The detective's bright flashlights seemed to be overcome by the room's darkness as they worked in that musty old chamber, lifting and opening each wooden container, one by one by one.

After several hours of investigation and inventorying the hidden attic's contents, Lieutenant Gerhard Hildebrandt, the Munich Detective at the crime scene, called his police desk sergeant and began the conversation: "Sie werden das nicht glauben... "

"You're not going to believe this..."

CHAPTER FIVE

The cobblestoned streets of Florence, Italy, were quiet that early Sunday morning, as the war-torn city had begun to show its wear and tear. It was early September 1943, and the Nazi army had just taken over the occupation of the ancient renaissance city. The resistance forces had fought gallantly against the Nazi's and its fascist regime, suffering severe losses. The 'partigiani,' or the Italian resistance, consisted mostly of anarchists, republicans and especially, devout Catholics. They aided in the war effort primarily by conducting espionage, sabotage, and guerrilla warfare behind enemy lines. These guerrilla soldiers operated deep within the mountains of Tuscany surrounding the ancient city, desperately trying to protect the Florentine region that they loved. There had been a considerable amount of fighting between the partigiani resistance forces and the Axis armies during the previous summer months, with many of its medieval buildings, ancient structures, and landmark bridges destroyed in the process.

Father Angelo Gentile was the pastor of the Basilica Della Santissima Annunziata, located far away from the central part of Florence. He was briskly walking through its piazza to conduct early morning mass for the few parishioners who were bold enough to attend that morning. The old church was a Renaissance-style basilica located on the northeastern side of the medieval city. The landmark cathedral was significantly away from the guerilla warfare and the continuous fighting that was going on in the surrounding town and mountainous areas.

As Florence had just fallen to the Fascist armies with its current manifest of Jewish persecution, Fr. Gentile was considerably apprehensive. He had been asked several months ago by Florence's cardinal, the

Reverend Elio Cardinal Della Croce, to do whatever possible or necessary to help and assist the sizeable Florentine-Jewish population in escaping their capture and abduction by the Nazi's.

It was almost seven o'clock that morning, as Fr. Gentile began to say early Sunday mass for the ninety or more parishioners who had arrived to worship that morning. Among those parishioners, sitting within the last several pews of the church, were several Jewish families, almost seventy in all, there to worship as well in prayer.

In an attempt to escape Nazi abduction and persecution, the Jewish families had been baptized as Catholics by Cardinal Della Croce several weeks ago. They had been instructed to 'religiously' follow the customs and guidelines of the Roman Catholic Church, which included praying, abstinence, acts of penance, the holy sacraments, and the attendance of holy mass every Sunday.

Fr. Gentile, with the aid of Cardinal Della Croce, had been providing housing, food, and clothing to these Jewish families, who had come to the Basilica Santissima Annunziata for sanctuary. The church had a large facility that was previously used as a convent and a school for the nearby children before the war and was a comfortable place for the Jewish refugee families to live until another safe place could be found for them.

Fr. Gentile had just finished distributing Holy Communion to the ninety or more parishioners who were there in attendance when he noticed someone wearing a red 'zucchetto' patiently praying in the very last row of the church. At the end of mass, Fr. Gentile approached him and sat next to him in the last pew.

"Buon Giorno, Your Eminence," as Fr. Gentile kissed his ring.

"Buon Giorno, Fr. Angelo. I truly enjoyed your mass this morning," the Cardinal said.

Cardinal Della Croce was an older man in his late fifties, with graying salt and pepper hair that seemed to blend well with his red cardinal cap and vestments. He was an ardent critic of fascism and made no secret of his opposition against its inhuman philosophies and merciless values. Cardinal Della Croce was entirely instrumental in spiriting away and granting sanctuary to many of Florence's Jews to neutral countries and Allied occupations within Europe.

"Come' va'?" he said in Italian. "How are things going here?" he eagerly asked the Basilica's pastor.

"We could use more food and medicine, Your Eminence. The Nazi's have currently blocked off all the incoming roads and trains coming into Firenze. We barely have enough to take care of the families that we now have," Fr. Gentile explained.

The Cardinal looked at the church pastor with begging eyes, knowing that he was about to make his current burden even more cumbersome.

"Fr. Angelo, I have come here to ask for your help once again. We have five more Jewish families, some thirty people in all, who need sanctuary here in your church. Your parish is the only facility that is large enough to house these misplaced fugitive Jewish families."

The pastor looked at the Cardinal, with an almost shocked look on his face.

"Your Eminence, how will this be possible? We are running out of food and are having difficulty feeding those who are here now," the pastor protested.

The Cardinal thought silently for a few moments.

"I have several farmers within the Tuscan region who have been providing wheat and vegetables to other poor families in the city, and I am sure I can get you more food and supplies from them."

"We have to be careful, Your Eminence. We cannot allow these 'fascisti' to discover and abduct the families

34

we now already have. Bringing in more Jews will only put the others at additional risk," Gentile protested.

"I understand, Father. But we cannot turn these people away. We are their last and only hope. I will bring them late tomorrow evening after dusk, and we will conduct and document their baptism immediately."

Cardinal Della Croce required that all Jewish families seeking sanctuary within the Catholic Church to be immediately baptized as Roman Catholics, which was actively endorsed and encouraged by Pope Pius XII and the Vatican.

"Please, Father, look into your heart."

Fr. Angelo faithfully nodded his head, knowing that it was his ultimate duty to take care of all of God's children, no matter what the cost of that burden. They both rose from the last pew of the church, and the priest escorted Cardinal Della Croce outside, past the old wooden oak doors, down the steps, and into the Piazza Santissima Annunziata. He genuflected and kissed His Eminence's ring, as Della Croce promised him that he would be hearing from him within the next few days.

By the following Tuesday, Cardinal Della Croce sent over thirty-six additional Jewish women and children, hungry and tired, barely wearing the dirty, ragged clothing on their backs. They had traveled from small neighboring towns, some coming from as far as Lucca. These tired mothers with their children were wearing old Nazi army boots and clothing that had been stolen from some of the dead soldiers that had been discovered along the way. Fr. Angelo took them into his makeshift dormitory, passing out used clothing that had been donated by other families within the parish. Cardinal Della Croce had sent over several chickens, some fruits and vegetables that were given from a farmer earlier that day, and they had enough eggs to make a large 'frittata' to feed everyone that evening.

The next morning, Cardinal Della Croce arrived at the basilica and assisted Fr. Angelo in baptizing all the newly arrived Jewish women and children, performing the Roman Catholic Rite of Baptism. They were all anointed, each having other parishioners as their Catholic sponsors, carefully documenting each sacrament. The new baptismal documents were then signed, copied, and registered with the Cardinal and immediately sent to the Vatican registrar's office in Rome.

His Eminence had been going door to door for several weeks within the various villages in a horse-drawn buggy, soliciting help. He had been traveling extensively to the different communities surrounding Florence within the Tuscany valley, asking for food and clothing donations to help feed the hungry Jewish refugees that Fr. Angelo and his parish were supporting.

Early one November morning in 1943, Fr. Angelo had arrived from his rectory apartment to find several Nazi jeeps parked in front of his church. He nervously took out his black beaded rosary and said several prayers before approaching the church steps.

"Are you Father Angelo Gentile?" asked a young, blonde-haired Nazi officer, as he came out of the church's front entrance, escorted by several other uniformed, Nazi officers.

"Yes," the pastor bravely said. "I am Father Angelo."

The Nazi officer glared coldly at the priest for several silent seconds.

"We understand you are hiding Jews here in your church, Father. Do you realize that such a blatant offense in the Third Reich is punishable by death?" the young Nazi proclaimed.

Lieutenant General Gerhard Wilhelm was a young, ambitious Nazi officer of the Third Reich. He had been recently transferred from Berlin to oversee the smooth transition of power within Florence and the

Tuscany region. He had a lot to prove to his superiors, the German 'Wehrmacht' and its associated Nazi officers. Lieutenant Wilhelm was considered extremely ruthless and had no issue with sacrificing human life to uphold the cruel edicts of Nazi Germany.

"That is not correct, Officer," the young priest explained. "We have a homeless shelter here for poor, Catholic refugees here at our church, most who have been displaced by this war, and have looked to me and our church for food, clothing, and a place to sleep."

The young officer glared at the priest. "Catholic refugees, huh?"

Four of the Nazi soldiers walked behind the priest and stood erect, as the Nazi Lieutenant continued to interrogate the church's pastor in front of the church steps.

"I can assure you, Fra' Angelo, that your sheltered guests here at your church are NOT Catholics," he replied. Two of the Nazis grabbed the priest's arms from behind him, as Fr. Angelo hastily dropped the black beaded rosary that he was grasping onto the ground. He was taken into custody and was driven to the make-shift Nazi German headquarters in a temporarily abandoned villa on the outskirts of Florence.

The Nazis frequently took over homes and villas for their use in occupied territories and this case, the old, antiquated farmhouse, and the villa was a perfect location for the Nazi's to convert into a military control center. The peasant Jews residing at the church were instructed to lock all their doors within their sectioned off living quarters and to stay inside in case of a German Nazi raid such as this one. A dozen or more Nazi soldiers surrounded the old cathedral parish, waiting for the orders to raid the church compound.

At about eight o'clock that evening, Cardinal Della Croce arrived at the makeshift Nazi headquarters in the Tuscan hills. He had been picked up and escorted by several Nazi officers and brought there to meet with the ruthless, young Nazi officer. The Cardinal had been in contact with the Vatican, and the Pope was negotiating with Heinrich Himmler regarding their Nazi demands of the release of the Jewish refugees hiding at the Florentine basilica.

"Heil Hitler," the young Nazi officer said to the Cardinal, who completely ignored his greeting.

"Buona sera," Della Croce said, as he calmly sat down in the living room converted office of the Third Reich. He was offered some coffee, which he quickly refused, and made himself comfortable in front of the young, arrogant German officer.

"Your Eminence, as you know, we seem to have a problem at the Basilica Santissima Annunziata. It has come to our attention that you and your pastor have been hiding Jewish refugees there, against the policies of the Third Reich. You do understand the consequences of these offenses, do you not?"

"I am aware, Lieutenant. However, a statement has been vehemently made by the Vatican in Rome, protesting these accusations. These poor refugees have come to our church wishing to become Roman Catholics. We have therefore baptized and consecrated them with the Holy Spirit, and these refugees have been practicing Catholics for the last several months. You or your authorities cannot call these Florentine refugees 'Jews'. They are documented, practicing Roman Catholics," the Cardinal loudly corrected the Nazi officer.

Lieutenant Wilhelm laughed out loud, as he put a cigarette into his mouth and lit up, blowing smoke circles towards the Florentine Cardinal.

"Your Eminence, you must take the Third Reich as complete and total fools. You cannot conveniently convert one hundred or more Jews into Catholics and expect our motherland to accept this conversion. I am very sorry, Your Eminence. A Jew is a Jew!"

He continued to laugh, as the Cardinal glared at the cocky young Nazi officer. Della Croce was finding it very hard to control his anger.

"Our authorities at the Vatican, specifically the Pope, have been in contact with one of your superior officers, General Heinrich Himmler, I believe. I was told by my contacts that a deal can be made," Della Croce exclaimed.

Wilhelm was silent for a few moments as he finished his cigarette, slowly extinguishing it on the ashtray in front of the Cardinal.

"Yes, Your Eminence. I was told this, as well. But keep in mind, we will drive a tough bargain for the hundred or more Jews which you wish for us to release."

Della Croce was aware of the art looting that the Nazi's had been performing throughout Italy and the rest of the occupied countries in Europe during the war. He knew it was only a matter of time before the Nazis would arrive to rob and pillage Florence of its' most precious renaissance art masterpieces.

The Cardinal glared coldly at the Nazis.

"One," he only said.

"One what?"

"Only one. I will only allow you to take one painting from the Uffizi Art Gallery in our city. As you know, each one of our renaissance paintings is worth millions."

The Nazis began laughing hysterically.

"You must be joking, Your Eminence. You wish us to release over one hundred Jewish refugees that are now our prisoners in trade for only one Uffizi painting? I am very sorry, Your Eminence. But we are way too far apart to make any such deals here tonight."

The Nazi officer then motioned several of the surrounding soldiers to begin to escort the Cardinal out of his office when Della Croce interrupted them.

"Wait! What were you told by Himmler?" The Cardinal demanded to know. The officer stared down at the Cardinal.

"General Himmler will take no less than one Uffizi painting for every prisoner that we release into your custody, Your Eminence." Della Croce's blood began to boil with anger.

"Lieutenant? Why not rob and destroy the whole Uffizi art museum?" the Cardinal angrily replied.

"That can be arranged, Your Eminence," the Nazi officer coldly replied.

The Cardinal began to count to ten under his breath, trying to control his rage. He then thought about the forty-two paintings that were entrusted to the Uffizi art gallery in 1938 by Pope Pius XI to Mussolini for 'safe-keeping,' in case of an 'art-raid' in Rome.

"There are forty-two paintings that have been consigned to us from the Vatican Museum in Rome, securely hidden in the museum basement. I will allow you to take those."

The young Nazi officer was suddenly offended.

"You will allow us to do nothing!" the power-hungry young officer screamed.

"You are in no position to negotiate. It is only by the kindness of The Fuhrer that he is even allowing you to negotiate for these Jews."

The Cardinal was silent, allowing the young Nazi to calm himself down.

"The Fuhrer will not 'rob or take' anything from you or your Uffizi Museum, Your Eminence." The Nazi retorted in a calmer voice.

"We will give you what we believe to be a fair price for your art masterpieces," Wilhelm stated, as he wrote a number down on a piece of paper and handed it over to the Cardinal.

"Really? For forty-two paintings that are worth millions? This is quite an insult!" The Cardinal protested.

"Seventy-eight thousand lire and the lives of 103 Jewish refugees, Cardinal Della Croce. Jewish pagans that you have consciously hidden away from the Third Reich. As I have said, we are offering you a fair, generous price and the freedom of your Jews."

The Cardinal silently glared at the young, cocky, Nazi bastard.

"You have ten seconds to accept my generous offer, Your Eminence."

Della Croce said a short prayer to himself, asking God to give him the strength from leaping across the desk of that Nazi officer and sending him down to the deepest depths of Hell.

"You have a deal," he slowly said.

"Good," the young German replied, offering his hand to Della Croce.

The Cardinal ignored his handshake offer, and coldly replied, "You may send your officers to the Uffizi Museum in the morning, and we will complete this transaction. When will you be releasing Father Angelo?" the Cardinal inquired.

"We will release your church pastor when this transaction has been completed."

"Fine. I trust that Fr. Gentile will not be harmed," the Cardinal sternly warned.

The Nazi officer only smiled at Cardinal Della Croce, knowing that he had full power and control of the entire situation here at hand. The young Nazi enjoyed all his newly acquired authority here in Florence, and he relished the demands and restrictions that his Nazi position brought to the occupied region of Florence.

Within the next twenty-four hours, the forty-two paintings from renaissance artists including Raphael, Giotto, Correggio, Botticelli, Lippi, and Tintoretto were boxed up, carefully wrapped individually and crated in wooden containers. They were then loaded onto military trucks and sent to Hamburg, Germany, where an excited

General Himmler was anxiously waiting for their arrival. Because these art masterpieces have initially been all consigned to the Uffizi from the Vatican Museum several years ago for 'safekeeping,' the Cardinal felt that he had negotiated away valuable art masterpieces that belonged to the Vatican Museum, not the Uffizi.

Della Croce was livid with the Vatican and extremely bitter. He felt he did not receive the support that he needed from Pope Pius XII in negotiating with the Nazis to spare the lives of these Jewish families.

Lasciate che il Museo Vaticano assorbire tali perdite, he said to himself.

Let the Vatican Museum absorb these losses.

The next day, one hundred and three Jewish refugees, consisting mostly of women and children, were loaded into the Nazi military trucks, with their intended destination to the border of Switzerland. Della Croce personally saw each one of the refugees onto the trucks, giving each of them some bread and wishing them safe travels for their long journey through the Italian Alps. They were to be safely sheltered there until the end of the war conflict. Himmler had personally, made the arrangements for the Jewish refugees to be safely transported there, Cardinal Della Croce was promised.

But they never arrived.

After seventy-two hours and a considerable amount of pleading by the Cardinal, Father Angelo was finally released from custody. Lieutenant Wilhelm felt it necessary to personally escort the pastor back to his church, along with several of his Nazi henchmen. As several military vehicles pulled up in front of the old basilica, Wilhelm got out and accompanied the pastor back inside of the cathedral.

"Welcome home, Father. You must now feel very grateful to be back in your church," Wilhelm observed.

"Yes," Fr. Angelo nervously responded.

"Shouldn't a religious man such as yourself, give thanks to your god for such a triumphant homecoming?"

The pastor fearfully looked at the Lieutenant.

The Nazi soldiers then pointed their rifles at Fr. Angelo.

"Go to the altar, Fra' Angelo…kneel, and give thanks," the insane Nazi officer ordered. Fr. Angelo began to openly weep, as the pastor was forcefully pushed to the front of the marble altar, then required to kneel.

"Pray to your god, Father," as the guns continued to be pointed at the back of Fr. Angelo.

Fr. Angelo, with tears streaming down his face, began to say the Lord's Prayer. The priest continued to say prayers of mercy, begging the Lord's forgiveness for his Nazi captors and what they were about to do. As the German Lieutenant patiently listened to Fr. Angelo pray, he withdrew his Walther P-38 semi-automatic pistol. Wilhelm then pointed the loaded gun directly up against Father Angelo's head.

Coldly smiling, he pulled the trigger.

Chapter Six

The day after Christmas was a colder, cloudy day on Belmont Avenue in Chicago, as the weather reports called for snow flurries and an inch of snow later that evening. It was past seven o'clock, as I arrived at the Belmont Funeral Home for Don Carlo Marchese's funeral wake. As I expected, there was a long line of people waiting to pay their respects to the well-known and well-loved Mafioso. The range of people going into the funeral chapel went outside, out of the door and spilled into the parking lot. I noticed a few familiar people in line waiting to pay their respects, including several Chicago alderman and a couple of state representatives.

I greeted everyone that I immediately knew in line, as it was too cold to be standing outside, waiting to go into the funeral home to view the body. I was glad that I had worn my heavy, mohair overcoat and brought along a hat and some gloves. I decided that I would rather mess up my combed, salt and pepper hair and put on my red, woolen Blackhawks hat than stand outside and freeze on Belmont Avenue.

It was almost forty-five minutes before I was close enough to get to the casket and view the body of the late Don Carlo Marchese. Having been at the funeral home before, I knew the owner there and wasn't surprised to see him standing in the hallway. He was happily directing the crowds of people, including many dignitaries, to the correct chapel. I then approached the body, and saw the old Mafioso, dressed in a tuxedo, peacefully laying in his black, ornate, silver-handled casket. I smiled to myself, knowing how prideful these Italian undertakers are with every detail, successfully making their subjects look as though they were only taking a long, peaceful nap.

At the front of the chapel, his son-in-law, brothers and several other gorillas that I didn't recognize were standing alongside the casket, greeting all of the mourners as they came through the reception line. One of them, who had seen me first, was Frank Mercurio. He was an underboss for the Marchese Family.

"Hey Paulie," as he greeted me with a kiss on the cheek, Italian style.

"What's up, Frank."

"You know I'm supposed to throw you out of here, you know this, right?" Mercurio was referring to the fact that syndicate crime families didn't approve of the press or media showing up at their loved ones' wakes and funerals.

"I know the rules, Frank. I respected Don Carlo. He was a good man."

"You're here as a family friend, Paulie...not, a reporter. Capish?"

"Got it, Frank."

"You're a fly on the wall. Don't write nuttin' down and don't take no pictures."

"I get it, Frank."

He then gave me a playful slap on my left cheek and smiled, knowing that he wouldn't have to worry about my breaking any of the family's rules. I finished shaking hands with the immediate family, including his son-in-law's and his daughters and went to find my place in the back of the chapel, near the back wall where all the flies were hanging out. I couldn't have been sitting there for more than five minutes when another one of my mobbed-up acquaintances sat next to me.

It was Salvatore Marrocco, who was the controller for the DiMatteo Tomato Distribution Company, and the alleged 'consigliere' of the DiMatteo Family. He was here on behalf of his boss, 'Little Tony' DiMatteo, who was considered the 'Capo dei Capi' of all of the Chicagoland crime families. I had met Sal several years ago while investigating a mobbed-up Teamsters story. Although we didn't see 'eye to eye,' he was always a gentleman and was very respectful of the job that I was trying to do at the time.

"Hello, Mr. Crawford," as he extended his hand in friendship.

"Mr. Marrocco...how are you?" as we exchanged formal greetings.

"I'm good. Too bad we see each other under these circumstances," Marrocco replied.

We continued to exchange pleasantries about our families, Chicago politics, and the economy when we began talking about the circumstances of Don Carlo's morbid death.

"How in the hell did he end up hanging out of the eighteenth floor of the Blackstone?" I sheepishly asked.

"No clue, Paul. Nobody knew anything about this."

"Really? You're trying to tell me that this *wasn't* a hit?" I asked.

"Off the record?" Marrocco looked at me, extending his hand as if we were now creating a mortal contract.

"Of course," I said, shaking his hand again.

"This was NOT a hit," he explained. "I heard two guys were waiting for him in his hotel suite at the Blackstone. They hung him outside and escaped downstairs out of the hotel and out of the back door. Not even his driver saw them come outside that day. The coppers said the surveillance cameras didn't get a good shot of them either."

"And you don't know who ordered this hit?" I asked him.

"It wasn't us. I've been told that the Roselli's, the DiNunzio, and the Lucatelli Families didn't order this hit either. And of course, the Marchese Family wouldn't order a hit on their own family 'Capo.' So basically, whoever killed him was outside of the five families here in Chicago," Sal explained.

"But it doesn't make any sense," I replied.

"I know. Like a said...this was definitely NOT an ordered hit."

We both sat there, as we were watching all of the people file past the casket. The people that were going through the funeral home that evening was a 'who's who' of Chicago celebrities. They included prominent politicians, gangsters, hoods, coppers, lawyers, judges, and everyone else in between. Judging from all of the people who had gathered that night at the Belmont Funeral Home, it didn't take a genius to figure out that Don Carlo Marchese was a much loved, well-respected gentleman.

But who would kill him? If it wasn't a mob ordered hit from another crime family, then who else would want him dead?

I sat there in the back of the funeral chapel for another half hour, while Marrocco and a few others gathered and socialized on the other side of the room. I saw several other news reporters there, including Chaz

Rizzo from Channel Eight Eyewitness News filing past the casket.

"What's up, Paulie?" as he sat next to me, showing off his ostentatious dress attire.

Chaz Rizzo was a flashy, well-dressed news reporter who never left his house without looking like he was modeling for a fashion show. I once saw him in a Hugo Boss men's clothing store on Michigan Avenue, getting fitted for some high-end suits that I couldn't afford even to touch, let alone buy. He probably dropped over ten grand on suits and clothing that day when I saw him, and he didn't think anything of it.

"How come you didn't get the 'Miranda' warning?" I immediately asked him, referring to the stern 'reporter' cautionary I received from one of the family henchmen.

"They caught me outside before I came in," he smiled, sitting down next to me and crossing his legs. Even his fancy, wing-tipped shoes shined and glistened of big money. We sat there together, people watching all of the so-called mourners file past the casket.

"What's your take on this, Chaz?" Rizzo looked at me, dead square in the eyes.

"He must have pissed somebody off," he slowly replied, shaking his head.

"What do you mean?"

He sat there and thought for a moment. "I've heard from other sources that Marchese had some intense, Vatican connections over the years, and had done a significant amount of business with the Holy See in the past."

"Really? What kind of business?"

"He's brokered some investments here in the United States and Italy, including some artworks that the Vatican needed to liquidate over the years, and he was able to arrange some buyers for."

"Really? And here I thought he made all of his money selling 'roll-offs' and garbage dumpsters." I smiled, listening intently to Rizzo's assessment.

"That was only a small part of his empire. He was born in Italy, and his family is originally from a small town near Rome. He has several uncles and family members who are distinguished monsignors and diplomats within Vatican City. He had a lot of Vatican connections because of his family ties there, which expands beyond several papacies," Rizzo explained.

"Several papacies? Really?"

"We were in Rome several years ago doing a feature story when Pope John Paul II passed away, back in April 2002. Marchese was a guest at the Pope's funeral and was sitting in the first two rows there in St. Peter's Square. He was sitting right alongside all of the other world dignitaries that were present. He had very profound Vatican connections in Rome."

"No, kidding?"

"It's been rumored that he brokered an enumerate amount of recent investment deals with the Holy See. There is gossip that he negotiated several deals, selling off some of their Vatican museum masterpieces within the last few years. With the onset of these various diocesan lawsuits going on around the world, the Vatican has had to have a few 'garage sales,'" Rizzo explained.

"You're referring to these pedophile priest lawsuits?"

"Well, yeah, Paulie. All of these archdioceses are getting sued up the ass and going bankrupt. Who do you think is bankrolling all of these lawsuit settlements? And the Vatican is one of the richest sovereignties in the world. Whenever they need liquid assets, they start selling off priceless works of art and masterpieces from all of their art galleries and museums."

"I'm surprised that none of these 'art sales' has hit the media," I observed.

"And that's the point, Paulie. The Vatican needed a discrete 'art broker' that they could trust, and thanks to his family connections, Marchese was the one that the Vatican trusted to help them unload their paintings and priceless artworks."

"Wow," was all I managed to say. "And you think there might be a connection here?"

Rizzo looked at me for a few silent moments, initially not saying a word.

"As I said, Carlo Marchese must have pissed somebody off."

I looked at Rizzo, remembering what an encyclopedia of information he has always been, especially when it came to Chicago crime syndicate families and their connections to the Catholic Church. With all of the reports and investigations that he has done on them over the years, I wouldn't be surprised if he were formally excommunicated someday or found in the trunk of somebody's Cadillac.

"You're not going to report any of this on your six o'clock news report, are you?" I jokingly asked.

"Are you kidding? I wouldn't dare. Like I said, Marchese's murder is coming from some very deep shit...someplace and somewhere much bigger than any of these Chicago wise-guys."

He got up and shook my hand as he went off to socialize with several of his mobbed-up pallies standing outside of the funeral chapel. With all of the syndicate stories he has done over the years, I was surprised even to find him here, let alone allowing him to hang out at Marchese's wake.

After a while, I looked at my watch and realized it was almost 8:30, and I needed to get home to my dog. Being single and living alone in Lincoln Park, I didn't have anyone else that I could depend on to take care of my yellow Labrador, Bruno. I had an early day tomorrow, and I probably got all the information I was going to get on the late Don Carlo Marchese.

As I was walking outside to the parking lot of my car, I found another surprise. He was sitting in a black Ford SUV in the corner of the parking lot, quietly observing everyone going in and out of Belmont Funeral Home. I decided to walk over to his car and blow his cover, as he reluctantly rolled down his window.

"Detective Dorian...what a pleasant surprise. Are you here writing down license plates and doing 'copper surveillance?'"

Detective Philip Dorian was a seasoned investigator out of the Sixteenth District in Jefferson Park. He was one of the more experienced veteran police detectives whom the Chicago Police Department used to crack their significant cases. We had mutual respect for one another, although I got a distinct impression that he didn't like me.

"Get lost, Crawford. I'm trying to do a job here," as he jokingly smiled and shook my hand.

"You look very conspicuous sitting out here alone in your unmarked cop car. If I noticed you out here, I'm sure all of the other wise-guys inside know you're here too."

"I'm just here to keep everybody honest, Crawford. What the hell are you doing here?" he eagerly asked.

"Just here to snoop around. Did you see your buddy Chaz Rizzo?"

I knew about the contentious relationship between Dorian and Rizzo from the several run-ins I heard the two of them had with one another over the years.

He just smiled. "Yeah, he waved to me as he was going inside."

It was getting cold standing outside, so I walked over to the other side of his unmarked squad car and very aggressively, invited myself inside, sitting on the passenger side of his squad car.

"What's the latest and greatest on this homicide, Detective?" I boldly asked. He looked at me, surprised that I dared to invite myself into his squad car.

"Do you think I'm going to volunteer any information to you, Crawford? The last thing I need is to be quoted in your paper."

"Come on, Dorian. We're at a funeral, paying our respects. Anything you say to me is off the record."

Dorian laughed out loud. "Yeah, I've heard that before."

"Seriously, Phil. I've been ordered just to be a 'fly on the wall' tonight. I'm not even here."

"Yeah, okay," as he smiled. I noticed a half-eaten Subway sandwich sitting on the dash of his car.

"Do you think this was a mob hit?" I point-blank asked him.

"No, definitely not. All the 'families' are playing 'nice in the sandbox.' They're all getting along. Everyone is minding their own business."

"Then who do you think did this?"

"I'm baffled. I can't figure this homicide out," Dorian replied.

"Do you know anything about Marchese's Vatican ties?"

Dorian looked at me as if a light switch had gone on in his head. "What have you heard?"

"Your pallie, Chaz Rizzo, was telling me inside that Marchese had some profound Vatican connections. He was an 'art broker' of sorts, helping the Holy See unload of some of their priceless art masterpieces over the years," I eagerly volunteered.

I was hoping this new information to the detective would, at the very least, earn my keep while trying to stay warm in his squad car.

"We only know that he made a lot of trips back and forth to Italy. He supposedly has a lot of family in Rome and a summer villa in his hometown. We never made a big deal out of his numerous European trips abroad," Dorian answered.

"Well, that's an angle you may want to pursue. But of course, you didn't hear this from me, Dorian." I recused myself to the detective, hoping I could pump some information out of him later in this investigation.

"Between you and Rizzo, I don't know who is worse," he smiled.

I put my red, Blackhawks woolen cap back on, knowing I had to get back out there and warm up my car for the ride home.

"Keep me in the loop, Detective. The coppers and the reporters gotta watch each other's backs in this town."

"Yeah, sure. Stay warm, Crawford," as he shook my hand.

I got out of his unmarked squad car and encountered my cold, lifeless vehicle, waiting to be started and warmed up for the long ride home. As I was driving to Lincoln Park, I was turning Rizzo's words over and over in my head, wondering what he was eluting to when he replied that Marchese must have 'really pissed someone off.'

But who could that someone be? Who was the person who ordered a hit on a Chicago 'Capo' who was obviously very well-loved and well respected in this town? Whoever it was, he had to be from a significant association, a large group of people far more prominent than all of the five crime families in Chicago combined. That person had to be part of a large union of killers, more significant than all the wise guys, all the hoodlums, and all the criminals who ever did business with Don Carlo Marchese over the years.

And at that moment, I could only think of one.

CHAPTER SEVEN

It was a cloudy morning last July as the taxicab pulled into Terminal One at O'Hare Airport. Wolfgang Schmidt instructed the cab driver to park as close as he could to the United Airlines departure lane, as he wanted to check his luggage with the attending baggage clerk outside. The Chicago Police were performing security in front of the terminal as always, and the cabbie knew he had a limited amount of time to drop off his passenger and unload the luggage from the trunk of his car. The art dealer handed him a fifty-dollar bill, then checked his bags in front of the terminal.

Schmidt had a 9:45 flight scheduled to Munich, Germany that morning, and had less than an hour to go through the long, TSA security lines and find the departure gate to his destination. The flights were running on time that day, as he checked his sport coat pockets. He wanted to make sure he had his passport and boarding pass in hand. Schmidt checked the electronic departures board. United Airlines' 1114 direct flight to Munich was departing from Gate A-12, on time.

The German art dealer fumbled through security, taking his time to put back on his brown, wing-tipped shoes and briskly walked toward the Gate A-12. Arriving at the departure gate, he gave the airline attendant his boarding pass, airline ticket, and passport. This trip to Munich was a last-minute flight, which he had only booked two days ago. Although he had made several trips a year to Munich, Germany, this trip was a rather sudden, unexpected one.

His first cousin, Hermann Kalkschmidt, who was eighty-one years old, had suddenly passed away and was found dead in his apartment earlier that week. He communicated with his cousin often and had done some business with him over the years. Although he felt that he needed to express his condolences to his distant family in Germany personally, there was also another significant reason for his visit to Munich.

Apparently, he received a long-distance telephone call from a Lieutenant Gerhard Hildebrandt, a Munich detective who was investigating the sudden death of his first cousin. The detective was informed by Hermann's neighbor, Wilhelm Guerling, whom Schmidt had met often, to contact his cousin in Chicago regarding any family emergency immediately. Hermann once mentioned to his caring neighbor to contact his cousin Wolfgang should any emergency occur regarding his well-being.

Detective Hildebrandt had called Schmidt not only to express his condolences on the loss of his cousin but to discuss the circumstances of his death. There was a powerful, gas odor that was more than distinctive when the Munich police responded to the emergency call placed by his neighbor. The detective was uncertain as to whether this was an accidental death, a suicide, or, more importantly, judging from the discovered contents of the older man's apartment -a murder.

The detective had his suspicions. Hildebrandt suggested that Schmidt fly into Munich as soon as possible to assist him in this investigation and to help him in sorting out the discovered contents of the older man's apartment. It seems Detective Hildebrandt had some serious questions. Lots of questions.

Because the discovered 'Uffizi Gallery' paintings had been in storage in the old man's apartment, Wolfgang knew he had better have the right answers and the proper documentation to prove that those stolen paintings initially from the Uffizi were rightfully the property of Hermann Kalkschmidt and his family.

Schmidt always had reservations about his cousin's decision to store and oversee those stolen paintings in his apartment personally. His old cousin never trusted anyone with these inherited masterpieces from his father, and never wanted these art gallery paintings to be very far from his sight. Wolf remembered the countless number of times that he 'loudly' suggested to his cousin that these Uffizi paintings would be far better off being stored elsewhere. Wolf argued with his cousin that these paintings would be safer in a secured storage area, where they could still be secretly hidden away from the rest of the world. Those Uffizi paintings were a burdensome heirloom that his family chose to keep hidden and concealed away for so many, many years.

But his old cousin Hermann was stubborn. He had inherited these valuable items from his father, Klaus, once a highly ranked, Nazi German soldier. His old cousin wished to continue his father's tradition and personally hide and stash these valuable masterpieces in the same manner his father had done for over the last eighty years, far away from the public eye and the rest of the world. And Hermann Kalkschmidt trusted no one.

As the United Flight 1114 began boarding, Wolfgang found his aisle seat E-14 of the Boeing 747 and began to make himself comfortable. He had brought along a book and some Vicodin to help him sleep his way through the long, nine-hour flight to Munich. He and brought along some legal documents and some files which he knew would assist him and the Munich detective.

But he kept turning the circumstance of his cousin's death over and over in his head. Did his cousin so irresponsibly leave the gas stove on and then fall asleep in his bed? Did Hermann appear to be suicidal?

Not likely, Wolf laughed to himself. His old cousin Hermann was far too mean and egotistical to perform such a selfish act. Would his death look like an accident to the detectives? His old cousin had lived alone for many, many years, and had cooked and cleaned for himself without incident. His cousin was not likely to cook in the kitchen and then forget to shut off the stove. If this didn't look like an accident, would he be a possible suspect?

He wondered what was going through the Munich detective's mind: Could he now be a suspect? How would the detective suspect him in being involved in his cousin Hermann's death, with his being in Chicago? Who else knew about those hidden paintings? Why use the gas stove to kill him? Why didn't the killer strangle the helpless older man and rob his valuable Uffizi paintings from the bedroom attic?

These were all questions Wolfgang Schmidt did not have the answers to, and he continuously pondered them while in flight to Germany. His grandfather, Hans Schmidt, and Hermann's father, Klaus Kalkschmidt, were brothers. Grandfather Hans had shortened his name when he immigrated to the United States after the First World War.

Although he immediately obtained his U.S. Citizenship, his grandfather was always a Nazi sympathizer and justifiably supported his younger brother Klaus as he served as a lieutenant in the Nazi Army. He had proudly endorsed Klaus as he rose through the Nazi ranks, becoming the personal secretary to Heinrich Himmler. His uncle Klaus knew a significant amount of classified Nazi information that was only available to Himmler and his immediate staff. Detailed information regarding the next striking areas which the Nazi intended to invade, especially during their failed Russian, first offensive. Uncle Klaus was also familiar with the Jewish civilian raids, which occurred throughout the occupied territories of Europe. And Uncle Klaus was more than acquainted with the various art museum raids and robberies which the Nazi Army helped themselves to.

When Himmler was in Florence, he became especially fond of the valuable masterpieces of Raphael, Caravelle, Giotto, and other artists most popular during the Italian renaissance period. He requested his secretary to assist him in acquiring and storing these art masterpieces in 1943. Because of the distinct threat of any of the Allies or other Nazi officers getting their hands on them, Klaus arranged with his brother to have the masterpieces discretely shipped away, via Naples by boat in several large containers, to Buenos Aries, Argentina until after the war. It was not until after 1953 when Klaus Kalkschmidt felt it was safe enough to slowly, over two years, ship these paintings by boat back to Munich, where he oversaw their safety and security ever since.

Since the Second World War, there had been a significant number of claims of missing, stolen, or destroyed property, especially by the Italian, French, Austrian, and Belgium governments, for the safe return of these priceless artworks and masterpieces. It became necessary for the German government to begin to wash their hands of the past sins of the Nazi armies and its soldiers during World War Two.

The German government declared that it would no longer assist or address these outstanding claims or demands from these other countries and especially, from the United Nations. They took a "finders, keepers" attitude in 1961 after the Berlin Wall was erected, to any and all parties looking for their missing artworks and their stolen family heirlooms. Unless the claimants or their government could prove their ownership beyond a shadow of a doubt, the Germans now washed their hands of the matter.

The German government realized that it neither had the human resources or the financial resources to reclaim and return all of these priceless works of art stolen by the Nazis during World War Two. So, they turned a deaf ear to the cultural art world and its rightful owners.

The nine-hour flight was grueling, as Schmidt had trouble falling asleep, even after taking two Vicodin pills after takeoff. There was a significant amount of turbulence, and Wolf's stomach started to feel queasy as the pilot adjusted the flying attitude from 28,000 feet to 32,000 feet. The pilot was hoping to avoid some of the air pockets and the bad weather that was brewing over the Atlantic Ocean. Wolf ordered a whiskey on the rocks, hoping the stiff drink would settle his nerves.

It was almost midnight Munich time when United Flight 1114 landed at Munich's International Airport. Wolfgang grabbed his luggage from the carousel at the baggage claim and then went through customs without incident. He expected to take a taxicab to the Hilton Hotel in downtown Munich, where he had made reservations for the next five days. But as he exited the baggage claim area, he saw a well-dressed gentleman in a light beige raincoat standing near the exit door, holding a sign with his name on it.

"Herr Schmidt?" The man exclaimed as Wolf approached him.

"Yes. I'm am Wolfgang Schmidt."

"Good Evening, Herr Schmidt. I am Detective Hildebrandt of the Munich Police Department. I thought it would be a good idea to meet you here at the airport and drive you to your hotel if you didn't mind."

Wolfgang was a little startled, as he was looking forward to retiring to his hotel room before dealing with the police investigation of his cousin's death.

"Please accept my apology, Detective Hildebrandt. But I am a little exhausted from the long plane ride from Chicago. There was a significant amount of turbulence," he explained.

"I understand. But our department wanted to extend the courtesy of picking you up at the airport and bringing you to your hotel this evening," the Detective explained.

Schmidt thought that it was a little weird, but he accepted Hildebrandt's ride invitation. He helped Schmidt load his suitcase, and his briefcase into the back of his unmarked Mercedes squad car and they proceeded through the autobahn to his waiting hotel.

"I am sorry for your unpleasant flight, Herr Schmidt. I hoped you would be feeling more energetic when you arrived. I wanted to bring you directly to the crime scene, which we successfully sealed off from the public. It seems these large crates of art paintings have been starting to stir some publicity. We have been asked to give a statement in this regard, but we have been waiting for your arrival from Chicago," Hildebrandt explained.

Schmidt was quietly sitting on the passenger side of the Mercedes, and because of the unpleasant plane ride, he had very little patience for the detective or his intense questions.

"I must apologize again, Detective. This will all have to wait until the morning. I am exhausted. I wish to retire to my hotel room immediately."

"I understand, Herr Schmidt."

"Thank you," he replied in an anxious voice.

Hildebrandt continued to drive his squad car through the Munich traffic until pulling in front of the Munich Hilton Hotel. He exited the vehicle, assisted Schmidt, and retrieved his luggage from the back.

As Wolfgang grasped his bags and walked through the entrance door, the Detective wished him a good night.

"Do get some rest, Herr Schmidt. Tomorrow will be a hectic day. I trust you have brought with you the necessary documents to verify the ownership of these paintings," he mentioned.

Wolfgang glared at the Detective, desperately trying to keep from losing his temper.

"I will be ready at 9:00 am after breakfast. Good night, Detective," he coldly replied. He quickly entered the Hilton entrance and walked directly towards the concierge at the front desk, hoping that the Detective didn't follow him in.

Schmidt knew he would have his hands full in trying to acquire the release of those stolen Uffizi paintings from his cousin's sealed off the apartment. But he had done a significant amount of business with the German government before and specifically, with the Munich local government.

He had dinner with Mayor Bertram Kossel on a few occasions over the last three years, and he was confident that he could persuade him and acquire his assistance in releasing the stolen Nazi paintings. Herr Wolfgang Schmidt wasn't worried. He opened up his luggage before retiring and took out two large, white bulky envelopes which he had hidden in one of the compartments, tightly wrapped with clothing. Schmidt was very grateful that his luggage wasn't opened or inspected as he placed the large envelopes in his briefcase.

He had a few tricks up his sleeve.

CHAPTER EIGHT

The telephone of Wolfgang Schmidt's hotel room on that July morning was ringing loudly at 8:55 am. He had risen early before six o'clock that morning and had showered and dressed before ordering room service. He was just finishing a light breakfast of bagels, lox, and cream cheese when the hotel room phone started ringing. The Chicago art dealer knew immediately who it was and hesitated for a few long seconds before answering.

"Hallo?" he responded in German.

"Guten Morgen, Herr Schmidt. I trust you are rested this morning." It was Detective Hildebrandt, arriving early to pick up Schmidt from his hotel room.

"Danke dir, Detective," replied Schmidt, thanking him for his concern. "You are downstairs?"

"Yes. I am near the coffee shop at the front desk."

"I will be down shortly," he replied.

He expected the detective to arrive at his hotel room to pick him up. Although he knew Hildebrandt needed his help in his cousin's death investigation, he was a little startled at his overzealous presence since picking him up at the airport last evening. Wolf had brought with him several files and documents ascertaining the original bills of lading and shipping documents from Argentina in 1953 for the discovered paintings in Hermann's apartment. Schmidt had copies of the document transactions from the Uffizi Gallery and the Nazi's as well. He had acquired copies of these documents many years ago from his cousin when they were preparing the estate and trust documents for his older cousin.

It was always agreed and therefore stated in Hermann's will, that Wolfgang would be the sole executor and beneficiary to his cousin's valuable estate. Hermann did not have any children or any other close family members other than his Chicago cousin. Although Wolf did not approve of the manner and means to which Hermann secured and maintained the Uffizi art pieces, they still supported a close and respectful relationship.

Wearing dress jeans, a white button-down shirt, and a black corduroy sport jacket, Wolfgang arrived downstairs with his briefcase to meet Hildebrandt.

"Did you have breakfast?" the detective asked.

"Room service.... I did, yes. Thank you," Wolf replied.

They both then exited the Hilton Hotel and drove twenty minutes through downtown Munich to his cousin's sealed off the apartment. It was a rather sunny, warm day, and Wolf had brought along his Ray-Ban sunglasses for the glaring, bright sunlight. The traffic was rather light that morning, and they conveniently located a parking space in front of the dark brown, old apartment building at 67 Barer Street. The front door of the second-floor apartment was sealed off, and there was a unique lock on the door. Hildebrandt unlocked the apartment door and broke the seal as they both entered Hermann's old, musty living quarters.

There were assorted boxes, magazines, books, and other miscellaneous items scattered everywhere in no real order within the apartment. There was also a small pathway from the living room to the bedroom, where Hermann usually slept.

"It's surprising to me that this place has never caught fire," the Detective observed, as he tried to make

65

his way around the assorted junk scattered everywhere around the living room floor.

"Yes...I have fought with my cousin for years to clean this place up. This was always a fire hazard," Wolfgang remembered.

He explained to the Munich detective that he had gotten into a heated argument with his cousin the last time he was in Germany several months ago, knowing that it would not take very much to set the old, antediluvian apartment ablaze.

"He seemed to be quite a 'packrat' of sorts," Wolf said.

"Did you know about the old paintings stored in the attic bedroom?" Hildebrandt wasted no time asking questions to the Chicago art dealer.

"Yes. Those paintings were a family heirloom that was passed down to him from his father."

The two of them made their way through another path to the doorway, in which the door locks had been broken, and walked up the short flight of stairs to the attic bedroom. The three crates had been broken, and a few of the paper-sealed paintings had been unwrapped, exposing several identities of the hidden pictures. All three boxes were stamped with the word 'FIRENZE' in the front of each container.

"A family heirloom? Really?" The Detective started to smirk. "Is this why the containers are still stamped "FIRENZE" on each crate?"

"They were acquired by my uncle during the Second World War, as he was a high-ranking Nazi officer. He purchased this art from the German Army, who acquired it from the Uffizi Gallery in Firenze, Italy."

The Detective looked at Schmidt, somewhat perplexed.

"Are you trying to say that your uncle purchased all of this art and these valuable masterpieces during the Second World War? You must have had a wealthy uncle." Hildebrandt observed.

Schmidt glared at the Detective.

"Are you familiar with the way and means of how the Nazi Army acquired valuable art masterpieces during the war, Detective?" he asked.

"I have heard stories."

"Adolf Hitler and his associates did not 'steal' these works of art from these art galleries and museums. The curators were 'forced' to sell Hitler these works of art at hugely discounted prices, and proper bills of sale were transcribed and documented between the Nazi Army and these museum curators. The Uffizi Gallery was 'paid' for these works of art, and my uncle, Klaus Kalkschmidt, legitimately paid for these items."

The Detective looked at the Chicago art dealer, thoroughly confused.

"You are saying that these valuable art masterpieces were legitimately sold to Hitler and his officers during the war?"

"That is correct. The museum curators were involuntarily forced to sell these masterpieces to the Nazi's. But these items were legitimately 'sold,' and I have brought along the proper documents and bills of sale supporting these transactions."

Herr Schmidt opened his briefcase and took out the various files, which included typed documents dating back to November 1943. The 'bill of sale' contained a detailed listing of each painting, which was being sold at their 'fair market value' at the time of sale, forty-two paintings in all, totaling seventy-eight thousand lire. The copies of the documents, although typed and faded, were legitimate, being stamped and notarized by several signatures that appeared to be other Nazi officials. By all appearances, these documents seemed authentic and genuine.

The detective put on his reading glasses and perused through the official wartime documents, slowly reading and looking over each manuscript.

"I must apologize, Herr Schmidt, but I will have to submit these documents to the proper authorities. As you understand, even though our government has taken an inactive role in the repossession and recovery of any prior Nazi 'acquisitions' during the war, we will need to submit these documents, showing their proper ownership," Hildebrandt stated.

"I understand your position, Detective. But as the rightful owner and heir of these valuable properties, I cannot allow these valuable artworks to stay here in this apartment and risk their potential damage. These valuable art pieces must be relocated to another location in an environment that is more secure. These priceless masterpieces need to be moved immediately where the potential damage to them will be far less at risk," Schmidt made his point.

"Really?" Hildebrandt observed.

"Herr Schmidt, why are you in such a hurry to move these paintings? They have been created and sitting in this musty old apartment for how many years? Why the sudden rush?"

"As I have said, Detective. There is a risk of potential environmental damage in allowing these paintings to stay here. They need to be moved to a location where the air and temperature are controlled, preventing minimal impairment to these masterpieces."

"I see," Hildebrandt replied.

The Munich Detective began to casually walk around the old musty attic, looking into each opened crate and admiring the beauty of each of the Renaissance masterpieces.

"Herr Schmidt, can you tell me about this painting?" he removed the artwork from the crate. "That is a priceless masterpiece from Sandro Botticelli, circa 1495. It is called the 'Chart of Hell' and is one of the most powerful visual representations of Dante's Inferno ever made," the art dealer recited.

"This artwork, which was done with pen and brush on vellum, portrays the descent made by the poets Virgil and Dante through what the latter called the "abysmal valley of pain." The artist envisioned hell as an abyss leading to the center of the Earth, and he imagined nine rings of hell, each representing a different category of sin."

"I see," the detective slowly replied, not taking a whole lot of interest in the personal art lesson the knowledgeable art dealer was giving him.

He then walked over to another crate, removing another half-unwrapped painting.

"Please be careful with that, Detective."

"Of course, Herr Schmidt," ignoring the art dealer. "And what painting is this?" he inquired.

"The 'Demons of Divine Wrath,' painted by Fra Filippo Lippi, a Carmelite monk from Tuscany who painted this priceless masterpiece back in 1459," Schmidt immediately responded.

Hildebrandt glared at the Chicagoan, impressed by his comprehensive art knowledge.

"I'm impressed, Herr Schmidt. You know quite a bit about art and especially these masterpieces." The detective walked around the several opened 'Firenze' marked wooden crates.

"It must have bothered you to witness your cousin blindly storing these art masterpieces in dark wooden crates in a musty old attic, in such an uncontrolled environment. Did you protest your dismay to your cousin?" The detective's questions were turning from curious inquiry to a police inquisition.

Schmidt looked at the detective, knowing exactly where he was going with his line of questioning.

"As I have said to you, I had many disagreements with Hermann regarding the manner to which he was storing these paintings."

"And at your last visit, you mentioned that you both had a rather loud disagreement regarding the subject of these Uffizi masterpieces?"

Wolfgang put his briefcase down and walked closer to the detective, his face within centimeters of his.

"I would never wish any harm on my cousin, Detective. Will my lawyer's presence here be necessary?"

"Oh no, Herr Schmidt. I am making no such implication," Hildebrandt said, with his tongue in cheek. "It just seems rather unusual that your cousin Hermann, who was allowed to hold and maintain these paintings for so many years in this musty old attic in this manner, would suddenly be found dead in his room, with the stove gas still on," the Detective observed.

"You're such a passionate and knowledgeable art dealer from Chicago, it must have been killing you, knowing that these paintings were secretly being stored here all of these years in this manner," Hildebrandt was making his accusation. "Especially, these missing and stolen art paintings from the Uffizi Gallery in Florence." The two were still exchanging dialog, locking their eyes on each other.

"I believe this conversation is over, Detective. As the proper heir to my cousin's estate, I must ask you to leave," Wolf demanded.

"I'm sorry, Herr Schmidt. But this is still a crime scene investigation. And this apartment and its contents will remain so until I say otherwise," Hildebrandt pointedly stated.

The Chicago art dealer only smiled. "We will see about that, Detective."

Wolfgang took the files and proof of ownership documents, which he was still holding and placed them back into his briefcase.

"I will hold you and your department personally liable for any damage done to any of the contents here in this apartment, Detective. I suggest that we leave together before I call your commander," Schmidt demanded.

The detective, knowing that Schmidt was well connected within the German government, didn't want to stir unwanted publicity regarding this art finds anymore. He already knew that this unaccounted-for death and suspected homicide were already leaked to the local papers, and he did not want to have an immediate confrontation with Schmidt at this time. They both left the apartment together, and Hildebrandt resealed and locked the apartment.

They both silently walked down the flight of stairs and outside onto Barer Street.

"I am sure we will talk again, Herr Schmidt. Have a good day." The detective concluded, as he entered his unmarked Mercedes squad car and drove off, leaving Schmidt there alone in front of the old brownstone apartment building.

Wolfgang put on his sunglasses and walked several blocks to a local café nearby. He ordered a German coffee, which is a type of cocktail made with *Kirschwasser*, coffee, and whipped cream. Wolfgang sat at the table outside and pulled out his cell phone. He needed to make a phone call.

"I am here on Barer Street. How quickly can you get here?" he asked his colleague, still keeping his briefcase very close to his side. He had another meeting scheduled that morning and had some important business to discuss.

Apparently, the Chicago art dealer had an envelope to deliver.

CHAPTER NINE

The next day, Wolfgang Schmidt had been patiently waiting for the late arrival of his colleague that morning at the Munich café. He had been sitting outside, enjoying his second coffee, when a white, new model BMW M6 convertible pulled up across the street from the Café Sommerlicher. The driver of the vehicle was hesitant at first to exit the car, until he recognized Schmidt sitting at the outdoor café, waiting for his arrival. The dark-haired young man with slicked-back 'Elvis-style' hair, wearing a white Polo shirt, dress jeans, and sunglasses crossed the street to greet his late morning appointment.

The two gentlemen made eye contact without even saying a word. The young man only sat down next to him and ordered a strong, 'German-style' espresso. After making himself comfortable, he took the first sip of his caffé. He then grimaced.

"You damn Germans never learned how to make espresso," he loudly observed.

Stefano Iannucci was a young, tall, good looking Italian from Acerra, near the outskirts of Naples. His official job occupation was that of a 'contractor' of sorts. But his actual job duties, in real terms, was that of a hired, professional killer. He and his sorted gang of professional murderers were discretely hired out by very wealthy families and businessmen to eliminate any person or persons who may be getting in the way of a 'business transaction,' which usually involved a considerable fee.

They were considered an 'elite' squad of 'hitmen' who traveled throughout Europe to perform these professional 'contracts' on the guarantee that the job would be accomplished without discovery or prosecution by the authorities.

"You damn Italians never learned how to be on time," Schmidt noting that Iannucci was almost a half-hour late for their appointment.

Stefano was more than qualified to be a 'murder-for-hire' contractor. He was in the military as part of the Italian Special Forces, or a CUMSUBIN (Comando Raggruppamento Subacquei e Incursori) soldier, the Italian equivalent of a Navy Seal. He received long and extensive training in expert target, rifle, commando, and assault weapons training, with more than one hundred successful 'special op' assignments to his credit. In his specially trained unit, each commando soldier was considered 'a human assault weapon,' with specially trained technologies and tactics associated with the Italian Naval Assault Division and Naval Special Forces.

After leaving the military, he worked as a 'carabinieri' or a police officer for the City of Naples for four years until being terminated for assaulting and injuring one of his superior officers. He then became a very successful 'contractor' over the last several years. Stefano developed a favorable reputation among various wealthy individuals and Italian crime families who needed an 'expert killer' who can professionally, get the job done. His 'fees' were equivalent to the required job and difficulty of the assigned task, and his fees were always paid in cash, preferably in U.S. Dollars. He made monthly visits to his Swiss bank in Zurich, Switzerland, of whom he was asked no questions when depositing large amounts of American currency.

Besides being handsome, young, and rich, Iannucci also was a third-degree black belt in several martial arts. With his quick-triggered temper, his special combat abilities, and his various assault skills, Iannucci was a dangerous man indeed.

"How did it go with Hildebrandt?" Stefano eagerly asked.

"He sounds a little suspicious. Should I be worried?"

The casually dressed Italian only smiled. "It will be a frozen day in hell when you start to worry, Wolfgang. You have ice-water running through your veins."

"A lesson that perhaps you should learn, young man," Wolfgang answered, making a note of Iannucci's famous, uncontrollable temper.

"Your detective friend will soon discover that there were broken gas lines in the apartment. You have nothing to worry about," the young Italian reassured him.

Wolf then picked up his locked briefcase and withdrew a bulky, white 8 ½ x 11 envelope. He then placed it on the café tabletop.

"It's all there," he only said.

Stefano picked up the envelope, opened it, and peeked inside. He took a visual inventory of the five stacks of US currency, tightly wrapped one-hundred-dollar bills, each in ten-thousand-dollar bundles and neatly placed inside of the white envelope.

"Our agreement was fifty thousand dollars plus expenses, Herr Schmidt," the young assassin stated.

"Fifty thousand dollars, just for turning the gas on?" Wolfgang protested as if to complain about the fee arrangement with his hired killer.

Stefano coldly glared at the Chicago art dealer for a long minute, making sure that his dead silence made a loud statement to Wolfgang Schmidt.

"You may submit your operating costs for this engagement at our next meeting, Stefan," the Chicago art dealer curtly said. Although he grumbled, he knew that the price of hiring Iannucci to eliminate his old cousin Hermann for the sole custody of his hidden artworks was more than a bargain.

Schmidt was now close to having complete and total control of the forty-two Uffizi art masterpieces that have been in the Kalkschmidt family since the end of the war. He had been fighting with his cousin for ages as to the storage and safekeeping of those art masterpieces, and Schmidt wished him to begin selling off those works of art years ago. But his old cousin Hermann wouldn't hear of it. He was physically and emotionally attached to each art masterpiece and preferred to leave them crated up in his dusty old bedroom attic, rather than to sell and share them with the rest of the world.

The art dealer also knew that, with the passage of almost eighty years or more, that the art world would pay dearly for any auctioned off renaissance paintings stolen by the Nazis during the war. The applicable documentation associated with these paintings would allow all of them to be legally sold at any art auction. There was a king's ransom to be made when the sale of these priceless artworks is finally liquidated, and Wolfgang Schmidt was more than happy to begin their sale.

"I was surprised but happy that you were able to grant old cousin Hermann a quiet, peaceful death," Schmidt observed.

"I thought about it," answered Stefano. "Those ancient apartment buildings have old, leaky gas stoves that can fill up with a gas odor very easily. It was a much cleaner kill."

"Just because a murder weapon wasn't used does not mean you get a discount," smiled Iannucci.

Schmidt smiled back at the young assassin, obviously pleased with the results of this operation.

"Thank you for your efforts," as the two shook hands.

Stefano then confidently grasped the white envelope and rose from the café table, without finishing his German-made espresso. He then walked across the street to his awaiting convertible and quickly drove away.

Almost a block away, sitting in his unmarked Mercedes squad car, Detective Hildebrandt was observing the whole transaction at the Café Sommerlicher. He noted the Italian license plates of the white BMW convertible and took pictures of the man holding a white envelope, entering his sports car to leave.

Later that afternoon, Herr Schmidt had an appointment at the municipal and administrative building within the City of Munich. The New Town Hall is a longstanding administrative building located in the northern part of Marienplatz in Munich. Built-in 1874, it hosts the local city government, including the city council, the office of the mayor, and the administrative offices of its native government. He entered the hallowed halls of the old building and, after several minutes, negotiated his way to the Mayor's office.

"Burgermeister Bert Kossel, bitte. Ich habe einen termin 03:00," he asked in German to his receptionist, requesting to see the mayor.

She cheerfully noted his presence and kindly asked him to be seated, contacting him in his office. Schmidt found a comfortable leather chair within the opulent municipal office, with its ornate custom woodwork and dark oak, wooden walls. He patiently waited for the mayor to see him for almost twenty minutes when his receptionist finally called him to follow her into his office.

"Good afternoon, Herr Schmidt," as the two hugged. It had been over a year since Wolfgang and the mayor had been in contact. They both conversed in German, making small talk about the weather, their careers, and their families. After several minutes of pleasantries, Mayor Kossel broke the ice:

"My deepest sympathies on the loss of your dear cousin, Herr Schmidt. I know the two of you were close."

"Indeed," Wolfgang thanked the Mayor. "It was a shock to see how he had so tragically died," referring to the gas leak in his apartment.

"We sent our Building Department there to the apartment building. There were some broken gas lines located in the utility room, leading to your cousin's apartment. There were also several building code violations, including the carbon monoxide and fire alarm detectors that were not functional. It is no wonder that the whole apartment building didn't blow up," the Mayor mentioned.

"Really?" Wolf exclaimed, silently noting in his head that he was officially off the hook. "I am thankful for your efforts by your department in properly investigating my cousin's death."

"It is regrettable. My sympathies again, Herr Schmidt."

The two of them sat there in silence for several moments until Wolf brought up the subject of his visit.

"I will need access to my cousin's apartment and all of its contents."

Kossel looked at the art dealer, expecting him to address the subject.

"I am sorry, Herr Schmidt. There have been some implications made that the hidden artworks in your cousin's apartment were stolen Nazi masterpieces from the Uffizi Gallery during the war. According to the Washington Principals Agreement established in 1998, our country now must return all recovered stolen cultural art to their rightful owners," the Mayor explained.

The Washington Principals on Nazi Confiscated Art Agreement is an international treaty regarding the restitution of art confiscated by the Nazi regime in Germany before and during World War Two. It was a conference established in Washington, D.C., back in 1998, where a treaty signed by forty-four countries pledged international cooperation in returning stolen Nazi artifacts to their rightful owners. Germany was encouraged by NATO and its allies to cooperate with this extensive, international treaty.

"My dear Mayor," Herr Schmidt began to make his argument, "there has been a considerable amount of debate as to the cooperation of such an encompassing treaty upon the recovery of these stolen artifacts over the years. The Washington Principals Agreement applies to 'stolen art.' I can assure you that this is not the case here. Hitler and the Third Reich did not 'rob' or 'steal' a good portion of these artifacts, especially during the latter part of the Second World War. Many of these art masterpieces were 'purchased' by Hitler and his staff."

Mayor Kossel was listening attentively.

"And in this case, I have in my possession a bill of sale, signed by General Himmler and Cardinal Della Croce from Florence's Uffizi Art Gallery, along with its curators at the time. It is dated November 14, 1943, and lists the forty-two art paintings that were properly sold for seventy-eight thousand lire," Schmidt explained.

The Mayor listened attentively to the Chicago art dealer. He was sympathetic to Schmidt and believed that he had a right to the paintings. But his office had been getting inundated by telephone calls and emails from Florence's police department along with several messages from the board of directors of the Uffizi Gallery, demanding the return of these valuable artworks. They also received a call from the Vatican Museum, claiming these stolen paintings as well.

"I am sorry, Herr Schmidt. Until we can sort all of this out, I have been recommended by our legal department to keep the apartment sealed until we can figure out the rightful owners of these stolen masterpieces," he explained.

Wolfgang Schmidt sat there silently for a moment. As he had expected, it was time to play 'hardball.'

"Bertram, we go back several years, correct?"

"Correct."

"You and I both have relatives and descendants who were forced to do some very questionable things during the last war. My grandfather and my uncle have both been accused of being Nazi art thieves. Do you recall who your grandfather was?"

Schmidt was referring to his grandfather, SS-Gruppenführer Gerhard Kossel, a former Nazi General who was considered the Amtschef (Department Chief) of the Auschwitz concentration camp located in southern

Poland. He was the superior officer who oversaw and signed off on many Jewish persecutions and deaths that occurred from 1940 until 1945. His grandfather disappeared after the war and escaped, like many former Nazi's, to South America. He was found dead, apparently from a self-inflicted gunshot wound in Buenos Aries in 1953, before the Jewish 'Nazi-Hunters' could capture him and bring him to trial for his Nazi war crimes.

Kossel had enjoyed a very successful political career, first as a city councilman and then as Munich's Burgermeister for the last ten years. It has been rumored that he had political aspirations of national politics in Germany. But needless to say, his grandfather's Nazi affiliations have never been mentioned or publicized, and they both knew the damage such a revelation could make on his political career.

"I would hate for your grandfather's Nazi affiliations to be revealed to the local media with all this art discovery frenzy," Schmidt boldly stated.

The mayor's facial expression and demeanor changed from cordial to irate as his face started to turn several shades of red. At that moment, Kossel was speechless.

Schmidt then reached into his 'magic bag of tricks' and withdrew another bulky white envelope with an undisclosed amount of U.S. currency inside. He carefully placed the envelope on the Mayor's desk.

"I am sure that you are accepting political donations for your next campaign, Mayor. There are more 'white envelopes' where this came from."

The Mayor glared at the Chicago art dealer.

"I will need your assistance in helping me clean up and discreetly remove the contents of my cousin's apartment," Schmidt demanded.

Mayor Kossel grasped the envelope and looked inside for a moment, then quickly put it inside of his bottom desk drawer.

"I will see what I can do, Herr Schmidt. You will be hearing from me in the next few days," as the Mayor rose from his desk, eager to escort the Chicago art dealer out of his office.

"I look forward to hearing from you very soon." The two coldly shook hands.

Schmidt then exited the Munich Town Hall and returned to his hotel room at the Hilton. He later had dinner with 'a friend' whom he periodically met with when he was in town. She was a young, beautiful, married art collector by the name of Ingrid Von Stueben. They had several cocktails after enjoying dinner at the hotel restaurant and then went upstairs, spending the evening together in his hotel room.

Over the next few days, Wolfgang Schmidt finally got the release of his cousin's apartment and its contents, despite the protests of the Uffizi Museum, the city council, and more specifically, Detective Hildebrandt. He had his suspicions of Wolfgang Schmidt all along and wished to continue and pursue his investigation into the precarious circumstances involving the death of Hermann Kalkschmidt. But he was ordered by the Munich mayor to 'back off,' allowing Schmidt to go forward with his plans of 'cleaning up' his cousin's estate.

With the help of the Mayor's office, Schmidt discretely hired several German contractors in Munich to clean and repair the apartment, and more precisely, remove and relocate the forty-two art masterpieces to a small, warehouse location within the outskirts of Munich. The warehouse had a controlled, humidified environment that is more conducive to the secured storage of forty-two, five-hundred-year-old Renaissance masterpiece paintings.

There had been several leaks to the media regarding the discovery of these hidden paintings that were recovered in his cousin's apartment. Several news media stations and some newspaper coverage had descended onto Munich to do a thorough investigation of the story. One reporter from the New York Times had approached the Mayor's office to inquire about the disposition and ownership of the hidden, discovered paintings.

Kossel was careful to brief his associates and detectives, especially Hildebrandt, in making sure that no information leaked to the press as to whom had laid claim to these stolen masterpieces. Because the apartment and the immediate area was sealed off by the police, the media had no access to this sensational discovery. Except for the stolen paintings unearthing, their disposition and whereabouts were kept secret from the rest of the world. With the thanks of Mayor Kossel, Schmidt was able to acquire these hidden masterpieces and to make them again, 'disappear.'

After spending a week managing and cleaning up the affairs of his deceased cousin, it was time for Wolfgang to return to Chicago. He arrived early at the Munich International Airport for his mid-afternoon flight, checking his bags and going through security. He sat down and made himself comfortable at the departure gate and was casually reading a magazine when he heard someone calling his name.

"Wolfgang Schmidt?" the Munich detective was standing directly in front of him, within inches of his chair.

Startled, Schmidt began to stand up.

"Oh no, please sit down, Herr Schmidt. This will not take long."

The detective sat next to him in the vacant available chair next to his.

"Please understand that, after doing some investigation, I have come to believe with certainty that you are the one responsible for your cousin's accidental death."

Schmidt sat there silent, as the detective let his statement slowly sink in.

"I ran the plates of your 'Italian friend' a few days ago, and my compliments on your choice of professional killers. He not only managed to turn on the gas stove on that day when your cousin died, but also managed to disconnect and tamper with some of the gas lines in the building's basement leading up to your cousin's apartment."

The Munich detective continued. "Iannucci did quite a professional job in making your cousin's death look like a believable accident, and there isn't a damn thing that I can prove."

Schmidt intently glared at the detective at first, but then only smiled, careful not to say a single word. The look on Wolfgang's face only continued to mock the detective, as if to say, *'Catch me if you can, asshole.'*

The two sat there silent for several long moments, and both men continued to glare at each other.

"My regards, Herr Schmidt. You have friends in very high places."

The detective then slowly stood up.

"We are not done here, Herr Schmidt. Whatever you did or wherever you are storing those paintings, I will find them. I will be all over your ass every single time you return here to Munich. I will hunt you down like an animal. I will follow you, and I will be all over you, every single time you come into town."

Schmidt stood up and smirked at the detective. He then offered his hand for what he hoped would be a friendly handshake. The detective looked down at his hand, coldly ignoring his offer.

"If you're smart, you won't be returning to Munich anytime soon."

Wolfgang broadly smiled as his two o'clock United Airlines flight to Chicago that afternoon was about to start boarding.

"I look forward to seeing you again, Detective." Schmidt gleefully exclaimed, as he grabbed his carry-on bag and briskly walked towards the entrance gate door to the waiting Boeing 747.

Hildebrandt watched Schmidt board the plane and slowly, smiled to himself. Despite not having the evidence to apprehend and arrest the art dealer on murder charges, he decided to be patient. Hildebrandt chose to play it very, very cool.

The detective knew he had the home-court advantage.

CHAPTER TEN

It was just after nine o'clock in the morning as I was settling in my office with my usual Starbucks coffee. It had been a few days since Don Marchese's funeral, and I had finished the feature stories on his murder investigation and its' aftermath. By all accounts, I went pretty easy on him. It was a very respectable news story and biography on the life and death of the well-respected Mafioso. Even my assistant editor, Mike Daudelin, thought it was a very classy and respectful piece. The headline for the leading news story for that day was "Death of a Gentleman Mafioso," and I received some complimentary emails on the story, including one from his daughter, Anna Maria.

I had been turning over the mobster's alleged Vatican connections over and over in my mind, and I couldn't get it out of my head. It amazed me that a local Chicago man of his stature would have been able to pull off the sale of the art investments of the Vatican without the rest of the world knowing about it. It was a very intriguing story indeed, and I decided to walk over to the office of the 'Editor of the Daily Planet' and pick his brain.

"What's up, Chief?" as I walked into his usually disheveled office. He was on his feet at that moment with some paper towels in his hand, drying off some spilled coffee that had accidentally splattered on some various documents on his desk.

"Son-of-a-bitch," he was cursing. "I always know it's going to be a bad day when I start off spilling coffee,"

"Why don't you clean off your desk for a change, so you can keep your office from being declared a federal disaster area?" I retorted as I made myself comfortable in front of his desk. I felt like every time I entered my assistant editor's office, I was putting my health at risk and needed to take a bath in Lysol afterward.

"Shut up, Paulie…I know where everything is."

"Of course, you do," I agreed.

He was situating himself while discarding his coffee-soaked paper towels.

"Maybe you should do a 'Brawny Paper Towel' commercial," I sarcastically suggested.

"You're working on your stand-up routine, I see," as he finally made himself comfortable behind his desk.

"What's on your mind, Paulie?"

Mike and I had this telepathy thing going on, so he immediately read my mind, knowing I was ready to bounce something off of him.

"I've been thinking about my favorite wise-guy lately," as I started.

"Marchese? What about him?"

"Chaz Rizzo made mention of something that I thought was a little unusual at the wake over at Belmont the other night, and I haven't been able to get it out of my head."

Mike was intently listening while trying to finish what was left of his coffee.

"Chaz Rizzo? From Channel Eight?"

"Yep."

"Be careful of whatever comes out of that guy's mouth. I think he starts more rumors that anything else. I often wonder sometimes whether he creates a lot of bullshit and convinces his newsroom to let him pursue all of his wild goose chases," Daudelin replied.

"Yeah, Mike. I would sometimes agree with that," I slowly answered, thinking for a few moments while Mike finished drying off his coffee-stained white shirt.

"But Rizzo said something that took me for a loop the other night."

"Like?"

"Did you know anything about the Vatican Museum having a 'garage sale'?"

"What? What are you talking about?" Mike Daudelin had a shocked look on his face, looking at me with three eyes.

"You heard me. Do you know anything about the Vatican selling and brokering off fine art to pay their various lawsuits and legal bills?"

Mike looked at me closely for a few minutes, not knowing where this information came from.

"Are you kidding? Chaz Rizzo told you this?"

"Yes."

A few more moments of silence before Daudelin responded.

"Coming from someone else, I might believe it. But from Rizzo? Sounds ridiculous."

I looked at him and shook my head.

"Why?"

"Did you have your 'bullshit meter' off while he was selling you this crap?" he asked.

"Why do you think that?" I ignorantly asked.

"First of all, Rizzo has a terrible habit of creating rumors and innuendos and trying to find later or create the facts to back them up. They should have fired him and sent him to the 'National Enquirer' years ago. His news reporting is usually very sloppy at best."

"And you know this from experience?" I innocently asked although I did remember Channel Eight putting out a news story retraction on a political bribe headline that he supposedly 'broke wide open' from City Hall.

"Please, Paulie. Don't make me go there. We almost took the bait a few times on his breaking news story bullshit," my assistant editor recalled.

"So, you think the Vatican having a 'garage sale' is a load of crap?"

"Of course. Do you realize who we're talking about here? The Vatican is the richest, wealthiest sovereignty in the world, and if they sold off all of their assets, they could probably eradicate world poverty with just one check." Mike started fidgeting with his automatic pencil, trying to get it to work.

"Ok, but let's say there is some truth to it. How would we go about verifying this story?"

"Paulie? Why? Why would the Vatican bother to finance all of these 'soon-to-be-bankrupt' archdioceses? Selling off valuable artworks and masterpieces that have been part of the Vatican Museum for centuries? Just to pay off all of these child molestation lawsuits. Why not let them go broke, file bankruptcy and be done with it as Boston and Portland did? It makes no sense."

I was silent for a few moments, contemplating my bosses' thought process.

"I don't know, Mike. Where would Rizzo hear such a rumor? I saw him getting friendly with some of the Marchese Family soldiers at the funeral home the other night, so he's gotta know or must have heard something."

"Then why isn't he reporting it?" Mike asked.

"Maybe he's scared, Chief," I replied. "Maybe he doesn't want to do an unscrupulous news story on Don Marchese, especially so soon after his death."

"Chaz Rizzo scared? He's too vain and too stupid to be scared," he started to laugh. "That will be the day when Chaz Rizzo is scared."

We both sat there silently for a few moments, turning the subject over and over in our heads.

"Unless you have something solid, Paulie, I'm not sure we should do another story on him either," Mike replied.

"Listen, Mike, ...suppose there's some truth in this rumor. How could we go about verifying this?"

"It's bullshit, Paulie. Get it out of your head."

"No," I exclaimed. "Chief, I'm serious. What if it's true? What if some foreign henchman, or maybe even the Vatican, is behind Marchese's murder? Nobody knows who put the hit on him, and everybody agrees it was a professional job, and it probably wasn't local. What if the killer or killers is someone big? Someone bigger than any of the crime families here in Chicago?"

Mike started to laugh. "I think you've been watching 'The Godfather' movies way too many times."

"I'm serious. What if there is some truth to all of this? How could we go about verifying this story?"

Mike put down whatever he was fidgeting with and sternly locked his eyes with mine.

"Paul, I won't have you wasting your time or this paper's money trying to chase down one of Rizzo's bullshit stories!"

I then got up from his office chair, as I was starting to get irritated. I had an acute feeling, a sixth sense about this story, and I wanted to pursue it.

"Chief, I got a funny feeling here. Who else would have put out a hit on Marchese? Rizzo kept saying that he must have really 'pissed somebody off." Maybe it was someone from a European crime cartel that had an interest in some of these sold Vatican paintings? Maybe he double-crossed somebody?"

My assistant editor looked at me, shaking his head. There was a long delay in his response.

"I'm not crazy about this, Paulie. But just to show you that I trust you, see if you can get more information out of Rizzo, and bring back some ideas on how you plan to conduct this news story investigation. When you come back with some solid leads or some other evidence confirmed by anyone other than Rizzo, we'll sit down and talk," Daudelin reasoned.

"So, you're going to make me have sex with Rizzo to find out where his sources are coming from? Come on, Chief. How far do you think that will take me?"

"That's your problem, Paulie. But if I go to the editor and tell him that you're working on a Vatican murder connection to Don Marchese's death, we'll both get fired."

I thought about this alternative for a few moments.

"Okay, Chief. I have a few ideas. I will make some phone calls and see if I can corner Rizzo. Maybe I can get some information out of him and a few other wise-guy friends that I know."

Mike emptied his coffee cup in the garbage. He then started playing with his computer mouse, pretending that he was doing an honest day's work, which he seldom did. Although I loved and respected my assistant editor, I often wished he would spend more time writing and editorializing some of these stories himself, instead of ordering around his reporters to do it for him. Mike spent way too much time logging onto social media, on his Facebook, Instagram, and Snapchat accounts.

He then caught me as I was leaving.

"Paulie, you're on a short leash on this one," he firmly reminded me.

"I get it, Chief," as I quickly exited his office. I had a couple of ideas, and I knew exactly where to start.

At that moment, I had no idea what I was about to discover.

CHAPTER ELEVEN

It was past noon on that July day in the ancient city of Florence. The summer Tuscan sun was recklessly beating down on the medieval countryside, making the afternoon heat almost unbearable.

Don Rodolfo Giammarco, a wealthy Florentine businessman, was sitting on his second-floor terrace patio within his villa that muggy, hot day last July. He had just finished his midday 'cinetta' of 'Linguini Alla Pescatore.'

'Don Rodolfo' as he was often called, was a very influential entrepreneur. The spacious Tuscan villa of the latter sat on the foothills of his ninety-five-acre winery, growing the Sangiovese grapes that produced the superb Chianti wines in the region.

The Giammarco family lineage went way back to the 15th Century, with maternal bloodlines to the wealthy Medici family of Florence. Giammarco, now in his early eighties, was considered the patriarch of one of the oldest, most influential families in the Tuscany valley, and he reveled in the immense respect that was given to him from all those whom he was associated with.

Giammarco was well esteemed within the community. He was an extremely wealthy venture capitalist, known for his financial and political influence in and around 'Firenze.' He had several profitable bars and restaurants, real estate developments, and other businesses located within the city and its surrounding villages. Giammarco was also known for his 'ruthless' reputation, which was all connected to his very profitable loan sharking business. Although he never considered himself as the head of a 'crime syndicate' organization, he had a dozen or more henchman ('associates' as he liked to call them) who were all too willing to exert whatever physical means were necessary to make sure Don Rodolfo

Giammarco had his way. The Italian newspapers often referred to Giammarco's association as the 'Firenze Mafia.' It had been rumored that he once stabbed to death a delinquent business associate who refused to pay an outstanding juice loan in the middle of one of his restaurants. He then had one of his culinary associates slice up the poor bastard's body and then, thrown into the River Arno.

It has been often said that there are those men at the twilight of their lives, who wish to be well-loved and fondly remembered when they leave this world and ascend into the next. In the case of Rodolfo Giammarco, although he wanted to be loved and well-respected, he was above all else...enormously feared.

Despite his dark side, Giammarco was also known for his philanthropic efforts and activities in and around the Tuscany province. He served on several director's boards of various banks, not-for-profit foundations, and disabled children's homes and orphanages.

But there was one organization that he was particularly fond of and proud to be a part of, and that was his position as the board chairman of Florence's Uffizi Museum. This was a coveted position that had been held in his family for several generations, and as a cultural donor and benefactor to the Uffizi, took an extreme interest in its operational policies, art acquisitions, and all its executive decisions. Don Giammarco was also an avid art collector, owning several expensive masterpieces of his own. He appreciated the fine cultural arts that the medieval city had to offer to a respectable and affluent man of his means.

Don Rodolfo was enjoying his espresso that early afternoon, when one of his young associates, Mariano, brought him the afternoon edition of the 'La Repubblica' newspaper.

"Il tuo giornale, Zio Rodolfo."

"Grazie, Mariano," he said to his favorite nephew with gratitude.

Mariano Giammarco was the son of his oldest brother, who had passed away from lung cancer at a young age when Mariano was only six years old. Because he was without a mother (she abandoned him and his father when he was born), Don Rodolfo accepted sole custody of young Mariano and raised him like a son, and that he had no children of his own. His young nephew, now in his late twenties, had completed his law studies at the University of Padua a few years ago, and Don Giammarco was grooming Mariano to become his business 'consigliere' and eventually, sole heir to the family business and its fortunes.

"Have you heard the news this morning, Zio?"

"No, what news are you referring to?" he patiently asked.

"CNN reported the death of some old man in Munich the other day. He was found dead in his apartment, apparently due to a gas leak from a faulty stove. When the Munich police went over to investigate, they found forty-two paintings, crated up, and stamped "Firenze" on them. The old man had been stashing these paintings in his attic since they were stolen from the Uffizi during the Second World War," Mariano explained.

The older man's face changed colors and began to turn red. He had always taken a keen interest in any news regarding the Uffizi Museum. He became shocked when his nephew explained the details of the news report from the worldwide cable news network. Don Rodolfo put on his reading glasses and hurriedly, rampaged through the first several pages of the Italian newspaper.

There on the second page was a detailed news article describing the Munich art discovery:

Stolen Uffizi Masterpieces Discovered in Munich

Don Rodolfo carefully read the article several times, making sure he had not missed, skipped, or misunderstood a single word. His nephew was sitting at the table with him when Rodolfo made a directive.

"Mariano, go on the internet and see whatever else you can find out about the information regarding this Uffizi discovery. Also, contact all the Uffizi board members. We need to have an emergency board of directors meeting tomorrow morning."

"Yes, Zio," he obediently replied to his uncle.

The rest of that afternoon was spent making telephone calls to the other board directors of the Uffizi Museum, several of the curators, and the legal counsel to both the Uffizi and the Giammarco family. He directly ordered one of the assistant curators, Claudia Romanelli, to research the stolen Uffizi masterpieces and to possibly, provide a list of those missing artworks and see if they corresponded to the recovered Munich paintings. Within a few hours, Signorina Romanelli had reconstructed the list of those missing pieces, which were extensively documented by the Most Reverend Elio Cardinal Della Croce, who was the Cardinal of Florence during that period in November 1943.

Before five o'clock that afternoon, Don Giammarco had a comprehensive list of those forty-two stolen artworks with the accurate description and the artist of each painting. Those paintings were notoriously sold by the Uffizi to the Third Reich in November 1943 for seventy-eight thousand lire.

Claudia Romanelli called Don Rodolfo to give him another update on the information she had gathered on the stolen masterpieces.

"Don Giammarco," she reminded the influential Chairman of the Board that afternoon, "these paintings were the same Vatican Museum paintings that were consigned to the Uffizi in May 1938 by Pope Pius XI to Mussolini for safekeeping, away from the Germans.

According to the museum records, these paintings were 'sold' at a discounted price to the Third Reich in exchange for the trade-off of 103 Jewish refugees that were being protected and hidden by the Catholic Church."

"Really," responded Giammarco, trying very hard not to get upset upon hearing this news.

"Cardinal Della Croce sold off these paintings, thinking the Vatican would not miss them."

There was a long silence on the phone.

"And by the way," she continued. "Those Jewish refugees that were traded for those paintings? They never made it to the border of Switzerland. They were later shipped off to Auschwitz, where they were all eventually murdered."

Giammarco silently listened to the assistant curator, his blood beginning to boil with anger.

Romanelli then added, "The pastor of the Basilica Santissima Annunziata, his name was Fr. Angelo Gentile, according to our records, was also shot and killed by the Nazis in retaliation for hiding those Jews in his church."

Giammarco started boiling with rage upon listening to this information.

'Quei figli di cazzo puttane,"he swore out loudly.

"Those goddamn Nazi bastards! And now, they still have our paintings," he vociferously exclaimed over the telephone.

Don Rodolfo's next telephone call was to that of his old friend, the Chief of Police of the Florence Police Department.

"Ciao Giuseppe," as Commander Giuseppe Maffei answered the telephone.

"Ciao, Don Rodolfo. I presume you are calling me regarding the Uffizi discovery in Munich."

"Of course. In what regard can we begin an investigation into the theft of these missing artworks from the Uffizi?"

Commander Maffei began to laugh loudly at the Don.

"You wish to file a police report regarding the theft of these paintings, almost eighty years after they've been stolen?"

Giammarco was silent for several moments, allowing Maffei to get the amusement of his request out of his system.

"Giuseppe...we can do this the clean and legal way, or we can do this 'my way.' Which method do you prefer?"

The Commander thought about it for several moments.

"I will send over a detective to the Uffizi Museum tomorrow morning, bright and early. We will see how far we can go and how much progress we can make with the Germans."

The Don loudly replied, "These people are not Germans, Giuseppe. They are Nazi's. Damn ruthless Nazi's, who ripped off the Uffizi Museum and killed 103 Jews and a church pastor in the process."

Commander Maffei patiently listened to Tuscany's most influential businessman.

"That was a long time ago. That was the war, Rodolfo."

"FUCK THE WAR!" he loudly screamed.

Giammarco rose from his patio table, grasped his espresso cup, and threw it down onto the marble patio, as it exploded into a thousand pieces. He was still holding his cell phone while loudly exerting his explosive temper.

"Those Nazi bastards raped and pillaged our town of its artworks and killed over one hundred local Jews in the process. Now all you can say is *that was the war*?"

The Police Commander tried in vain to calm down the Tuscan Mafioso.

"Rodolfo, we cannot hold the Munich government responsible for the actions of several callous Nazi soldiers who have since been either tried for their war crimes, have either died or have been killed long since the war's end. We cannot 'declare war' on the Munich government if they do not release those paintings to us," Commander Maffei tried to reason with Don Rodolfo.

Giammarco was unsuccessfully trying to control his anger.

"As I said, Giuseppe," the Don loudly reiterated his point. "We can do this the legal way, or we can do this *my way.*"

There were several more silent moments over the phone.

"I will send over one of my detectives, and we will see where this goes," Maffei said in closing, as he politely ended the conversation.

Bright and early the next morning, Detective Mario D'Agostini was at the Piazza Della Signoria in the center of the city, in front of the ancient brass doors of the Uffizi Museum. The assistant curator, Claudia Romanelli, was expecting him at the early hour of 7:00 am.

She began to escort him through the Vasari Corridor, making small talk. At the same time, they walked through the elevated enclosed passageway connecting the Palazzo Vecchio to the Palazzo Pitti within the medieval structure of the Uffizi building. This massive, renaissance museum, constructed in 1564 by the Medici Family, still contains all the numerous, antiquated colossal windows, allowing the morning Tuscan sun to illuminate its long, gigantic corridors brightly. From the left side of these hallways, one can see the glistening River Arno, as it follows its northern bank near the Ponte Vecchio. They walked along the ancient corridor to the Palazzo Pitti, eventually ending their ten-minute walk to the massive, large conference room located just east of the Torre dei Mannelli.

Romanelli knocked on the large, ornate rosewood door, escorting the detective to the enormously long, antique wooden conference table, where the assembled board of directors were anxiously awaiting D'Agostini's arrival.

"Buon Giorno" greeted Don Giammarco, as the detective introduced himself and shook the hands of each one of the twelve Uffizi's board of directors. They were all brought together for an emergency meeting called by their board chairman.

After Romanelli brought over caffe' and refills to those already gathered, Don Giammarco began the business at hand.

"Detective, as you are aware, the news of these stolen Uffizi paintings discovered in Munich the other day has been quite alarming to those of us here at the museum. These paintings were mostly 'stolen' by the Nazis in 1943 in exchange for the lives of 103 Jewish refugees, who were eventually shipped off to the death camps in Auschwitz and were murdered," the Chairman of the Board explained.

"I have been made aware of the circumstances, Don Giammarco. Commander Maffei has briefed me on the details of this Munich discovery," D'Agostini replied, as he was emptying a packet of sugar into his small, espresso cup. The smell of the Italian caffe' that early morning began to take over the musty odor of the ancient, renaissance conference room, complete with Botticelli paintings and large, picture windows overlooking the lush, ornate Uffizi gardens.

"What other information do you have?" inquired Alberto Piacenti, a wealthy local businessman who was one of the board members.

"I have made a telephone call to the Mayor of Munich, a gentleman by the name of Bertram Kossel. We discussed in detail the circumstances at hand. I then reminded him of the international treaty, called the Washington Principals on Nazi-Confiscated Art Agreement which addresses the confiscated art by the Nazi regime during World War II. As you all know, this international treaty was encouraged by the United Nations and NATO to return stolen Nazi artifacts to their rightful owners. His response was not encouraging," D'Agostini clarified. Giammarco looked intently at the detective.

"And what was his response?"

"He stated that the heirs to the estate of this deceased old man produced a legal bill of sale for the purchase and acquisition by the Nazi's of these paintings, dated November 1943. Because this 'bill of sale' appears legitimate, according to Mayor Kossel, the Washington Principals Treaty does not apply, as a fair price was paid for them at the time and signed by the rightful authorities of the Uffizi Museum."

"A rightful bill of sale?" The chairman replied.

Giammarco rose from the head of the table and slammed his open hand, shaking and startling everyone within the room.

"He calls the lives of 103 Jewish refugees, a Catholic priest, and seventy-eight thousand lire a legitimate, fair price? He calls this a legal bill of sale?" he screamed from across the conference chamber.

Signore Piacente chimed in, "So mostly, the City of Munich, along with the German government, has told us to 'go play with ourselves.' Is this correct, Detective?"

"That is correct."

"What information do we have regarding the deceased and his estate, and who is the executor?" asked Dottore Marco Fanizza, an affluent physician in Florence.

"Interesting that you should ask that question," D'Agostini began to elaborate. "The executor and sole heir to the Estate of Hermann Klackschmidt is his American cousin, a Chicago art dealer by the name of Wolfgang Schmidt. My sources have revealed that he is currently there now settling his cousins' affairs and that he has been allowed to take full possession of the decedent's assets, which includes these forty-two stolen Uffizi paintings. Schmidt is the one who possesses the original Nazi 'Bill of Sale', which he presented to the City of Munich and its Mayor Kossel. They have now recognized this document as the right deed to the ownership of these rediscovered paintings."

Giammarco was silent for a moment. "I have heard that name before," he quietly said. "He is well known within the art world and had brokered, sold, and acquired priceless masterpieces all over Europe and the States. It is no coincidence that Schmidt is the one to conveniently handle his cousin's estate and the possession of these paintings," Don Rodolfo recalled.

"I also made a phone call to the Chief of Police there in Munich." D'Agostini continued.

"There seem to be some suspicions as to the nature of this old man's death and the involvement of his cousin regarding this sudden event. The Klackschmidt family, we have come to learn, have owned these Uffizi paintings since the Second World War, as his father was the personal secretary to the Nazi General Himmler," the Detective summarized.

101

"Maybe this Wolfgang Schmidt has run out of inventory and decided to bump off his cousin to have access to the hidden, stolen paintings," Fanizza observed.

"One would think," observed Piacente.

Don Giammarco then looked over to the other end of the conference table, and into the eyes of the Uffizi Museum's legal counsel, Dottore Edoardo Giannini. He was an older man in his late fifties, a former practicing attorney, and currently, the magistrate judge within the Tuscany province. Giannini was well versed in the rules and practices of international law.

"Dottore Giannini, what is your take on all of this?" asked Giammarco.

"Quite frankly, Don Rodolfo, this is a matter of international law. Although the Washington Principals Treaty has been signed and agreed upon by the NATO nations internationally, the German government is under no obligation to seize and return those stolen paintings to us. This treaty, quite frankly, is under the guidelines of interpretation. If the German government would rather accept a Nazi 'bill of sale' over the treaty guidelines that were signed and agreed to internationally twenty years ago, there isn't much that we can do," replied Giannini.

"And we cannot file any legal motions preventing anyone else from seizing those paintings?" Piacente asked.

"On what grounds? The Italian government has no jurisdiction over the City of Munich or the German government for that matter. The best we can do is to apply international pressure to convince them to do otherwise," the magistrate judge observed.

Don Rodolfo sat there, shaking his head. "So, this Washington Principals Treaty isn't worth the goddamn paper it was written on," he observed.

"That is correct," replied Giannini.

D'Agostini emptied his espresso cup and looked over to the Chairman of the Board while attempting to make his final point.

"Don Giammarco, I was informed by Mayor Kossel that we are not the only ones laying claim to those stolen paintings," he interjected, knowing that his statement would enrage the chairman even more.

"How so?" Giammarco was pretending to play stupid.

"I was informed by Mayor Kossel that the Vatican Museum is also claiming these stolen paintings as well. These paintings were originally consigned by the Vatican to the Uffizi for safekeeping back in 1938," D'Agostini replied.

Giammarco looked around the conference table, completely frustrated. There were several moments of silence, and everyone in the conference room was exasperated in finding a solution to the problem of recovering these stolen and now rediscovered, Uffizi Museum paintings.

"Thank you, gentlemen. We will be in touch." Giammarco said, as he rose from the head of the table and called the meeting adjourned. Don Rodolfo then wished each one of the board members a pleasant rest of their day as they all left the elegant conference room to begin their daily routines on that sunny, pleasant Tuscany morning in Florence.

Detective Mario D'Agostini was the last one to leave the conference room, as he noticed Don Giammarco, standing in front of the conference table facing the picture window, staring off at the green, lush Uffizi gardens outside.

"Have a good day," D'Agostini wished Don Rodolfo.

He only glanced at the detective, making eye contact and granting him a pleasant nod. He then continued to stare out at the well-manicured gardens outside.

D'Agostini realized that Don Giammarco was more than upset. He recognized that Giammarco had looked upon those stolen Uffizi masterpieces as a personal assault upon his beloved museum, his city, his heritage, and, most of all, his home.

It was as though, the recovery of those paintings had become a personal vendetta by the most powerful man in Florence against a ruthless, former Nazi regime, with its ruminants still deeply intact within the city walls of Munich. Detective Mario D'Agostini now understood that, according to Giammarco, that this was now very personal.

The recovery of those stolen Uffizi paintings would promptly be dealt with personally by Don Rodolfo Giammarco...

"My way".

CHAPTER TWELVE

Pope Emeritus Honorius V was sitting in the study, enjoying his second cup of espresso on that hot summer day in his papal apartment. It was a warm, July day in Vatican City, as St. Peter's square was alive with hundreds of tourists bustling down below.

There was a loud knock on the door.

"Your lunch is here, your Holiness," the older nun exclaimed.

Sister Giovanna was a small lady in stature with a big smile and seemed to enjoy looking after "Papa Onorio" in his papal apartment, looking after his every need.

"Molto Grazie, Suora," he exclaimed with a smile on his face.

He was sitting at a table in front of the window of his papal apartment, watching the crowds of people gather at the Vatican Piazza down below. The heat index was beginning to climb past the point of being comfortable as he sat there with the veranda window open. He had the "La Repubblica" newspaper folded on the table, along with several other publications that he spent most of his time reading in the morning, including the "New York Times" and the "Die Welt" in his native German.

The former Josef Claus Schroder had just celebrated his 90th birthday last week. Although the former pontiff had some coronary disease issues and had three heart stents installed a few years ago, he was very much in perfect health for a man of his age. He walked his usual ten kilometers early every morning in the Vatican garden and around Vatican City and was very

105

conscious of his diet. His lunch on that day consisted of some minestrone and a small lettuce salad. He seldom ate red meat and enjoyed those delicious pasta dishes prepared by Sister Giovanna on only rare occasions.

Sister Giovanna set up his napkin and silverware and placed his lunch tray on his veranda table overlooking St. Peter's Square.

"Grazie," he replied again as she left his room.

Papa Onorio continued to stare out of the window of his papal apartment, slowly picking at his lunch. He was not very hungry on that day. The Pope Emeritus was very depressed and had not had much of an appetite over the last few days. The Italian newspaper, "La Repubblica," had published some slanderous editorials a few days before, criticizing him of his papal resignation in 2013 and his very questionable, very secretive Nazi background.

The young Josef Schroder was only fourteen years old when Nazi Germany came into power back in his native Hamburg, Germany. Like most children his age, he was inundated with the questionable intonations and mantras of the Third Reich. Young Josef was conscripted into the Hitler Youth, as membership was required by law of all German boys his age. He resented the policies and doctrines of the Nazi's during that period and even experienced the murder of one of his mentally disabled cousins by a Nazi soldier. But against his will and moral scruples, he was drafted into the German aircraft corps as a 'Luftwaffenhelfer' while still in the seminary and began training in the German infantry.

As a German soldier, he was interned in a prisoner of war camp when the American troops captured him and his unit in 1945. He was released a few months later at the end of the war in May 1945, then re-entering and continuing his seminary studies until his ordination in 1951. Although he enjoyed a very long and influential career as an archbishop, and later as a Cardinal of Munich, his dubious Nazi background during the Second World War had always been questioned. The former Josef Schroder publicly and privately disavowed the intonations of the Third Reich throughout his lifetime and career. Still, he has never been able to escape the dark, Nazi shadows of his past life.

As he continued to pick at his meal, there was another knock on the door.

"Permesso, you're Holiness," announced his papal secretary, Monsignor Gianpaolo Iacobelli, as he opened the door to his papal apartment.

"Accomadi," the former pope replied in an almost inaudible voice.

"You wished to see me, Your Holiness?"

"Yes. Have you written my response to that slanderous editorial, which was published by the 'La Repubblica' newspaper last week?"

"Yes, Your Holiness. As you recall, I gave that document to you yesterday."

Papa Onorio walked over to his adjacent office and searched across his desk. As expected, the Pope Emeritus did not own or operate a computer and did not receive or acknowledge e-mails. He did business 'the old-fashioned way' and depended on his papal secretary to draft and read all of his correspondences and outgoing communications.

"I do not see it here, Gianni. Could you bring me another copy?"

"Yes, your Holiness," he replied, ready to exit his papal apartment.

"Eh, Gianni," a name which the former pope fondly called his secretary, "what did it say?"

"Only that you vehemently deny any of the editor's accusations regarding any Nazi doctrines or policies during your time in the Second World War," Iacobelli replied.

"Okay. Please send it out immediately. What is that editor's name again?"

"Massimo Gianforte, Your Holiness."

Papa Onorio sat back on his chair facing the window, as he motioned his secretary to sit next to him at the table.

"Please sit down," as he pointed to the chair. The Monsignor made himself comfortable.

"Gianni, I have prayed and prayed over these needless, blasphemous editorials that have been written about me over the years, especially since my resignation. How can I continue to go on while my defamation by these reckless newspaper editors, especially those like Gianforte, continue to be published?"

Iacobelli sat there and nodded his head, feeling sympathy for the former Pope Honorius V.

Monsignor Gianpaolo Iacobelli was a very well-educated cleric within the Vatican See, who attended the University of Rome and graduated with a doctoral degree in canon law from the Sapienza Universita' Di Roma and its seminary. Because of his legal background, he knew that there was some factual basis for the slanderous comments and the editorials that the newspaper had published. But even if Gianforte's accusations were indeed reckless and critical of the former pope, the facts were correct. By all historical accounts and by the retired pope's admission, the Pope Emeritus was a former German soldier who fought for Nazi Germany during the Second World War and at one time, was a 'Nazi.'

"I will do whatever I can to assist you, your Holiness, and your plight will always be in my prayers," he replied.

"Thank you, Gianni."

The Pope Emeritus continued to stare out of the papal apartment window, as Monsignor Iacobelli continued to sit with him in his study.

"Have you heard about that news article from Munich?"

"What news, Your Holiness?"

"There was an old man who had been found dead in his apartment in downtown Munich two days ago. When the authorities were called, they discovered forty-two valuable, priceless paintings which have been stolen and missing since the Second World War," Papa Onorio explained.

"Really? Where were these paintings from?"

"These paintings were masterpieces stolen from galleries and museums by the Nazi's and have never been discovered or resurfaced until now."

Monsignor Iacobelli was inquisitive.

"Who was this old man, and how did he die?"

"I don't recall. He was found dead, not sure if it was a homicide," Papa Onorio answered. "Nobody has any other information on how or why it happened."

"Where were these paintings from?"

"The article says that these paintings were crated and stamped "FIRENZE." It looks like these had been missing from the Uffizi Gallery in Florence since the Second World War."

Iacobelli was silent, and he tried to study the facial expressions of the former pontiff.

"Do you remember your renaissance art history, Gianni?"

"Regarding?"

"Regarding the Vatican artworks that were sent on consignment to the Uffizi Gallery in 1938 by Pope Pius XI to Mussolini, for his 'Black Shirt Army' to guard and protect? Do you recall that information?"

Iacobelli sat there puzzled for a minute.

"I remember reading something about it."

Papa Onorio looked directly at the Monsignor, ready to make a poignant demand.

"Gianni, I want you to go through the records of the Vatican Museum, and scour all of the documentation and letters that you can find. I am sure there must be some detail of the priceless museum artworks that were sent up to Florence by Pope Pius XI. There must be some letter of proof or documentation that the Pope kept, a shipping letter, a bill of lading...something."

"What are you thinking, Your Holiness?" Monsignor Iacobelli seemed perplexed.

The Pope Emeritus suddenly changed facial expressions, and the shadow of a smile began to appear on his face, He was about to drive his point home with his papal secretary.

"I believe that there is a possibility those artworks discovered in Munich, apparently stolen from the Uffizi Gallery, are those missing Vatican art paintings that were sent up to Florence before the war."

Monsignor Iacobelli tried to follow the former Pope's train of thought.

"And you believe that these missing art pieces belong to the Vatican, and not the Uffizi?"

"Once these artworks are identified, yes...I do believe these are true. I believe those paintings belong to the Vatican Museum."

Papa Onorio started eating his lunch, consuming his almost cold minestrone and his green salad. He enjoyed talking with his brilliant papal secretary, who has been with him since his early days at the Vatican.

"Do you not think, that if I, as the Pope Emeritus, reclaimed these stolen, missing art pieces from the Vatican almost eighty years ago, now discovered in Munich, that the Roman press might begin thinking differently of me? What if I brought these valuable masterpieces back here to Rome, do you think that this could restore my reputation and help secure my papal legacy here at the Vatican?" he asked his Papal Secretary.

Iacobelli sat there silent. At that moment, he was without words.

"Gianni, we must make the press finally understand that I am not a 'Nazi,' and that I am no longer a 'former Nazi soldier.' We must recover and bring those missing art pieces back home to the Vatican?"

They both sat there, as Papa Onorio finished his lunch. He was now getting excited about the idea that he had in restoring his papal reputation. The Italian press was never kind to the Pope Emeritus since the time of his papal election. As the papal conclave elected the former Josef Cardinal Schroder in April 2002, his reputation as a Vatican enforcer was always criticized.

It was his strict policies and doctrines in upholding the current philosophies of the Roman Catholic Church and those specifically related to the handling of the "Pedophile Priest Scandals," which attracted the most criticism. There seemed to be no room for compromise as his clergy, his staff, and his various Vatican diplomats dutifully followed his orders. They made sure that those deviant priests were pulled from their predator environments and reshuffled into other Catholic communities. His German and Nazi soldier background only made him an easy target for the Italian press, as they were always extremely critical of the Vatican's past handling and protocol of those enumerated sexual abuse scandals.

Papa Onorio's reasons for resigning as pope was officially attributed to his health, as he always maintained that he no longer had the physical strength to perform his papal duties. But judging by his age and his present good health, the press has had their suspicions. The 'La Repubblica' published a slanderous editorial several days after his resignation in 2013, accusing the former pope of conceding to the pressures and past cover-ups of those many sexual abuse scandals now plaguing the Catholic Church. That article accused him of being the 'architect' of that scandalous policy under the reign of Pope John Paul II. It was a policy that specifically directed the transfer and relocation of those priest pedophiles, secretly forcing them to leave the church without prosecution, and paying off its many sexually abused victims.

"Perhaps, I can be remembered as the Pope Emeritus, who recovered the stolen Nazi art masterpieces from the Vatican. We could have a triumphant homecoming at the Vatican Museums, and we could do a press conference displaying these stolen pieces of art from the Nazis."

Papa Onorio now displayed a gleam in his eye, as he began to fantasize about the probability of his bringing home those missing art masterpieces.

"Your Holiness? How do you expect the Munich authorities and especially the German government to release those missing works of art? I am sure the Uffizi has already laid claim to them. How would these missing masterpieces be properly returned, with the media headaches and the potential bad publicity that could also be associated with your involvement in this?" Iacobelli asked.

"We must find a German diplomat or a German art expert who could negotiate and acquire these missing art pieces that properly belong to the Vatican, on our behalf."

Papa Onorio sat there silently for several moments, continuing to stare out of his papal window.

"I read somewhere of a German art dealer in Chicago, who has dealt and specialized in acquiring and selling valuable artworks from museums in Europe," said the Pope Emeritus. "I do not recall his name at the moment. The article stated that this art dealer was very successful in negotiating with the German government in the release of other missing, valuable masterpieces."

He got up from his table by the window and walked back to his office desk, frantically searching for the saved newspaper article, which he cut out concerning this Chicago art dealer. After fifteen minutes or so, he returned to his study where the Monsignor was patiently waiting.

"Here, Gianni...I have it here," as the Pope Emeritus sat back down.

"His name is Wolfgang Schmidt. He is a German art dealer out of Chicago who specializes in European artworks," as he handed the newspaper clipping to Monsignor Iacobelli.

"We must contact him. Discretely, of course."

Monsignor Iacobelli scanned the article after putting on his reading glasses, quietly considering Papa Onorio's request.

"Perhaps my cousin from Chicago could help us," referring to Don Carlo Marchese. "He has been very successful in assisting us in the past. He has been very discrete in all of our prior transactions as well," he stated.

"Yes, Gianni," Papa Onorio exclaimed. "That is an excellent suggestion. You must contact your cousin. I am sure he can help us."

Papa Onorio smiled at his papal secretary's suggestion. He was now excited to finally find a solution to all of the bad, ugly press of which he has been a victim since his papal election and his resignation afterward. He could now, perhaps, embrace his legacy as the righteous Vicar of Rome that he always felt he indeed was. He could soon be the Pope who recovered Nazi stolen Vatican art and rightfully returned this famous art and cultural masterpieces to the Vatican Museum.

Papa Onorio smiled to himself. His rightful place in papal history was now at hand.

CHAPTER THIRTEEN

The Michigan Avenue traffic was flowing slowly that early Tuesday morning last summer, as the assistant curator Veronica Giancarlo was arriving to work. She had just picked up a Starbucks coffee, her usual grande flat white, and was trying hard to walk up the grand steps into the front entrance of the Art Institute of Chicago without spilling her beverage. The sun was already beating down that weekday morning, as she anticipated it to be another scorching hot, July summer day.

Veronica had worked for the art museum since getting her master's degree from the University of Michigan twenty years ago and enjoyed her position as assistant curator of the European and Contemporary Art Departments at the museum. Her job was quite extensive. She assisted the head curator in overseeing more than 300,000 artworks and masterpieces within the museum and was a curatorial expert in those artworks from the Renaissance period. She arranged for special exhibits, managed the maintenance of these various painting displays, and was in charge of acquiring new and exciting art pieces that would blend and fit in with their current collections and presentations.

Veronica enjoyed her museum position, as one would consider her a modern scholar of the art world. She had written several books on her favorite subject of the European Art Renaissance, and was a free-lance, contributing writer to the Chicago Sun-Times, assisting them in all topics concerning the art world. Veronica periodically taught classes on contemporary art at the adjoining art school and headed seminars at local school libraries.

She lived a quiet single life, maintaining a condo in Logan Square occupied by only her and her two golden retrievers. Being in her middle forties, Ms. Giancarlo enjoyed the quietness, and the peace that her current prescribed lifestyle and looked forward to every quiet day of her career at the Art Institute of Chicago. She spent her vacation every summer in Europe, visiting and studying the various artworks of such famous painters like Michelangelo, Rembrandt, Caravaggio, and Donatello.

Ms. Giancarlo was a gorgeous brunette, in an almost nerdy, librarian sort of way. She wore her red, horn-rimmed glasses and her long dark hair in a bun as if it were a mask, trying to intentionally hide her Italian, olive skin and her stunning good looks. Her big, beautiful brown eyes were hidden behind her glasses, and her conservative Anne Klein suits did little to enhance her shapely figure.

Because she was married and divorced many years ago and having no children, she had no interest in pursuing anything or anyone outside of her curatorial art career. Her biological clock had ticked out and exploded a long time ago, and she was in no hurry to engage in anything outside of her quiet, conservative life. Other than work and her running along the lakefront three or four times a week, her life was smooth and uneventful. She had very few friends that she engaged with, and outside of her job, did very little socializing. Veronica couldn't remember the last time she had been on a date, and actively discouraged anyone who considered asking her out on one.

As she settled into her office that morning, she was attending to her job duties of planning the next art exhibit, when she received a long-distance phone call from

Florence, Italy. It was her friend, Claudia Romanelli, who was a fellow curator at the Uffizi Gallery.

"Ciao Claudia," she excitedly answered her desk phone, as she was very proficient in the Italian language.

"Ciao Veronica," her friend responded, as they both started to engage in small talk, updating each other on their current jobs and Veronica's lack of love life.

"Have you heard the news?" she excitedly asked her long-distance, Chicago friend.

"No, Claudia. Are you and Roberto finally engaged?"

"No, that will never happen. He is too much of a 'mammone' ever to get married. He will never leave his mother."

Veronica laughed. She often corresponded with her friend on Facebook, and it was a rare occasion when they talked over the phone.

"The Uffizi has made demands of the German government to return the stolen paintings the Nazis robbed from the gallery during World War II. It's been on CNN and all over the news."

"Really? How interesting," Veronica answered.

She was very familiar with the robbed and missing Uffizi art pieces that were stolen and disappeared from the art gallery back during the war. She had studied the recovery of many of the missing art pieces that the "Monuments Men" of the American army had recovered both during and after the war. She was well aware and familiar with the many stolen masterpieces that Hitler and his "SS" army had robbed from Florence, Paris, Moscow, and many of the other reputable art museums throughout Europe.

"What was the Germans response?" she eagerly asked.

"They're playing stupid," she replied. "They are pretending they know nothing about them. They are probably sitting in some rich German art collector's basement somewhere, making sure no one knows where they are."

Veronica smiled as she 'Googled' the current art news on her computer while still on the phone. She had found the article in the New York Times and was reading it simultaneously while conversing with her friend.

"Are you surprised?" she asked her friend.

"Of course not. The German government has been denying the whereabouts of those and other famous works for decades. The only difference now is that our gallery is now putting the public, worldwide pressure on them. It amazes me that they continue to play the denial game," Claudia observed. "We haven't heard the last of this."

Veronica smiled, trying to finish the conversation. "' Stay tuned' as the Americans would say," as they both laughed over the phone.

They both continued their brief gossip regarding their curator jobs until Veronica cut her off on the phone.

"Arrivederci," Claudia formally replied before ending their phone call.

Veronica put some thought into the New York Times article still on her screen. She wondered and fantasied the whereabouts of those priceless, missing art pieces that the Nazi's made disappear so many years ago. Veronica had spent a considerable amount of time studying those lost masterpieces, works of art ranging from Rembrandt and Giotto to the many priceless works of Raphael. The world is now deprived, she thought to herself, of the fantastic masterpieces that Nazi Germany had so expertly made disappear and would probably never be introduced back into the art world again.

As Veronica Giancarlo continued her curatorial duties that day, she continued to think about missing Uffizi masterpieces. Being an experienced curator, she was very familiar with all other art dealers and world-wide players within the art world, and she began to wonder. What did the other art dealers think of the Uffizi demand of their artworks from Germany? What were their thoughts?

It was just after four o'clock that late afternoon when Veronica decided to make some phone calls to her fellow newspaper colleagues at the Chicago Sun-Times. She wondered if anyone in the contemporary lifestyle department was planning on following up on recent Uffizi news.

"Tom, have you heard anything about the Uffizi news story out of Florence today?"

Tom O'Conner was the assistant editor in charge of the Contemporary Section of the Chicago Sun-Times, whom Veronica had worked with quite often when contributing to a news story concerning the art world.

"Just heard," he answered.

"Are you planning a write up on this soon?" she asked, hinting on maybe being a contributing reporter on this news story.

"Thinking about it. However, the Germans' denial of these missing art pieces is nothing new." Tom answered. "What's your take on this?"

Veronica thought about her answer. "I think we should do a story on it. We need to continue to put pressure on the Germans to come up with some answers on the whereabouts of these missing art pieces."

"Really? And you think we should do another 'Monuments Men" story on a subject that has already been extensively covered?"

"Tom? We both know that there are so many missing pieces of art that the Nazis stole that has never been recovered, especially those pieces from the Uffizi."

"And you think another story on this is going to make these missing pieces reappear? Come on, Veronica. We have so many more social and contemporary issues to cover." O'Conner replied.

"We need to help put pressure on the German government, Tom," she replied, regarding a subject she felt so strongly about.

There were several moments of silence as the assistant editor considered her request.

"Okay, Veronica. I promise I'll think about it," he said, giving her the answer that she didn't want.

"Come on, Tom. Think hard. Please?"

"You know,

Veronica, since you're on the paper's payroll, why don't you do some investigating of your own here and write up the story. If I like it, I'll print it."

"Really?" she was excited at his response.

"Sure. Start with that German art gallery big shot over on North Wells Street. What's his name again?"

"Wolfgang Schmidt?"

"Yeah, that's it. Give him a call. Maybe he can magically tell you where these Uffizi art pieces are, and then we can make a long-distance phone call to Florence and tell them that we've found their missing masterpieces," he sarcastically said.

"You're a funny guy, Tom," as she abruptly hung up the phone.

The assistant curator gave her colleague's suggestion more serious thought, thinking that perhaps, she could make some phone calls to some of her art world connections. Maybe, she could put together an interesting article that could get some local news coverage. It was necessary, Veronica thought, to continue the pressure on the current German government. Maybe she could get a comprehensive list of all of the prominent art collectors in Europe and start to pressure them? She decided to take her colleague's suggestion and left work early.

It was almost five o'clock that afternoon when Veronica exited the taxicab at the storefront Kunstgeschäft Art Gallery, at 524 North Wells Street. The storefront was a small, quaint retail gallery of almost two thousand square feet, with many art displays and paintings of both contemporary and modern art, all from established and new artists. She had known Wolfgang Schmidt for many years and was well familiar with his art store and his family's well-established reputation.

"Good afternoon," said a loud, deep voice from the rear of the store as Veronica entered the old, antiquated art gallery. "To whom do we have this honor?" Wolfgang Schmidt hugged Veronica as he displayed his sudden surprise at her unannounced visit.

"Hello, Wolf...how are you?"

"Has the Art Institute run out of inventory?" he jokingly asked.

"You know that will never happen," as she smiled.

The two of them exchanged small talk, as Wolfgang pulled out his cell phone and proudly showed off recent pictures of his beautiful, one-year-old granddaughter. After about ten minutes of pleasant conversation, Veronica decided to confront Schmidt regarding the subject at hand.

"Wolf...have you heard about the Uffizi's demands of the German government regarding their art pieces stolen by the Nazis?"

Schmidt started to laugh immediately.

"The Uffizi has been demanding the return of those masterpieces for decades. It's an old story getting some new media press," he replied.

"But the people in Florence are pushing the Germans a little harder now and hoping that world-wide pressure from the art world will make them succumb this time."

Schmidt squarely looked at her, trying to be a voice of reason.

"Veronica? How is more pressure going to force the Germans to make disclosures regarding stolen Nazi art pieces that they know nothing about? How will all of this recent news coverage make the Germans do otherwise?" Schmidt asked.

"Would you like an espresso?" Schmidt was graciously trying to change the subject, as he walked over to his espresso coffee bar in the corner of his store.

"An Italian girl never says 'no' to espresso," she replied, following him over to the far side of his art gallery.

As he was making her an espresso doppio, Veronica decided to push the subject. She had heard rumors of Schmidt's grandfather being a Nazi sympathizer and often wondered if his family had any knowledge of the missing, stolen masterpieces that the Nazi's so successfully stashed from the rest of the world.

"Wolf? Did anyone from the Uffizi ever contact you or your family over the years?"

"Of course not," he immediately answered, his back turned away from her while he answered her question. "Why would they call us?"

"I don't know, Wolf. Maybe your status in the European art world? You are quite a player, and your family is very well known and established."

"Or the fact that I'm German?" Schmidt looked at her point-blank, as he offered her the espresso, he so carefully prepared for her.

"Come on, Wolf. You know where I'm going here. I have a good friend who works at the Uffizi, and she gives me the inside scoop of whatever is going on at her gallery and in Florence. You shouldn't be surprised here with my questions," she replied as she was putting a packet of sugar into her espresso.

"Signorina…as you know," Wolf explained, "I would be more than happy to assist the Uffizi in recovering those missing, stolen pieces. It would be very profitable for me to do so. But I have no current connections in Bonn or in Munich that could assist the Uffizi in this recovery."

Veronica continued to study Wolf as he answered her questions, slowly sipping her evening coffee. Somehow, she wasn't surprised at his reluctance to answer her questions and assist her honestly. He was not about to volunteer any information, considering the importance and the value of any evidence regarding those missing art masterpieces.

"The Sun-Times has asked me to do an article to follow up on the Uffizi's German request," she informed the art dealer.

"Good luck with that," Schmidt smiled as he finished his coffee. "If there is any other information that you may need, I will be happy to help you," he pleasantly offered.

Veronica finished her espresso and gave Schmidt a long, five-second stare.

"I'm sure you will, Wolfy," as she kissed him on the cheek. "We'll be in touch."

She walked out of the downtown Chicago art gallery, more convinced than ever that the German art dealer was not telling her the truth. But she also knew that, unless there were more evidence suggesting otherwise, her getting correct facts out of him would be next to impossible. She would have to pursue her other art world connections and get them to assist her in her quest to discover this stolen art reality.

These missing Uffizi masterpieces had now become her obsession, and she was fixated in solving the mystery of these Nazi stolen art pieces. But she had to find another angle.

One way or another, she was going to find out the truth.

CHAPTER FOURTEEN

Munich International Airport was quite busy that summer afternoon, as Don Giammarco arrived at the gate from his short, one-hour flight from Florence. He had boarded an Alitalia Boeing 747 at 12:30 pm that day, carrying only his black satchel. The Don traveled very light that afternoon, as he was only there for some brief business in Munich and was not planning on staying overnight. Although his German was very limited, he was able to hail a taxicab that was waiting outside of the arrival gate of the airport.

"Munich City Hall, please."

"Of course," the cab driver replied in German, as the Mercedes sedan quickly exited out of the arrival traffic and onto the Autobahn, paying a toll along the way. Within fifteen minutes, Don Giammarco was at the front steps of the New Town Hall on Marienplatz, at the northern point of the city.

Don Rodolfo quickly exited the Mercedes taxicab and entered the front doors of the local city hall, negotiating his way to the Mayor's office.

"Mayor Kossel, bitte," he politely asked the young, blonde receptionist in his very limited German.

She looked at the older man whom she had never seen before and wondered why he was demanding to see the Mayor immediately.

"Wem soll ich sagen, anruft," she politely asked. Don Rodolfo looked at the receptionist, and she immediately knew he didn't understand her question.

"Whom should I say is calling?" she asked again, only this time in very distinct English.

"Signore Rodolfo Giammarco, from the Uffizi Museum," he politely replied.

She got up from her desk and disappeared in back for what seemed a very long time. Within ten minutes, she had returned, knowing that she now had a direct order to try and get rid of him.

"I'm sorry, Signore Giammarco, but the Mayor is at the conference at the moment, and he will be in meetings all afternoon."

"This will not take long, Madam. I have traveled directly from Florence today, and I only wish five minutes of his time."

The blonde receptionist was taken aback by this traveler's demands, wishing to immediately see the most important man in Munich without an appointment.

She had no idea who he was.

"I will see what I can do, Signore Giammarco."

She went back to his office, and he could hear some loud commotion going on in the back room. He casually found a black, leather chair at the far wall of the reception area and sat down to patiently wait for Kossel to see him.

"He is still in conference," she managed to say twenty minutes later when she returned to her desk. Don Giammarco politely responded to the young receptionist, who had no idea who he was.

"I will wait, Madam...all day if I have to."

"As you wish," she replied.

The older gentleman withdrew some reading materials and a magazine from his satchel. He began his long wait in the reception area, wondering if he should have confirmed an appointment first before hastily, traveling to Munich from Florence for an unscheduled

126

meeting. He had called Mayor Kossel several times over the last couple of days since he had heard about the rediscovery of the Uffizi Museum art pieces. Although he had left several messages, the Mayor wasn't gracious enough to even return his telephone calls, let alone speak with him.

He obviously had no idea who he was.

It was closer to 4:30 pm, and Giammarco had been patiently waiting in the reception area for over three hours, not any closer to seeing the Mayor of Munich than when he arrived. The attractive, young blonde receptionist had given him some bottled water to make him comfortable during his wait and had gotten up several times from her reception desk, walking directly into the Mayor's office. She was probably trying to convince Kossel that Don Giammarco was not going anywhere.

At 4:45 pm, Mayor Kossel came out of his office and into the reception area to meet Don Giammarco.

"I am very sorry, Signore Giammarco, to make you wait," he apologized after they both shook hands.

"I have been swamped in budget meetings all day, and I just don't have time to meet with you," as Giammarco politely handed him his business card.

The older gentleman only glared in silence at the Mayor for a few moments.

He definitely had no idea who he was.

"Mayor Kossel, I think it would be in your best interests if the two of us met in private, immediately," as the two of them shook hands again. This time, Giammarco very tightly gripped the Mayor's right hand, while he put his left hand into the right side of his suitcoat pocket as if to demonstrate to the ignorant politician that he was carrying a weapon.

Kossel silently looked Giammarco straight in the eyes.

"Cancel my next appointment, Emma," as Giammarco released his firm grip, and the two of them proceeded into the Mayor's office.

The two of them made themselves comfortable, and Don Rodolfo was offered another beverage, which he refused.

"Mayor Kossel, I believe you have some things that belong to us," Giammarco began.

The Mayor only smiled, knowing immediately what the Florence businessman was referring to.

"You are referring to the discovered Uffizi paintings?"

"Those indeed," Rodolfo curtly replied.

"I am very sorry, Signore Giammarco. But those paintings were released yesterday to their rightful owner. We were presented with papers and documentation that supported the correct ownership of those rediscovered paintings. We had no choice but to release them," Kossel explained.

"What documentation was presented, may I ask?"

"I am not at liberty to say, Signore."

Giammarco leaned closer to the mayor's desk while still sitting in front of him.

"Please, Mayor Kossel...let's be informal here. Call me Don Rodolfo," the old man confidently said, his

Beretta weapon now distinctively bulging from his suit coat pocket.

"Tell me, please. What documentation was presented?" he asked again.

The Mayor looked at him and was now very fearful of whom he had irresponsibly let into his office. He soon realized who Don Rodolfo was, and being in a closed office with a very dangerous man like Rodolfo Giammarco was not a very pleasant position to be in.

"We were presented with a proper bill of sale," he only said.

Don Rodolfo knew immediately what Kossel was referring to, and he glared at the Kossel.

"My dear Mayor. You are saying that you accepted that ridicules Nazi 'Bill of Sale', which was dated in November 1943 for seventy-eight thousand lire, as the proper documentation to release those paintings immediately? Forty-two masterpieces that are the rightful property of the Uffizi Museum?"

Kossel immediately turned several shades of red, now knowing that Herr Wolfgang Schmidt did not put him in a very pleasant position.

"I will need to know where those paintings are, Mayor Kossel," Giammarco immediately responded.

"I am not at liberty to say," the Mayor immediately said.

Suddenly, Don Giammarco reached across the desk and grabbed Kossel by his red, Windsor knotted tie, pulling him closer to his face as he leaned as close as he could to the Mayor's face. He then reached to his pocket and pulled out his Beretta APX Compact pistol and shoved it into Kossel's mouth, ready to pull the trigger.

"Ascoltemi, you Nazi son-of-a-bitch! Those paintings belong to our Uffizi Museum, and I suggest you do everything in your power to recover those paintings. Otherwise, your fucking head will be splattered all over that Nazi bill of sale," he sternly warned.

Kossel could distinctively smell the garlic breath of Don Rodolfo and taste the rustic metal of his pistol. The Florentine Mafioso continued to tightly grab his tie, making sure the barrel of his Beretta was well inserted down his throat. There were several silent moments of terror.

He then released the Mayor and asked him again, "Would you now care to answer my question? Where are the Uffizi paintings, Herr Kossel?"

The Mayor of Munich was terrified, afraid than the next syllable that he uttered could quite possibly be his last.

"67 Barer Street," he replied with a frightened voice. "They were claimed by a man named Wolfgang Schmidt from Chicago."

Don Rodolfo put his gun away and rose from the chair facing Kossel's desk. He then glared at the Mayor of Munich, silently letting him know that any result other than the immediate recovery of those Uffizi paintings in that apartment would be unacceptable. There would be a grave price to pay for the release of those paintings.

Giammarco then casually walked out of the Munich City Hall and hailed a taxicab, disappearing into the bustling urban traffic.

Mayor Kossel sat at his desk in silence, almost traumatized, for more than ten minutes. He then picked up his desk phone and made a phone call to Detective Hildebrandt.

"Detective...I just had a visitor by the name of Rodolfo Giammarco from Florence. What can you tell me about him?" the Mayor ignorantly asked.

That late afternoon, Giammarco took a ride to the 67 Barer Street address, where the Uffizi paintings had been hoarded and were supposedly located. He walked up to the dark brown, old apartment building, which looked very drab, abandoned, and unusually quiet. He rang several doorbells until one of the tenants came downstairs to answer the door.

An older woman opened the apartment building entrance door to inquire what the stranger wanted. "Kann ich dir helfen?"

Don Giammarco looked at her, feeling ridiculous. "I am sorry to bother you, Madam," as he immediately knew the result of his inquiry.

"If you are looking for those paintings, that apartment has been cleaned out, and those art pieces were removed days ago," she curtly said in German. She looked haggard, tired of answering the door for inquiring newspaper reporters asking the same questions.

"Danke dir," he politely replied. He now knew that his abrupt and sudden trip to Munich was a huge mistake. He realized that this was going to be an international wild goose chase, with no immediate result insight.

Don Rodolfo was outraged. This incredible mistake in releasing those Uffizi paintings to whoever laid claim to them was an erroneously gross blunder made by the Mayor of Munich. He was livid, and Giammarco held Kossel responsibly. Don Rodolfo had now the name of the art dealer from Chicago who had laid claim to those paintings and realized that he would have to travel much farther than Munich, Germany, to find him. He hailed a taxicab and returned to the Munich International Airport. The old Mafioso, feeling angry and frustrated, patiently waited to board his Alitalia flight back to Florence.

Three days later, Emma, the attractive blonde receptionist, arrived at the City Hall parking lot very early that Friday morning to begin her shift. There was only one other car, a black Volvo parked on the other side of the parking lot, which she immediately recognized as the Mayors. She had left Mayor Kossel at his office at 7:00 pm last evening. He was working late at the time and was surprised to find his car in the parking lot still.

She opened the rear entrance door and entered the municipal building, arriving at her desk a few moments later. She immediately noticed the light still on in the Mayor's office, with the door closed. She walked over and knocked a few times on the door.

"Mayor Kossel?" she inquired as she continued to knock with no response. She then pushed open the Mayor's office door and suddenly screamed at the top of her lungs.

There at his desk, was Mayor Kossel, slumped over in a pool of blood. He had been shot in the back of the head, and the dripping blood oozing from his head wound had spilled over his desk and onto the carpeted floor. The bloodied area had begun to dry up around Kossel's desktop as if he had been dead for several hours. The receptionist frantically ran out of his office and dialed '911'.

The Munich police arrived at the victim's office and pronounced Mayor Kossel dead at the scene, with Detective Hildebrandt coming several minutes later. When the coroner finally arrived, they removed the dead body, having estimated Kossel's time of death at 8:00 pm. There were security cameras located around the City Hall

Municipal Building, but the detectives discovered nothing unusual. There were no intruders parked anywhere in the parking lot or around the municipal building, which may have entered the Mayor's office. The killer must have entered the building through an open window, they reasoned, and was able to avoid being spotted by the security cameras located around the building.

Having received a phone call a few days earlier from Kossel reporting that he had been threatened, the Munich detective had his suspicions as to who was responsible for Mayor Bertram Kossel's death.

Detective Hildebrandt now knew that the price of those recovered Uffizi paintings could only be paid for...with blood.

CHAPTER FIFTEEN

It was about one o'clock in the afternoon when I parked my car on West Grand Avenue in Elmwood Park. There was a social club that some of 'The Boys' used to hang out at, and I was looking for one 'wise-guy' in particular. The faded address of 3745 West Grand Avenue was barely readable on the unmarked, red-bricked building near the railroad tracks. It had been an unassuming social club for many years. I liked to call it a 'man-cave for grease-balls,' where many Italian men hung out to play cards, drink espressos, watch the soccer games, and spend hours playing the slot machines in the back room. Most of the guys there found it to be a great place to hang out and escape their nagging wives.

When I opened the entrance door, probably two dozen or more guys were sitting and standing around the bar, all of their eyes looking directly at me like I was an 'alien from outer space.' I casually walked up to the bar.

"Espresso doppio," I loudly ordered, knowing that in a place like that, you never asked for 'cappuccino.'

"Molto bene," the barista answered, assuming that I was Italian.

I looked around the room, finally locking eyes with the very man I was looking for. Frank Mercurio was a large, barrel-chested, older man in his late fifties, who was barely five feet, eight inches tall.

Frank was the family underboss and a very dangerous member of the Marchese Family. I knew that he had always been very close to Don Carlo and was even his driver for a short time. I waited for my caffe' and walked over to the table where he was playing some Italian card game with an Italian deck of cards. He was sitting with three enormous 'gorillas,' pretending not to know who I was.

134

"Hey, Frank," I casually said, trying to get him to take notice of my presence.

"In a few minutes, Paulie. I'm busy here," as he slammed a few cards on the table and rattled out some Italian swear words I had only heard from my mother when I was a little kid.

Being half Italian from my maternal side, I was very familiar with some of that Italian vulgarity when I was a kid growing up in Park Ridge. My mother, who spoke fluent Italian, directed her obscene, Ivy League repertoire at my innocent father, who was of Scottish descent. She was a gifted 'wordsmith' of sorts. In both languages, she could insert and put together swear words into names and sentences that I never thought were even possible.

I watched him finish playing their card game while I sat at another empty table. I was still feeling all the other sets of eyes staring back at me, glaring and practically 'burning holes' into my skull with their laser vision.

"Cazzo di mama," Frank loudly yelled out, as he threw his failed hand of cards on the table. He threw out a twenty-dollar bill, then got up and smiled at his 'gorilla' friends, who were all too happy to take his money. Frank then walked over to my table, where I was sitting.

I immediately got up to shake his hand, but he was all too eager to pull me towards him and kiss me on both cheeks.

"Hey, what's up, Paulie?"

"Hey, Frank, how are you?"

"Great. Hey, I read that article you wrote on the Don. It was very 'articulate.'"

I looked at him strangely for a minute, then realizing that he was using an unfamiliar fifty-cent word and had no clue what it meant.

"Articulate? Do you mean to say 'eloquent'?"

"Oh yeah, that's it. You know what I meant, Paulie. Thanks for the nice words."

"It was my pleasure. The Don was a good man," I exclaimed.

"Hey, with a name like Crawford, how come you look more like a 'dago-kid'?" Frank innocently asked.

With dark olive skin and hazel brown eyes, I hardly took after my father's Scottish heritage.

"My mother, Elsa, was born in Rome."

Frank started to laugh. "You look more Italian than I do," as we both chuckled.

"I just wish you wouldn't use that M' word when you're writing about the Don," talking about my news story and referring to the word 'Mafia.' They always preferred to use the words 'Family' or 'La Cosa Nostra' when referring to their all-too-powerful-and-sometimes-very-violent street organization.

Frank sat back down and ordered us both another espresso. We then exchanged personal greetings, and he talked about his grown-up kids and his marriage to his wife, Phyllis. After a few minutes, Mercurio broke the ice.

"So, what's up, Paulie?"

"Frank, do you know anything about a 'Vatican Connection' with the Don?"

Mercurio paused and looked at me for a moment, as his dark, olive leather skin started to turn red. He then looked around the room.

"No," he bluntly said as he looked at me straight in the eyes, while finishing his coffee. His blank, cold stare almost looked scary, as we both knew he wasn't telling the truth.

"What do you mean, 'no'?" I pressed.

"Paulie, I just told you. No. No means no. I don't know nuttin'."

Mercurio looked at me again, and I could tell he was starting to get uncomfortable with the conversation. I decided to let the silence sink in as I was finishing my second cup of espresso. I then suggested that Frank and I go outside and talk.

As he followed me out to the side of the building where the parking lot was located, I suddenly realized that I was asking some very personal questions to a terrifying guy like Frank Mercurio. He had quite a violent reputation, and allegedly had a few hits of his own under his belt. Being in the middle of Elmwood Park, standing outside in a parking lot in the cold winter air was probably not such a good idea.

"Look, Paulie. You can't come in here and start asking those kinds of questions about the Don," he explained with a very stern tone in his voice.

I looked at him, figuring I could get him to calm down with my usual, 'reporter's charm' without him getting too excited.

"Come on, Frank. I'm not trying to ruffle any feathers here. I was just asking you because some rumors are flying around town that I thought you should know about. If there is any truth to any of them, I would think you would want a 'friend of the family' like myself dispelling any bad gossip and setting the truth straight." I could see him starting to 'chill down' as I was calmly reasoning with him.

"Would you rather have a sleaze-ball like Chaz Rizzo from Channel Eight reporting on these rumors and stirring up some bullshit on the street that isn't true?"

He stood there, silent for a moment.

"No, Paulie. You're right. You've always been a good 'friend of the family.'"

We both stood there in the cold, as I was starting to wish we were having this intense conversation inside the club rather than outside in the white graveled parking lot.

"Don Carlo spent a lot of time flying back and forth to Rome with his wife over the last several years. He always brought his wife along as an excuse that he was

137

spending quiet time at his villa in Casalvieri. After a while, we all figured out that the Don was doing business out there. He visited with his cousin a lot at the Vatican," he explained.

"Really? Who is his cousin?"

"Iacobelli. Monsignor Iacobelli. Don Carlo has several priests in his family in Italy, but Iacobelli was the one he did most of his business with. I only know this because he asked me to get involved in getting several documents and transactions notarized at customs for some 'things' he was bringing over from Rome."

"What 'things,' Frank?" Mercurio hesitated and looked at me as though he had realized he had already said too much. Several moments passed as Mercurio only stood there, silent.

"I better go inside. It's getting cold out here."

"Frank," I followed after him as he was heading back to the front door of the club.

"What things?" I loudly pressed.

"Get out of here, Paulie. You're asking too many questions. I've gotta go."

I realized that Frank Mercurio was worried about others overhearing our intense conversation, especially those men he was playing cards with. There were a lot of men in that club who were affiliated with the Marchese Family.

"Frank?" I said again before he entered the building, trying to get his attention back.

"Was it art?" I said in a softer voice, knowing he was the only one who could hear me.

The family underboss looked at me, then looked around to make sure no one else was watching or listening. He then nodded his head and quickly went back inside.

I immediately knew that there was way more to this story than anybody was talking about or willing to admit to. I had a feeling that the Marchese Family had more than a few suspicions as to who was responsible for the murder of their family 'capo.' They weren't talking about it, but they were probably planning their own 'vendetta' in avenging the death of their beloved family patriarch. Judging by the nervousness displayed by Frank Mercurio, I had a distinct feeling that I was definitely 'barking up the right tree.'

This investigation was starting to take some twists and turns that I certainly wasn't prepared for.

CHAPTER SIXTEEN

The pigeons were circling St. Peter's Square on that hot July summer day, dashing across the Roman sky in large droves as the bells from the Vatican bell tower sounded off the midday hour of noon. It was a bright, sunny day in Rome, as the large crowds of people were continuing to crisscross the ancient Vatican piazza as tourists, visitors, and various Catholic clergy were ascending upon St. Peter's Basilica.

Pope Emeritus Honorius V had just finished his second cup of espresso that early afternoon and was observing the crowds below from his papal apartment. As he sipped his caffe', he continued to study the faces of each of the famous apostles and saints, whose statutes have been honored around Vatican City's most magnificent piazza. 'Papa Onorio' studied each one of the erected structures as if to find the answers to the slanderous media statements that have been made against him and his character by the Italian press.

There was a knock on the door. "Permesso."

"Accomadi," answered Papa Onorio.

Monsignor Gianpaolo Iacobelli entered the papal apartment, holding several folders and some notebooks, along with variant notes loosely attached and sticking out of each binder.

"Buon Giorno," he said with a smile, as he knelt to kiss the Pope Emeritus's right hand.

"Buon Giorno, Gianni. Have you brought those documents that I asked you to find for me?"

"Yes, Your Holiness. I have been researching these documents and referencing them to the Vatican Library for the last two days, as you requested."

"Thank you, Gianni. What do you have for me?"

Monsignor Iacobelli sat down at the small table in front of the veranda, looking over the Vatican Piazza, and began situating his files and documents around Papa Onorio's lunch tray and his half-filled espresso cup. He then grasped a specific binder and opened up to an extensive, legal-sized report, which had been yellowed and tarnished over the years.

It was the original transfer manuscript, detailing each of the forty-two paintings that had been effectively transferred and consigned to Benito Mussolini and the Uffizi Museum by Pope Pius XI. The old, notarized document, originally signed and stamped by the Pope himself, was dated May 22, 1938.

"Your Holiness, this document details the transferred paintings to the Uffizi that you are referring to. As you can see, each painting is accurately described in detail by the painter, the type of painting, the date of each masterpiece, and its subject matter."

Papa Onorio put on his wired reading glasses, and Iacobelli carefully handed him the yellowed manuscripts, which were enclosed in thin, plastic notebook liners that had been attached in a black, three-ring binder. Monsignor Iacobelli removed each document and handed it to Papa Onorio. The latter slowly read each antiquated record, reading the accurate descriptions of each Vatican masterpiece, line by line, one by one.

After twenty minutes or so, Papa Onorio took off his glasses and smiled at the Monsignor.

"This is a precious document indeed, Gianni. It details the consigned paintings to the Uffizi, which were, in turn, traded and sold to the German Army," he happily exclaimed. Papa Onorio was always very careful not to refer to the German army soldiers of World War Two as 'Nazis.'

"We now need to verify that these paintings and those discovered in Munich are the same," he pronounced, taking a sip of his now, very cold cup of espresso.

"This will not be an easy task, Your Holiness. There have been reports that, even if we could verify that these paintings are indeed the same, that the City of Munich is turning a blind eye to those demanding their return," Iacobelli observed.

"Who else is demanding these paintings?"

"The Uffizi, of course."

"How can the Uffizi demand the return of these paintings, when they know that these were only theirs on consignment?" Papa Onorio inquired.

"These paintings were traded to the Germans at the time for seventy-eight thousand lire and the lives of 103 Jews, who were being hidden inside one of their churches by then, Cardinal Della Croce as refugees at the time."

The Pope Emeritus listened intently to his papal secretary, then glanced out to the Vatican Piazza down below.

The Monsignor continued. "Those Jews never made it to their destination in Switzerland, Your Holiness. They were sent to Auschwitz and eventually murdered. The pastor, who was hiding the Jews in his church in Florence, was murdered as well."

Papa Onorio only listened attentively, as he was without words. He continued to glance outside his papal apartment. Monsignor Iacobelli watched the Pope Emeritus, as he continued to silently stare at the Vatican crowds down below, wiping a tear away from his eye with his right hand.

"The war was brutal, Gianni," as he continued to shake his head. "We cannot begin to understand the atrocities that occurred to so many innocent people during that terrible war," His Holiness managed to say.

"But those atrocities do not give ownership rights to the Uffizi Museum. Those consigned masterpieces belong to the Vatican, and that pre-war document affirms that" Papa Onorio declared.

The Pope Emeritus began to pace his small papal apartment, walking back and forth between his papal office and study, his bedroom, and the attached living room with its magnificent veranda overlooking the famous Roman piazza. He was dressed casually that day, wearing a pair of dark slacks and a beige, short-sleeve shirt, and leather sandals. If one didn't know otherwise, one would easily mistake the former head of the Roman Catholic Church as a leisurely, summer tourist. He was usually dressed informally around his papal apartment. But due to security purposes, his physical activities were always confined to the immediate boundaries of Vatican City. Since his resignation, he could count the number of times on one hand that he ventured outside of the small, sovereign state. Outside his papal apartment, Papa Onorio still wore his papal whites and the pectoral cross, holding himself as the current Bishop of Rome.

When Pope Honorius V unexpectedly resigned his papacy several years ago, he was the first Pope to do so in nearly 600 years. After his resignation, he did not, as many within Rome expected, fly off to some obscure Bavarian

143

monastery somewhere in Germany. He did not distance himself away from the controversies of the current Vatican Curia and the Roman Catholic Church that some believed he created.

That didn't happen.

He stayed put, imbedded in his papal apartment, still accepting the title "His Holiness." He was again writing and publishing, still massaging his dismal papal record and reputation, still meeting cardinals, even making statements and, unfortunately, still being involved. He took on the role of overseeing the operations and management of the Vatican Museum and its ancient treasures, and has made himself annoyingly involved, despite his designated background role as 'Pope Emeritus.' His very existence within Vatican City encouraged conservative church critics who wished to undermine the current liberal pope's preaching, his presence, and his present papal reign. And with the former pope's past reputation, as the so-called 'architect' of the current pedophile priest scandals plaguing the Catholic Church today, has made his very involvement in the affairs involving the Vatican Curia a breeding ground for continuous controversy and criticism by the Italian news media.

'He was too sick to continue as Pope, but well enough to be Pope Emeritus and mettle in the affairs of the Vatican,' the Italian newspapers were quoted as saying.

'The Nazi Pope needs to return to Germany,' the La Repubblica Newspaper recently published in one of its controversial editorials.

Although he stated in his resignation that he would dedicate the rest of his life to solemn prayer, Papa Onorio's daily activities have been anything but. Except for his brief time praying in his private Vatican chapel at the beginning of each day, the Pope Emeritus has actively involved himself in various Vatican affairs that, quite frankly, are no longer his business. His new fixation with the recovery of these consigned Vatican masterpieces, now being claimed back by the Uffizi in Florence, is just another example of Papa Onorio's sick, obtrusive obsessions. Pope Emeritus Honorius V had become the Vatican's 'loose cannon.'

Monsignor Iacobelli was well aware of the unordinary, various passions of his papal superior. He had been in conference with the current pope and other different cardinals regarding the Pope Emeritus's extraordinary, contradictive behavior. But since there have been no other established precedents regarding the conduct and actions of any prior 'former popes,' he knew that Papa Onorio had been given full reign within the Vatican to say and do whatever he pleased, despite the operational tensions of having 'two popes' still involved in the functioning affairs of Vatican City.

The Monsignor was instructed to keep a 'close eye' on Pope Emeritus by the current pope and to report back to him regarding any unusual statements or behavior that he needs to be aware of. But Iacobelli, despite Papa Onorio's complex behavior, felt a unique loyalty to him, having been his secretary for the last twenty years. He was not afraid to travel outside of the Vatican to do his bidding, in whatever diplomatic means were necessary to discretely assist the former pope in any of his various personal projects, desires, or eccentric impulses. And Papa Onorio knew that he could completely trust the Most Reverend Monsignor Gianpaolo Iacobelli...without exception.

"Does the current mayor of Munich, this Mayor Kossel...does he realize that I was the former cardinal of Munich before my election as Pope, Gianni?"

"I am sure he does, Your Holiness."

"And does he understand, that I have influences and connections that reach far beyond his functional powers and duties as mayor?"

"Yes, Your Holiness. I am sure he does."

"Then perhaps, Gianni, you should visit this Mayor Kossel. He needs to understand that these paintings rightfully belong to the Vatican Museum, and need to be returned immediately," Papa Onorio exclaimed.

The Monsignor sat there silently, and there was a long pause in the conversation as the Pope Emeritus continued to pace his papal apartment.

"But what if this is not possible?"

Papa Onorio briefly stopped pacing and glared intently at his trusted secretary.

"Then we must afford other means in securing these paintings, and to make them understand that we will stop at nothing until those masterpieces are rightfully returned," the former pope loudly stated.

Iacobelli raised his eyebrows. "Other means?"

Papa Onorio sat down at the chair of his small dining table overlooking the veranda. He quietly addressed his papal secretary in a loud whisper, as if his papal apartment were bugged.

"We are both aware that there are those gentlemen who make themselves available to eliminate those others who stubbornly stand in the way of doing the 'right thing,' am I correct, Gianni?"

The Monsignor knew precisely what the Pope Emeritus was referring to, and he thought immediately of his Chicago cousin.

"Are you asking me to involve my cousin Carlo in such a request?"

The former pope quickly answered, "No, Gianni. I do not wish to involve your cousin for his services in this matter."

He then got up from the table and walked over to his office desk, rumbling a few desk drawers for about five minutes or so. He then returned to his table at the veranda, where Iacobelli was still sitting.

"I may wish for you to visit this Mayor Kossel. I would like you to strongly encourage him to release those paintings to the Vatican immediately."

"I would be happy to travel to Munich on your behalf, if necessary, Your Holiness."

Papa Onorio smiled at his faithful assistant, then handed him a business card with his fist closed over it, as if he were trying to hide the card from anyone who might be invisibly watching.

"I would also like you to call this gentleman. I have been told that he would be willing to render his services if he were needed."

Monsignor discretely looked at the business card. At first, he was confused as to what the former pope was referring to. After several silent moments, Iacobelli re-read the business card again and looked intently at Papa Onorio.

"I will call him, Your Holiness."

"Thank you, Gianni. I know that I can always trust you," as Papa Onorio grasped the Monsignor's right hand with both of his.

They then said a quick prayer of thanks together, and Iacobelli gathered his large files and documents and exited the papal apartment.

As Iacobelli began to descend the stairwell leading down from the papal residences, he stopped midway down the stairs. He looked at the business card again, making sure he understood his papal superior's request. He read the name on the business card several times, imbedding his name and number into his memory. It simply said:

Stefano Iannucci - Contractor

CHAPTER SEVENTEEN

The Chicago summer was in full swing on that hot July day, as the city was enjoying a very long, pleasant, string of warm, rainless days. The most significant weather complaint on the local news channels was the lack of rain that summer, and how everyone, especially in the suburbs was slowly watching their manicured green lawns die from the lack of water.

Veronica Giancarlo had just enjoyed her lunch, a quick Jimmy John's turkey sandwich, which she had taken to go and shared it with the ducks and swans at Grant Park. She had been working on the Uffizi story for the last couple of days in her spare time, piggybacking a lot of information from the New York Times and CNN. She had a relationship with a CNN reporter named Laura Perotti, who was very eager to share whatever she had learned regarding the Uffizi Art Discovery. Both resources verified that a man was hoarding the Uffizi paintings by the name of Hermann Kalkschmidt, who was found dead in his apartment last week, apparently from an internal gas leak in the building. Although there were some possible signs of foul play (like an opened gas stove), the Munich police were refusing to call it a homicide. Only a regrettable accident, they claimed, due to the faulty leaking gas pipes that were found down in the basement of the apartment building.

She decided to make another phone call to the news reporter again from CNN and see if she could acquire more information.

"Hey, Laura, its Veronica Giancarlo from the Chicago Sun-Times."

"Veronica, what's up?"

"How is your progress going on the Uffizi Art Discovery in Munich a few weeks ago?"

"We're getting stonewalled at every angle by everyone at the Munich Police Department. We've been trying to acquire information on who claimed the paintings after the apartment was unsealed, but no one will give us any information. It's as if the paintings disappeared," Perotti said.

"Laura, do you have any information on the deceased?"

"Only that he worked for the City of Munich administrative office for years, and his father was a Nazi officer during the Second World War. The 81-year-old man had a very private funeral service, and we haven't been able to get any information from the coroner's office as to who claimed the body. The old man was cremated a few days after his death."

"Really?" Veronica listened.

"Veronica...it's like the whole City of Munich has been paid off to make this old man and his circumstances disappear and go away without a trace," Laura explained. "We're at a dead-end, right now."

"Thanks, Laura. Let me know if you find anything else out."

While Laura was talking and explaining the latest information on this story, Veronica was silently thinking. Who else that she knew of, could make the administrators and all the local 'big-shots' within the City of Munich completely silent and to play 'stupid' regarding the death of Hermann Kalkschmidt? Veronica went online and 'Googled' his name, which turned up almost nothing. She then tried to get into the City of Munich administrative records, which only listed him as a waste management

150

department administrative clerk for the City of Munich for forty-five years. She was at a dead end and couldn't find out any more information about him online.

Being a part-time genealogist with her family tree, she had an idea. She logged onto the website *FindYourRoots.com* and entered Hermann's personal information that she was able to come based on the information she had retrieved online. A family tree was started on the genealogy website by another Kalkschmidt family member and had traced its roots through several generations throughout the years. By looking at all the detail, Veronica was able to ascertain that the family tree had an American side, relatives, and cousins who had shortened their ancestral name from 'Kalkschmidt' to 'Schmidt.' She was surprised to find who had turned up as one of Hermann's cousins:

Wolfgang Schmidt - Born: July 31, 1959, in Chicago, graduated from DePaul University in 1981, married in 1985, with three daughters. Lives and operates an art dealership in Chicago.

Amazing! Veronica smiled to herself, now knowing that she could go directly to her friend Wolfgang and inquire about whatever information he may have on these stolen Uffizi art paintings. Being that the deceased man hoarding the stolen pictures was a cousin of Wolfgang Schmidt puts a direct connection between him and the possible whereabouts of these stolen masterpieces.

Veronica decided to make another surprise visit to the Kunstgeschäft on 524 North Wells Street. She left her office at 4:00 pm, and with traffic in the Chicago Loop, was at his front door at 4:15 pm. When she approached the front door, there was a sign that displayed only the words ON VACATION. She then tried calling the art store from her cell phone. She got a prerecorded message that simply said that the store was closed and that they would be on vacation until August 15th. That was almost a month away. Veronica was suspicious, knowing that Wolfgang's cousin was found dead last week, and the Chicago art dealer was nowhere to be found.

All this only seemed to point directly to Wolfgang Schmidt as the new owner of the newly discovered stolen Uffizi art paintings.

"Pronto?"

"Ciao, Claudia...It's Veronica."

"Ciao, Veronica...Come va'?"

"Molto bene," Veronica eagerly replied, as she had called her Uffizi curator friend for a favor.

"Are you extremely busy these next few days? I have some vacation time coming, and I would like to fly into 'Firenze' for a visit. Can I take you up on that offer?"

"Of course, Veronica...you are welcome at any time. Is this about the stolen Uffizi painting discovery?" she excitedly asked, knowing that she was going to receive a visit from her Chicago friend.

"Yes," the Chicago curator replied. "I am writing a story for my paper, and I need you to help me put the pieces together."

"Would love to," Claudia replied.

By that following Thursday morning, Veronica was on a United Airlines direct flight to Rome, with a connecting flight to Florence. She was anxious throughout the entire trip, writing and working her newspaper story, trying to make the connection between the Chicago art dealer, the death of his cousin in Munich, and the rediscovered stolen Uffizi paintings. She knew that as an art curator at the Uffizi Gallery, her friend Claudia could give her a significant amount of help and assistance in tracing the ownership of those paintings, and where they may now be.

The Amerigo Vespucci Airport in Florence was bustling on that late, dark Thursday evening, as the apprehensive Chicago curator exited the arrival gate of the airport. She looked at the texts on her iPhone, making sure she hadn't misunderstood Claudia's instructions upon her arrival. As she looked around for several minutes, she heard a car horn beeping.

"Veronica!" a loud voice was coming from an adjacent white Fiat.

"Veronica! Qui dentro!" as she saw where the strange voice was coming from. She quickly crossed the busy airport traffic and made her way to Claudia's makeshift taxicab.

Claudia Romanelli excitedly exited her car and ran over to hug Veronica. She hadn't physically seen her Chicago best friend in almost four years, and she was more than enthusiastic to see her in person finally.

"You haven't changed, Claudia. You're beautiful as always," Veronica said.

They continued to hug and kiss each other, with the Fiat door still wide open and various cars beeping their horns, trying to drive around her. Claudia was wearing a tight pair of jeans and a white, half-buttoned blouse, which accentuated her shapely, European figure.

Claudia was in the same 'sexy-model-turned-nerdy-art-curator' category as Veronica was, and she could have passed for a shapely Paris model or a sensuous Italian actress. She had large blue eyes and blonde hair that went well with her light red lipstick, as her dark, seamless suntan brightly reflected the esthetic traffic lights off of her olive skin. The assistant Uffizi curator, even with her geeky glasses on, was still drop-dead gorgeous.

"Sei bella come sempre," Claudia replied, complimenting Veronica on her beauty as she helped her load up her luggage. They then sped off to Claudia's apartment. The two of them made small talk and exchanged pleasantries in both English and Italian, as Claudia negotiated the Florentine traffic with ease.

Veronica had studied languages while she was a student at the University of Michigan. She was quite proficient in Italian, thanks in part to her Tuscan roots. Her parents had immigrated to the United States several years before she was born, and Italian was her first language growing up in the Bridgeport neighborhood of Chicago. Her background and her proficiency in speaking other languages (she spoke Spanish and French as well) made her a valuable asset at the Art Institute of Chicago.

Over the next few days, Claudia and Veronica studied all the records of the stolen Nazi Uffizi paintings. They scoured through the Florentine gallery documents, reconstructing the circumstances of the discounted sale to the Nazi's, and how over one hundred Jewish refugees helped pay for those paintings with their lives. The two art curators found the infamous 'bill of sale' for seventy-eight thousand lire to the Nazi's, and documentation by the Cardinal of Florence, letters signed by His Eminence Cardinal Della Croce at the time, vehemently protesting the sale.

There were also letters written and saved by the Cardinal to the Vatican. They went on to explain the circumstances of that art transaction, the destiny of the Jewish refugees, and the murder of their beloved pastor.

Veronica was also able to interview the Uffizi's board member, Dottore Edoardo Giannini, regarding his thoughts concerning the rediscovered paintings. The veteran board member freely discussed his opinions, openly accusing the Munich government of hiding and giving away those rediscovered Uffizi artworks.

"We will find where those paintings are, and we are determined to bring them back to the Uffizi Gallery where they belong," Dottore Giannini was quoted as saying.

They also found the consignment documents from the Vatican Museum to the Uffizi, signed by Pope Pius XI in 1938. There were attached letters and records discussing the safety of their misguided consignment to Mussolini and his 'black shirt' army, hoping that these valuable artworks would never be in the hands of those 'art-thief Nazis.'

Veronica obtained a copy of the press release from the papal secretary to the Pope Emeritus, Pope Honorius, reiterating the ownership of those forty-two paintings as belonging to the Vatican Museum.

"Pope Honorius, our Pope Emeritus, has made the return of these rediscovered paintings in Munich the focal point of his post papal duties. His Holiness strongly urges that those who possess these forty-two rare masterpieces, return them to the Vatican Museum, their rightful owners," the press release stated from Monsignor Gianpaolo Iacobelli, papal secretary to the former Pope Honorius V.

Claudia and the free-lance Sun-Times reporter researched the current situation in Munich and inquired with the Munich police department for information regarding the murder of Mayor Bertram Kossel. After several telephone calls back and forth, she was able to get in touch with Detective Hildebrandt regarding the status of this homicide investigation.

"We have no new leads at the moment," the Detective said to Veronica, "as we have not confirmed a motive as to why Mayor Kossel was killed," he said over the phone.

"Do you believe that the rediscovered stolen paintings from the Uffizi may have been the motive, blaming the Mayor and his staff for letting those paintings disappear again?" Giancarlo blatantly asked the detective.

"We have our suspicions, but we cannot confirm that at the moment. Mayor Kossel had a lot of enemies, and we are investigating all potential leads in this case," he politely stated.

After spending a full week in Florence, researching, and investigating this story, Veronica Giancarlo thanked her girlfriend for all of her assistance and helped with this case. She took an early flight back from Florence to Chicago, with a two-hour layover in Rome. Veronica spent the next twelve hours writing in detail her complete story. She laid the blame of the disappeared masterpieces directly upon Munich's local government for not taking proper care in their safekeeping. Giancarlo mentioned in detail the consignment transaction between the Vatican Museum and the Uffizi Gallery back in 1938. And lastly, she hinted to the Chicago connection, and how a 'certain local art collector' may know where those stolen paintings are.

The following afternoon, Veronica Giancarlo personally delivered her investigative story to Tom O'Conner, the assistant editor in charge of the

Contemporary Section of the Chicago Sun-Times. Veronica had worked with him on other stories before, and she felt there would be no problem in getting her story printed for this Sunday's edition.

"I've got this 'Stolen Uffizi Painting Scandal' all figured out," she excitedly said to her assistant editor, showing him the two-thousand-word article, along with the suggested headlines:

Stolen Uffizi Art May Have Chicago Connection

Veronica was very proud of her investigative story as she watched her assistant editor read the printed article. After several minutes, he looked at her with a disappointed look on his face.

"Veronica, I'm not sure we can print this. You make a lot of presumptions here without any proof as to who or where these paintings are. We can't write a story accusing a local art dealer of having anything to do with a German relative's death and the discovery of his hoarded paintings," O'Conner stated.

"But Tom, it's so obvious. This old man was a close relative of Schmidt, and he has been on vacation and temporarily closed his art gallery when these paintings went missing in Munich," she protested.

"It doesn't mean he has them. You can't print such an accusation, even if you imply this. We will have lawsuits up the ass if we print this story."

"Tom...I worked hard on this. These missing Uffizi paintings are becoming quite an international mystery, with the Uffizi Gallery and the Vatican trying to get their hands on them."

"I'm not sure we can print this, Veronica. Besides, I don't think our readers are interested in these missing paintings. Where these paintings are or who has them is of no real interest to anyone other than the upper-class art collectors of the world," he coldly exclaimed.

Veronica looked at her assistant editor, her eyes starting to well up with tears. It was unusual for her to let her emotions and her feelings take over when submitting a news assignment. The assistant editor, feeling bad about expressing his opinion on her well-worked story, qualified himself.

"I will have another reporter look at this article, as see if we can rework it. We will need to omit some of your presumptions here and see if we can fit it in somewhere."

Veronica, not having any other choice, politely thanked her assistant editor and quickly left his office. She was having trouble controlling her anger as she left the Sun-Times building on North Orleans Street, and took a taxicab directly back to her office at the Art Institute of Chicago. She was disgusted, knowing now that her assistant editor and his staff would completely ignore her hard work.

Tom O'Conner called another one of his associate reporters, George Shea, and had him read and review the story. After a few hours, the reporter returned to O'Conner's office.

"So," he asked Shea, "what are your thoughts?"

"Veronica Giancarlo makes a lot of 'wild goose chase' presumptions that are unsupported. All this article consists of is a lot of finger-pointing. Besides, I don't think our readers care about who or where these stolen Uffizi paintings are."

The two seasoned reporters looked at each other silently for a moment. "Nobody gives a shit," Shea said.

"Then it's total garbage," O'Conner concluded, as Shea smirked and nodded his head.

They both laughed as the assistant editor archived Veronica's article from his open news files, and then physically tore up her printed piece.

He then correctly disposed of it in the circular file next to his desk.

CHAPTER EIGHTEEN

The blue, cloudless sky flowed freely around the beating sun, overlooking its majestic dome as the weekday mass at the Basilica of St. John, the Lateran in Rome, was just winding down. Monsignor Gianpaolo Iacobelli had just completed dispensing communion to all of the worshippers at early morning service that sunny, Tuesday morning. The July sun was already beating callously on that ornate, weathered piazza in front of the ancient church, which after St. Peter's Basilica, is considered the holiest of all the Roman Catholic churches in the Eternal City.

Don Carlo Marchese was finishing his espresso doppio at a nearby café, watching the surrounding tourists throw breadcrumbs on the ground for all the pigeons in front of the church. The birds were flying recklessly around the ancient basilica, as weekday worshippers were beginning to disband after mass. He had an appointment with the Monsignor, who was the Papal Secretary to the Pope Emeritus, his Holiness Pope Honorius V, and was patiently waiting for him to complete his morning service.

He had ordered his second cup of espresso when Monsignor Iacobelli walked over to the nearby café to meet his beloved cousin from Chicago.

"Ciao, Cugino," the Monsignor exclaimed as he greeted and kissed Don Marchese on both cheeks.

"Ciao, Gianpaolo, so nice to see you again," as he ordered his cousin a cup of espresso coffee.

"How was Mass?"

"I expected you, Carlo. I hoped you would surprise me. You would have been the first in line for communion," the Monsignor jokingly smiled.

"With all the blessed vocations of our uncles and cousins, I think I've done enough holy masses for a lifetime," as another espresso doppio magically appeared on the café tabletop. The two of them began exchanging family gossip concerning the Chicago and Roman sides of the family, both enjoying the picturesque, outdoor café located adjacent to the famous Renaissance church.

"How long are you here in Rome for?"

"Only a few days. My wife and I will be returning to Casalvieri to visit family before we return to Chicago next week," Don Carlo explained. He went on to confirm the many family visits and dinners he had obligated himself to when visiting his birthplace, which was only 178 kilometers south of Rome.

"Well, I have asked you here to discuss some important business regarding Pope Emeritus," the Monsignor began.

"Papa Onorio?" as the Italians called him, referring to Pope Emeritus Honorius V.

"Yes. As you know, you have assisted us in selling several museum masterpieces which we needed liquidating in the past," the Monsignor started.

"Of course. These transactions have been very profitable. My thanks again to you and Papa Onorio for allowing me to be of assistance."

Pope Emeritus, since he resigned from the papacy in February 2013, has had the sole duty of overseeing the Vatican Museum, the Sistine Chapel, and the management of its business affairs. As the Pope Emeritus, he is in charge as the chairman of its excessive art masterpieces, sculpture, exhibits and art galleries. His role regarding his managerial duties includes the advisement and directorial input in handling the operations of these extensive art galleries.

Although 'Papa Onorio' has had limited responsibilities in this regard, he has had the 'last say' in any significant decisions concerning the management of these world-renowned museums.

One of these significant decisions has been the offering for sale of limited art pieces displayed within the Vatican museum. The current pope decided to explore the possibility of liquidating several of these art masterpieces, to raise the money needed to fund these various sexual abuse lawsuits which the Catholic Church has been inundated with over the last twenty years. With the direction of these many lawsuits pointed directly to various archdioceses around the world, and especially in the United States, these urban dioceses have looked for financial assistance from the Vatican. These variant pedophile lawsuits have now totaled in the billions of dollars worldwide, and the Vatican is now forced to find other means of assisting these dioceses without financially impacting the IWR or the Vatican Bank.

Because of the public relations nightmare that these art museum 'sales' may cause, the Vatican has had to investigate another means of discretely liquidating these masterpieces. To this end, Don Carlo Marchese has been dramatically utilized for his services. Because of his international connections to wealthy investors within the United States and elsewhere, Marchese has been able to find buyers for these artworks. He has been able to single-handedly assist the Vatican in solving its financial issues, without the public relations fiasco that these valuable art transactions may cause. And with the excessive commissions that the Marchese Family has earned in these artwork sales, Don Marchese has been more than happy to assist the Vatican in accomplishing its financial goals.

The bell towers of St John the Lateran began to toll loudly, as the two cousins continued their intense conversation.

"Cugino, I have been asked by Papa Onorio if you could be of assistance again for another great favor."

Don Carlo nodded his head while fumbling with the sugar packets, carefully emptying them into his espresso cup.

"Are you familiar with the missing artworks of the Uffizi Gallery in Florence?"

"Vaguely," the Don replied.

"In 1943, the Nazi's during World War II robbed the Uffizi Art Gallery in Florence of many valuable art pieces and artworks, valued now in the millions of euros. It has come to our attention that several of these missing art pieces have resurfaced in Munich."

"Okay," the Don curiously responded.

The Monsignor took another sip of his caffe'.

"Papa Onorio would like your assistance in acquiring back these art pieces for the Vatican Museum."

Don Marchese looked at his cousin, completely perplexed, taking another long sip of his espresso doppio. There were several moments of silence, as the Don displayed a confused look on his face.

"He wishes to acquire art now?"

"Yes."

There were more silent moments, as Don Marchese blankly stared at the Papal Secretary.

"I thought the Vatican and Papa Onorio wished to sell art and raise money, not buy and acquire art," he replied.

Monsignor Iacobelli finished his expresso and began to explain.

"Many years ago, before the war in 1938, Mussolini persuaded Pope Pius XI to send up various priceless Vatican Museum artworks to the Uffizi Gallery in Florence in anticipation of Hitler invading Rome and the Vatican. The dictator convinced the Pope that these different art pieces would be far safer in Florence under the security of his 'squadristi' or 'black shirt' army. Believing that Hitler would 'rape and pillage' valuable artworks of the Vatican, 'Il Duece' convinced Pope Pius XI that these Vatican artworks would be far safer under his security at the Uffizi. The Black Shirt Army could aggressively defend any Nazi invasion of the Tuscan province," Iacobelli carefully explained.

"As you know, the opposite happened. When Pope Pius XII ascended the papacy, he was able to convince Hitler to spare the Vatican and its many valuable ruins and art treasures. But Hitler and his 'SS' army robbed and looted the Uffizi Galleries when the 'black shirt' army disbanded in 1943. Many of these stolen masterpieces were Vatican artworks from Rome."

"Really?" Don Carlo replied, listening attentively to his cousin's history lesson.

The two of them sat in silence, and Monsignor Iacobelli waited attentively for his cousin's reaction to the conversation thus far.

"Gianni, I think I know where you are going with this, and I don't think I can help you," he immediately reacted.

Iacobelli looked at him and smiled.

"I haven't asked you yet."

"I know where this is going, and I am not sure I want to get involved."

More silence.

"Let me guess," Marchese continued, "Papa Onorio wants my help in getting back these missing Uffizi art pieces," as he fidgeted with his empty espresso cup, still shaking his head. "But why?"

Iacobelli looked at his cousin and explained.

"Papa Onorio, if you haven't heard, has been having a public relations problem here in Rome. Due to his German background, his participation in a Nazi youth group has left him to be unfairly labeled by the Italian newspapers. He has never been able to shake off the stigma of being a sympathizer to the Anti-Semitic and Aryan race ideology that was so much a part of Nazi Germany's manifest during the Second World War. He has been called the 'Nazi Pope' by the press here in Rome and has been hugely criticized for abdicating his papacy several years ago."

"Okay...so?"

"The Pope Emeritus feels that reacquiring this stolen Vatican art, which was robbed from the Uffizi by the Nazi's during the war, would be an excellent media détente for him and the Italian press. He feels this could be a way to repair and restore his papal legacy, so to speak," Iacobelli concluded.

"Is that even possible?" he remarked. Don Marchese started to laugh again, as he continued to look towards the piazza while carefully formulating his words.

"Cugino, I'm not sure I can help you."

Monsignor Gianpaolo Iacobelli carefully studied his cousin for a few long minutes until he broke his silence.

"Perhaps you can."

"How?"

"There is an art dealer in Chicago who is rumored to have special, political connections to Munich and the German government. It is rumored that his family has had access to many of these stolen Nazi art pieces in years past."

"Who?"

"His name is Wolfgang Schmidt, and he owns an art gallery in Chicago. Since the discovery of these Uffizi masterpieces in that old apartment in Munich last week, the German government has sealed off the location, not allowing anyone to lay claim to these stolen paintings. The Pope Emeritus cannot directly contact the German government and cannot appear to be involved initially. But he has heard of the rumors of this art dealer in Chicago, and he has asked me to ask you to intercede and assist us."

Don Carlo looked at his cousin and shook his head. "First of all, I do not know this man. Secondly, even if I were to intercede, how would I be able to help?"

"Convince Wolfgang Schmidt to help you recover these Uffizi works in Munich on behalf of the Vatican. There would be a lucrative price for his and your trouble."

Don Marchese called over the waiter and ordered his third espresso doppio.

"Cugino, it will be challenging to force this Schmidt-guy to do something this complicated for a stranger such as myself. There would have to be a lot of money involved."

"I am told this would not be a problem," the Monsignor replied.

Marchese slowly drank his coffee after inserting his packets of sugar, staring off at the adjacent, picturesque basilica. The crowds of morning tourists were beginning to ascend onto the church and its picturesque piazza.

"I will see what I can do. You do understand Papa Onorio will owe me for this. I am sure the commissions to reclaim these valuable works of art will be excessive."

"The Pope Emeritus would be greatly in your debt," he replied.

Marchese took the last swallow of his espresso and rose from the table.

"If my hands start shaking today, I will blame you for making me drink all of this espresso," Marchese joked, as he kissed his cousin on both cheeks.

The Monsignor smiled, shaking his cousin's hand with both of his.

"We will be in touch?" Iacobelli asked.

"You will hear from me," Marchese said, and he walked away from the café', catching a taxicab to his Hotel Adriano on Via Vittorio Emanuel.

As he sat in the taxicab, Don Carlo Marchese smiled to himself. He was considering his options in the new task his cousin and the Vatican had now given him. Marchese knew that getting close to this Wolfgang Schmidt character and his art gallery would be a difficult task, without raising suspicions. He would have to do his homework, he privately thought. But the Don also realized the excessive commissions he could accrue in accomplishing such a transaction.

The Roman Curia, he thought to himself, had just handed him a blank check. Doing business with the Pope Emeritus had indeed, become quite a profitable business venture. The Vatican, he smiled, was turning into quite a 'cash cow.'

Don Carlo Marchese had no idea this transaction would eventually cost him his life.

CHAPTER NINETEEN

The summer traffic on the Tri-State Tollway was light that early evening last July, as Caroline Tortorici was maneuvering her black, BMW sedan towards the O'Hare Airport exit. She was told by her married boyfriend, Carlo Marchese, to pick him up at the airport at United Airlines' arrival gate at 7:15 pm.

Caroline Tortorici was a gorgeous brunette in her middle forties. She was well educated, having graduated from the University of Chicago, and worked at Northwestern Hospital as a dietician for the last twenty years. She had never been married or had any children. Although several of her friends were more than aware of her long-term, intense relationship with a married man, she enjoyed the diversity and freedom that having a relationship with a married man brought into her life. She had the liberty and independence that she could enjoy while Marchese was home, spending Sundays, holidays, and most weeknights with his wife and family. Over the last several years, she had even enjoyed an outside relationship or two without Marchese's knowledge. And because her married boyfriend was a multi-billionaire, there was nothing that she could want that Don Carlo didn't provide for her. He had even purchased a new BMW as a birthday gift for her and surprised her last year as well.

She was looking forward to seeing him exclusively, after his being in his Italian villa vacationing with his wife for the previous three weeks in his hometown of Casalvieri. He told Caroline that he left his wife to vacation there alone for the remainder of the month at their summer villa until the end of August.

Casalvieri is a small village located within the province of Frosinone, Italy, situated over the mountains near the large city of Cassino. It is also adjacent to the famous Benedictine Abbey of Montecasino, which sits high up above the sprawling urban town.

She pulled her BMW up to Terminal One at O'Hare Airport and waited for him to come outside, carrying his bags in tow finally. She got out of her car and opened her trunk, then giving Don Carlo a long, passionate kiss.

"I missed you, honey," she exclaimed, hugging him excessively while the City of Chicago coppers were clamoring to get them along and move her car from the restricted parking area in front of Terminal One. They both got in, with Don Carlo taking over the driver's side of her car, and the two of them drove off to their exclusive downtown suite at the Blackstone Hotel. After spending several hours together in their luxury hotel room getting reacquainted, Don Carlo got up to light up a cigarette and to make a phone call from the other room. He called his trusted underboss, Frank Mercurio.

"Frank, we need to talk. Can you do breakfast tomorrow?"

"Sure, Don Carlo. Where at?"

"Meet me at Granny's Pancake House in River Forest, on North Avenue. Eight o'clock sharp."

"Ok...sure thing."

The clouds that early Thursday morning seemed to consume the Chicago summer sky, as everyone seemed to be grateful for the brief rain that was expected to come. Don Marchese was picked up at 7:00 am by his driver Paolo at the Blackstone Hotel, and they were promptly there at 7:45 am, despite the heavy outbound traffic on the Eisenhower Expressway.

Knowing that he was early, Don Marchese went inside and ordered a bagel and a cup of coffee from the hostess, and brought it out for his driver, knowing that he had a long wait that morning. He afterward went back inside at his usual table. Don Carlo was a regular there, having many of his breakfast meetings at Granny's because of his addiction to their potato pancakes. It was only a few minutes later that Frank Mercurio arrived. He saw Don Carlo sitting at his usual table in the east corner of the restaurant and walked over to greet him.

"Buon Giorno," he said in his most annunciated Italian.

"Buon Giorno," Don Carlo answered, taking a sip of his well-deserved caffeine. He was still a little jet-lagged, having gotten up at 3:00 am and had a difficult time falling back asleep.

"How was your trip?"

"Very relaxing, thank you, Frank. I couldn't wait to come back home. There seems to be quite a heat spell going on in Italy," he exclaimed.

"Well, it hasn't been much cooler here either. Everyone is outside doing a rain dance this morning. They're predicting a rainstorm," Frank answered.

"That would be nice. I am not looking forward to my water bill, as I'm sure the sprinklers have been working overtime lately."

"Of course. I'm sure that your grass is dying like everyone else's," Mercurio commented.

The two of them ordered breakfast, with Don Carlo curing his craving for the potato pancakes that he had come so far to enjoy. Frank liked his three eggs 'lookin' at him', and he needed a half a loaf of fresh, toasted bread to just clean off his plate. They made small talk, with the Don discussing his trip excursions to Rome and Caserta, visiting the ancient castles there. Mercurio had been spending his summer watching his grandsons play little league baseball and had spent one hot July weekend at the Wisconsin Dells with his wife, Phyllis, and their four grandchildren.

Afterward, Don Carlo changed the subject.

"Frank, have you heard anything about a missing Uffizi art collection discovered in Munich?"

Mercurio thought about it for several seconds.

"I had heard something on CNN about an old man, who was found dead in his apartment. They reported that there were some Florence masterpieces discovered in his attic. It was on the news last week," he answered.

"I met with my cousin, Monsignor Gianni, in Rome last week. It seems he has a special favor to ask," Marchese began to explain.

"In 1943, the Nazi's during World War II robbed the Uffizi Art Gallery in Florence of some precious paintings and artworks, valued now in the billions of euros. These missing art pieces have resurfaced in Munich in this old man's attic."

"Yes, that has been reported." Mercurio held up his coffee cup as the waitress brought over another refill.

"Well apparently, before the war in 1938, Mussolini persuaded Pope Pius XI to send up many valuable Vatican artworks to the Uffizi Gallery in Florence in anticipation of Hitler invading Rome and the Vatican. They believed that Hitler would 'rape and pillage' invaluable artworks of the Vatican. Mussolini convinced Pope Pius XI that these Vatican artworks would be far safer at the Uffizi," Marchese explained.

Mercurio was listening attentively, still munching on the last piece of dry toast.

"The opposite happened. Now the Pope Emeritus believes that these missing paintings discovered in Munich are those consigned artworks from Rome and that they belong to the Vatican Museum, not the Uffizi," Don Carlo concluded.

"Really?"

"Pope Emeritus has asked us to get involved. There is an art dealer in Chicago who may have a connection in all of this. His name is Wolfgang Schmidt, and he owns the Kunstgeschaft art gallery on North Wells Street. Since the discovery of these Uffizi artworks in that old apartment in Munich last week, the German government has sealed off the location, not allowing anyone to lay claim to these missing art pieces. The Pope Emeritus has asked us to intercede and assist them in acquiring back those paintings."

Mercurio had a confused look on his face, shaking his head.

"How can we help? We don't know anything about this guy."

"We are going to have to do our homework, Frankie. I didn't want to say anything to my cousin, but I believe I know who this Schmidt guy is. I believe my daughter has a friend that she has gone to school with, who is this art dealer's daughter. I may have an idea on how to approach this guy. According to my cousin, this gentleman may have some direct information on accessing these missing masterpieces. He is very well connected in Munich." Don Marchese called over the waitress and asked for the check.

Mercurio thought about the Capo's unusual request.

"What do you need from me?"

"I need you to find and start tagging this guy for a few days, presuming that he is in town. See if our IT guy can get into his place and plant a few bugs. Maybe he can get a clone on his cell phone."

"Being that we don't have any connections or business with this guy, that might be difficult," Mercurio answered.

"Papa Onorio has his checkbook ready, and Cousin Gianni says he's ready to pay handsomely to get these paintings back."

Mercurio looked perplexed. "Why? I thought the Vatican was selling, not buying."

Don Marchese chuckled to himself as he finished explaining.

'I guess the old bastard is having public relations problems. The Italian newspapers have been beating up on him, calling the old son-of-a-bitch a Nazi and telling him to go back to Germany. He thinks acquiring these stolen Uffizi masterpieces are going to save his reputation at the Vatican."

Mercurio laughed. "Is he out of his goddamn mind? The damn Mona Lisa couldn't save his shit-hole reputation. The press has been saying that he assisted the Vatican in shuffling around all those pedophile priests when he was a cardinal," Mercurio observed.

Marchese finished his coffee and then pulled out a money clip of cash, inserting a clean, crisp twenty-dollar bill into the billfold. The bill was $19.45.

As they both got up to leave, Frank Mercurio embarrassingly threw a five-dollar bill down onto the table while Marchese walked out ahead of him.

As they strolled onto the parking lot, the Capo reiterated.

"See what you can find out for me as soon as you can, Frankie. I need some information on this 'kraut bastard.'"

Frank looked at him, still confused.

"Don Carlo, why are we getting involved in this shit? We don't need any of this crap right now. We've got our hands full with our other operations."

Don Carlo looked at his family underboss.

"There is a lot of money to be made on these paintings, Frankie...with or without Papa Onorio's checkbook."

Mercurio kissed Don Carlo on both cheeks as he got into his black, four-door Buick and sped off, eastbound onto North Avenue.

Frank Mercurio stood there alone for a few moments in the parking lot, perplexed and confused, as he stared off at the North Avenue traffic. The summer raindrops were beginning to fall as he stood there for a few long seconds, getting wet.

He began to think out loud: *What the hell is Don Carlo getting himself into?*

Pope Emeritus was enjoying his espresso that late morning, as he had just finished his morning walk of seven kilometers around the Vatican gardens. The summer sun was already beginning to beat down on Vatican City, even though the Roman lunch hour had not yet arrived.

He picked up the 'La Repubblica' newspaper and read the headlines:

Vatican Demands Return of Masterpieces

Papa Onorio put on his reading glasses and smiled to himself, knowing that his papal secretary had done an excellent job. He had asked Monsignor Iacobelli to put out a press release the other day, to put the Munich government and everyone else on notice that the Vatican originally consigned those stolen Nazi paintings to Florence's prestigious art gallery before the war. He perused through the first several pages of the Italian newspaper, making sure he had read all of the detailed news coverage describing the Munich art discovery.

"Auguri, Gianni," he immediately replied when his papal secretary abruptly entered his apartment.

"You did a fine job on this press release," he smiled, as he was pleased with the news article that the Italian newspaper had written.

"They have finally written something positive about their Pope Emeritus," he said, referring to himself in the third person.

"We have successfully put the world on notice that those forty-two paintings belong to the Vatican, and not the Uffizi galleries."

Monsignor Iacobelli smiled back at the former pontiff. "I wish a Vatican press release was all that was needed to secure those Uffizi paintings back."

"Uffizi? No, Gianni!" Papa Onorio corrected him. "You must refer to those paintings as stolen 'Vatican' paintings. You will no longer use that reference."

"Yes, Your Holiness."

Papa Onorio seemed to be in a happy mood. He carefully read the article several times, giggling to himself as he mentally quoted and memorized every word within the article, making sure he had not missed or misunderstood a single syllable. His papal secretary was sitting at the table with him, waiting for his next directive.

"When will we be granting an interview to RAI or CNN? We must continue the momentum of this news," Pope Emeritus explained to his papal secretary.

"They have been contacted as well, Your Holiness. So far, La Repubblica is the only media outlet that has elaborated and given us any news coverage on our press release."

"Well, Gianni, you must be the one to grant the interviews. Make sure you explain the Vatican history of those paintings. The world must understand that those masterpieces were stolen from the Vatican and not the Uffizi galleries," he reiterated.

The Monsignor was carefully trying to be reverent, as he had noticed that the Pope Emeritus was showing definite signs of his ninety-plus years. The former pontiff was showing signs of severe psychological, bipolar disorder. His moods were becoming very volatile, being joyful and happy at one moment, then becoming angry and annoyed the next. He was always repeating himself, saying the same statements and directives over and over. He was displaying significant displays of decline and dementia, not remembering his previous instructions and forgetting the previous tasks and remarks that he was saying and doing moments earlier. This worried Iacobelli immensely, as he knew that whatever the former despot pontiff said or previously did would never be consistent with what he was saying or doing now.

Putting the former pontiff in charge of the Vatican Museum and all of its business affairs was undoubtedly a mistake by the current pope. Papa Onorio was not a harmless, retired older man, as the Vatican hoped he would become when he initially resigned. He was becoming a senile, former prelate who still had a tremendous amount of power, control, and influence over the Roman Catholic Church. Leaving him alone to play in his 'sandbox' was a colossal mistake by the Vatican. The papal secretary was now regretting that he had gotten his cousin involved in the Pope Emeritus' mission to recover those stolen paintings in Munich.

Monsignor Iacobelli now realized that the former pontiff was a very dangerous, unpredictable man indeed.

CHAPTER TWENTY

It was almost four o'clock in the afternoon, as I had been sitting at my usual table at the Fullerton Avenue Starbucks for a few hours. The coffee shop was several blocks away from my townhouse on Wrightwood Avenue in Lincoln Park, and I spent a lot of time writing and researching my news article projects while drinking my usual grande, extra wet cappuccino.

I knew everyone there, including all of the morning customers, the employees, and even the 'baristas' behind the counter. Everyone in the neighborhood knew that I spent my early morning hours there at that Starbucks, and I was surprised that the manager had not handed me an invoice for rent by now. I needed a place to start putting my ideas down on my laptop that afternoon, and I wasn't about to fight the rush hour traffic going back to my office at the Sun-Times building.

I needed to make a phone call, so I started fumbling with my iPhone at that moment, wondering if I still had his cell phone number in my phone directory.

"Hello?"

"Hello, Chaz? It's Paul Crawford from the Sun-Times."

"Hey, Paul, what's up?"

"Did I catch you at a bad time?"

"No, Paulie. I was just starting to wind things down here in the newsroom. What's up?" he eagerly asked. I could hear a female voice in the background while he was talking, and I started to wonder if he was at his Channel Eight newsroom.

'Hey, I know this is short notice, but do you have any dinner plans tonight? I wanted to hook up and discuss a few things with you," I eagerly asked.

177

There were a few moments of silence, and he was probably weighing all of his social options for the evening.

"Well…I've got dinner plans at eight o'clock. But if you want to hook up for drinks somewhere…that would work. What time are you thinking?"

"Where are your dinner plans?"

"I have a date at Tuscany's on Taylor Street," he replied.

"Is she hot?" I jokingly asked.

"Oh yeah, this is the third date. Her name is Yvonne. Met her on Match.Com. You know what they say about third dates."

I smiled to myself. Heaven forbid anyone to get in the way of Chaz Rizzo's dinner date plans or encroach on the possibility of his 'getting laid' later that evening.

"Okay…there is a bar on Halsted Street nearby, called Cleary's Bar and Grill. Have you heard of it?" I asked.

"Oh yeah, I've been there…know exactly where it is. Does six-thirty work?"

"That's perfect, Chaz. See you there."

I figured I better rush home and clean-up before getting together for drinks at Clearys. Knowing that Rizzo always made a fashion statement, I didn't want to look or dress like 'trailer trash,' even though it was just for cocktails.

I pulled my car into a parking space in front of Cleary's Bar and Grill and walked very gingerly into the dark, shadow forecasted doorway. I arrived a little early for our meeting that night, so I quickly found my way to the bar. The blaring sounds of the jukebox seemed to overtake the darkness of the drab saloon, as the early dawn of that December sunset had overcome that cold winter evening. It wasn't quite New Year's Eve yet, but there were 'Happy New Year' decorations scattered everywhere around the bar. An Andy Williams Christmas tune was blaring from the jukebox, as the traditional holiday song was reverberating loudly off of the walls.

My eyes adjusted to the darkness as I found my way to a barstool and waited patiently for the attention of the bartender. She was an older blonde lady, who looked as though she was slinging drinks as a part-time gig to make up for the shortfall of her social security checks. The make-up on her face was way over-done. I had a hard time distinguishing what red blush and blue eye shadow was and what was over-applied war-paint. She was wearing a short-sleeve blouse and had various colorful tattoos posted over both of her arms. She noticed me at the end of the bar and walked over and smiled.

"Welcome to Cleary's Bar and Grill. What can I get you?"

"Grey Goose and Tonic, with a splash of water."

"Did you want a lime with that?" she asked.

"Absolutely."

I figured I would start easy while waiting for Rizzo and keep my present state of mind, not over-doing it. She mixed my drink in front of me, and I peeled off a twenty-dollar bill from the roll of singles I had stashed in my sports coat.

"Start a tab, please." I innocently requested, hoping she didn't see the other small bills I had attached to my twenty.

"Oh sure," she smiled as if to play along.

I took a few swallows of my watered-down vodka, hoping that someone would walk over to the jukebox and make another selection, other than Andy William's "It's the Most Wonderful Time" song. I looked around the drab, haggard bar, noticing a few televisions playing a football game of some kind, although I was not familiar with who was playing that night. Since the Chicago Bears weren't in contention for the playoffs after another losing season, I had lost interest in football.

It was an ancient, very antiquated tavern. The place looked like it hadn't seen a coat of paint since Roosevelt's New Deal back in the Depression days. I had heard from another patron a while back that this place was a hang-out for Dion O'Banion's s gang back in the day. There was a faint smell of old stale cigars as if the 'No Smoking' laws didn't apply to old, dilapidated Halsted Street taverns.

It was almost 7:00 when Rizzo finally came strolling in, dressed in a long, camel haired overcoat and his usual spiffy, Hugo Boss tailored blue suit. I stood up, and we shook hands, doing the 'man-hug' thing, and he sat down and ordered a Crown Royal on the Rocks.

"I forgot what a dump this place is," he observed, as he made himself comfortable on the barstool next to mine. We did a 'holiday toast,' clinging our drink glasses, and we made some small talk. He was busy at the newsroom, explaining that he was doing some political piece on the dubious background of one of the mayoral candidates. He started talking about his 'hot date' later on, and he had his sights on taking her clothes off after wining and dining her that evening.

I wished him luck.

"So, what's up with you, Paulie?"

"Riz, do you remember our conversation at the funeral home regarding Don Carlo?"

"What part?"

"The part about Marchese peddling off Vatican art pieces?"

He looked at me silently for a moment, as he probably wished he hadn't said anything that evening. He was twirling the ice cubes of his already consumed cocktail.

"Okay, what about it?"

"What else do you know, and who's your source of information?"

Rizzo laughed one of his girlish giggles as if to almost ridicule me for even asking the question.

"Come on, Paulie...you know I can't tell you that. I made some promises."

"What kind of promises?"

He paused from his ice cube twirling competition and stared at me, squarely in the eyes.

"The kind of promises that you make to some dangerous people when you stumble on some information that you're not supposed to stumble on...then you give them your word that will hopefully save your ass."

I quietly looked at him, taking another sip of my drink.

"Those kinds of promises," he finished.

I decided to push him, knowing that it would cost me another drink. I looked over at 'Trixie, the Dinosaur Bartender' and motioned another round.

"Look, Chaz, I was already over at the 'Boys Club' this afternoon, and I already got confirmation from one of their 'gorillas' that Marchese was involved in importing some high-priced art pieces from Rome. It seems he had a cousin that works over at the Vatican, named Iacobelli. What do you know about him?"

He took a long swallow from his second drink, and I could see his tongue starting to loosen up.

"Monsignor Iacobelli is the papal secretary to the Pope Emeritus."

"The Pope Emeritus? You mean Pope Honorius?" I asked.

"Yep. That's him. The Pope Emeritus is on the board of directors for all of the Vatican Art Museums and the Sistine Chapel in Vatican City. It was a position created for him by the Pope after his resignation to give the old Nazi something to do."

"Really? So now he's running 'garage sales' out of Vatican City, liquidating pieces of art to raise money for their numerous pedophile priest lawsuits?" I was immediately putting all of the pieces together.

"Bingo."

"So how did you stumble on all of this?" I pushed.

"I have a connection over at O'Hare Airport. Some women I used to date is a U.S. Customs Agent there. I was doing a drug trafficking piece a few years ago, asking about any large crates that have been stopped and searched from South America and Europe over the years. She made mention of a few large wooden crates, originally shipped from Italy, that had some priceless masterpieces in them. I acquired and traced the Illinois Use Tax on those shipments. They were imported by an LLC, which was registered to Marchese's attorney. I did some more digging and brought it to the attention of one of my Marchese Family connections, hoping I could do a feature story on it. That was canned quick."

"Is that why you didn't pursue the news story?"

"Well, ...yeah. Don Marchese didn't want the whole world knowing that he was involved in brokering off these art pieces. The whole reason why he was involved was that the Vatican needed discretion and didn't want anyone to know what they were doing. If the art world were made aware of these expensive art pieces being sold off to private collectors, it would probably create a cultural, international war."

"And Monsignor Iacobelli was Marchese's Vatican connection?"

"Yep."

Rizzo took another long swallow of his second drink, and I realized I was going to have to 'pop' for another round.

"What do you know about this, Monsignor Iacobelli?" I asked.

"Only that he's a first cousin to the Don and has some pretty powerful connections over at the Vatican. The Don was involved in finding new owners for these

182

expensive art pieces, and they were willing to pay top dollar for them," Chaz explained.

"Then who did he 'piss off'? And who put the hit on him? What did Marchese do to get himself killed?" I was asking him rapid-fire questions.

Rizzo made another girlish giggle between gulps, then a short period of silence.

"Those are excellent questions, my friend." He put his empty glass tumbler onto the bar, and then he motioned to the bartender for one more Crown Royal.

"Easy on the juice, Chaz. Are you trying to 'drink her cute'?" I joked.

"I do better in bed when I'm sauced," he boasted, making me realize that his 'hot date' may not have been so hot after all.

"Who gave you all of this information?" I pushed him again.

"Tony DiNapoli. He's one of the Marchese Family lieutenants. I did him a favor once and helped him with a criminal attorney that I'm good friends with. My attorney friend did me a favor and helped him with some assault and battery charges, which he needed help with."

"Who's your attorney friend?"

"Michael Prescott. He's a criminal attorney on North LaSalle Street. Good guy."

"I've met him before," as I recalled the name.

Rizzo was gulping down his third drink, while I was gingerly sipping on my second. By this time, Rizzo was feeling pretty good, and I could have probably gotten him to give me his Hugo Boss credit card and his social security number.

"So, what is your take this, Riz? Who do you think Marchese pissed off?"

He sat there silently for a few more minutes, still twirling his ice cubes and pretending to be interested in the football game. It was a Green Bay-New Orleans game, and the Packers were up 24-14.

"Do you recall that missing art discovery last summer? That story about an old man who was found dead in his Munich apartment and there was, something like, millions of dollars' worth of missing artworks that were stolen from the Uffizi Gallery during World War II?" Rizzo was feeling really good, I could tell.

"Yes, I think so. I think the Chicago Tribune did a story on it. I had heard that one of our reporters attempted to submit a story on it, but according to my assistant editor, it was never printed. I forget her name. She's one of the curators over at the Art Institute of Chicago," I was trying hard to recall the Tribune story.

"Veronica something...she has an Italian name, right?" Rizzo remembered, recalling that he had asked her out on a date a few times, but was turned down.

"Yeah, something like that. She's that cute curator over at the Art Institute," I recalled. "She's a freelance reporter for our cultural arts section. Why?"

"You may want to look her up, Paulie. I heard Marchese was involved with that scenario as well."

"Involved? How so?" I asked.

"Not sure. I just recall DiNapoli telling me that the Don made a special trip to Rome last summer. He also got chummy with that German art dealer on North Wells Street," Rizzo was starting to slur his words.

That evening, I sat there at Cleary's and watched him suck down three Crown Royals in less than twenty minutes. By that time, I was starting to worry about my favorite Channel Eight news reporter leaving the tavern and driving over to Tuscany's on Taylor Street. I looked at my watch and noticed it was almost eight o'clock.

"I've got an idea, Chaz. Let me drive you to Tuscany's tonight, so you're not late for your 'hot date.' Leave your car parked and 'Uber-it' back here when you're done with dinner. By then, you'll feel good enough to drive."

He insisted on driving off alone at first, but I convinced him that dropping him off was no trouble. I settled the bar tab, and we left Cleary's. I figured with all of the juicy information that I had pumped out him, that driving him to the restaurant was the least I could do.

I pulled my car in front of Tuscany's on Taylor Street. By then, Chaz Rizzo had a worried look on his face.

"Paulie? How are you going to write this story? You do realize I can't be involved. DiNapoli will cut my balls off."

"Don't worry, Chaz. I've got your back. I have a few more leads I need to investigate. But don't worry. I won't disclose my sources to anyone. I'll keep you informed."

"Thanks, Crawford...I trust you," he said, knowing that it was the alcohol talking. I then wished him luck on his romantic endeavor.

The restaurant valet opened the passenger door of my Cadillac SUV and let out Rizzo, who was all too eager to make a grand entrance for his waiting date inside. I then temporarily parked my car in Tuscany's parking lot. With the car still running, I pulled out my notepad and wrote down all of Chaz Rizzo's valuable information. I figured I would impress 'The Chief' will all of this new material on Don Marchese's murder, and I knew I had more than enough to start a very intense investigation.

At that moment, I had no idea what I was getting myself into.

CHAPTER TWENTY-ONE

BIRTHDAY PARTY – LATE JULY 2018

As Wolfgang Schmidt pulled into the circular driveway of his expansive Winnetka mansion last summer, he noticed a large foray of Mercedes, Maserati's, Rolls Royce's and Bentley luxury vehicles that he didn't recognize, parked in front of his home. There was a large trampoline and blow-up air balloon of some obscure cartoon character he didn't recognize in his backyard. Hundreds of people were already congregating in his vast and spacious two-acre yard. His wife Dora greeted him at the front door and pleasantly admonished him for arriving late to his only grandchild's birthday party.

'Wolfy,' as some of his friends and close family liked to call him, fixed himself a Manhattan at the bar and began socializing with some of his daughter's guests.

"Thank you, Daddy" as his daughter Lisa kissed her father on the cheek, for allowing her to open their house to all of her guests for his granddaughter's first birthday party. She placed her daughter Emily into her grandfather's loving arms as he doted on her while socializing with the other guests.

Lisa began 'working the party' with her father, introducing him to her many, many close friends. One of the friends she had introduced him to was Anna Maria Marchese, with her fiancé' Anthony Fanelli, and her mother and father, Carlo and Angela Marchese, who was also invited and attending the party.

"It's a pleasure to meet you," Wolf extended his hand to the elder Marchese. He had heard about the reputation of Carlo Marchese from his business associates and whatever he had read in the papers, but also heard that he was a 'stand-up guy' and a gentleman.

"The pleasure is mine," Don Carlo reciprocated. The two of them made small talk and exchanged pleasantries, complimenting each other on their established business endeavors and their foregoing reputations. 'Grandpa Wolf' turned over his granddaughter to Dora, and he began having an expansive conversation with Don Marchese. He decided to show him around his Winnetka mansion, as he abandoned socializing with the other guests.

"Do you enjoy cigars?" Wolf asked.

"Of course, I do. Especially Cubans," he replied.

"I just received a shipment of Romeo y Julietta's I would like you to try."

Wolfgang then brought the elder Marchese down to his smoking and humidor room, over in the western wing of his mansion, far away from the children's ongoing birthday party. He offered Don Marchese a Cuban cigar and a brandy sifter, filled with three fingers of Remy-Martin Louis XIII Baccarat Cognac.

"Cheers, Don Marchese...to your good health," he addressed his esteemed guest.

Carlo was somewhat surprised at his host's formal salutation, addressing him as the "Don."

"And here is to yours, Herr Schmidt," Don Carlo reciprocated. The two of them shared a light as they cut and began smoking their Cuban cigars.

They continued to make small talk, each of them becoming more and more familiar with the other's infamous reputations. They continued to talk in private in the Schmidt's cigar room for over an hour when Don Carlo began to 'break the ice.'

"So, tell me, Wolf, who are your clients these days?"

"I sell artwork to art collectors and museums all over the world," he mentioned.

Don Marchese took a long drag from his cigar, making smoke circles in the air.

"Art collectors all over the world?" he inquired.

"Yes. I have access to art pieces that no other art dealer in the world has access to," Schmidt bragged.

"And you have access to all of these invaluable art pieces?"

"Of course."

"Would any of those art pieces be stolen works of art looted by the Nazis from the Uffizi Gallery in Florence during the Second World War?"

Wolf turned three shades of red. He quickly became silent and studied his guest, sitting across from him in his cigar room. He had heard about the resourcefulness of Don Marchese and was now about to find out about his ruthless reputation firsthand.

Don Marchese had more than done 'his homework' that afternoon before accepting the invitation to his granddaughter's birthday party. He had heard about the Schmidt family's art world reputation and the access to the stolen Nazi art pieces that only Wolfgang Schmidt had access to. Marchese always made it a point to do 'his homework' before sitting on the other side of the negotiating table of his adversaries.

Knowledge is power, he would always say. Before sitting on the other side of the table to make a deal, make sure you know the '*color of his underwear*.' To that end, Don Marchese knew confidential information about the Schmidt family and their Nazi stolen art connections that was not readily available to others.

"Complimenti," Wolfgang Schmidt said in Italian to his guest of honor, after several moments of intense silence. "You've done your homework, I see."

"Danka dir," Don Marchese replied in German.

The two gentlemen smiled at each other in silence, both enjoying their Cuban smokes and taking small sips of their expensive brandy sifters. After several quiet minutes, Don Marchese again broke the ice.

"Herr Schmidt, I did not come here to your home in honor of your granddaughter and to insult you. Just the opposite. I've come here to inquire about the possibility of the two of us doing business together," as he took a long drag from his Cuban cigar, which he was thoroughly enjoying.

Wolfgang Schmidt only glared at his guest in silence.

"You have my attention, Don Marchese."

"I have associates and business connections that may be interested in acquiring back some of those stolen art pieces that were originally looted from the Uffizi and ultimately, from the Vatican in Rome."

"The Vatican? What do these Uffizi art pieces have to do with the Vatican?" Schmidt inquired, although he knew precisely what Marchese was referring to.

"Many of the artworks that were stolen from the Uffizi in Florence during the war were on consignment from the Vatican. The Vatican sent an enumerate amount of these artworks at the request of Mussolini before the onset of the war in Italy. After these art pieces were looted, Pope Pius XII had made inquiries of 'The Fuhrer' to return these valuable works of art. Do you know what Hitler's reply was to the Pope?"

"No, I do not." Herr Schmidt was pretending to play stupid.

"Dies ist der Preis, den Sie für den Frieden zahlen," Don Marchese replied in flawless German.

Schmidt sat there motionless, as Don Marchese translated.

"'This is the price you pay for peace,' was his reply to the Pope. As you know, the Vatican had an agreement with the Nazis that they would spare Vatican City from any of the war activities and violence that was transpiring in Rome and throughout Italy at the time."

Again, Schmidt was silent, attentively listening to his guest.

"You may also know, the Vatican and specifically, Pope Pius XII personally oversaw the escape of many Nazi criminals to Latin America and other parts of Western Europe, by supplying them with fake passports and documents. False identities of deceased priests and monsignors were used to escape the wrath of all the Jewish Nazi hunters and American spies that were directed to bring these Nazi war criminals to justice," Marchese lectured.

"I have heard this before...yes," Wolf slowly replied. Don Marchese was not educating him about anything he didn't already know.

The two of them sat silent while finishing their cigars. Don Carlo chose these few quiet moments to let the seriousness of this conversation sink into the art dealer's head.

"Would you say that, perhaps, the officials at the Vatican have a right to have these valuable pieces of art stolen from the Uffizi during the war, returned to them without question?"

Wolfgang Schmidt lost his patience and suddenly stood up from his chair. He was desperately trying to hold his temper, holding his lit cigar in one hand and his brandy sifter in the other.

"I am not at liberty to answer that question, Don Marchese," he loudly replied. At that moment, he was not about to let himself be played by this Mafioso or anyone else.

"Besides, how deep do your Vatican connections go?" There were several moments of silence.

Don Marchese then smiled and quietly pulled out his iPhone. After sifting through some pictures, he displayed a recent photo of himself, posing with the current pope in Rome. After presenting this photograph, he showed several other images of his posing with Pope Emeritus Honorius V and Pope John Paul II several years ago. His cell phone with these photographs was passed back and forth in silence to Wolfgang Schmidt, without mentioning a word.

"So, you are friends with the Pope?"

"The Pope Emeritus," he replied. "I have deep connections within the Vatican and know most everyone within the Holy See. It has been mentioned several times that the Vatican would be interested in the return of some of these Uffizi stolen art pieces."

More silence as Don Marchese finished his cigar and swallowed the last drop of his expensive cognac.

"This could be a very profitable transaction for both of us, Herr Schmidt. I never said that the Vatican wanted them back for nothing," he inserted.

Wolf then smiled at his guest as he too finished his drink.

"Perhaps...we can do business together." Schmidt stood up as he shook Don Marchese's hand. They looked at each other in the eye, knowing that the Don's proposal could be a very profitable transaction for both of them. They both exited the cigar room and returned to the children's birthday party at hand.

At that moment, neither one of them understood the real meaning of the words 'divine wrath'.

CHAPTER TWENTY-TWO

DINNER WITH THE ART DEALER – THE NEXT DAY

The bright lights were glaring in his eyes on that late summer evening, as the cars were traveling quickly down Belmont Avenue. Don Carlo Marchese was sitting at a booth, dressed in his usual seventies garb, next to the window of one his favorite little Italian restaurants.

La Zingara was a small, quaint little trattoria just east of Belmont and Central Avenues with twelve, checker cloth tables. The décor of the restaurant looked like a scene from one of the Godfather movies, set in the 1940s, where Michael Corleone came running out of the men's bathroom with a gun in his hand. It still had a jukebox in the corner, and the wooden chairs looked so old that they would probably collapse if an overweight patron ever utilized them. Several customers were enjoying their pizza, and pasta entrée's, as the aroma of freshly cooked Marinara sauce from the kitchen, filled the room.

Don Marchese knew the owner, Carmen Mastroangelo, very well. Since he was also the chef and did most of the homemade cooking himself, he kept sending samples calamari fritti and freshly baked ziti over to the Capo's table. At the same time, he waited for his guest to arrive on that muggy, last night of July.

Wolfgang Schmidt came strolling into the small restaurant at almost nine o'clock that Sunday night, thirty minutes late for his dinner meeting with Don Marchese. He rose from the booth and greeted his new friend with a customary hug, as the art dealer apologized profusely for being late. Wolf was coming from his home in Winnetka and wasn't familiar with the area. His GPS wasn't working correctly; he kept exclaiming, as the Capo asked Chef Carmen to make something special for his German friend.

Wolfgang had spent his birthday on that Sunday assisting his wife and daughter clean and rearranging their house after his granddaughter's backyard birthday party the day before, and lost track of time.

On that hot Sunday evening, Wolfgang was dressed in a crisp pair of light khaki trousers, beige Dockers, and a well-pressed blue Polo shirt, which showed off his flat stomach and lean figure. Don Marchese, in contrast, was wearing a pair of plaid, checkered pants, white shoes, and a gold, polyester short-sleeve shirt. Even when it called for casual attire, the art dealer always took pride in his modern fashion. He was taken aback that evening by Don Marchese's appearance and his penchant for flashy, seventies-style clothing.

They both ordered a glass of red wine while they chit-chatted about their businesses and Wolfgang's birthday party for his little granddaughter the night before. Wolfgang had asked Don Carlo to meet him that evening to discuss further his plans of 'doing business' together, as Schmidt was planning to return to Munich within the next few days.

Don Carlo decided to try the baked ziti while Chef Carmen made Wolfgang his specialty: linguini with stuffed shrimp in a red clam sauce. Wolfgang broke the ice as the food entrées arrived.

"I understand today is your birthday," Don Marchese said to the German art dealer.

"Happy Birthday."

Schmidt looked shocked, as no one other than his family even remembered his special day, let alone acknowledge it.

"Thank you, Don Carlo. How did you know."

"Facebook," Marchese joked. He made it a point to remember birthdays and knew about his while researching his background. In reality, Carlo Marchese had no desire or nothing to do with social media.

"So, Don Marchese, tell me about your Vatican connections," the art dealer inquired.

"I come from a long line of Catholic priests in Rome," the Capo started. "Three of my uncles were Catholic priests, and I have a brother and three cousins who are priests as well. One of them is the personal secretary to Pope Emeritus."

"Pope Honorius? The German pope who resigned?"

"Correct," as Don Carlo was thoroughly enjoying his baked pasta dish.

"Okay..." Wolfgang replied while tasting his linguini and stuffed shrimps. He was waiting for Don Marchese to elaborate.

"My client, the Vatican, is interested in your paintings."

"Which ones?" Schmidt knew very well which ones he was referring.

"Your Uffizi paintings. The ones you acquired from your cousin in Munich who just passed away."

Schmidt was taken aback at how much information Don Marchese knew, considering that this whole transaction just occurred two weeks before.

"Okay…Which ones?"

Don Marchese grasped his glass of wine, taking a final sip, then motioned the waitress to bring them two more drinks.

"All of them." Don Carlo was looking at the art dealer dead square in the eyes.

Wolfgang laughed. "Your Pope Emeritus wants *all* of the paintings?"

"Herr Schmidt, I must correct you. First of all, Pope Emeritus Honorius V is probably more your pope than mine, considering that he is one of your *paisani* from Germany. Secondly, Papa Onorio wishes for the Uffizi paintings, which were originally Vatican Museum artworks consigned to Florence's Uffizi Gallery before the war erupted, to be returned to the Vatican," Marchese patiently explained.

"Don Marchese, forgive me for asking. You did mention that the Vatican was willing to purchase these artworks, correct?"

"Correct."

"You talk as though these paintings should be returned *au gratis.*"

"Papa Onorio wishes to purchase those forty-two paintings back from you at a fair price, considering those paintings belonged to the Vatican, to begin with. There is documentation proving this, Herr Schmidt," Marchese pointed out.

Schmidt didn't remember telling Marchese how many Uffizi paintings he had in his possession and wondered how the Capo got his information.

The art dealer took another sip of wine. "*Congratulazioni*, Don Marchese. You've done your homework, I see."

The Don smiled and nodded his head.

"To begin with, Don Marchese, I have a bill of sale, dated November 1943, authenticating the sale of those forty-two paintings from the Uffizi Art Gallery to the Nazi's for seventy-eight thousand lire. The Nazis stole nothing. It was a legitimate transaction," taking a sip of his red wine.

"Let me make this very clear. I went through a lot of trouble to acquire those paintings from my cousin," Schmidt paused for a moment and looked at Don Carlo as he nodded his head once again.

"I am not about to give them away to your Pope, the Vatican, or anyone else now for less than fair market value," he started to say.

"I have appraised those paintings at no less than two hundred million dollars, and I am confident that I can receive every dollar of that amount in any art auction that I place those paintings in. I have prospective art galleries, wealthy investors, and many art collectors who have expressed their interest and are more than happy to give me my price. I don't need the Vatican, and I certainly don't need your Papa Onorio," Wolfgang Schmidt spoke bluntly to the Capo.

"And..." he added, "I don't give a shit that your Pope Emeritus is a German or not."

Don Marchese smiled, taking another hearty bite of his baked ziti, which he was more than enjoying.

"You must admit, Herr Schmidt," as the Don continued eating his dinner. "The food here is pretty good," he said, complimenting the chef and trying his best to irritate the art dealer.

"Herr Schmidt...go back to what you previously said."

"Back to what?"

"Back to the part of...' all the trouble you went through to get those paintings,' you know...that part," Don Marchese was still chewing, pointing his fork at Schmidt at the same time.

"What about it?"

The Capo coyly smiled. "You do realize we have a common friend, correct?"

"Which friend is that?"

The Capo said, "Stefano Iannucci."

The art dealer turned several shades of red at the sound of the hired assassin's name. He suddenly became very uncomfortable, and he was starting to sweat, as the Mafia family capo casually continued eating, almost finishing his baked ziti entrée.

"Boy...this is delicious. The food is delicious here, wouldn't you agree, Herr Schmidt."

The art dealer silently sat there in the booth of that quaint, Italian restaurant, totally motionless. He was starting to feel nauseous. He became very apprehensive of what Don Marchese had in mind.

"May I call you Wolf?"

Schmidt nodded his head.

"I don't think it's a really good idea for you to be talking smart and cocky about how you received those paintings and how much you intend to sell them for. Please understand, Wolf, the underworld is a very small world indeed, where everybody knows everybody. Mr. Iannucci has done some work for our family as well,"

Don Marchese was mentioning his influences and connections very casually, as sweat started to bead down Wolfgang's forehead.

"Now, understand, Wolf...we don't want those paintings for nothing. But we certainly are not going to be extorted for them, either. And you do realize; those paintings originally belonged to the Vatican."

Schmidt sat there silently, not mentioning another word.

"I also understand that the Munich Police Department...Detective Hildebrandt is his name? I understand that they are very interested in speaking with you after you bribed their mayor to release those paintings after your cousin's death and later was found shot to death at his desk two days later."

More silence, as Don Marchese let his words sink in with the international art dealer.

"You see, Wolf, I have many, many friends all over the world. I have friends in Munich. I have friends at Interpol. I have friends in Scotland Yard. I have lots of friends in the Chicago P.D., the FBI, and the CIA. And I also have friends like Stefano Iannucci, who says you still owe him some money, by the way," taking his last sip of wine.

"So, you see, my friend," he continued, "I wouldn't talk too smart if I were you."

Don Carlo Marchese had the art dealer right where he wanted him. Information is power, Don Carlo always believed. He had been doing an incredible amount of research on the Chicago art dealer and his business dealings, especially in Munich over the last few weeks. He had accumulated a great deal of information on him. By the time Schmidt had walked into that restaurant that evening, Don Marchese had turned on his x-ray vision. He could see right through his fancy Hugo Boss frigging underwear.

Wolfgang glared at him. "What do you fucking want from me? Do you want me just to give those paintings away to you?"

"No, Wolf. Just offer them to us at a fair price, and I will go to the Vatican. If I can get Papa Onorio to agree on a price tag, then maybe we can all make some money here. We can make a deal for all forty-two for your Uffizi paintings."

Wolfgang became very angry with the tone of the whole evening's dialog, and he had heard enough. He was not about to sell his soul to Marchese, the Vatican, or anyone else, for a low price. He knew what those paintings were worth and intended to get every dollar.

"I don't think we can do business here, Don Marchese. I am not going to be threatened or pushed around by you, the Vatican, or anyone else," he said as he threw his napkin down on the table and was about to leave.

"I wouldn't go anywhere if I were you, Wolf."

"Your problems are far from over. Just because you have those paintings stashed in some warehouse in Germany somewhere, doesn't mean you are going to be able to get them out," he coldly said.

"The Vatican is the best, most realistic buyer you're going to get on those paintings...presuming we're still friends, of course," he reiterated.

"If you walk out of this restaurant, my offer to buy those paintings from you is off. I can then assure you; we will no longer be friends."

Wolfgang angrily glared at Don Marchese.

"And the minute you walk out of this restaurant..." he sternly warned, holding up his cellular phone, "I am going to immediately make some phone calls that will make your life a very miserable one indeed."

There were several long moments of silence as the waitress came over to ask if everything was okay with their meals.

"Everything is wonderful, honey," the Mafioso smiled.

The two men continued to glare at each other in silence, as they were at an impasse. Neither man said a word, as Wolfgang finished eating his linguini. He then wiped his mouth with his napkin, finished his wine, and held up his index finger to Don Marchese.

"One," the art dealer calmly replied.

"One what?"

"I will sell the Vatican one painting, for one million dollars. If this transaction goes smoothly, we will negotiate a fair price for the other forty-one paintings."

More silence.

"Which painting would that be?"

"'The Demons of Divine Wrath,' by Fra Filippo Lippi. It was painted in Florence in 1459 by the famous painter, depicting St. Michael the Archangel slaying the devil and its demons as they're emerging from the deepest depths of hell," Wolfgang proposed.

"Look it up on the internet. The painting is worth between three to four million dollars on the open market. It is the most valuable painting of the total Uffizi art collection. I will sell it to your pope for one million dollars. If we can complete this transaction smoothly, then we will go forward with the rest."

Don Marchese was deep in thought for several moments.

His expression quickly changed, and he suddenly looked very pleased with Wolfgang as he extended his hand.

"I think we can make a deal here," Don Marchese replied, as Wolfgang accepted his handshake offer.

"I will contact Papa Onorio," Marchese said, as Wolfgang threw a couple of one-hundred-dollar bills on the table and began to get up and leave.

"Call me before Thursday. I leave for Munich then, and if I don't hear from you, I will presume your pope is not interested," Schmidt clarified.

"I'm sure we'll be talking," Marchese replied.

Schmidt began to walk towards the exit door, and Don Marchese continued to sit there at the booth, waiting for him to leave so that he could start making some phone calls. As he approached the door, he looked back at Marchese.

"Presuming that we can complete this deal for all of the paintings, you must give your Pope Emeritus a personal message from me," the art dealer requested.

"Of course."

"You will tell him I said, 'fuck you.'"

Don Marchese smiled, shaking his head. "Should I tell him in English or German? Or in Italian, perhaps? Which language do you prefer?"

"You can tell him in any goddamn language you like," Wolfgang coldly replied, as he exited the door towards his new Mercedes S-Class convertible.

Don Carlo Marchese watched Wolfgang pull away and then pulled out his cellular phone, dialing a telephone number overseas. He checked his watch. It was almost eleven o'clock Chicago time and was seven o'clock in the morning where Marchese was calling. He dialed the number and waited for a response.

"Detektiv Hildebrandt ... Sie werden sehr bald einen Besucher empfangen,"

"You will be receiving a visit very soon."

CHAPTER TWENTY-THREE

Don Marchese arrived at Rome's Leonardo DaVinci Airport on that Tuesday afternoon and was well familiar with the gate exits and luggage claims of the airport layout and Alitalia Airlines. The overcrowding of the 'ferroagosto' tourists was overwhelming, as it seemed as though everyone in Rome was trying to catch a flight out of the Eternal City during the first week of August.

Marchese had called his cousin, Monsignor Iacobelli, after his meeting with Wolfgang Schmidt at the La Zingara last Sunday night and demanded him to schedule an immediate exclusive audience with the Pope Emeritus. The Mafioso did not want to waste too much time going back and forth between Schmidt and Papa Onorio unless he knew that he had a deal for the Uffizi paintings. Carlo Marchese was not a man of texts, cellular phones, and emails if he could help it. He preferred doing business the old-fashioned way, and when there was a considerable amount of money involved, he wanted to transact his business face to face with his clients.

After going through customs, he took a taxicab to the Hotel Quirinale on Via Nazionale and checked into his hotel room. He was tired after his long, grueling flight, which originated at O'Hare Airport at 10:00 pm the prior evening with a brief layover in Newark. He wanted to freshen up and take a nap before heading over to the Vatican to the Pope Emeritus's papal apartment at 6:30 pm.

After a few hours of rest and getting cleaned up for his meeting, Don Marchese dressed up in a black

Canali pin-striped suit, a crisp white shirt, and a black-tie for his papal appointment at the Vatican. He didn't need to disguise himself as an old, penniless vagabond the way he usually did in Chicago. Don Marchese learned many years ago that when he dressed in old, worn-out clothing from years back, he was often left alone by the media, the politicians, and anyone else looking to stop him for a favor. Wearing his old, gaudy clothing was a masquerade of sorts, and as a result, very few people recognized him.

The taxicab pulled into St. Peter's Square at 6:15 pm and circled towards the back of Vatican City, as the Vespas and bothersome little Fiat's tried in vain to cut them off. Driving in the Eternal City and around the 'spaghetti bowl' was always a challenge, as every vehicle driving on their ancient cobblestoned streets had to compete with each other to get to wherever they were going.

The taxicab pulled up in front of an old rustic brownstone building, with two Swiss Guards standing in front of the doorway. One of them quickly opened the taxicab door and requested the name and identification of the Chicago Mafioso.

"Signore Marchese? Benvenuto, il Papa Emerito vi aspetta," the Swiss Guard replied, letting him know that the Pope Emeritus was waiting.

Don Marchese was grateful that his cousin had made the necessary arrangements for his security clearance. For a moment, Marchese was starting to enjoy this up-scale diplomat treatment as he climbed out of the car and was motioned inside. Don Carlo was escorted to an elevator, which brought him up three floors. He exchanged 'buongiorni's' with several other papal associates, who then accompanied him through several dark rooms, until opening two large oak doors into a spacious, brightly opened great room.

The large, lavish great room was decorated in Italian white, Carrera marble, with wide-open ornate ceilings and art décor statutes neatly placed upon several glass tables. Numerous, large Renaissance masterpieces were hung intermittingly around the towering walls of the papal apartment. There were several black leather chairs and a large black sectional couch set up in the middle of the room. Across from the entrance door were two twelve-foot windows that opened to an expansive veranda, which boasted a beautiful, scenic view of St. Peter's Square.

"Caffe?" he was politely offered by an associate priest as Don Marchese made himself comfortable in a chair facing the open windows.

"Si, per favore."

Not more than thirty seconds passed before Monsignor Iacobelli came dashing out of a backroom from the other side of the papal quarters.

"Cugino!"

"Ciao Gianpaolo!" They quickly embraced and kissed each other on the cheek.

"Come' va?"

"Molto bene. Grazie Cugino!" Don Carlo excitedly replied.

"I trust your flight here to Rome was a safe and enjoyable one?"

"Yes, Gianni...I am a little tired, though."

At that moment, an associate priest entered the great room, bringing over Don Carlo's espresso, along with two small packets of sugar. Marchese placed them on the small glass coffee table in front of the leather chair he was sitting in, and quickly poured the packets into his evening coffee. The rich aroma of Italian caffeine seemed always to have a different flavor and smell when enjoyed in the Eternal City, and Don Carlo was more than grateful for the delicious cup of espresso that early evening.

The two cousins continued to make small talk for several minutes when Pope Emeritus finally entered the room.

"Good Evening, your Holiness," as Carlo Marchese knelt and kissed the ring on his right hand. He had met the former Pope Honorius V several times before and were always friendly and cordial with one another, almost on a first-name basis.

"Buona Sera, Carlo. It's so nice to see you again," as Papa Onorio gave him a firm hug, kissing him on both cheeks.

The associate priest had Papa Onorio's espresso doppio all ready for him as he sat down at the black leather chair next to his.

"How are things in Chicago?" he excitedly asked.

"Very warm, Your Holiness. We are in dire need of rain."

"I wish I could travel again. I have not seen Chicago in over thirty years. What a beautiful city," he exclaimed. "I sometimes feel like a prisoner here in Vatican City, unable to leave and travel without the whole Swiss Guard following me around."

"I suppose this is your cross, Your Holiness," as Don Carlo was trying to be cordial.

The two exchanged pleasantries and more small talk while Monsignor Iacobelli sat at the other leather chair facing the two of them. The young, associate priest, who looked to be Latino and spoke Italian with a thick Spanish accent, stood guard to attend to any of the former pontiff's needs that evening.

"That will be all, Gustavo," Papa Onorio curtly said, as the young associate bowed and excused himself. At that moment, the three of them were alone in the great room, enjoying their caffe', ready to attend to the business at hand.

"Thank you, Your Holiness, for agreeing to see me at such short notice."

"Thank you, Carlo, for all that you have done for us here at the Vatican. I can assure you that we are very grateful for your services in helping us raise the funding that we have needed over the last few years."

"The pleasure is mine, Your Holiness," smiling at his cousin.

"I understand that you have some wonderful news for me regarding the return of those forty-two Vatican paintings that have finally been recovered."

Don Marchese looked at the Pope Emeritus with a confused look on his face.

"Well, yes....," he slowly replied.

"I understand that the German art dealer in Chicago has them stored near Munich. That will make it easy to have them transported back here to the Vatican Museum," the former Pope presumed.

"Well..." Marchese looked over to his cousin, who mutely sat there without a word.

"Your services to me and the Vatican have always been exemplary, as you have been a gift from heaven. We are so grateful to you and the fine job you have done for us as always..." Papa Onorio continued.

Don Marchese only sat there, speechless. He now realized that his debriefing of the Uffizi painting situation that he had explained to his cousin over the phone late Sunday evening had not been communicated to the Pope Emeritus. Carlo looked over at the Monsignor as if to express his astonishment using his eyes only.

"So, Carlo, when will these paintings be delivered? We will need to plan their arrival," he excitedly stated, then looking over to Iacobelli.

"We have much to do, Gianni. We will need to inform the press and especially the La Repubblica Newspaper. They must be the first to know that their Pope Emeritus has finally brought back home, the missing Renaissance paintings stolen by the Nazis during the Second World War..."

The former Pope was smiling from ear to ear as if he were standing in front of all forty-two missing paintings himself, for all the world to see.

"Your Holiness?" Monsignor Iacobelli interrupted the over-excited Pope Emeritus.

"My cousin Carlo has other news for you..." trying to gently break the update to him, knowing that the former pontiff would soon be very disappointed.

"What other news?"

"Your Holiness," Don Marchese began, "we have not secured the return of all the paintings as of yet. I was only able to make a deal for one painting. Once we have secured payment delivery of this painting, we can begin negotiating for the other forty-one masterpieces."

The Pope Emeritus sat there in silence.

"The 'Demons of Divine Wrath," painted by Fra Filippo Lippi, was the only one I was able to make a deal for, so far."

There were several long moments of silence. Pope Emeritus glared at Don Marchese for a few, long uncomfortable moments.

"One painting? Only one painting? You flew all the way here from Chicago to tell me about one painting?" The old prelate was trying very hard to control his all-too-famous Bavarian temper. His eyes began to bulge, and he was trying to temper his words carefully.

"Carlo, did I hear you say, 'secured payment'?"

"Yes, Your Holiness. Herr Wolfgang Schmidt is asking one million dollars for the painting. He claims the 'Demons of Divine Wrath' is valued at four million to five million dollars. It is the most valuable masterpiece of the art collection."

The Pope Emeritus shook his head, still glaring at the Chicago Mafioso.

"Secured payment?"

The Monsignor tried to interject.

"Your Holiness? My cousin Carlo here has tracked down and found where these missing paintings are and befriended the Chicago art dealer who has them. He has gone through a tremendous amount of trouble to find those paintings and secure a deal for one of them. As he has stated, a deal for the rest of them can be made once we pay for the first painting."

"Pay? Who said anything about 'paying' for these paintings? Those forty-two Vatican masterpieces were stolen by the Nazi's in Florence when they were consigned to the Uffizi in 1938."

"I asked for those paintings to be recovered. I never said anything about paying for them."

The Monsignor was appalled, as he looked over to his cousin, who could not believe what he was hearing.

"Those paintings have been recovered, and now need to be returned to their rightful place at the Vatican Museum. We will not be extorted to pay for stolen property that originally belonged to Rome and the Vatican all along," the Pope Emeritus sternly responded, trying very hard to control his temper.

"But Your Holiness...you cannot expect an art dealer to freely give away forty-two Renaissance masterpieces that are worth over two hundred million dollars or more back to the Vatican after more than eighty years of being missing and stolen by the Nazi's. Besides, he has a bill of sale, dated November 1943, where the Nazis paid seventy-eight thousand lire for those paintings to the Uffizi Gallery," Don Marchese tried to say.

"THEY WERE NOT THEIRS TO SELL!" he stood up and screamed as he grabbed his espresso cup and threw it onto the marble floor, exploding into a million pieces.

The associate priest heard the commotion and came rushing into the great room, ready to clean up the mess.

"LEAVE IT!" he yelled, pointing his finger, as the poor young priest froze in his tracks.

"What makes you believe we at the Vatican should pay for something that already belongs to us? Do you believe that we are interested in buying back our stolen paintings? Those paintings belong to the Vatican, and you were asked to recover them!" he loudly and angrily stated. His voice was vibrating, and one could hear the trembling of the delicate art statutes poised on their glass stands.

Don Marchese was speechless. He turned to his cousin and openly complained.

"You told me that the Pope Emeritus would be willing to buy back those paintings when they were recovered. I was under the impression that buying or repurchasing them would not be an issue."

"So was I," Iacobelli replied, looking back at Pope Emeritus.

"I never told you, Gianni, that I would be willing to pay for the return of those paintings. A finder's fee, perhaps," he said, his loud voice coming down a few decibels.

"But, I never agreed to be extorted!"

The Chicago Mafioso looked at his cousin with a confused look still on his face and then stared back at the Pope Emeritus. At that moment, he decided to take the high road and try to appease the former pontiff.

"I understand, Your Holiness. I will see whatever it is that I need to do to 'recover' those paintings for you," he calmly said. He then kneeled before him and kissed his ring.

"Please excuse me, Your Holiness, as I must return to my hotel room. It has been a very long day."

The Pope only answered, "I trust you will return here with better news, Carlo. I will be anxiously awaiting your response."

"Buona Sera, Your Holiness," he politely said, as the young priest escorted both he and Monsignor Iacobelli out of the opulent papal apartment.

Feeling embarrassed, the Monsignor and the demoralized Mafioso said nothing to each other while in the elevator. They were careful to stay silent until they were both outside in front of the ancient, brownstone Roman building.

"I believe your Pope Emeritus is losing his goddamn mind," Don Marchese stated. "Does he expect me to recover those paintings for nothing?"

"I don't understand, Carlo. He must be getting senile. He originally mentioned that he would be willing to repurchase them..." the Monsignor recalled.

"Perhaps..." Iacobelli continued to speculate, "he figured that, with your underworld connections, that you could recover those paintings, and intimidate the Chicago art dealer into freely giving them to you on our behalf..."

"What? Intimidate? What are you talking about?" Marchese was perplexed at his cousin's assumption.

"Does he expect me to 'whack' this guy for the damn paintings? Is he out of his goddamn mind?" Carlo loudly responded. "Tell your senile pope that those days of Al Capone are over. We don't go running around 'whacking people' anymore. Those days in Chicago are long gone, Cugino."

"I don't know, Carlo. I don't understand. I am so sorry. I did not expect him to react this way," Gianpaolo apologized.

Carlo Marchese looked at his cousin, knowing that he had no control over any of this. He took a very long, deep breath and sighed. He put his hand on the Monsignor's shoulder and patiently smiled. Carlo then asked one of the Swiss Guards to hail him a taxicab.

"This is not your fault, Gianni. I don't blame you. I will salvage this deal, don't worry," as he hugged and kissed his apologetic cousin on both cheeks.

The yellow Fiat taxicab pulled up in front of the brownstone building, and Marchese climbed inside.

"I will do whatever it is that I need to do. Thank you, Gianni," the Mafioso said.

"When will you be calling back the Pope?" he innocently asked.

Don Carlo Marchese looked back at his cousin, smiling.

"I won't be," he said with a smirk on his face, waving his middle finger up in the sky towards the papal apartment of the Pope Emeritus.

"Ci vediamo dopo," he said out of the taxicab window as it drove away towards Via Nazionale to his hotel. Unbeknownst to anyone else, Don Carlo Marchese had a 'Plan B' in mind.

And it had nothing to do with the Vatican.

CHAPTER TWENTY-FOUR

The American Airlines Boeing 777 Airbus made a smooth touchdown onto Detroit's Metropolitan Airport on that late Wednesday evening, as it was then immediately taxied over to Gate 17. Marchese had probably traveled over ninety-six hundred miles over the last two days, taking a direct flight to Detroit after spending only one night in Rome. With the collapse of the painting deal with the Vatican, he was not about to waste any more time in Italy, relaxing at his villa in Casalvieri. There was an opportunity to make some serious money here, and time was of the essence. He was not going to let his cousin at the Vatican, or the arrogant Pope Emeritus get in his way. After grabbing his only luggage, he went through the U.S. Customs line.

"Where are you coming from, sir," the U.S. Customs Agent asked Marchese.

"Business in Rome, returning to the United States," he politely answered.

The customs agent thumbed through his passport, noting that he had a significant number of 'customs stamps' from Italy, the most recent two days ago.

"How long were you in Italy, sir?"

"Twenty-four hours," he brazenly said, knowing that he had done nothing wrong.

The customs agent scanned his American passport through the computer, and there was a notification code that transpired on the screen. After

215

several long minutes, the U.S. Customs agent asked Carlo Marchese to escort another customs agent into a small adjacent room, off to the side of the luggage claim area. The Mafioso was asked to sit down and wait until another U.S. Customs Agent came into the room, and they both started asking him questions.

"Why were you in Rome for only twenty-four hours?" One of them asked.

"I had an audience with the Pope Emeritus, regarding some future business that the Vatican wished to consult with me," he calmly replied.

"What was your rush to come back?"

"I have more business to transact here in Detroit, before returning to Chicago tomorrow."

"What kind of business?" The U.S. Customs agent began to pry.

Don Marchese became irritated with the questions and fired back.

"Look, gentlemen...I am a U.S. Citizen, and as you can see, I fly quite often into Italy on business. I am a legitimate entrepreneur, and I run legitimate businesses here in the United States. So, if you wish to ask me any more questions, I can call my attorney and have him here at Metro Airport in an hour."

The two customs agents looked at each other. They were probably notified that Marchese was traveling overseas for some reason, as a unique code came up when his passport was scanned. But they later realized after checking his luggage, that he had not transported anything over from Rome. After another thirty minutes or so, Marchese was released.

A long, black Cadillac limousine was waiting for Don Carlo when he appeared out of the arrivals exit at the airport. A young, well-dressed driver was standing alongside the opened front door, waiving to Marchese as he walked towards the car. As he was greeted, the chauffeur opened the rear entrance door of the stretch limo, welcoming him to Detroit.

"Benvenuto, Don Marchese," said a low soft voice from the other side of the car. Two familiar gentlemen were sitting in the very rear seat in the back of the luxury limousine, as they both leaned over to kiss Don Carlo and shake his hand.

"I apologize for your hold up at customs," said Don Pino, "we are not starting our visit on the right foot."

"No worries," Don Marchese smiled, as the stretch limo pulled out of Metro Airport and onto the I-94 expressway towards downtown Detroit. "The customs agents are not used to Detroit travelers taking frequent trips to Italy."

The other passenger, Caesar Giordano, made light of it. "Such stereotyping. An Italian businessman arrives at the airport from Italy, and he is already presumed to be in the Mafia," he laughed, as Don Marchese made himself comfortable.

There were three glasses of Dom Perion champaign already poured and waiting for their consumption, as the three of them made a toast.

"Here's to doing business again, Don Marchese," Don Pino raised his glass, as Don Carlo thanked his gracious hosts for patiently waiting for him at the airport.

Don Pellegrino Licovoli, or 'Don Pino' as he was affectionately called, was the Capo dei Capi of the three crime families doing business here in Detroit. His associate, Caesar Giordano, was the family consigliere, who always accompanied Don Pino in all of their business transactions. He was the head of the elite Licovoli crime family. They made their money in olive oil importing and Italian food distributions, with an expansive 'juice loan' and gambling racket on the side.

Don Carlo had called Don Pino while he was in Rome and requested a meeting. They had done a significant amount of business in the past and asked Don Pino to tap into his cultural connections in helping him sell off the Uffizi paintings. The three men exchanged pleasantries, and then Marchese gave them the background information regarding the discovery and proposed sale of those recovered Renaissance masterpieces.

Within thirty minutes, the black Cadillac limousine pulled into the parking lot of Sogni Per Tutti, an upscale Italian restaurant located on Michigan Avenue in Corktown. As the three men sauntered into the restaurant, they were escorted by an older gentleman wearing a black tie and tuxedo, to their secluded table in the corner. Two other well-dressed men were already patiently waiting for them, enjoying their glass of wine.

Don Pino promptly made the introductions. Mr. Peter Cataldi, a prominent Detroit attorney and older gentlemen who did a significant amount of business with the Licovoli Family, and Mr. John Males, the director and board chairman to the Detroit Institute of Art, were both at the table. Both men had been previously briefed as to the reason for this meeting and had expressed interest in assisting Don Marchese.

Three bottles of the Belle Glos Pino Noir were swiftly brought to the table, and Don Pino asked the chef to prepare 'something special' for his guests. They made more small talk, and after some light conversation regarding Don Carlo's brief encounter with U.S. Customs, the discussion became serious.

"Gentlemen, as you have been made aware, I have the possibility of acquiring forty-two Renaissance paintings, which were stolen from the Uffizi Gallery by the Nazi's during World War Two," Marchese began to say.

"These forty-two priceless, oil masterpieces include the works of Raphael, Rembrandt, Donatello, Giotto, Botticelli, Caravaggio, Lippi, and other prominent Renaissance period, artists. Their current, realizable value in today's market is probably over two hundred million dollars or more."

John Males immediately asked the question that was on the minds of everyone at the table.

"Are these the same paintings that were discovered in Munich last month, and smuggled out of some dead old man's apartment before the Mayor of Munich was found murdered?"

"They are the same," Don Marchese replied.

Cesare Giordano, the Licovoli family consigliere, had done some homework on the paintings as well and had made some long-distance phone calls before their evening encounter.

"Those stolen Uffizi paintings are a hot commodity right now, Don Carlo. Everybody in Italy is looking for them. The Uffizi Gallery wants those paintings back, after being sold to the Nazi's for a discounted price during the war. The Uffizi Gallery and its board chairman, Don

Rodolfo Giammarco, who is the head of the Giammarco Family, has put the word out that the Uffizi gallery is demanding the unconditional return of those paintings as well," he began to summarize, fidgeting with his fork.

"The Ambassador from Italy has also appealed to the German Chancellor to enforce the Washington Treaty and return those paintings to Florence," the consigliere continued as he took a brief sip of his wine.

"And now, the Pope Emeritus, Pope Honorius, has also made a demand for those paintings too. Those masterpieces were initially consigned to the Uffizi before the war by the Vatican, hoping that they would be safer there with Mussolini when the Nazi's invaded Rome. Papa Onorio has even gone as far as to say that he may have already acquired them, through the help of a 'Chicago art broker.' The rumors are that those paintings are still in Germany." Giordano finished saying.

"The Pope Emeritus wants those paintings back for nothing," Marchese interjected, as everyone at the table attentively listened.

"I do not believe that I can get the Chicago art dealer to sell me all of those paintings for less than one hundred million dollars. He is currently asking over two hundred million dollars for all of them," Marchese clarified.

"That goofy, goddamn pope thinks we should whack him for the paintings!"

Don Pino pointedly looked at Marchese. "For two hundred million dollars, maybe we should," he suggested.

At that moment, their food entrées had arrived. Delicious dishes of bruschetta, Linguini con Zupa di Mare, Calamari Alla Griglia, and Crostini di Polenta were among the Italian specialties enjoyed by all at the table.

Everyone had brought along their late-night appetites, and the intense, business atmosphere was quite jovial.

By then, it was close to eleven o'clock, and the restaurant had closed their door to other patrons, allowing for the five men to finish their dinner.

They talked intensely while savoring their late-night 'cinetta,' appreciating the restaurant's secluded privacy for their meeting. The affluent businessmen all continued to discuss the pros and cons of assisting Don Marchese in helping him sell-off those valuable, rediscovered Uffizi paintings.

"What do you have right now?" Mr. Cataldi asked.

"I can have the painting "Demons of Divine Wrath" by Fra Filippo Lippi at your museum within the next few weeks."

"That is quite a beautiful painting," John Males stated. "For how much?"

"Two million dollars...cash," Don Marchese replied, looking at Don Pino without saying a word.

John Males looked puzzled for a moment.

"I would have to get a commitment from our Board of Directors before spending that kind of money. That would have to come out of our board endowment fund," he replied.

"I have authorization for one half million dollars, no questions asked. Your cash request would not be a problem," Males stated.

"But two million dollars? I would need board approval."

Don Pino looked at Carlo Marchese, knowing that he could count on splitting the one-million-dollar mark-up with him without any questions. He had a very close, very personal relationship with the Chicago Mafioso, and knew there would be no issues cutting up the profit.

"What if I loaned the art institute a short-term loan until you got approval?" Don Pino asked.

"If the Art Institute isn't interested or can't afford the price tag, I am sure the Cleveland or Toledo art galleries could come up with the money without any problems."

"A loan to the Art Institute? At what rate?" Males asked.

"Our usual rate, twenty percent," Licovoli replied.

Males considered the options, expressing the desire to acquire that painting for the Detroit Institute of Art.

"I am very familiar with the Renaissance paintings of Fra Filippo Lippi. I do not believe that we have many masterpieces in our art gallery from that popular Florentine artist. Having another acquisition of his would put our gallery on the same upper echelon as New York and Chicago's art galleries," Males observed.

"How about the rest of the forty-one paintings?"

"If you purchase this one, I will give you an option for the other forty-one masterpieces," Don Marchese replied. Again, he made eye contact with Don Pino.

"For how much," Attorney Peter Cataldi asked.

"That I don't know. That would depend on how or when I could get my hands on the other forty-one paintings. Could be well over one hundred million dollars or more."

John Males and his attorney looked at each other, as the chairman of the art institute continued to weigh his options. There were several moments of silence.

"We will purchase the Lippi painting for your asking price of two million dollars in cash. I will secure the approval of this purchase from the board," Males finally committed, making eye contact with Cataldi.

"So, we have a deal?" Marchese asked.

"Yes, we have a deal."

All at the table shook hands and raised their wine glasses.

"Here's to the 'Demons of Divine Wrath!'" John Males triumphantly made a toast.

"I am sure that beautiful painting will be a wonderful addition to your art gallery," Don Marchese observed.

The men at the table were more than happy to celebrate their new cultural transaction. It was a win-win for everyone. The Detroit Institute of Art got a new addition to their Renaissance displays with the supplement of a noteworthy painting by the famous Florentine artist. The Marchese and Licovoli Families would split the profit of this sale, and Wolfgang Schmidt had a new buyer for his paintings.

When Don Marchese was dropped off at his hotel room at the Detroit Marriott in the Renaissance Center, it was almost two o'clock in the morning. He was still a little jet-lagged and decided to make a phone call to the Chicago art dealer, even though it was very late in the evening. Don Marchese never had a problem or any boundaries when it came to waking someone up in the middle of the night.

When there was no answer, he left a voice mail message, confirming his intent to purchase the Lippi painting for the agreed-upon price of one million dollars, with delivery to be made within the next few weeks.

Back at the Vatican, a restless Pope Emeritus was anxiously waiting to hear back from Don Carlo Marchese. He had called his papal secretary two to three times daily, demanding to know why he had not heard back from his Chicago cousin. Within several days, the Pope Emeritus had realized that he had been deceived and that the stolen Uffizi paintings would not be returning to Rome...not by Marchese anytime soon.

The Pope Emeritus had been made a complete and total fool of by the Chicago mafioso. He was embarrassed. He was mortified. But most of all, he was fuming mad.

At that moment, Papa Onorio picked up his private line and made a phone call.

CHAPTER TWENTY-FIVE

The crowds of people around the arrival gate were overbearing, as Wolfgang Schmidt exited the United Airlines Gate 12 of Munich International Airport that summer afternoon. Everyone was trying to board their flights for their August summer excursions, as Schmidt found it challenging to maneuver his way around the crowded airport towards the baggage claim area downstairs.

After claiming his luggage and going through German customs, he hailed a taxicab to bring him to his hotel.

"Le Meridien, bitte," he asked the cabbie in German, "Bayerstrasse 41."

"Bestimmt," the cab driver responded, as Wolfgang was transported through the bustling Munich traffic on that hot, muggy afternoon. The twenty-minute drive to his hotel allowed him to sort through his personal belongings as he fidgeted with his airline ticket, his passport, and boarding pass, which he still had folded in his light blue summer sports coat.

The airline flight on the Boeing 737 Max 8 Jetliner was quite turbulent, as Schmidt was not able to rest or acquire any sleep throughout the nine-hour trip from Chicago's O'Hare airport to his arrival at Munich. Wolfgang's mind was in a trance and was hardly paying attention to the conversation coming from the front of the taxicab. The cab driver was trying in vain to make small talk with Schmidt, even complimenting him on his flawless German after he briefly explained to the cabbie that he was here on business from Chicago. Wolfgang's mind was elsewhere, as he had only one reason for this visit to Munich: To relocate the hidden Uffizi paintings.

The art dealer was not only tired from his long, turbulent flight, but he was also very much on edge. He had received the late-night message from Don Marchese the night before, so he knew that he now had to deliver one painting to the Chicago mobster.

Wolfgang also heard about the recent murder of Mayor Kossel two weeks ago and was extremely nervous. He had read and heard about the public demands of both the Uffizi Galleries and the Vatican Museum regarding the return of his late cousin's hidden paintings. Privately, he was beginning to feel a tremendous amount of pressure to disclose and return those paintings to their original owners publicly.

There had been both written and verbal appeals made at the United Nations by the current Ambassador of Italy, Maurizio Dresti, to the German government to actively participate in the return of those forty-two priceless Uffizi masterpieces. Ambassador Dresti publicly addressed the United Nations and accurately, the current German Chancellor, Rudolf Ludendorff, to follow and adhere to the Washington Principals on Nazi-Confiscated Art Treaties signed over twenty years ago.

Although this agreement specifically addressed the restitution of any confiscated art by the Nazi regime during World War II, the German government, despite the NATO treaty, continued to stall and turn a 'blind eye' to their whereabouts. The German government seldom cooperated regarding the return of many stolen Nazi art pieces and particularly, those stolen Uffizi paintings.

Several of Schmidt's art world colleagues had been contacting him as well, bluntly asking him if he had any information on the whereabouts of those missing Uffizi masterpieces. Although Schmidt continued to deny their location or have any information about them, he knew that his denials explanations and regarding the disappeared paintings were not believable.

He was playing stupid, and everyone knew it. Every single art collector and museum curator in the international art world knew of the Schmidt family's cultural reputation. They found it very hard to believe that the Uffizi paintings would just suddenly disappear again, of all places but in Munich, without the German art dealer's knowledge.

Schmidt was also aware of Detective Hildebrandt's recent murder investigation. The detective made public inquiries and interviews on CNN concerning the homicide and shooting death of Mayor Kossel. There was an open investigation in Munich, headed by Hildebrandt, in trying to solve the Mayor's gruesome killing. It didn't take a genius to figure out that the missing Uffizi paintings had something to do with his murder.

Although Schmidt, being in Chicago, had the perfect alibi against any possibility of his being considered a murder suspect in the Mayor's homicide, he had absolutely no idea who would be willing to kill someone for those paintings.

The pressure was on, and Wolfgang Schmidt was now 'feeling the heat.' He knew that the stakes were high in his hiding these Uffizi paintings, and he had to be extremely cautious as to where and how he transported these four, post-war wooden crates containing these cultural masterpieces. The hidden location of those forty-two paintings, for which he was only one of two people to know their place, was not only becoming a much sought-after international secret...it was becoming a dangerous game of 'hide and seek.'

It also didn't help that the New York Times ran an article last week containing the headline:

Stolen Uffizi Masterpieces Disappear Once Again

The article addressed the sudden loss and disappearance of the rediscovered Uffizi paintings. It made the direct connection between their recent recovery in his cousin's apartment attic after his sudden death and Mayor Kossel's imminent murder.

Wolfgang Schmidt was a very nervous man indeed.

The taxicab pulled in front of the Le Meridien Hotel on Bayerstrasse, double parking in front of the hotel's revolving door entrance. Wolfgang paid the cabbie with a fifty-dollar bill, grabbed his luggage, and entered the five-star inn, walking past its opulent modern décor of white leather couches and open fire-pits neatly placed around its atrium.

"Guten Tag," the very pretty, but older lady from behind the hotel desk greeted him, wearing a name tag, 'Olga.' She looked like a much older version of Annamaria Sciorra, with sagging wrinkled skin and misplaced Botox injections. The dark-haired concierge politely asked Schmidt for his reservation information, his passport, and credit card, for which he retrieved after fumbling through his inside jacket pocket. After exchanging several pleasantries to the aging hotel desk clerk in German, she gave him his hotel room key.

"Room 522, Mr. Schmidt," she said in flawless English after looking at his blue passport.

"Thank you," he exhaustedly responded.

He then picked up his luggage and walked towards the adjacent hotel elevator to his hotel room. Wolfgang was wholly jet-lagged and was extremely tired, barely keeping his eyes open in the middle of the afternoon.

He decided that he would make his business phone calls later that day. Wolfgang had previously planned to head over to the warehouse, which was located in the outskirts of Munich, to take inventory of his precious, much sought-after Uffizi paintings later that evening. But for now, he thought to himself; he would take a short, well deserved 'power-nap.'

As Wolfgang disappeared into the hotel elevator, a young man was casually sitting in the large, hotel

228

reception lounge, perusing the German newspaper Die Welt. The gentleman looked to be in his late twenties and was sporting a thick, coarse beard and short black hair. He was wearing a dark sports coat and dress jeans, disclosing his stripped alligator socks and light brown leather shoes as he crossed his legs. He had been waiting for Schmidt to arrive at his hotel from the airport that afternoon, as he was hired to perform surveillance on the art dealer's every move. He then pulled out his Apple iPhone and dialed a phone number.

"Pronto," he said in Italian, announcing the art dealer's arrival. "Il commerciante d'arte è arrivato."

Detective Hildebrandt was extremely busy at his desk at the Munich Police Station on that August afternoon, when he received a telephone call from a customs security officer at the Munich International Airport.

"Detektiv Hildebrandt? United Flight 731 aus Chicago ist gerade am Gate 12 angekommen, " the security officer said.

He had asked a customs security officer from Munich Airport to keep watch on the arrivals of the flights coming into Munich from O'Hare International Airport that day, as he was anticipating the arrival of Herr Wolfgang Schmidt. Although he had not been in contact with him since his last confrontation at the airport, he had been keeping tabs on him from afar. He was watching his activities through his art sales online. Hildebrandt had been surveilling him and any possible travel back to Germany.

The Munich detective's investigative methods were very much in line with taking the 'playing it cool" approach. He knew that Schmidt would have to return to

Germany soon to take inventory and to keep watch over his late cousin's stashed Uffizi paintings. He knew that somehow, he was going to have to try to transport those paintings out of Germany and begin liquidating his newly acquired priceless masterpieces. The German detective knew that it was only a matter of time before he could make good on his promise of "hunting him down like an animal" and being all over him every time he came into town.

Hildebrandt jumped into his unmarked Mercedes squad car and quickly drove out to the Munich International Airport to try to apprehend Schmidt. The detective wanted to get to him before he went too far, following him to his hotel and eventually, to the location of the stored Uffizi paintings. When Hildebrandt arrived at the Munich Airport, the detective double-parked his squad car in front of the baggage claim area outside and quickly entered the airport. As he approached security, he was told that he was too late and that all of the passengers from the United Flight 731 from Chicago had already claimed their bags and gone through customs.

The detective then pulled out his cellular phone and made a call to the front desk clerk at Le' Meridien Hotel. He had placed surveillance on Wolfgang Schmidt's credit cards earlier that month, and the hotel reservation at the Le Meridien came up on his computer when the art dealer made the reservation earlier that week.

"Olga, das ist Detektiv Hildebrandt," as he knew the desk concierge by her first name.

"Hat Herr Schmidt noch eingecheckt?" he courteously asked if the art dealer had recently checked in.

"Ja, er kam vor zehn Minuten," replying that he had arrived ten minutes earlier. "Danke," he responded politely.

All Detective Hildebrandt had to do now was to keep surveillance on Schmidt while he was here in town on business, starting from his hotel room at the Le Meridien and then follow his every move. Whenever Schmidt planned to go to wherever he was stashing those stolen Uffizi paintings, the detective would know about it. He only smiled to himself as he shook his head:

This was going to be way too easy.

CHAPTER TWENTY-SIX

It was frigidly cold and snowy outside on that last day of the year as I entered the Chicago Sun-Times building, my Cole Hann leather loafers covered with snow. The Weather Channel had called for a winter snowstorm that was expected to drop more than six to eight inches of snow in the Chicagoland area that day. It looked like the best option for everyone, including myself, was to stay home and celebrate New Year's Eve in front of a warm fireplace and a single bottle of champagne.

I got into the newsroom early that day, knowing that I would have probably been better off working from home, despite the weather. But I wanted to talk to the 'The Chief' and give him an update on the Marchese Murder investigation after I met with Frank Mercurio and Chaz Rizzo the day before. I sat down at my desk and started to read and dissect my notes, putting some statements and sentences together while sorting out both of their conversations, trying to 'connect all the dots.'

There were so many open-ended questions regarding this case that I just didn't know where to start. Like who did Marchese piss off and double-cross? Why was he involved with the Vatican? Where and how did he manage to sell off Vatican Museum art paintings and to whom? How were the Uffizi painting discoveries last summer related to this murder?

I was still staring at my computer screen when I saw Mike Daudelin walk into his office from the wintery cold outside, his black leather jacket covered in snowflakes. I figured I would watch him enter his office, take off his coat, then try to figure out where his coffee cup was hiding on that war-torn, disheveled office of his. I decided to wait several minutes before assaulting him with my news assignment issues.

"Good morning, Chief," as I walked into my assistant editor's office. Mike was standing behind his desk, removing foreign debris from the inside of his cup with a tissue.

"Dammit, Crawford? Can you at least wait until I get my cup of coffee before you attack me this morning?" he jokingly asked.

"Come on, Chief. You looked like you might need some help on that scavenger hunt you were conducting on your desktop," I joked, as he took his somewhat clean coffee cup and began to walk towards the newsroom cafeteria in that elusive search of a fresh cup of coffee. I followed him into the kitchen with my notepad, like a little puppy dog wagging his tail, trying to get his attention.

"I had a chance to talk to Rizzo last night," I mentioned as he was grasping the Bunn coffee pot from the still-brewing coffee maker. He sloppily placed his coffee mug underneath the dripping coffee pot and struggled to pour some freshly brewed coffee into his ceramic cup. Daudelin looked reasonably desperate for some caffeine that morning.

He only glared at me, while I continued to brief him on my previous night's cocktail engagement and conversation with Channel Eight's star reporter. He maneuvered himself around the kitchen, throwing in a splash of spoiled cream from the refrigerator and walking quickly back to his office without saying a word. After I finished mentioning all the facts I had gathered from both Rizzo and Mercurio, we both sat down at his desk as I watched my assistant editor's brain start to de-crystalize with every fresh gulp of his morning caffeine.

"Okay, Paulie. Where are you going with this, and what's your theory?" He was moving some papers out of the way to make room for his clean, ceramic cup of coffee.

"I think Marchese could have been working for the Vatican, and he must have pissed someone off there big-

233

time. He probably double-crossed them in an art deal, and someone decided to take revenge against him," I theorized.

"So, you're saying the Vatican had something to do with Marchese's murder?" The Chief summarized. "Do you have any idea what a stretch that is? How in the hell are you going to prove that? And what does all this have to do with those Uffizi paintings that were discovered in Munich last summer? How is all of that connected to Marchese?"

Daudelin was asking me the same questions that I was asking myself, and I didn't have the answers to any of them.

"I get it, Mike. There are a lot of holes that need to be filled here. But I need to push this investigation full-throttle, and I need your blessing. I have no idea where all of this is going, and where any of this is going to end up." I began to plead with my favorite newspaper chief from the Daily Planet.

"Crawford? I think you have been hanging around Chaz Rizzo for too long. You seem to be buying the admission tickets to all of his 'wild-goose chase' investigations," Mike replied.

We both smiled at each other as he sat behind his desk, fidgeting with his computer mouse and probably trying to log onto Facebook.

"How is Rizzo anyways? Is he at least getting laid?" Mike was referring to his all too infamous serial dating reputation.

"That I can't confirm, Chief. Nor do I want to," as I laughed out loud.

"Well, that's all part of Rizzo's game plan, Paulie. He sleeps with most of his news sources, you know," Mike pointed out.

"I've gathered that. I only hope he isn't playing both sides of the street," I wondered.

The assistant editor shuffled around some more papers on his desk and was trying to look busy, then looked at me intently as we both made eye contact.

"How much time do you need on all of this?"

"At least a week for sure. But seriously? I have no clue."

Mike took another long swallow from his coffee cup, emptying its contents. My assistant editor seemed to really enjoy his cups of java, especially first thing in the morning. I've counted his trips to the cafeteria coffee pot at least a dozen or more times a day, especially in the morning. I've often wondered if they could run a three-hundred-foot garden hose from the Bunn cafeteria coffee maker directly to his office desk.

"Okay, Paulie. Do what you have to do. But don't make a career out of this. You're still on a short leash," Mike reiterated.

I rose from his office chair immediately, as if the words 'on your mark...get set...go' had been loudly announced as I darted out of his office.

"Keep me posted!" I could faintly hear him say, yelling out from behind his desk.

I took a taxicab to 524 North Wells Street; an art dealer store called the Kunstgeschäft, which meant *art store* from the limited German I had learned in high school. I had previously looked up and 'Googled, 'the art dealer's owner, Wolfgang Schmidt. He was quite a prominent art dealer here in the United States and Europe and had an established, world-wide reputation in the cultural art world.

I heard the jingle of the doorbell behind me as I entered the small, quaint art store, with its elaborate displays of both modern and old, renaissance art. There were art paintings exhibited everywhere around the store as if the empty wall and floor space was a priceless commodity.

"May I help you?" I heard a deep voice from the back of the store. "We'll be closing soon, due to the weather," a tall, good-looking older man in his late fifties came out to greet me. He had salt and pepper hair and had a slight resemblance to the actor Michael Caine from twenty feet away. He was well dressed, wearing a black, vee-neck sweater and a button-down, grey, untucked shirt. Schmidt was wearing red, reader's glasses, balanced on the edge of his nose. His designer shoes looked like they had the same price tag as some of his expensive paintings hanging on the elaborate walls of his store.

"Are you Wolfgang Schmidt?" I eagerly asked the approaching gentleman.

"I am indeed," as he extended his hand.

"I'm Paul Crawford, from the Chicago Sun-Times."

"Pleased to meet you," the art dealer exclaimed. "May I offer you an espresso?" he immediately walked directly to his espresso coffee bar in the back of his store.

"On a snowy day like this? Of course." I eagerly answered, even though I didn't need the caffeine.

"It's going to be a cold, messy New Year's Eve," Schmidt observed, as he was busy brewing two small cups of some tremendous smelling espresso coffee.

"Absolutely," I answered as I continued to engage in small talk with the art dealer regarding his New Year's Eve plans.

"So how can I help you, Mr. Crawford?"

"Our newspaper is doing an article on the Marchese Murder investigation and wanted to ask you a few questions concerning the story we're doing. Did you know him?"

"Yes. I met him a few times," he answered blatantly. "His daughter went to Loyola University with my daughter, and we've had the family over at our house a few times."

Schmidt continued. "He was a good man. I was sorry to hear about his passing."

I was temporarily being sidetracked by the intense flavor of his freshly made espresso, almost wishing for another cup.

"This is great coffee," I observed.

"I know. I bought this espresso machine at Macy's for one hundred bucks. It makes better coffee than those expensive, five-thousand-dollar espresso machines at the restaurants."

"I agree," as I was sucking down the last drop of my espresso.

"So, Mr. Schmidt...did you have any business dealings with Carlo Marchese?"

"Business of what sort?"

"You know," I reiterated, "any business with him?"

Schmidt looked at me suspiciously, knowing where the direction of this conversation was going.

"No. We only had a personal relationship. As I said, we had him and his wife over for dinner a few times, on the count of his daughter is my daughter's best friend. Otherwise, I've never dealt with the man."

"I see." I knew he was friggin' lying.

"Have you heard anything about Carlo Marchese selling any art paintings on behalf of the Vatican?"

Wolfgang Schmidt started to turn red as if he had consumed five more extra shots of espresso.

"No," he slowly said. This bastard wasn't a very good liar.

"Well, that's interesting. From what I've read and heard, Mr. Schmidt, nothing happens in the cultural art world without your knowledge. You seem to be the 'go-to' guy for anyone looking to buy or sell expensive art masterpieces," I eagerly pointed out.

"I appreciate the compliment, Mr. Crawford."

I was walking around his small little art gallery, admiring some of the paintings and their absurd price tags, some in the hundreds of thousands.

The art dealer was suddenly in a hurry. "Mr. Crawford, I need to close the store now, due to this inclement weather and my New Year's Eve plans. I won't make it home to Winnetka in this traffic if I don't leave now," he said, looking at his expensive Rolex watch, noticing it was already past three o'clock.

"I understand, Mr. Schmidt. Perhaps I can come back the day after tomorrow. I want to ask you about those expensive, Uffizi paintings that were discovered in Munich last summer."

Wolfgang Schmidt turned red again, and this time, I knew I had hit a nerve. He approached me within inches of my personal space and smiling, extended his hand.

"Happy New Year, Mr. Crawford," leaving me no choice but to shake his hand and to leave his exclusive art store graciously.

"Happy New Year, Mr. Schmidt," as I turned to leave.

"Stay safe in this bad weather," he said, completely ignoring my last statement regarding the Uffizi.

As I was leaving his art store and trying to hail a taxicab, I knew that Schmidt was only the tip of the iceberg in pursuing this story. I knew the art dealer had whatever information I needed concerning those discovered Uffizi paintings last summer and Don Marchese's art dealing for the Vatican.

I was confident that Wolfgang Schmidt would be a treasure trove of information regarding any recent buying and selling of any masterpieces in the art world. But he was also going to be very uncooperative, and trying to get him to volunteer any information would be difficult. Unless I could find another angle, trying to approach him again would be a total waste of time. I was on the right

238

path to getting whatever information I needed to pursue this story, but I also felt very nervous and apprehensive.

Like walking into a darkened room without a flashlight and listening to the closing of a steel door...locking me inside.

CHAPTER TWENTY-SEVEN

There was over an inch of rain on that late summer morning last August, as the torrential downpour forced many of the Vatican tourists without an umbrella to take cover. It was the beginning of 'ferroagosto,' where most Italians took the month of August off for the remainder of the summer. Vatican City was enjoying an increase in tourism that season, as there seemed to be in increased interest in the religious affairs of St. Peter's Basilica and the featured activities of the Vatican Museums.

Pope Emeritus Honorius V was sitting by his veranda window, watching the summer rain drench the Vatican visitors down below. He had just finished his ten kilometers walked through the Vatican gardens that morning and was feeling somewhat exhausted. He was also slightly apprehensive that morning, as he remembered a special appointment that his secretary had scheduled at his papal apartment for him at one o'clock.

"Permesso, Your Holiness," as Monsignor Iacobelli barged into the papal apartment without knocking.

"Accomadi," Papa Onorio replied. He was in a good mood that late morning, happy that he was able to get in his brisk morning walk before the torrential rain.

"Just a reminder of your afternoon appointment, Your Holiness."

"Yes, thank you, Gianni. Please remind Sister Giovanna that I would like to have my lunch before then if it is possible?" Papa Onorio requested.

"Yes, Your Holiness." Monsignor Iacobelli was all too happy to assist the Pope Emeritus in his desire to meet with his next appointment.

The papal secretary then exited the former pope's apartment and continued to his outstanding tasks at hand.

Iacobelli was somewhat annoyed by the constant interest that Pope Emeritus continued to place upon those rediscovered Uffizi paintings in Munich several weeks ago. He had him contact his cousin, Don Carlo Marchese, earlier last month, then track down a list of those consigned paintings to the Uffizi back in 1938. He then had him place several calls to some authorities in Munich, including the Mayor, to retrieve the necessary information needed for the recovery of those outstanding forty-two paintings and the status of their ownership.

Pope Emeritus had just learned last week that those paintings had been surrendered to the 'Chicago Art Dealer,' and Papa Onorio was not happy. He was interested in doing whatever was necessary for the return of those lost Vatican artworks back to the Vatican Museum, and he was obsessed with their recovery. It was as though there were no other religious mandates for the former pope to attend to, as Monsignor Iacobelli's s desk phone was constantly ringing, with Papa Onorio making constant demands regarding the status of those consigned Vatican art pieces.

"Gianni, any news of those paintings?" was the daily morning greeting of the Pope Emeritus, every day since he was informed of their recovery.

"I am working on it," was Iacobelli's daily response, as he was continually barraged with orders and tasks by the assertive former pope.

After enjoying his light lunch of minestrone and a small salad, the Pope Emeritus cleaned up and dressed for his one o'clock meeting. He had heard about what a sharp, clean-cut young man his upcoming appointment encounter was, and Papa Onorio wanted to look his best.

"Permesso," the Monsignor formally knocked on the apartment door. It was a little after one o'clock.

241

"Entra," Papa Onorio loudly demanded.

The monsignor entered the papal apartment and announced the Pope Emeritus's upcoming guest.

The handsome young gentlemen, with slicked 'Elvis' style black hair, was wearing a sporty blue Valentino dress suit, a crisp white shirt, and black tie. He genuflected and kissed the papal ring.

"It is a pleasure to meet you finally," the young man said.

"The pleasure is mine, Signore Iannucci."

Stefano Iannucci stood at attention until the Pope Emeritus motioned him to sit down at the black leather chair in his study.

"Gianni...allow us some privacy, please," Papa Onorio motioned Iacobelli to leave the two of them alone. Sister Giovanna arrived just then with some espresso coffee and some freshly baked 'cornetti' from the Vatican bakery downstairs.

The two them sat down and exchanged pleasantries, with Stefano enjoying his Italian espresso and, of course, encouraged to have this opportunity for this unusual papal audience.

"Signore Iannucci, your reputation precedes you," the former pope complimented.

"Likewise, Your Holiness."

The Pope Emeritus finished his espresso and continued to speak.

"You have come highly recommended."

"Regarding what, Your Holiness?"

The Pope Emeritus stared at him silently for a few moments.

"Your services."

Stefano looked at Papa Onorio in total confusion.

"My services?"

"Yes...may I call you Stefano?"

"Please."

242

"Stefano...I am well aware of your 'contractor' services, and the Vatican may be in dire need of them," Papa Onorio began to explain.

"It seems that we have some precious property that the Vatican Museum would like to recover."

Stefano looked at the former pope, still confused. There were a few moments of silence as he finished his cup of expresso.

Papa Onorio began to explain the circumstances of the recovered paintings in Munich, for which Stefano silently acknowledged. He did not disclose his prior connection to Herr Wolfgang Schmidt and the murder of his cousin to the former pope. After Papa Onorio completed discussing the scenario of the rediscovered Uffizi paintings, Stefano only sat there in silence.

Unlike an attorney interviewing a prospective client, a professional killer does not have any ethics or scruples when it comes to conflicts of interest. Far from it, Stefano smirked to himself. A contract is a contract, and Stefano Iannucci had no 'professional rules of ethics' when it came to accepting his next professional assignment.

Iannucci had been involved in many professional contracts involving anyone from white-collar 'criminals' who needed to be eliminated, to 'Family Mafia' assignments, where the syndicate was incapable of performing the 'hit' themselves without being suspected or discovered. Being a 'Killer for Hire' meant that one needed to be extremely selective in accepting the contract assignments that he participated in, and Stefano always did his homework.

As a result, Iannucci's reputation was a flawless one. In other words, anyone who hired him to perform a contract would almost be guaranteed the strictest confidentiality and the total assurance that the authorities would never discover who the killer was or the party who had hired him.

At 35 years old, Iannucci considered himself to be a very shrewd, conscientious businessman. He did business the 'old fashioned way,' dealing strictly with cash and never using a credit card or a checking account. Stefano opened cellular telephone accounts in other people's names, all short-term, month-to-month contracts. He often disposed of these cellular 'burner' phones after a few months, making sure that he always changed his telephone numbers. He didn't own anything, not even his car. He often leased these vehicles with fake identifications, false passports, and some else's credit cards if it was necessary, all on a short-term basis. He owned no real estate, renting a small apartment in Naples, Italy on a month to month basis. His bank account in Zurich, Switzerland, had been opened under another close family member's name, using their passport and identification. He made monthly trips to Zurich to make deposits and withdrawals, driving for hours to most of his destinations. He took air travel only when it was necessary, whenever he felt he could go through the security lines without his true identity being discovered. He communicated and accepted referrals using one of several active email accounts, accepting new clients by recommendation only.

By all accounts, Stefano Iannucci was an invisible man on paper, and he liked it that way. His goal was to accumulate as much cash reserves as possible, and then to go off to some South American country somewhere and spend the rest of his life in luxurious retirement. He had over seven million dollars in his Swiss bank account. He figured that if he could double that amount over the next few years, he could retire on his fortieth birthday and live the comfortable lifestyle that he was accustomed to. He knew that the longevity of his career as a hired killer was not a long one, and he had to be careful of his every step. He was extremely cautious, making sure that no one was ever following him or was watching his every move.

Even though Iannucci was vigilant that he could never be traced on paper, he was conscious of the fact that the international authorities knew his identity. He was informed last year by a 'clandestine agent' working for Interpol, that the Federal Bureau of Investigation and Scotland Yard were well aware of his professional, covert activities. But he was assured that as long as he wasn't a terrorist, didn't participate in any terrorist activities, and accepted assignments on criminal subjects that the authorities could never get enough evidence to prosecute themselves, that they were willing to 'look the other way.' But he still had to continually watch his own back, always making sure that as a professional murderer, no evidence could ever be directly traced to him or his clients.

A highly skilled killer must frequently redefine the word 'ruthlessness' when it came to accepting any contract. Truth be told, if their referrals and references checked out, Iannucci would take a professional contract on his mother if the price was right. Indeed, he thought to himself, he was a cold-blooded killer, and he had no trouble accepting any lucrative contract from anyone even if his next client was the Pope Emeritus and the Vatican Church.

"My services are costly, Your Holiness. And they do not include the recovery of your paintings."

"I am not asking you to recover them. I am asking you to find the person who has them and strongly convince him to return these paintings to their rightful owner. At any cost," Papa Onorio exclaimed.

"In this case, as I have explained, we at the Vatican are the rightful owners of these consigned paintings that were sent to the Uffizi in 1938."

Stefano sat there with his legs crossed, showing off his dark brown Louis Vuitton leather shoes and his bright blue striped alligator stockings.

"Again, your Holiness. Your request comes with a price," Stefano sternly replied, not paying attention to the fact that he was talking to a man who was once considered the holiest human being on earth.

"And quite frankly, I don't give one damn about your paintings," he replied.

Stefano then pulled out a small notepad and took out his silver-plated Mont Blanc pen. He then wrote a figure on a piece of paper and handed it over to the Pope Emeritus, who quickly glanced at it. He then folded the piece of paper and put it in his white jacket pocket.

"I see no problem with your price, Stefano, presuming that you can convince this gentleman to return our forty-two paintings properly."

"If I do recover those paintings, you will pay me my asking price for those paintings,"

"Plus, my fee and expenses," Stefano added.

Papa Onorio nodded his head. The two of them shook hands to consummate the deal before Iannucci zeroed in on the specific terms of this contact.

"I will need a deposit of my fee of fifty percent, in U.S. Currency, wired to my bank account in Zurich."

Papa Onorio raised his eyebrows.

"That may be a little steep, Stefano. I will not give you five hundred thousand dollars upfront. For that price, I will send someone else to Chicago and find some cheap thugs on the South Side to accomplish this task," Papa Onorio sternly answered.

"I will give you ten percent, or one hundred thousand dollars, as a deposit. You will receive the remainder of your contract price when the job has been finished, and your work has been completed."

Stefano glared at the Pope Emeritus, beginning to think that this over-rated papal audience was a colossal waste of his precious time.

"As you wish, Your Holiness."

Stefano shook his head and stood up from his chair, ready to walk away from the Pope Emeritus's hard bargained counteroffer.

"But, I'm sorry."

He was walking towards the exit door when the former pope called him back.

"Stefano?" The professional assassin turned around, looking directly at the former pope.

"Very well. I will have my associates wire your deposit of fifty percent into your account in Zurich," the Pope Emeritus acquiesced.

"You will work out the details with my secretary, Monsignor Iacobelli, immediately. With complete discretion, of course."

"Of course, Your Holiness."

The two of them stood up, and once again, Iannucci genuflected and kissed the pope's ring. They both smiled at each other before leaving the papal study, as Stefano shook hands one last time with the former pope. It was an infamous image that would have captured the imagination of any Christian follower within the Holy Catholic Church.

The 'Nazi Pope' was now shaking hands with 'The Devil.'

CHAPTER TWENTY-EIGHT

Wolfgang had fallen asleep in his hotel room that night in August when his cellular phone rang loudly next to his bed.

"Hello?" He was still tired and dizzy from all of the jet lag and momentarily, didn't realize where he was.

"Hello, darling," a sexy, female voice responded. "I was waiting for you to call me when you got in."

Wolfgang was still groggy, rubbing the sleep from his eyes.

"Oh, shit...what time is it?"

"It's 9:00, my dear."

"It's only 9:00? Great! Now I'm going to be up for the rest of the night," he whimpered as he continued to rub his eyes.

Wolfgang groaned as he looked at the clock next to his bed. It was indeed nine in the evening. He must have fallen asleep when he checked in his room when arriving in Munich and figured on only taking a short nap.

"This is why I hate traveling...all of this damn jet lag," he exclaimed, realizing that his quick 'power-nap' lasted approximately six hours and that he had been asleep for the whole afternoon.

The familiar female voice, on the other end, started laughing.

"You must have been tired, my love. Does this mean that you'll be nice and rested for me tonight?"

Wolfgang smiled. He had forgotten how much he had missed Ingrid, his German girlfriend while he was away. She was his lover and close companion whenever he came into Munich. Their marriages and wedding vow to their spouses didn't seem to be a deterrent from their having a very close, very intimate physical relationship.

Ingrid Von Stueben was a wealthy, stunning art collector who had made her money the old-fashioned way: she married it. She had met Wolfgang at an art auction in Munich two years ago and enjoyed a steamy relationship whenever he came into town. She was currently married to a wealthy investment banker and lived in an eight thousand square foot mansion in the older section of Neuhausen, an affluent suburb of Munich.

Ingrid was a blonde, blue-eyed, shapely ex-model for Vogue Magazine, and although she was now in her forties, could still turn heads on any fashion runway. She had once posed nude for Stern Magazine twenty years ago and had actively modeled for several other fashion periodicals before contracting exclusively for Vogue. Her exquisite, blonde beauty and shapely figure had afforded her a very lucrative career before cashing it all in to marry a billionaire almost twice her age. She enjoyed the privileges of her open marriage with her very rich, but ancient husband, Piotr Von Stueben. He was in his late seventies, and although he had very little control over his very beautiful trophy-wife, his only rule was he forbade her from bringing her boyfriend's home while he was out of town, which was quite often.

They exchanged some romantic pleasantries over the phone while Wolfgang got up to splash some water on his face. They then agreed that they would get together downstairs for a late-night dinner at 10:00 pm.

Ristorante Dei Massimo was a Northern Italian, avant-garde restaurant located within the Le Meridien Hotel, which seemed to be well attended almost every evening. As Wolfgang came downstairs to meet his lovely girlfriend, he noticed something peculiar.

The gentleman in the hotel lobby sitting on a chair reading a German newspaper was still sitting there, with his legs crossed, showing off his alligator striped socks. Wolfgang remembered the gentleman because he recalled the same man wearing those same fancy socks, sitting at

249

that same chair when he had checked in earlier that afternoon. It was the same man.... he was sure of it. Wolfgang stared at him, and they briefly made eye-contact before the young man went back to preoccupying himself with his intensive, newspaper reading.

Schmidt became very suspicious. He now realized that there would probably be some convert surveillance occurring while he was in town, perhaps by Hildebrandt and the Munich Police Department. Wolfgang continued to stare at him for several moments until Ingrid arrived at the restaurant.

"Tisch für zwei, bitte," Wolfgang politely asked the hostess for a table for two, as Ingrid gave him an intense kiss at the door.

"I missed you terribly," she said in flawless English, as the two of them followed the hostess to a quaint, secluded table near the window facing one of Munich's busiest boulevards.

Ingrid wore her platinum blonde hair at shoulder length and, with her bright red lipstick, could have passed for Charlize Theron from a distance. She was wearing a sexy, black, Karl Lagerfeld sequined cocktail dress, which was open in the back, exposing her deep, dark, Mediterranean tan. The neckline uncovered her gorgeous cleavage, dipping just low enough to tease anyone as to how beautiful her well-endowed breasts were. Adorning her tanned skin was a string of white pearls that reflected the bright, traffic lights from the window next to their table. Her fragrance was mesmerizing, as she was wearing a Creed Acqua Fiorentina that smelled amazing. On that evening, Ingrid looked incredibly sensuous.

The two of them held hands as they talked and caught up on each other's present lives. Ingrid never had children and, when she wasn't shopping in Munich's high-end clothing stores, spent the majority of her time volunteering for several non-for-profit children's charities and organizations. She was also on the board of directors of the Pinakothek der Moderne, Munich's modern art museum.

"You have way too much money, and way too much time on your hands, my dear," Wolfgang used a German endearment as the waiter brought over a bottle of Salwey Spatburgunder Trocken 2017 Baden, Germany's exquisite version of a red, velvety Pinot Noir.

"That's what makes it fun, honey," she laughed as she raised her glass, making a toast.

"Here's to time and money. May we always abundantly have both," she said with adoring eyes.

"Cheers," as they both made intense eye contact while taking their first sip of wine.

At that moment, Wolfgang felt Ingrid's barefoot rubbing up against his leg as he was trying to order an entrée from the menu. It was probably fair to say that Ingrid had more than her share of boyfriends in her life, both past, and present. But at that moment, she had missed Wolfgang Schmidt the most, and couldn't wait to escort him upstairs. To say that she had truly missed and cared for him was an understatement.

They had ordered their entrées of Linguini al Diavolo and Rigatoni al Sugo di Manzo when Wolfgang brought up the main reason for his visit to Munich.

"Darling, I am going to need your help in moving those paintings," he mentioned after taking a long sip of his German Pinot Noir.

Ingrid was well aware of the circumstances of his late cousin's hidden Uffizi paintings. Wolfgang had privately complained to her several times of how often he tried to futilely convince his cousin, Hermann Kalkschmidt, to relinquish and sell those forty-two valuable masterpieces, each one of them worth millions. Wolfgang could not understand the sentimental value that each one of those paintings had to Hermann, who could have significantly upgraded his life and improved

251

his lifestyle, even if the old man had only sold one picture on the black market.

His arguments with his cousin became verbally abusive, and he was barely on speaking terms with him before his death. He was frustrated with the older man, living like a hermit in a musty old apartment, almost in poverty, while hiding and stashing away millions of dollars' worth of priceless masterpieces.

Wolfgang had used Ingrid as a sounding board in the past, always complaining to her about Hermann's stubbornness and trying to find some other useful solution. It was Ingrid who had finally introduced Schmidt to Stefano Iannucci, who was eventually hired by Schmidt as his 'contractor' to do his bidding.

Ingrid sympathized with her Chicago art dealer boyfriend and pledged her allegiance and support to do whatever she needed to do to assist him. She helped him find the secluded warehouse located 90 kilometers north of Munich and made sure that the warehouse was environmentally controlled. The storage location had to be well secured, and there had to be enough camera security to keep the Uffizi paintings safe and out of the public eye until Wolfgang was ready to transport them out of the country. Ingrid was Schmidt's overseas assistant, and she was more than helpful in making sure that the paintings were in a safe and secure place. It was self-evident that Wolfgang trusted her completely, as she had given him the only key to the storage warehouse before he had left the last time he was in town.

"How is your pasta," Wolfgang asked his lovely dinner date, her barefoot still rubbing up against his crotch.

"Just wonderful," enjoying every mouthful of her entrée and looking forward to the main course upstairs.

"I take it you were satisfied with Stefano's services?" she innocently asked.

"Indeed...he was a little too pricey, perhaps. But he did the job."

Ingrid looked at him and smiled. "Should we include that comment on his customer survey?"

Wolfgang quickly became irritated.

"Come on, Ingrid. Fifty thousand dollars in cash for breaking into his apartment and turning on the gas stove? Don't you think that's a little pricey?"

"Considering that your dear cousin Hermann would have probably outlived the both of us, and considering the amount of damage he may have continued to cause storing those priceless paintings in that old, musty attic?" Ingrid reasoned.

"No, Wolfy...I don't think you were overcharged. Besides, honey, look at the trade-off?" she pushed her bare foot even harder against his crotch while clutching his hand in a firm grip.

"You have over two hundred million dollars in priceless paintings that you can now sell at a very handsome profit. I would say your contractual fees to Iannucci are a minimal cost of doing business, wouldn't you say?" Ingrid astutely pointed out.

"You forgot your commissions, my dear," Wolfgang corrected her. He had promised her a handsome commission for an amount yet to be determined, once the paintings were 'state-side,' and he was able to broker them off to a market of frantically interested buyers he anticipated having.

"My commissions...of course," she smiled, taking another long sip of her Pinot Noir.

Wolfgang was finishing his linguini while massaging his dinner date's right foot, propped up nicely between his legs.

"What are your commissions, by the way?" The art dealer inquisitively asked.

The beautiful German ex-model was intelligent enough to know not to mix business with pleasure and never to interact with those serious discussions in the middle of a lovely, romantic dinner. If Ingrid intended to take him upstairs and have her way with him afterward, bringing up her commission demands at that moment would not have been a good idea.

"Let's just say I will accept a deposit in the form of your services for now," she perceptively replied, winking her eye.

Wolfgang peered back at her and laughed. "Good answer."

When the couple finished their entrée's, Ingrid ordered each of them an amaro after-dinner drink, and they both continued to make small talk regarding Wolfgang's plans to market the rogue Uffizi paintings. As Schmidt continued to talk, Ingrid saw her iPhone vibrating on the floor next to her purse. She conspicuously looked down at the text message for a brief moment while Schmidt wasn't noticing:

Text me when he's on his way.

Schmidt paid the waiter, and the two of them walked out of the restaurant and towards the lobby elevator to his fifth-floor hotel room. Ingrid was holding his hand, rubbing herself as firmly as she could without taking her clothes off in the middle of the hotel lobby. As they were both holding hands, Wolfgang pushed the elevator button and looked over his shoulder towards the hotel entrance. He then looked where the white leather couches and chairs were neatly situated, where all of the hotel guests were typically seated.

At a different chair and a different location, the young man in the striped alligator socks was still sitting there, fidgeting with his cell phone, pretending not to notice Wolfgang standing by the elevator doors.

He was either a private detective, a cop, or someone who had nothing else better to do, he thought to himself.

Wolfgang dismissed it. He decided at that moment to not give it a second thought and to take care of the business at hand. It was quite apparent that the Chicago art dealer was doing his most resolved, most intellectual thinking with something other than his brain.

That would prove to be one of his many, careless mistakes.

CHAPTER TWENTY-NINE

It had been a quiet, snowy New Year's holiday, with over ten inches of snow on the ground. I had spent all of New Year's Day visiting with my mother and father, having dinner with them, and spending the first day of the year in Park Ridge. I had spent most of the afternoon fixing their snowblower, then cleaning and shoveling the accumulated snow off of their driveway.

I had grown up in that modest home on Courtland Avenue, spending my childhood going to grade school at Mary Seat of Wisdom and then to Notre Dame High School in Niles. After graduating with a Bachelor of Arts degree in English and Journalism from DePaul University, I pretty much had my fill of the City of Chicago. I took a job as a correspondence reporter with the Boston Globe and lived in Cambridge, Massachusetts, for several years, with my parents calling me daily.

As an only child and having gone to parochial school my whole life, I always had this 'catholic guilt' thing going on. It finally caught up with me in the early nineties. My parents were getting on in their years, and when my father began suffering from the initial effects of Parkinson's disease, I realized that there was no one else around to look after them. I moved back to Chicago, bought a townhome in Lincoln Park, and took a job as a desk reporter with the Chicago Sun-Times. I've been gainfully employed there ever since.

Not having a wife or family to look after has been an advantage in my journalism career. To the dismay of my Italian mother, I never got married.

I've done enough dating in my lifetime and had been involved in enough toxic relationships to realize that keeping the opposite sex at arm's length was a far better option. I didn't need to go through the pain and difficulties of an emotional breakup, or more specifically, a marital divorce. A good number of my high school friends and fraternity brothers had gone through several marriages and divorces, some two and three times. They seemed to have nothing to show for it, other than some ungrateful, millennial children with a wicked sense of entitlement and a monthly alimony bill.

I was engaged once to a beautiful Italian medical student that I had met after I moved to Boston. She was from the city's North End or 'Little Italy,' and was a third-year medical student at Harvard Medical School at the time. We had been dating for a few years, and my mother adored her. We had planned our whole future together and had our wedding plans set in stone.

But three months before the wedding, just before the invitations were about to go out, she called off the engagement. She was cheating with another doctor that she had met while doing her internship at Massachusetts General Hospital and didn't see a future in our relationship anymore. My ex-fiancé concluded that being married to a newspaper reporter didn't fit into her long-term plans of an exclusive country club membership and a lavish, upscale mansion in the Hamptons.

But I have to say, I've had a pretty good run as a successful news reporter. The Editor-In-Chief told me that I would probably be considered for an assistant editor position within the next few years. Although I'm no 'Carl Bernstein,' I would have to say that my investigative reporting skills and intuitive instincts are right up there. My fine-tuned journalistic abilities have carried me pretty far within the newspaper, having broken several jaw-dropping stories and conspiracies within City Hall and in Chicago politics. My tenacious, probing talents have helped me earn the respect that I've needed within the paper to pick and choose the subjects that I want to be involved with as a Senior Correspondent.

I've also been involved in a few 'mobbed-up' syndicate stories as well. I knew all the 'capo's,' all the players, all the wise-guys, and most of the insignificant wanna-be's. Those contacts have greatly assisted me in getting whatever information I need to investigate a crime syndicate news story, such as this one.

I know all of the suburban police chiefs in Chicagoland and most of the Chicago coppers and detectives. I decided to pay a visit to one of my favorite detectives on that first working day of the new year and see if I could get a line on any updated information on this Marchese homicide. I parked my car in the parking lot of the Chicago Police Department Sixteenth District and approached the desk sergeant.

"What's up, Crawford? Happy New Year!" The gruff, six-foot, two-inch desk sergeant happily greeted me as I walked through the front door. Desk Sergeant Kathleen Hathaway was a very tall, not very pretty police officer in her late fifties, whose physical appearance could probably scare most career criminals into going straight. I never had the nerve to ask her if she had a sex-change operation, as there were remnants of her five-o'clock shadow starting to crop up on that early Wednesday morning.

"Happy New Year, Sarg. How many donuts am I going to have to bring to get in front of Detective Dorian this morning?" I replied.

"I would say your chances are pretty low, considering that you've walked in here with your hands empty. He's in a meeting right now with Commander Callahan and will probably be another half hour or so."

I looked at my watch and noticed it was almost eight o'clock.

"So then...what will it take?" I politely asked.

"If you come back here with a couple of sesame seed bagels and a large, black coffee from Dunkin'

Donuts, you might get five minutes of his attention," she suggested.

"And while you're at it, get me a large coffee too...cream and sugar."

"Sure thing, Sarg."

I jumped back into my car and arrived back twenty minutes later with a small bag of sesame seed bagels, a tub of cream cheese, and two large coffees. Dorian had just finished with his meeting, so I had timed it just right as she sent me the right direction to his office.

"Happy New Year, Detective," I brightly exclaimed, bearing gifts.

I set his coffee and cream cheese bagels on his cluttered desk, hoping to get some respect and maybe, some critical information.

"Yeah, right, Crawford. You come waltzing into my office with coffee and bagels, expecting to pump information out of me on your Marchese Murder Mystery," Dorian graveled loudly, as he didn't waste any time assaulting the Dunkin' Donuts bag of goodies.

"Would you like me to lie?" I said with a smile, hoping that my chirpy, bouncy sense of humor would charm him into giving me some information.

He reached into the bag, grabbed a sesame seed bagel, and slapped on some cream cheese. Dorian then quickly devoured it as though he were going to the electric chair.

"Thanks, Crawford," he replied, remembering to wish me a 'Happy New Year' as well. After he took his first gulp of coffee, I watched the caffeine do its magic.

"So, what can I do for you, Crawford?" he asked in a charming voice.

"How are you feeling these days, Detective?" I decided to ask upfront.

Detective Dorian was involved in the recent investigation of some serial killers, and the cruel deaths of four retired, pedophile priests last summer. He was stabbed and almost killed in the process, trying to solve that case.

"Feeling better now. Wearing that bag for six months until my stomach healed was no fun. I'm finally starting to gain some weight back."

"You look great, Detective," I complimented him.

Dorian grabbed another bagel, and using his formal manners, scooped some cream cheese with his finger and used it as a utensil.

"Stop sucking up, Crawford...I'm busy here. By the way, how's your buddy, Rizzo?"

"Oh, he's my buddy now? I heard the two of you have bonded. He talks about you like you're his BFF," I bantered back.

"I can take him or leave him. He's good for some Blackhawk tickets now and again," Dorian replied.

"It pays to be nice to the press," I reminded him, hoping that his cheerful, pleasant personality would continue to last as long as he had his Dunkin' Donuts coffee.

"So, Crawford, what's on your mind?"

"Where are you at with this Marchese investigation? Any new leads?"

Dorian glared at me, squinting his eyes. I knew a pleasant mood wouldn't last.

"Who are you, my damn Commander? I just had a meeting with him, and he was asking me the same thing," he gruffly replied.

I sort of sat there looking stupid, wishing I had brought along more sesame seed bagels. There were a few moments of silence, as Dorian was fidgeting with his automatic lead pencil.

"Have you interviewed that art dealer, Schmidt, yet?" I innocently asked.

"Why?"

"Well, I'm sure you knew about the Uffizi art painting discovery last summer, right? There may be a connection there."

Detective Dorian's eyes began to light up as if we were switching roles. At that moment, I felt as though I had more information on the Marchese homicide than he did. Maybe he should be buying me coffee and bagels.

"No, we haven't interviewed him yet. What's he going to tell us?"

"Maybe something to the effect that there is a connection between Marchese and the Vatican, who have been pushing hard for the recovery of those paintings."

"Why is the Vatican interested?"

"Not sure. That's what I'm trying to find out. I was hoping you would have some leads."

Dorian looked as though a light bulb had suddenly gone on in his head. He turned on his computer and started doing some internet surfing.

"I remember reading something about the Vatican trying to put in a claim for those recovered stolen Nazi paintings last summer. I didn't pay much attention to the article as I was too busy with those 'Pedophile Priest Murders,'" he said, as he continued to surf the web.

After several long minutes, he pulled up the article.

"Here it is."

It was a CNN article that was written by a reporter named Laura Perotti, published late last July. It stated that the recovered Uffizi paintings in Munich had disappeared again. It also reported that the Munich authorities were rather tight-lipped as to what had happened to them and were refusing to get involved. The article made mention of some very public international demands for those paintings, including those from not only Florence's Uffizi Museum but Rome's Vatican Museum as well.

He printed up the article, and I included it with my notes, highlighting some of the essential points. Dorian then continued to do some online research and discovered another interesting article regarding the homicide death of the Mayor of Munich, Bertram Kossel, last summer.

"The Mayor of Munich was found dead with a bullet wound in the back of his head, three or four days after those Uffizi paintings disappeared again," the Detective said, reading another CNN article.

"Think there's a connection?" I asked the Detective.

Dorian looked at me as if I had asked one dumb question too many.

"I need to do some serious research here, Crawford. I think there is a connection here. What I can't figure out is, what the hell do the Vatican and these recovered paintings have to do with Marchese's murder?"

"Well, I talked to his family underboss, Frank Mercurio the other day. He confirmed that Marchese was dealing with art paintings for the Vatican."

"Really?"

"There seems to be a connection between the art dealer, this Wolfgang Schmidt guy, those stolen Uffizi art paintings and Marchese. When I went over there to talk to him on New Year's Eve, he admitted to personally knowing him. But when I confronted him about doing any business with him, he lied to my face."

"How do you know he's lying? And besides, who the hell would want to talk to you on New Year's Eve?" he smiled. The caffeine was finally kicking his cantankerous personality into high gear.

"Just a hunch. He doesn't do well under pressure. I think you need to go over there and visit him," I suggested.

"He'll probably 'lawyer up,'" Dorian replied. "But you're right, Crawford...we do need to turn up the heat."

The detective finished the last drop of his miracle-working Dunkin' Donuts coffee and looked at me.

"So, let's get this straight, Crawford," the detective began to summarize.

"Carlo Marchese, the Capo of the Marchese Family on the North Side, has a Vatican connection...and you've confirmed that he's been dealing and selling off expensive art pieces. The stolen Uffizi paintings are rediscovered in some older man's apartment last July in Munich, are confiscated at the crime scene, and then quickly disappear again. The Uffizi Museum and the Vatican Museum are both making plays for these rediscovered masterpieces to be returned to them. Then the Mayor of Munich is found dead with a bullet hole in his head." Dorian was making notes and appropriately laying out all the facts of the case.

"Now we have a dead wise-guy hanging out of the window at the Blackstone Hotel just before Christmas, with none of the other families knowing anything about it or ordering the hit," I added.

Dorian began shaking his head. "And you think this local art dealer knows the score?"

"I would bet my last dollar on it, Detective. He's very well known in the art world and has an international reputation. He's also German," I replied.

"You need to do a background check on this guy, Phil. He's holding some missing puzzle pieces," I suggested. I decided that if I couldn't get any information out of Schmidt, I would let the Chicago P.D. 'pump it' out of him instead.

Dorian nodded his head in agreement. He then stood up from behind his desk and grabbed his gun from the desk drawer.

"Today might be a good day to visit him. Give me a call tomorrow, Crawford."

"Are you going to visit with him now?" I pointedly asked.

"Now? No," he replied.

"Now…I'm going to Dunkin' Donuts to pick up another bagel and some coffee. But I will go over there later today. Give me a call tomorrow."

"You should think about doing a Dunkin' Donuts commercial," I laughed, as we shook hands and I left his office.

I walked back to my car in the Sixteenth District parking lot and turned on the heat and seat warmer. I was desperately trying to warm up my body and my SUV from the frigid Chicago sub-zero temperatures outside. As my car was warming up and I was reviewing my notes, I realized that I had left one stone unturned in my search for information in this "Marchese Murder Mystery" and its connection to the rediscovered Uffizi art collection.

And that stone was lying right in front of the Art Institute of Chicago.

CHAPTER THIRTY

The sub-zero January temperatures of Chicago didn't seem to stop the crowds of people going about their day. Bundled up, pedestrians were negotiating their way around North LaSalle Street that late morning, as the vehicles and buses were causing traffic jams as they continued to fight for the right of way. I had been sitting in my car under a stoplight for several minutes, being careful not to hit any of the careless walkers that were trying to cross the busy intersection of Adams and LaSalle Streets.

I had just left the Chicago Police Department's Sixteenth District and was trying to find an open parking garage somewhere near Michigan Avenue. It was a convenient location to park my vehicle without having to go through the hassles of trying to get into the Grant Park parking garage. My past experiences have always been that every time I parked in that garage adjacent to the art museum on Michigan Avenue, I still had a tough time getting out.

I pulled into the self-parking garage on Adams Street, grabbed the metered parking receipt, and found a parking space high up on the sixth floor.

"6A," I repeated to myself.

I wrote that number down on my parking receipt in case I had a sudden episode of dementia and forgot where I parked like the last time. I found the elevator on the far end of the parking garage, which had 'Broadway Plays' music playing loudly as the themes for each parking floor. I pressed the first-floor button, now realizing that I wouldn't be able to get that 'Hello Dolly' song out of my damn head for the rest of the day.

I battled the crowds walking on the sidewalk towards Michigan Avenue, as the snowbanks from the

New Year's snowstorm were still piled up along the sides of each street. I frigidly negotiated my way to Michigan Avenue, just across the street from the Art Institute of Chicago. The sudden cold, glacial winds of Chicago pierced my whole body as I stood there on the intersection corner, waiting for the pedestrian traffic light to change. At that moment, the only thought going through my mind was why men didn't bother wearing 'long-john' underwear anymore, especially during these polar vortex winters.

Mental note to self: Go to Target and buy some 'long-john' underwear.

I negotiated the two dozen steps leading up to the main front doors of the art museum, noticing the landmark statutes of the two large lions that adorned the famous entranceway. I mentally wished each one of them a 'Happy New Year' as I entered the admission doors.

"I have an appointment with the assistant curator, please," I said to the admission clerk as I showed her my press badge. The vestibule of the famous art museum was jammed with kids, who were still off from Christmas vacation and were enjoying the 'Free Children's Admission' promotion that was still going on after the holidays.

I had called my office earlier while on my way downtown and gotten the name of the assistant curator from Mike Daudelin. She was also a part-time contributing writer for the Lifestyle section of our newspaper.

"Her name, please?"

"Veronica Giancarlo."

I had typed her name on my cell phone while I was driving so I wouldn't forget it.

At that moment, her name was very familiar, but I wasn't sure. I couldn't recall if I met her at the Sun-Times Christmas Party at the Four Seasons Hotel last month. If this lady was the same woman that I had met at the

266

holiday party, I should probably take inventory of my testicles immediately before entering the art museum.

This woman was a bitch, plain and simple: a card-carrying, dues-paying, member in good standing. I remember approaching her at the holiday party and introducing myself. I had offered her a cocktail and tried to make small talk with her while she was standing around, talking to one of the other reporters. She coldly brushed me off, saying that she was more than capable of getting her own cocktails. She then looked off into the other direction while I tried to make conversation, giving me a hint that she wasn't even remotely interested. I remember repeating several 'f-bomb's' under my breath as I walked away, feeling sorry for that poor bastard she was talking to.

"Her office is on the third floor...Room 317. Take the stairs up to the third floor and follow the signs to the curator's administrative offices," the admissions clerk politely directed me.

"Thank you."

I then darted up the three flights of stairs to the third floor. When I got there, I negotiated my way around to the administrative offices where the museum curators were located. I had asked Mike Daudelin on my way in to call Ms. Giancarlo in advance to let her know that I would be coming, but whether he did or not was another story. Pulling my assistant editor off of Facebook and getting him to do anything constructive was always a challenge.

"Ms. Giancarlo, please," I asked the receptionist.

"And your name, please?"

"Paul Crawford from the Sun-Times."

"Please be seated, and she will be right with you," as I found a black leather chair to sit in. It was a rather interesting reception area, with old pictures of the construction of the Art Institute of Chicago back in the late nineteenth century framed along each of the old walls. There were old, carved out oak trim moldings adorning the ceiling, with floor decorations and antique, Asian busts encased around the office. I couldn't take my eyes off of them. The reception room looked like a continuation of the art museum.

"Mr. Crawford?" I heard my name unexpectedly.

A slender, brown-eyed brunette was standing right in front of me, wearing her raven black hair up in a bun and red-framed glasses. She had on light red lipstick and an off-white, Anne Klein business suit that was doing a less than perfect job of hiding her gorgeous figure. She had beautifully tanned legs and a pair of Zegna black, high heeled shoes. Her dark olive skin had a mesmerizing effervescence, and she looked stunning. She looked like Jennifer Lopez dressed like a librarian. For five long seconds, I was speechless.

"Mr. Crawford?" She said again as she caught me in a trance.

"Yes, how do you do? I'm Paul Crawford, with the Sun-Times, pleased to meet you," as I graciously extended my hand.

She accepted my greeting with an odd look on her face as if she was trying to figure out where she had seen me before. Now I was sure of who she was. This was the same woman from the Christmas party. I quickly looked down and took inventory.

"What can I do for you?"

"I was hoping my assistant editor, Mike Daudelin, had called you to let you know that I was coming. I'm investigating the Carlo Marchese homicide that occurred a few weeks ago, and I was hoping you could assist me."

She coldly glared at me for about ten seconds as I stood there, holding my leather folder and writing pad. The way her eyes were fixated on me, I felt as though I was standing there naked.

"Follow me, please."

I followed her down a long hallway with several offices, equipped with ringing telephones, loud corporate meetings, and several associates walking around with half-filled coffee cups and clear water bottles. I felt like I was in an up-scale attorney's office on LaSalle Street, rather than in the administrative office of one of the country's most famous art museums. I followed her into her small office at the end of the hallway, which had a not-so-nice Hon black steel desk and two large wooden chairs.

'Please sit down," as she was forcing herself to be polite.

I looked on the walls and noticed several pictures of her posing in front of Paris's Eiffel Tower and Rome's Fountain of Trevi. She was posing in each photo with others who I assumed were her friends. I found it very hard to believe that this woman, with her cold, rattlesnake personality, had any friends at all.

"May I offer you something? Some coffee?"

"No, thanks." I wondered for a second if I had answered 'yes,' whether she would have probably spit in my beverage.

"So, what can I do for you, Mr. Crawford?"

"I'm investigating the homicide of Don Carlo Marchese two weeks ago. He was found dead at the Blackstone Hotel. Did you hear about it?"

"Yes," she coldly replied.

"I've uncovered some interesting facts about some of Don Marchese's covert activities, including the fact that he was dealing and selling art paintings and cultural masterpieces on behalf of the Vatican Museum. Being that you're one of the assistant curators here, I was wondering if you had any information or could offer up any leads that could help me," I explained.

She coldly looked at me without any reaction, and I began to feel very self-conscious. I looked down to make sure my fly wasn't open.

"No, I'm sorry. I can't help you," she said to me directly, without pondering her answer. She wasn't even helpful or pleasant about it, and her tone of voice made me feel as though I had said something that offended her.

"Oh, I see."

There was a long period of silence.

"You haven't heard of any such activity? You didn't know that the Vatican Museum was selling off their artworks?"

"No, I did not."

I decided to press forward. I figured she was probably going to throw me out of her office anyways.

"How about those stolen, Nazi Uffizi paintings that were recovered in Munich last summer and disappeared again? Did you hear about that discovery? And the death of the Mayor of Munich? Did you hear about that as well?"

Her face had started to turn colors as if I had poked the rattlesnake with a long stick. She began to get uncomfortable with my questions, and after a few silent moments, only shook her head.

"No, I have not," she said again. Now I knew she was lying.

"Really?" After binge-watching 'Chicago P.D.' episodes on television over the holiday weekend, I decided to push it.

"Ms. Giancarlo, being that you're in the cultural art world, I find it very hard to believe that you haven't heard anything about those rediscovered, stolen Uffizi paintings in Munich last July."

"No, I have not." She sounded like a broken record.

"Nor the murder of the Mayor of Munich? It was on CNN and in all the papers."

"No, Mr. Crawford," she coldly replied.

I just glared at her for several long seconds. For some odd reason, she was refusing to help or even to get involved. If she were a regular, run-of-the-mill, nerdy art curator, I would have possibly believed that she was ignorant of current events, didn't read social media and perhaps, didn't have cable TV. Maybe, I thought to myself; she wasn't made aware of international issues that were occurring in her chosen profession.

But being that she was a part-time, free-lance reporter for the Sun-Times, I wasn't buying it. For some strange reason, this woman had an appalling attitude, and I was starting to take it personally.

"What is your problem, lady? Why are you playing it 'stupid'? You look at me with a straight face and tell me that you don't know or haven't heard anything about any of these current events in the art world? This is your profession! And, you're a reporter, for Christ's sake!"

Her face was now starting to turn red, and her Italian temper was beginning to boil over. I was ready for the emotional typhoon that was about hit me 'right square in the face.'

Bring it on, baby.

"Excuse me, Mr. Crawford. You come into my place of employment and start asking me questions about things I know nothing about, and then you make accusations about what I should or shouldn't know?"

Veronica stood up from behind her desk and started to lay into me.

"I'm swamped here, Mr. Crawford, and I don't appreciate your coming into my office and verbally interrogating me. I believe this conversation is over. Please find your way out."

I got up and began to walk out of her office, dutifully. But then I thought to myself.

Why should I let her have the last word?

I turned around, took a shot back at her.

"Look, lady, I don't know what your damn problem is. If you're in the Chicago Man-Hater's Club, don't take your shit out on me. I'm just a reporter trying to do a job here."

I began to leave her office, with one last remark out the door.

"And a damn good reporter, too…something you'll never know anything about!"

Now I hit a nerve. She angrily walked around from her desk and started to lunge right at me verbally.

"Excuse me, Crawford. I investigated and wrote up a whole article on Uffizi art discovery and its possible connection to the Vatican last summer. I took it to my editor, who filed it away in the garbage. Nobody friggin' bothered even to read it. Nobody at the paper was even remotely interested in this story until some dead wise-guy shows up, hanging out of the window of the Blackstone Hotel," she loudly screamed.

The administrative office of the museum was dead silent, as our loud, verbal showdown was on display for everyone there to witness.

"And now I'm supposed to drop everything and help you? Now I'm supposed to answer all your questions and play 'nice in the sandbox' with you and the editors?" she yelled out, not caring about the interesting stares that she was getting from her fellow employees around the office.

"I worked hard on that story, and nobody at the paper gave it the damn time of day!"

"And how is that my problem?" I loudly retorted." For whatever reason, nobody at the paper was interested in your story last summer. Deal with it! But now I'm standing here, with my hat in my hand, asking for your help. If you have a bone to pick with the editors, throw your temper around at them, not me. I've done nothing wrong here, except politely ask for your help."

She was glaring at me without saying a single word.

'Don't sweat it, lady. I'll investigate this homicide and write up this story *without* your help," I loudly exclaimed.

"Thanks for nothing." I finally said.

I turned around, leaving her standing alone in the office hallway as I briskly walked out the door. I was livid. What a bitch!

Here she was, taking her anger out on me as if it was my fault that her story didn't get printed. I couldn't believe that Veronica Giancarlo had done a whole investigation on this Uffizi art discovery last summer, wrote up a story on it, and nobody at the paper ever mentioned anything to me about it. They discarded it and threw it away. Although I could understand her reasons for being upset, why did she have to dump on me about it? Why did she have to make it more difficult for me to do this story?

I was about to go down the three flights of stairs to the first floor and exit the museum when I heard someone yelling out my name.

"Crawford!"

I turned around and noticed the assistant curator approaching me. I was shocked, and I stopped dead in my tracks.

"Look, Crawford, I'm sorry," Veronica softly apologized.

"I didn't mean to take it out on you. I worked very hard on that story last summer, and I couldn't get anyone at the paper to give it the time of day. It has been bothering me for a long time, and I was hoping someone from the paper would approach me when Marchese was found dead," she softly reasoned, hoping she could make amends. As she was apologizing, she walked even closer to me while I was standing dangerously close to the edge of the marble stairway of the museum.

She extended out her hand as a token of friendship. I accepted her offer, and I stared at her for a few moments, suspicious of how to take this sudden change in attitude.

"I'm sorry, Crawford. Can I make it up to you?" she asked, showing off those gorgeous, chestnut brown eyes.

"Okay," I managed to say, my voice still feeling hoarse from all of the recent yelling in her office.

"Do you have plans tonight? Let me buy you dinner," she suggested.

I smiled, realizing it had been a long time since I was on the receiving end of a dinner invitation— especially one from a gorgeous brunette disguised as a mild-mannered, soft-spoken assistant curator of an art museum.

I nodded my head as I was temporarily speechless.

"How about that Ristorante Lo Scoglio on West Kinzie Street? I hear it's pretty good. Does seven o'clock work?"

I nodded my head again, making it apparent that I was more than interested.

"Okay," I managed to say.

"See you tonight, Crawford. Bring your notepad," she smiled as she turned away, walking quickly back to her office. I just stared at her gorgeous body rhythmically, walking back to her office, showing off her shapely model features as if she was on some Paris fashion runway.

I just stood there, less than an inch away from the stairwell. Here I was, being asked out to dinner by a beautiful lady. How cool was that? I became so happy with this sudden turn of events that I almost yelled out loud. I wanted to scream out 'YES' at the top of my lungs, filling up that empty marble stairwell with the sound of my voice, feeling euphoric. I couldn't remember the last time I had felt so happy. It was as though I could fly down those three flights of marble stairs without ever touching a step.

I later realized that I was about to embark on an incredible journey with the most interesting, most beautiful woman on Michigan Avenue.

CHAPTER THIRTY-ONE

The black leather chairs and modern décor of the upscale restaurant blended nicely with the ambiance and the casual atmosphere of Chicago's River North neighborhood. Ristorante Lo Scoglio is a well-attended, contemporary nightspot for those wishing to enjoy its top-shelf martinis and avant-garde food menu, along with its classy, elegant dining room design.

I arrived early that frigidly cold evening, having gotten there a little before seven o'clock, and placed my name with the hostess. I checked my London Fog cashmere coat with the coat-check girl, putting the ticket into my suitcoat pocket. I decided earlier to run home and dress up that evening. I was wearing a dark grey, Hugo Boss suit, with a crisp white shirt and black tie, and gold cuff links that I only wore on special occasions. I thought I would dress to kill that night, figuring that if I were going to sacrifice my testicles to this art curator, I would do it in style.

It had been a busy afternoon, and I had not had the chance to make reservations at this always busy restaurant. I was extremely nervous, as I crossed my fingers and hoped we would be able to get a decent table on that busy, winter evening.

"It will be a few minutes, Mr. Crawford," the hostess exclaimed. I stood around, trying not to look too anxious for my dinner date to arrive. It was almost fifteen minutes after seven before Veronica Giancarlo walked in through the revolving door off Kinzie Street.

"Good Evening, Ms. Giancarlo," I excitedly proclaimed, hugging her as she checked in her black, down-feather, full-length winter coat.

275

"Hey, Crawford...sorry, I'm late," she smiled, as the restaurant hostess immediately recognized that my elegant dinner date had finally arrived.

Veronica looked incredible. She was wearing a black, low-cut Armani dress, which stylishly showed off her shapely, well-endowed figure very nicely. She was extraordinarily well-dressed, and in anyone's most vivid imagination, could have passed for a Bond Girl. She looked as though she had just stepped off the French Riviera and through the doors of some chic, red-carpet style casino in Monte Carlo.

"Your table is ready, Mr. Crawford," the hostess promptly said, as I said a quiet prayer of thanks to the patron saint of dinner reservations.

"Did you make the reservations tonight?" Veronica asked.

"No, I didn't. It escaped my mind as I was so busy today."

"I didn't either. So glad we're able to get a table tonight. This place is always jam-packed," she observed.

We walked through the aisle of neatly arranged tables filled with well-dressed couples warming themselves with appetizers and very, very large glasses of wine. As we were following the hostess to our table, I heard my name being called out in the background.

"Paul! Paul Crawford!"

I looked to my left and noticed a beautiful brunette whom I hadn't seen in years. I had worked with her on an investigative news project with the Washington Post a few years back. At that time, I had flown out to Washington D.C. to meet with her on a Washington corruption scandal story that we were both working on, involving several Illinois legislators on Capitol Hill. We had gotten to be good friends and helped one another out a few times when we needed information on any news story we were reporting.

She was sitting at the table with a familiar, well-known attorney whom I had met a few times within the courtrooms of the Daley Center and at the Dirksen Building. We both walked over to say a quick 'hello' as our hostess patiently waited.

"Paul, it's so nice to see you," she enthusiastically hugged me, introducing us to her dinner date.

"This is my fiancé, Michael Prescott," she excitedly said as he stood up from the table and shook my hand.

"I've met you before, Mr. Prescott. How do you do?" I politely responded. "This is my friend, Veronica Giancarlo," as I introduced her to my newly encountered friends.

"This is Sienna DiVito. She's originally from Boston and is a reporter with the Washington Post."

We all shook hands and exchanged pleasantries, while the hostess patiently continued to witness our encounter.

"I *was* a reporter with the Washington Post. I just got a job here with the Chicago Tribune so that I will be your new, local competition."

"Really? You're living here in Chicago now?"

"Yes. I just moved here after Christmas," she said enthusiastically.

A moment of uncomfortable silence.

"Did I hear you're engaged? Congratulations," I finally exclaimed to them both.

"Thank you," she smiled. "We haven't set a date yet, but we're hoping it will be soon."

Michael Prescott was unusually quiet, only reacting with a slight smile. He always seemed to be somewhat arrogant, as he wasn't participating in our conversation as we all stood around their table and made small talk. Prescott never struck me as someone amiable. Although we were both aware of each other's well-established reputations, we never had the pleasure of sitting down and get to know each other very well.

By that moment, the hostess motioned us to continue to follow her before we lost our table. We sat down at a quaint little spot next to a large picture window opposite Kinzie Street, facing all the hustle and bustle of that typical winter evening in River North Chicago. We were given the wine list, and I immediately recommended the Belle Glos 2017 Pinot Noir Telephone & Clark vintage, which she was more than happy to try. I hoped that by my being brazen enough to immediately order an expensive bottle of red wine that our glasses would be well filled, and our conversation would stay light and breezy.

As we started to make ourselves comfortable, she gazed at me and took a long sip from her wine glass.

"Didn't I meet you at the Sun-Times Christmas Party last month?" she asked.

"As a matter of fact, you did. You were preoccupied at the time," I politely commented, not revealing the several words of profanity that crossed my mind after our first encounter.

"I remember you now. You were annoying me and insisted on getting me a drink while I was having this intense conversation with another reporter," she said, smiling as she sipped her wine. I was getting the impression that Veronica had an unusually dry sense of humor.

"I remember having this heated debate at the time about my 'Uffizi' story that was never printed," she explained.

"I wasn't very nice to you that night either, was I?" as she winked, still holding her glass.

"No, Veronica. I get it. You worked very hard to acquire some information on a story that would have been very informative and especially relevant to what is happening right now. The paper dissed you, I completely understand. I would have had a bad taste in my mouth too."

The wine was going down so smoothly, and I would have been agreeable to anything. I was trying very hard to distract myself from locking my eyes with hers. Her warm, chestnut brown eyes were mesmerizing and could have melted every iceberg on any ocean. She then held up her glass and made a toast.

"Here's to bitchy art curators," she kiddingly saluted, as I laughed along and raised my glass.

After a few long moments, she hypnotically stared into my eyes.

"Did anyone ever tell you that you could pass for Andy Garcia?"

I didn't know if she was sincere or if the wine was taking an early effect on her 20-20 vision. I smiled, trying not to blush.

"Now and again," I only said.

"He's very handsome, you know," she only said— what a difference from her throwing me out of her office that afternoon. After engaging in a conversation discussing our brutal Chicago winters, I thought for a moment before formulating my words.

"So, tell me about your Uffizi article, Veronica. What did it say?" I immediately noticed that her glass was empty, and I decided to make it my mission to keep her wine glass filled that evening.

"Well, you do know about that old man that was found dead in his apartment in Munich last July, correct?"

"Yes."

"Are you familiar with the art dealer here in Chicago by the name of Wolfgang Schmidt?"

"Indeed. I met him on New Year's Eve. I went over to his art gallery and tried to talk to him about his connection to Marchese and the discovered paintings in Munich. He was pretty tight-lipped," I summarized, still enjoying my smooth, satin red Pinot Noir.

Veronica only smiled, as if to say 'I know something you don't' before taking another sip. She then put her glass down on the table and made her pitch.

"I want in," she said. I looked at her, totally bewildered.

"What do you mean?" I had no idea at the time who I was *really* dealing with.

"I want in," she said again. Suddenly, I felt like I was in one of those elaborate scenes with George Clooney from the 'Ocean's Eleven' movie.

"I want to be a co-reporter on this story. I want to share this reporting assignment with you, and I want the paper to give me credit for assisting you with this investigation."

I looked at her for several long moments. This woman was not only beautiful and smart, but she was also very, very shrewd. She knew how to manipulate her beauty and brains to get whatever it was that she wanted out of any man. Yet, there I was, feeling like a defenseless victim, as I ignorantly sat there, holding my glass of wine.

I quickly looked down at my testicles, as I knew I was about to bargain them away.

But I also had no choice. She had valuable information that I needed to break this investigative story. With those incredibly sexy brown eyes, I immediately knew she could negotiate anything she wanted.

"Well, Ms. Giancarlo, that all depends on what information you have for me?" I wasn't about to make this too easy for her.

"Crawford, how long have you been working on this story now?"

"A few weeks. Why?"

"And all you have is a lot of unrelated information that you can't connect all the dots to, correct?"

I nodded my head. She was now going for the jugular.

"I can help you connect those dots, Crawford. I can help you tie the Vatican, Schmidt, those Uffizi paintings and Marchese all together in a pretty little box wrapped up in a nice red ribbon, ready for you to deliver."

"Really?" I took another long sip of my great tasting Pinot Noir, wondering if this would be my last. We both sat there in silence for a while, as I knew I needed to be careful with how I was about to respond. I needed her help, and we both knew it.

At that moment, the waitress arrived and saved the evening, taking down our entrée orders. She ordered the Branzino, Chilean seabass, while I ordered the special, the Pappardelle Con Sugo di Manzo. By then, my wine glass was empty.

"So, Crawford? Do we have a deal?" as Veronica extended her hand.

Right then and there, I knew I was screwed.

"I hope I'm not going to regret this," I smiled as I shook her hand.

She then grasped the Belle Glos wine bottle and poured the contents into my glass first, and then finished pouring the rest of it into her glass. Somehow, she knew I would need the alcohol to absorb the information she was about to reveal.

"Let's make a toast. To a beautiful partnership and the "Stolen Uffizi Painting Scandal," smiling as she held up her glass.

I curiously said 'cheers,' wondering what information she was about to reveal.

"Did you know that the old man that was found dead in that apartment in Munich and the art dealer are related?"

"Really?"

"Yep. They're second cousins. Both of their fathers and grandfathers were Nazi sympathizers during the Second World War."

"You're kidding."

"Nope. The old man's name was Hermann Kalkschmidt. His father and Wolfgang's grandfather were brothers. The art dealer's family shortened their name when they immigrated here to the United States many years ago. Hermann's father was a Nazi officer, who was the personal secretary to Heinrich Himmler," she explained.

"Do you recall who Heinrich Himmler was?"

"Vaguely," I responded, trying to remember what little I learned in my high school world history class.

"Himmler was one of the highest-ranking officers within the Nazi Party, second to Hitler. He was head of the SS Army and was later named as Minister of Interior. Himmler was directly responsible for the many various concentration camps and oversaw the capturing and transportation of millions of European Jews that were shipped off to those encampments," she was patiently explaining to her eager student.

"He was also very dominating in the Nazi Party's art looting. The Nazis stole many of the valuable art pieces and master artworks that were a significant part of the European art galleries and museums across Europe. Kalkschmidt's father assisted Himmler and the Nazi Army in hiding and stashing away many of those valuable, priceless works of art."

I silently sat there, now understanding how all of this was starting to tie out.

"After the end of World War II and the collapse of Nazi Germany, the 'Old Nazi' immigrated to Argentina for several years, then returned to his family-owned apartment in Munich. Hermann's father then passed that apartment and its contents down to his son after he passed away in the '70s. It was in the attic of that apartment that the forty-two stashed Uffizi paintings had been hidden for years until the old man died last summer."

"Okay," I agreed, "but how does all of this involve the Vatican and Marchese?"

Veronica only smiled as she continued reciting her history lesson.

"Marchese's cousin is the Monsignor Gianpaolo Iacobelli, the papal secretary to Pope Emeritus Honorius V. Since the Pope's resignation, he has been put in charge of the Vatican Museum. Because of all the recent 'priest pedophile' lawsuits against many of the catholic dioceses around the world, the Vatican has been running out of liquid assets. They have now started to sell off some significant paintings and masterpieces to various private art collectors around the world. Due to his connection to the Vatican, Marchese has been making millions in commissions by brokering off some of these paintings over the last few years."

I was intrigued. She was reciting all these facts of this investigation that I had discovered so far, but I was having a difficult time figuring out how all of this was connected. We continued to discuss facts of this Marchese homicide for another half hour or so until our entrée's arrived, and we were both feeling buzzed from all of the wine. It was turning out to be a cold but beautiful winter evening as the warmth of the adjacent fireplace near our table was radiating warm air across the room. I was enjoying our conversation while the pappardelle pasta was melting in my mouth. When the espresso coffee and desserts arrived, I asked the question that put it all in perspective.

"What is the connection between the Vatican, the Pope Emeritus, and the stolen Uffizi paintings?"

Veronica explained. "First of all, those forty-two paintings do not officially belong to the Uffizi. These paintings were initially Vatican Museum masterpieces that were consigned to the Uffizi Gallery by Pope Pius XI in 1938 to Mussolini, for 'safe-keeping.' The Pope intended to keep them away from the Nazi's in case they captured Rome and decided to rob the Vatican. In 1943, the opposite came true. When the Nazis occupied

Florence, those forty-two paintings were traded to the Nazis in return for the freedom of over one hundred Jewish refugees that were discovered hiding in one of Florence's churches. The Nazi's got the paintings at a discounted price, killed the church's pastor, and the Jews were shipped off to Auschwitz."

I was dumbfounded at the amount of detailed information that Veronica had regarding this homicide investigation.

"How did you learn all of this?"

"I have a good friend who is an assistant curator in Florence. She helped me research all of this information."

I was momentarily digesting all this valuable data. Veronica Giancarlo turned out to be an encyclopedia of information regarding the art world and particularly, those stolen Uffizi paintings. Veronica continued to talk about those rediscovered paintings with such excitement and passion as if she had each one in her possession. She was able to recite almost all the forty-two rediscovered paintings, by title and artist, that night at our table.

"Why does the Vatican want these paintings back now?" I ignorantly asked.

Veronica smiled. "It seems that the Pope Emeritus is having a little public relations problem with the Italian newspapers. Apparently, Pope Honorius was a former Nazi soldier during the Second World War, and the media has been hard on him. Since these paintings have been rediscovered, 'Papa Onorio' wants them back. He figures if he reacquires these paintings back for the Vatican, he can score a PR victory with the Italians and the Roman newspapers."

"So, the Vatican has been after them too?"

285

"Yes. And that's where Marchese came in. Don Carlo was the Vatican's art broker. For some strange reason, he was taken out and killed two weeks ago."

"Why do you think that happened?" I asked her.

"Good question. The only thing I can figure out was that he really pissed somebody off over in Rome."

"The Vatican, perhaps?" I was fishing for her opinion.

"Maybe," she replied.

"Angry enough to hang him outside of the eighteenth story window of the Blackstone Hotel?"

"To be honest, I don't know. No one has any idea what the Vatican is capable of doing?" she replied with a bewildered look on her face.

By then, our wine glasses and espresso cups were empty, and I didn't have another prop to fidget with while I continued to ask her these complicated questions.

"Where are those paintings now? I understand that they are no longer in Munich."

Veronica looked bewildered. "Correct, Crawford. Nobody knows where they are. Someone went into the old man's apartment and cleaned it out a few days after his death. The City of Munich has been tight-lipped as to who may have acquired them, especially since the Mayor was found murdered at his desk a couple of days later."

"Do you think that homicide is related?"

Veronica smiled, almost shocked at my question.

"Bet the farm, Crawford," as she was now sipping from her water glass, loudly twirling the ice cubes.

"Those paintings just disappeared. The Uffizi doesn't have them, and the Vatican is still inquiring about them. Our art dealer friend is playing stupid, and Don Carlo Marchese is now dead," she observed.

I just sat there for several long moments, shaking my head. When the bill finally came, Veronica wanted to make good on her offer to buy dinner, but I took out my American Express card and beat her to it. I was looking at this dinner as if it were a first date rather than a business meeting, and I wanted to make a favorable impression.

I helped her with her coat, and we both exited the restaurant. I called a taxicab for her, and as she was about to enter, I offered her my hand, trying to be cordial. She shook my hand at first, as I opened the passenger door.

But just before entering, she paused and looked at me for a second.

"I had a great time, Crawford. Thank you for dinner." Veronica then gave me a wet, passionate, three-second kiss on the lips. She tasted amazing.

"Call me tomorrow," she smiled as she got into the cab. She then closed her door, winked her eye, and waved as the taxicab drove off down Kinzie Street. The wet mud of the winter salt and snow splashed my shoes as I stood there, momentarily speechless. I felt my heart beating fast as the excitement from our wonderful evening was keeping me warm on that cold, January night. As I began to walk towards the nearby parking garage, only one happy thought kept going through my mind:

This was going to be a beautiful partnership.

CHAPTER THIRTY-TWO

The Midwestern polar vortex had a tight hold on the city, as the temperature had dipped down to minus 25 degrees below zero on that cloudy, January day. After the miserable snowstorm conditions from the New Year's holiday, schools and businesses throughout the area were either shutting down early or closing altogether. It was an unusually cold day.

Wolfgang Schmidt was bundled up in his art store office, trying to reconcile his checking account that afternoon. The heat was not working very well that day, and he had several space heaters scattered throughout the store and in his office to maintain the correct temperature for his art displays. He had been having trouble with the furnace downstairs and had called for service that morning. Schmidt was told that, because of the high volume of service calls from the inclement weather, a serviceman would not be able to get there for a few days.

Schmidt had always done a majority of his own bookkeeping. He was preparing his books and records for the preparation of the W-2's and payroll taxes due at the end of the month. He had gotten a business and finance degree from Northwestern University and was well versed in the principals of accounting. If it had not been for the recent changes in the tax laws, Wolfgang could easily prepare his own corporate and personal income tax returns.

He was coldly sitting at his desk with the space heater warming up his feet when he heard the jingle of the front door. Schmidt looked at the security monitor and saw two strange men dressed in dark black suits and ties. He quickly rose from his desk to greet his new visitors.

"Good afternoon, may I help you?" Wolfgang graciously asked.

"Good afternoon," as both men displayed their Chicago Police Department stars.

"I'm Detective Dorian, and this is my partner, Detective Morton. We'd like to ask you a few questions."

Wolfgang became immediately apprehensive and knew in the back of his mind what all of this was all about.

"Would either of you like an espresso?" Wolfgang asked. It was his usual manner to greet strangers in his store with an espresso coffee to make them feel comfortable, whether it was a potential customer who was about to spend thousands of dollars on an art painting or answering suspicious questions from Chicago coppers.

"Certainly," Dorian replied immediately. The seasoned Chicago detective never said 'no' to caffeine. Having several large cups of coffee a day, whether it was from Dunkin' Donuts or the precinct kitchen, was not unusual for him.

Schmidt had turned on his machine previously, and the water was set for him to make three, very long, hot espresso caffe's'.

"You seem to be the only one on North Wells Street to be open today. Everyone else is closed due to this frigid weather," Detective Morton observed.

"I have a lot of paperwork to do," Schmidt replied. "I have to close my year-end books for my accountant, who will be here next week."

The two detectives took a packet of sugar each and emptied them into their espressos. The art dealer then invited them both to sit down at the black leather chairs next to the marble coffee table adjacent to the espresso bar.

"How can I help you, gentlemen?"

"I'm sure you've heard of Carlo Marchese, the Chicago mobster who was found dead at the Blackstone Hotel just before Christmas," Detective Dorian began.

"Of course, it was all over the news," Schmidt replied.

"Did you know him?"

"Yes, I did," replied Schmidt, "Although not very well. His daughter went to school with my daughter at Loyola University, and we had them over for dinner a few times. I was sorry to hear about his death."

"Did you have any business dealings with him, Mr. Schmidt," asked Morton.

"No, I did not," the art dealer quickly answered.

"We've done some investigations regarding some of Marchese's activities, and we were surprised to learn he was involved in the sale of some art paintings on behalf of the Vatican. Were you aware of this?" Morton recited.

"Why would I be?" Schmidt replied.

"You're a 'mover and a shaker' in the art world, Mr. Schmidt. From what we've learned, nothing happens internationally without you knowing about it. So, we find it hard to believe that you weren't aware of the sale of any Vatican Museum pieces," Morton said in an accusatory voice.

Schmidt looked at the two detectives with a pleased look on his face.

"I appreciate the compliments, Detectives. But the Vatican doesn't call me regarding their art transactions," Wolf replied. "I'm a small businessman, and I don't venture too far away from this little store."

Dorian smiled, realizing right away that this 'art dealer' was full of shit.

"I believe that for about three seconds." Dorian was looking intently into Wolfgang's eyes.

Schmidt just looked back at Dorian with a slight smirk on his face.

"What can you tell us about those Uffizi paintings that were discovered and then disappeared in Munich last summer? We understand that you may have a connection to those," Dorian said in an accusatory tone of voice.

"Oh, really?" Wolfgang answered, trying to put a tone of surprise in his voice.

"Yes, really."

There were a few moments of silence, as the two detectives finished their espressos.

Detective Morton then got up from his chair and began perusing around the art store, noticing the expensive price tags that were attached to each painting.

"Do you sell a lot of these paintings, Mr. Schmidt?" Morton asked as he continued to walk around the art gallery.

"I do okay," Wolfgang replied.

"Yes, you do," Morton smiled. "A nice, large mansion in Winnetka, a brand-new black Mercedes sedan parked outside, lots of toys in the garage, a vacation home on Marco Island..."

Morton then walked closer to Schmidt, who was still sitting down, finishing his espresso.

"Yep...you do okay," Detective Morton said.

Detective Dorian played along, "That's a lot of paintings to sell every month, wouldn't you say? I don't see a lot of high-end customers lining up at the door."

Wolfgang laughed. "It's a little too cold for anyone to be lining up anywhere today."

Dorian tried to turn up the heat on the art dealer and their friendly little conversation.

"It's too bad about what happened to Munich's mayor," Dorian commented. "Those paintings were rediscovered one day, disappeared the next, and the Mayor is found murdered at his desk the day after."

The two detectives were studying Schmidt's reaction to their questions, as the art dealer was starting to appear a little nervous.

"Yes," replied Schmidt. "That was an unfortunate circumstance."

At that point, Dorian rose from his chair and faced the German art dealer. He immediately knew where this conversation was headed. He instantly realized that Schmidt had a lot more information about those rediscovered Uffizi paintings last summer, the Vatican 'garage sales' and their possible connection to the Marchese homicide.

"Any chance you may know where those missing Uffizi paintings are? Rumors are floating around that the discovery and disappearance of those paintings may have been a motive in Marchese's death," Dorian implied.

Schmidt looked at both detectives and nervously smiled, shaking his head without saying a word.

This guy was way too arrogant and extremely cocky, Dorian thought to himself. Trying to interview and interrogate him in the middle of his opulent art store in front of his snazzy espresso bar was not the way they were going to get any information out of him. This guy needed to be being 'shaken down.' There was a distinct possibility that he could be accountable and charged with Marchese's death. But they needed information. The two detectives were required to get a warrant to search his art store and his ostentatious Winnetka mansion if they wanted to find any direct connection between him and the Marchese murder. Getting at Wolfgang Schmidt and 'jumping way deep into his shit' was the only way they were going to do it.

"Mr. Schmidt, you need to come down with us to the district station and answer some questions," Dorian directly said.

"Now? Why?"

"We think there is a lot more information that you're not telling us," Morton explained.

Dorian completed the detective's sentence.

"Besides, we need to hold you at the station while we get

a warrant to search your store and your fancy little mansion in Winnetka."

Schmidt was suddenly feeling warm and became nervous. He looked at both detectives intently and immediately knew that he had to make a phone call. Schmidt needed to quickly take control of this situation before these coppers started 'having their way with him,' and things start getting out of hand.

"Would you both mind if I make a telephone call?" Schmidt innocently asked.

"Of course not," Morton replied. "You only get one."

He took his cell phone out from his pocket while Dorian quickly placed his hand on his gun holster. Schmidt then searched his cell phone directory and found the phone number he was looking for.

He needed to contact his attorney. A young, up-and-coming criminal attorney that was considered one of the best criminal lawyers in Chicago.

He had met him at a downtown Christmas party a few years back and always kept his office and personal cell phone number handy in case of any unfortunate situations that may arise. He had used him when he got into trouble in Munich a few months ago and knew that, although he was expensive, that he was one of the best.

He promptly dialed his office number, and his receptionist answered the phone.

"Mr. Michael Prescott, please."

CHAPTER THIRTY-THREE

Wolfgang looked at the clock illuminating on the nightstand in his hotel room on that hot, summer night last August in Munich. It was 2:04 am, and he was still wide awake.

The bedsheets were drenched with sweat and bodily fluids, as Wolfgang laid naked on top of the bed over the covers. He was lying next to Ingrid, who was fast asleep, with her pillow propped up against the edge of their large, king-size bed. She was clutching her pillow with her left hand while her right hand was conveniently placed just below Wolfgang's abdomen, ready to arouse him again when she woke up from her deep sleep. Both were exhausted, drifting in and out of romantic consciousness from their intense lovemaking after dinner.

Wolfgang glanced over at his beautiful lover, still fast asleep, while he studied her gorgeous, sensuous anatomy in the dark. Ingrid's body was tight and perfect, without an ounce of fat on her. Her size 36 D-cup breasts were still substantial for a woman her age, accentuating her rose-colored nipples and large, outlined areola. Her muscular abdomen was almost flawless, with a neatly placed birthmark strategically positioned next to her belly button. Her buttocks were hard and rigid, absorbing the periodic slaps that she insisted on receiving from him as they intensely made love throughout most of that evening. Their hot, continuous sex was long and passionate, lasting almost three hours, as they climaxed several times, then finally collapsing into each other's arms.

Wolfgang was still awake, realizing that his body was still on Chicago Central Standard Time, knowing that he would soon be exhausted within the next few hours. He couldn't sleep, as he got up to put on his underwear and bathrobe and walked to the large bedroom window facing downtown Munich. He could see the traffic lights and the bustling urban activity down below, understanding that downtown Munich never sleeps.

There was a lot on his mind that very early morning. He was thinking about the burden of keeping these Uffizi paintings away from public view, believing that this task was beginning to be too much for him to bear. He thought about the Vatican, considering that the paintings were still their property, always seeking to acquire them. He thought about the Uffizi Gallery, who had put out a press release recently stating that the stolen Nazi art belonged to them as well. And he thought about Marchese and his deal to sell one of those paintings. He did not know if he could be trusted and wondered if their initial transaction of one million dollars was a legitimate one. He knew he had to leave Germany with at least one painting. Wolfgang also knew he had to do it discretely before the Munich police or any other private investigators discovered the whereabouts of the Uffizi paintings.

At that moment, he heard Ingrid's cell phone loudly vibrate next to her nightstand. Who could be texting her in the middle of the night? It was well past two o'clock in the morning. Wolfgang very quietly rose from his chair facing the window and walked over to the nightstand where her cell phone was located. He momentarily paused, waiting for Ingrid to wake up from the vibrating noise.

She was still sound asleep. Wolfgang then picked up her cell phone to view the text. It only said:

Has he left to go to the warehouse yet?

He couldn't tell who the text was from, as it came from an unknown number that wasn't registered to her cell phone directory. Schmidt then memorized the phone number, then wrote it down on a piece of paper next to the desk lamp.

Who was inquiring about his whereabouts on Ingrid's cell phone? Who else knew that he was here at this hotel? Who else was aware of the warehouse location of those paintings?

Wolfgang's blood began to boil. Up until this point, he thought he could trust his girlfriend, Ingrid Von Stueben, completely. He could not believe that she had sold him out, revealing the location and whereabouts of these Uffizi paintings to another party.

"They're all the goddamn same," he whispered to himself.

Someone else was out there waiting for him, and he had no idea who. As Ingrid continued to sleep, he very quietly got dressed and grabbed his wallet and some other files that he could grasp out of his suitcase. He thought about packing but realized he would make too much noise and awaken her from her deep sleep. Schmidt then took his hotel key and very quietly exited his hotel room without making a sound.

"Excuse me," he said in English to Olga, the hotel concierge still on duty that very early morning. "Has my rental car been dropped off yet?"

"Yes, Herr Schmidt. They were here last evening to drop off a black, Volvo V40, parked in our downstairs parking garage. Here are the keys."

"Thank you, Olga. I will not be returning to my room. I will send for my luggage from another hotel. Please have the maid, and the bellhop appropriately clean out my room and have my luggage ready for pick up this afternoon," he cleverly stated, giving Olga a fifty-dollar bill for her trouble.

"Certainly, Herr Schmidt," as she proceeded to check him out.

Schmidt looked around the hotel lobby to see if he could locate the man with the alligator socks, still keeping surveillance. The young man with the beard was still sitting on the black leather couch on the far side of the atrium. His head was tilted back, and his mouth was wide open, looking as if he were sound asleep. No other hotel guests were sitting in the hotel lobby.

Wolf signed the credit card receipt and the hotel paperwork and then swiftly walked towards the revolving door without anyone else noticing his exit. He took an outside flight of stairs and descended to the underground parking garage, as he found his parked, black, Volvo rental car. He then proceeded to drive away quickly.

It was almost four-thirty in the morning when Ingrid was finally awakened to go to the bathroom. She was still tired and groggy, not immediately noticing that the right side of the bed was empty. Ingrid splashed some water on her face and then realized that Wolfgang was no longer there sleeping. She angrily comprehended that he had left her alone in the hotel room in the middle of the night without even saying 'goodbye.'

"That asshole bastard, son-of-a-bitch," she loudly cursed to herself.

She then grabbed her cell phone and noticed that she had received a cell phone text from someone almost two hours ago. Ingrid then texted back:

He's on his way.

Wolfgang was driving northwest down the A9 Autobahn turnpike at just after 3:30 in the morning, towards the warehouse where the paintings were being stored. The secured facility was located in Egenhofen, a village situated approximately 54 kilometers away from his hotel. It was roughly a forty-minute drive from the A-9 Autobahn turnpike towards the A-99 highway into the town to Neselbach Road. The warehouse was secured by cameras around the facility and warehouse building, with each warehouse properly heated and climate-controlled. Each person entering the gated storage facility needed a passcode to enter and exit the warehouse area.

When Schmidt arrived at the orange warehouse building, he immediately noticed that the entrance gate had been broken, allowing him to enter the area freely without his entrance code. He drove his Volvo around the storage facility, as each storage unit was individually locked and secured, and his unit was approximately 800 square feet. As he approached storage unit No. 31 in building C, he noticed that the opening overhead door was closed, but unlocked.

The art dealer's heart immediately dropped to his stomach, as he had suddenly feared the worst. He had no weapon or no gun to defend himself, and he thought long and hard before attempting to open that storage door. Wolfgang Schmidt must have stood at the storage unit door there alone for more than five minutes, debating whether he should open up that door.

Wolfgang finally opened the storage overhead door. It was completely dark inside, and Wolfgang had forgotten to bring a flashlight. The streetlights from the storage facility were his only source of light as he hesitated to enter the unit. He fumbled through his suit coat pocket in the back seat and miraculously found a lighter, which he usually carried around when he smoked his occasional cigar. He flicked the lighter and peered around the room.

It was empty.

Schmidt felt himself turn three shades of white, walking back and forth outside to check the storage unit number and made sure he was at the correct building. It was indeed Storage Unit Number 31, Warehouse Building C.

He checked his iPhone for the correct storage unit verification. He then remembered that he had a flashlight app on his cell phone, which he immediately turned on.

The concrete floor was all that was exposed as Wolfgang shined his light around the warehouse. His three wooden crates, storing the Uffizi paintings from his cousin's apartment, were no longer there, and he had no idea where they were.

He continued to strobe his light around the empty room, finding something looking like a dark pile of clothing in the corner. As he walked up closer, he noticed some large bloodstains coming from underneath the collection of clothing. When he walked ten feet closer, he realized what he was shining his flashlight on. The art dealer trembled.

There, in the corner of the empty warehouse, was a dead body lying face down in a fresh pool of blood. There also looked to be a revolver in his hand.

The victim had dark black hair, a black leather jacket, and blue jeans, and was wearing black shoes. He walked up closer and shined his phone flashlight on the victim's face. It was no one that he recognized. The large pool of blood was starting to dry up around the edges, and the victim's face, his torso lying face down in a red, crimson pool of blood. The victim had a severe head wound as if he had been shot. Blood had been gushing out of the man's head and torso.

Wolfgang completely panicked. Not only were his Uffizi paintings missing from the storage unit, but an unknown dead body had replaced them.

Wolfgang ran out of the storage unit and quickly closed the overhead door, whipping the door handles with his jacket sleeve. He looked at both ends of the building and noticed that there was broken glass on the ground, underneath the mounted security cameras perched on each corner of the building. Wolfgang immediately realized that all of the security cameras around the building had been shot out. He became terrified. Schmidt jumped into his Volvo and sped away from the warehouse facility as fast as he could.

He was anxious, worried, and scared, all at the same time. He was so panic-stricken that his vision was becoming blurry, as he could barely see the road ahead. Wolfgang didn't know who to call or what to do. He began driving aimlessly for over two hours or more until he decided to drive back to Munich to the Le Meridian Hotel. Schmidt would sort all of this out later, the art dealer thought to himself. Right now, he had to get the hell out of Germany.

It was just after 6:15 am as he was driving back that he called Ingrid at the hotel room. There was no answer. He then called her cellular phone and left a voice mail, telling her that the paintings were missing and that there was a 'miscellaneous surprise' waiting for him in the storage unit.

It was close to seven o'clock in the morning as he pulled into the hotel underground parking garage. He grabbed his coat and keys and casually walked up the stairs and through the revolving doors. He was about to approach the front desk when he saw several Munich police officers standing around the concierge's station. They were speaking to one of the desk clerks and the hotel manager when the concierge, Olga, looked at Wolfgang directly, pointing him out to the police officers. They then immediately approached him with their guns drawn.

"Bewegen Sie sich nicht, Herr Schmidt. Legen Sie Ihre Hände über den Kopf," as one of the officer's loudly ordered Schmidt to put up his hands and not to move. Wolfgang was terrified and froze in his tracks, as one of the officers approached him and grabbed both of his arms. He pulled them behind his back and handcuffed him.

Two more officers escorted him outside, as Detective Hildebrandt immediately pulled up in front of the hotel in his black, unmarked Mercedes squad car.

"Good Morning, Herr Schmidt. I see we had some fun last night, didn't we?" the detective said in a sarcastic voice to the art dealer.

Schmidt looked surprised and confused, as he glared at the Munich detective.

"What are you talking about? What happened?" Schmidt replied.

"You tell me, Herr Schmidt."

At that moment, an EMS truck pulled up in front of the hotel, and several firefighters and EMS attendants ran upstairs with a gurney. There were several firetrucks following from behind, as more firefighters ran upstairs.

"What is going on?" Schmidt demanded to know.

The detective smirked, "Looks like you and your girlfriend had some pretty rough sex last night."

"What are you talking about?" Schmidt demanded.

Hildebrandt walked over to one of the attending firemen and verified some information for about thirty seconds or so, and then walked back to where Schmidt was standing. He stood erect in front of Wolfgang, smiling from ear to ear.

"I told you not to return to Munich," he said, looking the art dealer straight in the eyes.

"We found your naked girlfriend upstairs in your room," he loudly stated.

"DEAD."

CHAPTER THIRTY-FOUR

The drab, gray walls of the ten by twelve-foot prison cell were dreary and dilapidated, as Schmidt sat on the single mattress situated within the middle of the room. He had been there for forty-eight hours, and other than trying to contact his attorney was given very few reasons as to why he had been taken into custody.

He found it hard to believe that Ingrid Von Stueben had been murdered, strangled in his hotel room right after he had left that early morning. And although he had mentioned to the arresting officers several times that he had checked out of the hotel that very early morning, his legitimate alibi seemed to fall on deaf ears.

Detective Hildebrandt was looking for an excuse to eliminate him and have him out of the way since acquiring those stolen Uffizi paintings. What better reason was there to get rid of him than to hold him in jail on first-degree murder charges?

Wolfgang had made a phone call to his Chicago criminal attorney, basically telling him that he needed him to fly out overseas here to Munich and to help him straighten out this whole mess. He needed his help to get him the 'hell out of prison,' and he didn't care how much it would cost. Because of his attorney's international criminal law experience, Schmidt was confident that his attorney would be able to help him sort through all of this.

In the meantime, who would have been motivated to murder Ingrid? What happened to his Uffizi paintings that were securely stored at the warehouse in Egenhofen? Who was the dead body inside of the warehouse? What did he have to do with all of this?

His attorney had told him that it would take a few days to fly out to Munich and try to straighten out all of this and asked him to patiently wait in his jail cell until he could discuss the charges with the Munich Magistrate. The Munich police had confiscated his cellular phone, and he was sure that Dora, his wife back in Chicago, was trying to get a hold of him. He didn't know how much she knew, or that she was even aware of his imprisonment. Considering that the police had found the body of a naked, dead woman in his hotel room, Wolfgang suddenly became worried about the status of his marriage. They were about to charge him with first-degree murder, and Wolfgang didn't need that information being volunteered to his innocent spouse.

Until his lawyer showed up, the art dealer had no other choice but to lay down on the flat, single prison cot, and rest. He had nothing else to occupy his time, other than to stare at the old, brutally ugly prison walls of his small jail cell. He had no telephone, no computer, no television, no newspapers, no magazines, no books, he had nothing at all.

Schmidt closed his eyes and tried to sleep. He kept hoping that this terrible, living nightmare would end very soon.

It was just after two o'clock local time when the jail attendant came into Wolfgang's prison cell.

"Wake up," he rudely shouted in German, as Wolfgang quickly sat up from his prison bed.

"Your attorney is here."

The Chicago criminal attorney, with salt and pepper hair and his George Clooney good looks, was casually dressed as he entered Schmidt's prison cell. He was wearing a dark, sports jacket, a white button-down shirt that was unbuttoned at the collar, and casual dress jeans that nicely matched his light brown, Rockport shoes. He was holding a large briefcase, as he politely thanked the correctional officer in German.

"Michael...I am so glad to see you," Wolfgang exclaimed, as he tightly hugged his travel-weary Chicago attorney.

"Wolfgang, what kind of trouble did you get yourself into?" the attorney inquisitively asked, even though the magistrate had already briefed him.

Criminal Attorney Michael Prescott had been traveling from Chicago's O'Hare Airport to Munich for almost twenty-four hours, since receiving Wolfgang's frantic phone call. He had already been in a brief discussion with the magistrate and was told that he would be returning later to confer with him and his client shortly.

After making sure that his client was comfortable in his German prison cell, he asked to be brought into a private room with Schmidt so that they could discuss the details of his case.

"Okay, Wolf...start from the beginning. How did a nice, successful Chicago art dealer end up in a jail cell in Munich on first-degree murder charges?"

Wolfgang Schmidt began to recall the events and details of the whole Uffizi painting scandal, starting with the death of his cousin Hermann, up until the night in the hotel with Ingrid and his arrival at the warehouse in Egenhofen, with the discovery of another dead body locked inside of the warehouse.

Although Schmidt knew he had client-attorney privileges with Prescott, he was suspicious of his surroundings, not knowing if the Munich police were electronically surveilling the room he was sitting in. The art dealer told his criminal attorney almost everything, conveniently leaving out his contractual transactions with Stefano Iannucci.

"So, let me get this straight," Prescott replied, after digesting all of Wolfgang's details.

"You have no idea where these paintings are and who has them? And the only one who knew about the whereabouts of those paintings, as far as you're concerned, was Ingrid?"

"As far as I know, yes."

"And she was found murdered in your hotel room after you checked out?"

"Yes."

"And when you went to the warehouse, there was a dead body there waiting for you?"

"Correct," Wolf replied.

"And you have no idea who it is?"

"No. I do not."

Prescott thought for several long moments, trying to decide the best strategy to approach this case and to get the art dealer out of this prison cell.

"Okay, then. I think I know what needs to be done here. But you gotta promise me that you are going to high tail it out of Germany the minute that I get you released from this prison cell," Prescott demanded from his client.

"Absolutely. I don't want to stay in this damn country one minute longer than I have to," Wolfgang replied.

"I don't want you to say another word to the German authorities. I will handle this," he instructed Schmidt.

The criminal attorney then shook hands again with his client, confident that the art dealer had made a promise to leave Munich on the next flight out to Chicago immediately, and that he would keep his word.

In making that promise, Schmidt knew that he would have to abandon those Uffizi paintings and not pursue whoever it was that might have confiscated them.

With those miscellaneous texts that Ingrid was receiving at the hotel, she must have been working with someone to acquire those paintings, and they decided to 'get rid of her' as well. She had probably made some demands to be paid off in some form of kick-back for the information on the whereabouts of those Uffizi paintings.

After an hour or so, Schmidt was escorted into another holding room, which he could see had a one-way mirror mounted on the right side of the cinder-blocked wall. Schmidt tried to make himself relaxed, even though he had not slept at all during the last forty-eight hours. He had not showered or bathed since arriving at his jail cell and was feeling dirty and uncomfortable in the dark grey, prison uniform. The guards were kind enough to undo his handcuffs and his ankle chains after transporting him from his jail cell to the interrogation room.

As Prescott and his client sat at the table for several long minutes, Detective Hildebrandt and Munich Magistrate Hugo Blaas finally arrived along with another officer.

"Good afternoon, gentlemen," Hildebrandt smiled, speaking English with a very thick German accent. He had a low, baritone voice that was unmistakable. "So nice to visit with you again, Herr Schmidt," he said sarcastically.

Michael Prescott stood up and shook hands with the Munich detective and the magistrate, whom he had met earlier.

"I trust you had a pleasant flight here from Chicago," Blaas inquired.

"It's a pleasure to fly Lufthansa Airlines to Germany, Detective. The airline scotch was top shelf, and my flight was enjoyable indeed."

"I am sorry we had to meet under these circumstances, Mr. Prescott," the detective stated while holding a large file filled with documents.

The criminal attorney nodded his head again, anxious to get to the business at hand.

"As you are well aware, your client here, is accused of murdering a very prominent woman in his hotel room the other morning, and we wish to pursue first-degree murder charges against him," Hildebrandt began the first volley.

"Herr Schmidt enjoys his sex on the rough side, and he conveniently strangled her in bed when he was finished," the magistrate smiled.

Michael Prescott smiled back at both men, after visually reminding Schmidt to stay quiet.

"And on what basis do you have for these charges?"

"His hotel room was spattered with his DNA." Hildebrandt pointed out.

The Chicago attorney laughed, almost mocking the Munich detective.

"Well, considering that they had non-stop sex throughout the whole evening, I would hope so," he replied. "That doesn't mean that he killed her, Detective."

The attorney then decided to volley back with Hildebrandt and Blass, knowing that they hadn't done their homework.

"My client had dinner with Ingrid Von Stueben the night before. As you both are aware, Ingrid was quite a Munich socialite with a wealthy husband and more than her share of sexual boyfriends on the side. My client happened to be one of them," Prescott started.

"After she went up to his hotel room that evening, my client checked out of the Le Meridian Hotel at 3:27 am early the next morning, leaving her to continue sleeping in bed," he explained.

He then pulled out a file with some documents out of his briefcase and placed them on the table.

Prescott, after receiving Wolfgang Schmidt's frantic phone call from the Munich prison cell, made some telephone calls to one of his private investigators, who was able to piece together the events of that morning. The investigator interviewed the hotel staff and, mainly, the bellhop who had brought her up to breakfast room service at 5:35 am.

"According to the hotel records, the murder victim called up for room service at 5:05 am. The hotel waiter brought up her breakfast, and he was the last one to see her alive at 5:35 am. The hotel cleaning lady was instructed to go up to his room to gather Schmidt's suitcases and belongings as he had already checked out that morning. When the cleaning lady arrived at 7:15 am, she had found her dead," Prescott explained.

"My client checked out of the hotel at 3:27 am. So how did you conclude that he killed her?"

Hildebrandt was starting to get annoyed, as he glared at the Chicago attorney.

"Herr Schmidt obviously must have returned to his room to commit the murder. He then exited the hotel after committing the homicide, returning to the hotel at 7:30 am."

Again, Michael Prescott seemed amused.

"So, your best explanation to all of this is that Wolfgang Schmidt, after checking out at approximately 3:30 am, returned to his hotel room between 5:30 am, and 7:15 am when she was found dead by the hotel maid," Prescott summarized.

"Of course, with security cameras located everywhere in the hotel, with several hotel security guards monitoring all of these security cameras, you have the tape footage to back up your claims, correct Detective?"

The Munich detective drew a blank for several moments.

"We will, Mr. Prescott. I have our detective working on it right now."

The Chicago criminal attorney is well known for doing his investigative homework, pulled out an encased computer disc, labeled by the Le Meridian Hotel. The computer disc included copies of the security tapes for the forty-eight-hour period, which included the time from which Wolfgang Schmidt checked into the front desk of the hotel until the time after Ingrid Von Stueben was found murdered.

He then politely offered the computer disc to the detective.

"Let me save you the trouble, Detective Hildebrandt. My private investigator has already done your detective work for you. Here are copies of the security tapes for all of the security cameras located around the front and back entrances. This also includes the fifth-floor hotel room from both sides of the east-west corridor and the security tapes around the hotel for the forty-eight period before, during, and after the murder."

Both the Munich detective and the Magistrate sat there in silence.

"Perhaps, Detective, Wolfgang Schmidt wore a cape and flew up to the fifth-floor window like Superman, entering the hotel through a hotel window, breaking the glass and murdering his lover for the evening," Prescott jokingly hypothesized.

"But we all know that didn't happen."

There were several moments of silence, as the Detective glared at the computer disc he was holding.

"Seeing that I have already done most of your investigative work for you, I can expect my client to be immediately released, correct?"

The detective and the city magistrate looked at each other, knowing that the evidence in their case against Wolfgang Schmidt was quite sloppy at best.

There were several moments of silence.

"I will expect my client to be released within the hour, Detective Hildebrandt," Prescott proclaimed.

The four of them all stood up from the table.

"Have a good day, gentlemen," after the Chicago attorney motioned the waiting security guard to return his client to his jail cell while he began the process of getting Schmidt released from prison.

It was almost six o'clock that evening, as Wolfgang Schmidt was patiently waiting at Gate 14-B of the Munich Airport. He was accompanied there by his attorney, after a few hours of going through the paperwork and process of getting him released. Prescott had taken a taxicab with him to the airport, intent on making sure that his client didn't meander off into some other art-finding adventure.

"Did the police mention anything about the body at the warehouse?" Wolfgang kept inquiring.

"No, Wolf. They've mentioned nothing, and neither will we. Your only goal right now is to get onto that plane and high-tail it back to Chicago as quickly as you can," Prescott ordered.

With the name and ownership of that warehouse rental contract under Ingrid Von Stueben's name, Prescott was confident that the authorities would have a difficult time tying his client to the warehouse or its contents. There was some press coverage on the body's discovery a few days ago, but no one approached Schmidt or Prescott regarding any connection.

"I have another flight to catch, Wolf. I need to be in Milan tomorrow morning for a client deposition. I trust you will board this flight to Chicago without any more incidents, correct?" Prescott reasserted.

"I have no desire to stay here any longer than I have to, believe me!" Schmidt proclaimed, holding up his ticket and boarding pass for his United Flight 522 at 7:20 pm, a direct flight to Chicago's O'Hare Airport.

The two of them stood up and shook hands, with Schmidt requesting his attorney to render his invoice upon his return to Chicago immediately. Within the next half hour, Wolfgang Schmidt was boarding the aircraft, immediately finding his window seat two-thirds down. He placed his carry-on bag into the overhead storage bin and then made himself comfortable. He quickly closed the window shade and then shut his eyes, waiting for the airplane to depart from Munich's International Airport.

He was thankful to finally be on that airplane, hoping that this would be the last of his Munich adventure. He wondered what had happened to the stolen Uffizi paintings and where they had disappeared. He thought about who that 'dead body' was and why he was at the empty warehouse. Schmidt had no clue who had killed Ingrid and how she had manipulated someone into stealing the paintings away from him. She paid for it with her life, Wolfgang thought to himself.

At that moment, Schmidt didn't care. He only wanted to go home.

Detective Hildebrandt was sitting at his desk that afternoon, pondering the events that had occurred earlier that day and how he was unable to make his homicide charges stick against the Chicago art dealer. Here was the body of a dead woman, naked and strangled in her bed, with no tapes, no evidence, and no indication as to who may have killed her. They had interrogated the hotel bell boy and the hotel maid for several hours, each coming up empty as to being viable suspects in this murder case.

Hildebrandt continued to play the hotel videotapes over and over, still not noticing anything unusual until he began to look closely at the stamped dates and times of the video tapping of the hallway corridor of the hotel's fifth floor.

He looked closely and documented their times. There were fifteen minutes of the corridor tapes missing, from 6:41 am to 6:56 am.

How could that have happened? The detective pondered. *Fifteen minutes?*

How could both of the hotel corridor cameras not be recording for those fifteen minutes? That would have been just enough time for a potential murderer to enter Ingrid's hotel room, strangle her, and then escape without anyone noticing. But by whom? And why was this break in the tapes not previously seen by anyone at the hotel security or the Munich police?

There were more questions than answers in this homicide case, as Hildebrandt buried his head in his hands. He was feeling frustrated, as he picked up his coffee cup and took a long, hard swallow of his cold, evening coffee. He placed his cup back down on the evening newspaper, which disclosed the headlines for that day:

Body Discovered at Egenhofen Warehouse

The dead victim apparently, was recently identified, according to the news article, as a 29-year old white male from Florence, Italy.

Hildebrandt picked up the newspaper and read the article, again and again, and again.

The victim's last name sounded familiar, but he couldn't remember at the time where he had seen that name before. He then grabbed a notepad and scribbled down the name of the identified victim:

Mariano Giammarco.

CHAPTER THIRTY-FIVE

The Florentine cemetery of Cimitero delle Porte Sante was filled with over two hundred attendees, as Don Rodolfo Giammarco sat at the head of the gravesite. He was grief-stricken, having to oversee now the funeral and burial of his beloved nephew and surrogate son, Mariano. His 29-year old lifeless body was found in an empty warehouse in Egenhofen, Germany, last week, having been shot in the head and left for dead in that warehouse for two days.

Don Rodolfo was feeling a sorted foray of intense emotions. He was grief-stricken and angry, of course, after receiving information on the whereabouts of the stolen Uffizi artworks. He sent his nephew and another associate to travel to Germany last week to retrieve them. He was confused, wondering how that confidential information that was provided by a discrete source had been leaked, and the paintings relocated from that remote warehouse in Egenhofen, Germany.

It was almost two weeks ago, when Don Rodolfo received information, through an 'anonymous' contact via one of the Uffizi board members, of the whereabouts of those stolen paintings. That contact, it turned out, was willing to render the exact location of those paintings upon payment of five million U.S. dollars, in cash, to be delivered upon receipt and confirmation of their precise location.

In reality, that anonymous contact was an affluent former German model, by the name of Ingrid Von Stueben. She was a Munich socialite who was quite active in the community and the European cultural art circles. A deposit of one hundred thousand euros was initially deposited after she had sent cell phone pictures of the three stamped crates and the contents of each container. Each wooden box was sealed "FIRENZE" with the Nazi swastika symbol, disclosing the total forty-two missing Uffizi masterpieces.

Don Rodolfo viewed the pictures along with Dottore Edoardo Giannini, who was the initial contact to Ms. Von Stueben. After seeing the pictures and ascertaining the authenticity of them, the one hundred thousand euros deposit was wire transferred into a Swiss bank account under her husband's name, Piotr Von Stueben. At that time, the German model contacted Dottore Giannini, verbally disclosing the exact whereabouts of the warehouse in Egenhofen, along with the electronic door lock combination and the unique security codes that were needed to access entry.

Last week, Don Rodolfo sent his trusted nephew, Mariano, to the warehouse location along with another associate, Vito D'Amore, to access the paintings and to make the necessary arrangements to transport them back to Florence safely. When he didn't hear from his nephew after frantically calling his cellular telephone for two days, he contacted the local authorities. A trusted associate of Ms. Von Stueben, named Marco Fontana, who had been surveilling Wolfgang Schmidt when he arrived in Munich last week, was supposed to meet his nephew and D'Amore upon arriving at the warehouse and calling in the remainder of the 4.9-million-euro balance.

Then last Thursday, he received a phone call from the Egenhofen Police Department, stating that his nephew was found dead in the warehouse, and there was no sign of Vito D'Amore. He also found out later that Ms. Von Stueben had been strangled to death in her hotel room in Munich, after spending the night with the Chicago art dealer.

He was also suspicious and vengeful, initially believing that Vito D'Amore must have engineered the whole scheme. He had suspected that D'Amore couldn't be trusted to accompany his nephew and to keep an eye on him during this very dangerous and very discrete transaction.

Vito D'Amore, up until last week, was a trusted associate of Giammarco crime family, the 'Firenze Mafia.' He was Don Rodolfo's consistent 'go-to' guy in doing whatever was needed to be done to complete whatever 'special project' the family needed to be accomplished. D'Amore had done an exceptional, professional job on the Mayor of Munich's assassination, making sure that he obverted the security cameras in accessing Mayor Kossel's office before murdering him. He had been professionally associated with the Giammarco family for over thirty years, and his loyalty was never questioned.

But recently, Vito D'Amore's problems were beginning to get in the way of his professional job duties. He was in the process of going through a very messy divorce with his third wife, Renata. Besides having to render her a substantial divorce settlement, he was being blackmailed by her to provide a significant amount of additional money, in the millions, in return for Blanca's silence regarding his professional 'hit-man' career. D'Amore discussed his plans of 'getting rid of her' in the past with Don Rodolfo, but he advised against it. He knew that such a domestic murder would bring about a tremendous amount of pressure and unwanted publicity on Florence's most powerful crime family.

Vito D'Amore went missing for several days, as Giammarco initially suspected him in his nephew's murder. That is until Vito's body was found yesterday, floating face down in the River Arno. It was a professional hit, with Vito having been shot several times in the head.

But Don Rodolfo had no idea of his whereabouts before the location of D'Amore's body, let alone authorize his murder.

There were suddenly, too many dead bodies and no paintings to show for them.

Don Giammarco sat there at the family plot, his gray hair slicked back, wearing a black Armani suit and dark sunglasses to hide his bloodshot eyes. Since the news of his nephew's death, he had not been able to stop crying. For him, his beloved nephew was the future of his Florentine enterprises and his crime family dynasty. For Don Rodolfo, his sudden death was an unexpected loss that was taking quite an emotional toll on him. He was eighty-one years old now, and with the loss of his young nephew and surrogate son, there was no one else left to take over his business ventures. The succession plan for his winery, his vast business holdings, and his family 'cosa nostra' was now in jeopardy.

His mind began to wander, thinking about his beloved nephew when he was a little boy. He thought about when he was helping him pick grapes and making wine with him every fall during the harvest, which he had done since he was seven years old until recently. It was part of the family business, but also a family tradition, as 'Zio Rodolfo' and his young nephew participated in picking and mashing the grapes, then bottling the wine months later after each harvest. Giammarco remembered watching his young nephew's soccer games at school, and what an excellent forward he had turned out to be for his academy soccer team. He remembered young Mariano helping him pick bushels of tomatoes from his elaborate garden. The two of them mashing the ripened tomatoes into the tomato sauce and jarring them each year. He also recalled how proud he was when he finally graduated from the University of Padua Law School, knowing now that, with his legal background, he could confidently participate as the family 'consigliere.'

Don Rodolfo Giammarco sat there grieving. His eyes were perpetually wet with tears, as a Roman Catholic priest blessed the wooden walnut casket, enclosing the body of his young nephew. The casket was then, slowly lowered into the shallow grave, inside of the concrete vault placed inside of the ground, as the two hundred or more guests placed their red roses on top of the ornate, wooden coffin. The vault was then sealed, and the two cemetery workers began throwing topsoil, with each shovelful, slowly filling up the burial site of young Mariano Giammarco. As the gravesite was nearly filled and completed, various attendees paid their final respects and condolences to Don Rodolfo. Each guest approached him, grasping his hand and giving him a quick kiss on each cheek. But Giammarco only sat there, completely motionless. He was devastated. He was shattered. He was utterly and emotionally destroyed.

As the rest of the funeral attendees left the cemetery, Don Rodolfo was the last one remaining, alone, solitary figure still sitting stoically in front of his nephew's grave. Two associates of his associates tried to help him rise from his chair, but he refused. He continued to sit at the head of the family plot, alone by himself, his eyes focused on the newly buried grave of his young nephew. His two associates only stood there alongside the family patriarch, patiently waiting for him to rise from his chair and leave the cemetery.

As he began to leave Mariano's gravesite, he turned to one of his associates.

"I want to know who did this to my nephew."

Both men looked at each other, one appearing more perplexed than the other. They didn't have a clue

317

where to start or who to suspect in the murder of their young associate, who represented the future of Florence's most powerful crime organization.

The three men walked over to the long, black Mercedes limousine, as one of them opened the rear passenger door for Don Rodolfo.

Before he entered the car, Giammarco looked at both of his associates and stood there stoically, without saying a word. And then, after a few long moments, he glared at them and simply stated:

"Chicago."

CHAPTER THIRTY-SIX

The isolated E45 German highway was dark and lonely that early morning, as the large white box truck was going southbound into Austria, then across the border through the mountainous Dolomites into the Italian Alps. It was a long, tedious four-hour drive into the northern South Tyrol region of Italy, into the town of Bolzano. Chicago's Marchese Family had instructed the two drivers to the specific warehouse in Bolzano, where they were asked to deposit the three Uffizi wooden crates.

One of the drivers was Marco Fontana, a young, ambitious 26-year-old man from Rome, Italy. He had a special connection to the Marchese Family and was all too eager to please his uncle Carlo Marchese. Marco was initially born in Casalvieri, Italy, and the only child to Don Carlo's youngest sister, Iolanda, and her husband, Ovidio Fontana. Marco was always a spoiled, hard-to-handle millennial that gave his mother and father an incredibly hard time.

He finished grade school in Casalvieri and was then sent to the Sapienza University of Rome to study engineering several years ago. Rather than his chosen field of study, he decided to acquire his 'associates degree in alcohol abuse and cocaine possession,' and was arrested by the 'polizia' several times on drug charges. After serving six months in the 'Prigione Romana,' his exasperated mother reached out to her older brother Carlo in Chicago to intercede. Marco flew out to Chicago a few years ago and stayed with his aunt and uncle at their lavish Sauganash mansion for several months. It was there that he realized that Chicago's underworld crime syndicate was his true calling. He worked for Don Carlo for several months, doing small family duties, which included assisting in some collections and overseeing some of the Marchese disposal routes.

It was during this period that Marco was allowed to assist his uncle in some of his Vatican painting transactions, assisting him in overseeing their safe transport from Rome to wherever the intended destination would be. Marco became familiar with Don Carlo's Vatican connections, which included those of his other second cousin, Monsignor Gianpaolo Iacobelli. Don Carlo was impressed with his young nephew's eagerness to please, and his keen eye for detail. But soon after that, young Marco wished to return to Rome.

Don Carlo gave young Marco several thousand dollars to restart his life, along with his promise to 'turn over a new leaf' and was sent back to the Eternal City. Marco acquired a luxury apartment near the posh, Trastevere area of Rome. He went back to his old habits of partying at the local nightclubs several nights a week and sleeping off his drug and alcohol hangovers during the day. Although he consistently disappointed his uncle and his parents, Marco continued to express his desire to return to Chicago and become a permanent member of the Marchese crime family. Don Carlo resisted, patiently explaining to him that he needed to 'prove himself.' Marco made no secret that he was a 'Chicago Mafia wanna-be' and wanted nothing more than to be a made member of his Uncle Carlo's esteemed crime family.

On New Year's Eve several months ago, Marco's lucky break happened at the posh, elegant Micca Club in the downtown Campo Marzio district. That event came in the form of a blonde, vivacious, former German model named Ingrid Von Stueben. She was there at an art auction in Rome along with a friend, when she immediately set her eyes on the young, handsome Roman. Although she was married and twenty years his senior, they hit it off immediately, with frequent marathon sex sessions between his apartment in Rome and her opulent Munich mansion when her husband was away. They became intensely 'in-love,' with the two of them traveling back and forth between Rome and Munich every couple of weeks.

It wasn't until several weeks ago, that young Marco realized that he was just another young, naïve, enumerate 'play-toy' within Ingrid's long list of extra-curricular lovers. They began verbally, then physically fighting, with Marco demonstrating his incredibly intense, hot temper and his uncontrollable, jealous rages. He became very possessive, very controlling, and began stalking her at every opportunity. Ingrid realized soon after that of her young boyfriend's intense, manipulative behavior, and how unstable he was.

But Ingrid also had a very intense sex addiction. She realized that having sex with a younger man twenty years her junior fulfilled many of her most private sexual fantasies, and she had a difficult time letting go of their volatile relationship. Their emotional ups and downs, along with their frequent break-ups, became a regular pattern of their unstable relationship, only to be resurrected by their intense sexual encounters.

During one of their marathon sex sessions two weeks ago, Ingrid received a phone call from Wolfgang, calling her from Chicago. While Ingrid took the call in the bathroom of the hotel where they were staying in Munich, Marco overheard their entire conversation. The art dealer was discussing specific information regarding the relocation of the Uffizi paintings from the warehouse in Egenhofen. After some coaxing, Marco got her to 'open up' regarding what she knew about the missing, Uffizi paintings, and the share of the painting proceeds that she would be paid once the forty-two paintings had been sold and liquidated.

Marco begged Ingrid to allow him to assist her in the relocation of these paintings, explaining to her that Wolfgang Schmidt was an unnecessary, needless component in this extremely lucrative transaction. He made her realize that, with her art world connections, that keeping Schmidt involved in this business deal was not a sensible option.

But Ingrid already explained that she had committed and received a deposit from the Giammarco Family in Florence and that they would be willing to pay her five million euros once they acquired the paintings.

Suddenly, Marco had a plan. He called his Uncle Carlo and was able to broker a deal with him where the Marchese Family would double her promised commission, or ten million euros, once the paintings were safely relocated out of Germany. The original plan called for the elimination of whoever showed up at that warehouse first and then transported the art out of the country.

But afterward, when realizing that Ingrid was also romantically involved with Wolfgang Schmidt, among others, Marco devised a different exit plan. This time, his dangerous jealousies kicked in once again.

He was in love with a married 'puttana,' he thought to himself. If he couldn't have the beautiful Ingrid exclusively, no one else would either.

Finding out where Schmidt and Ingrid were staying and their probable romantic rendezvous afterward, Marco created an ingenious plan. He approached the security officer of the hotel the day before to create a fifteen-minute 'power outage' within the security room of the Le Meridian Hotel during those early morning hours. Paying him two thousand Deutschmarks, those fifteen minutes was all the time that was needed for someone to get into her hotel room and to 'eliminate' Ingrid after acquiring the paintings.

Besides Ingrid's 'elimination' and the killing of whoever showed up to get the priceless pictures from the Giammarco Family, Wolfgang Schmidt was also supposed to be killed when he arrived at the warehouse. But he got there too late. By then, Marco had shot one of Giammarco's men at the warehouse, and took the other man as a prisoner, tying him up and gaged in back of the truck while transporting the paintings back to Bolzano, Italy. He would be disposed of later, he thought to himself. His friend, Maurizio Caravello, kept surveillance of Ingrid and Schmidt that evening, waiting for him to leave early that morning for the warehouse. Instead of tailing Schmidt, he was instructed to go upstairs and 'take care of Ingrid.'

Marco Fontana and the other driver, Franco Lucchese, had just crossed the Italian border on the Dolomite Italian Alps when Marco's cell phone began to ring.

"Pronto."

"Marco, è Zio Carlo. Voglio sapere che co'se' succeso" It was his Uncle Carlo, demanding to know what was going on.

"Zio, tutto va d'accordo...everything is working as planned," Marco lied in both languages. "Non-ti preoccupare...we have the paintings in the truck," he exclaimed, not mentioning the extra passenger tied up and gaged in back.

"Chi era presente della Famiglia Giammarco?" Don Carlo asked, wanting to know who showed up on behalf of the Giammarco Family.

"Not sure. We eliminated them both when we acquired the paintings!" Marco proudly proclaimed. He hoped that this transportation deal would finally get him into his uncle's good graces.

"Marco? You were not supposed to kill anyone," Don Carlo said, this time in English. "I only wanted you to tie them up until Schmidt discovered them at the warehouse," Don Carlo was angry, realizing that his overambitious nephew had considerably gone off-script.

"What happened to the girl?"

"She's dead too," he said, confirming the text he had just received from his friend Maurizio.

"What? Why was she killed?" Don Carlo angrily replied.

"I thought you would rather have her dead than to pay her an extra ten million euros for the paintings," Marco explained.

"Stronzo! I am the one who decides who will be eliminated! Not you, Marco! Do you realize what you have done? You have now started a dangerous war with the Giammarco Family of Florence?" Don Carlo, at that point, was screaming on the phone.

Don Carlo Marchese was very familiar with his nemesis, Florence's influential Rodolfo Giammarco. Although the Marchese Family of Chicago was more extensive and more prominent in the States, the Giammarco Family, known as the 'Firenze Mafia,' was far and away the most brutal and the most ruthless in the Tuscany region. They would stop at nothing to settle a claim or a vendetta against anyone who placed any harm on anyone in their family.

Later that day, Don Carlo came to find out through his various sources, that the man murdered at the warehouse was the beloved nephew of Don Rodolfo Giammarco, Mariano. He then became extremely angry with his nephew Marco, now realizing that his recklessness would probably cause a price to be placed on his nephew's head by the Giammarco Family, and there was nothing that he could do about it.

The white box truck pulled into the empty warehouse in Bolzano, Italy. Acquiring the keys and the necessary entry codes to the remote warehouse located in the outskirts of the city, Marco and Franco unloaded the three crates with a hand dolly, then initiated the security alarm and locked up the entry doors to the warehouse.

They then had the unpleasant task of figuring out what to do with Giammarco's other henchmen, Vito D'Amore. Marco figured that the best method would be to unload him at Giammarco's front doorstep in Florence, Italy. Not knowing exactly where Giammarco lived, they did the next best thing: They drove their truck to the Ponte Vecchio Bridge in the middle of the night and threw his body off of the bridge after conveniently depositing a bullet into the back of D'Amore's brain.

Having accomplished what he thought was an excellent service to his uncle, Marco and Franco drove their rented truck back to Rome. Marco Fontana was quite proud of himself, knowing that he was a great assistance to his Uncle Don Carlo Marchese in locating and delivering the famous, once stolen Uffizi paintings to his grateful crime family in Chicago.

Knowing now that no one else could have his girlfriend any longer, Marco smiled to himself. He looked up at the star-studded sky of the Eternal City and waved good-bye to his married lover, knowing that her promiscuous actions behind his back could never hurt him again.

Don Carlo was at the Blackstone Hotel that early morning in the middle of August, enjoying his espresso doppio. It had been a few days since his reckless nephew picked up and delivered the Uffizi paintings to the Bolzano warehouse when his cell phone started ringing.

It looked like an unknown long-distance telephone number with the '011' area code, indicating that it was from Italy. He looked at the phone intently, letting it ring several times before finally answering.

"Hello?"

"Pronto...Signore Carlo Marchese?"

"Sì'."

"Sono Rodolfo Giammarco."

Don Carlo's heart dropped down to his stomach. He knew precisely why he was calling him and was unprepared to answer for the reckless death of his nephew at the Egenhofen warehouse.

There was a long silence on the phone.

"I am sure you know why I am calling. I understand that we are now trading our nephews for these stolen Uffizi paintings, is this correct?"

Don Carlo was speechless, realizing that the Giammarco Family had now discovered his nephew's actions.

"I must compliment you, Don Carlo. You have a very ambitious nephew. He is quite an enterprising young man. He even killed one of my associates the other evening and dumped him into the River Arno near the Ponte Vecchio Bridge."

Carlo began to sweat, and his hands were starting to shake as he continued to hear the low, ruthless voice of his Florentine nemesis.

"Signore, Giammarco, I can explain..."

"There is nothing to explain, Don Carlo," Giammarco coolly interrupted him.

"I am only making this courtesy call to let you know of our intentions. Unless you would rather start an intercontinental war and we both start losing more family soldiers over this huge misunderstanding," he said.

"We have your nephew here," declared Don Rodolfo, "and we will be exchanging his life for the life of my Mariano's later this evening. I will have one of my associates send you the video."

"A meaningful swapping of chess pieces, one would say..." Giammarco calmly clarified long distance. "A trade of my knight, for one of yours."

Don Carlo Marchese was in shock, not believing that the Florentine Mafioso would announce the upcoming death of his nephew over the cell phone long distance as if he were taunting the Chicago capo. His nephew had just been kidnapped and was being held against his will by the Giammarco Family.

This had now become a dangerous chess game, indeed. There were additional moments of silence, as Don Carlo was speechless.

327

Giammarco continued. "Now mind you, I am not asking for your consent. Unlike your family murdering my beloved nephew without notice, I am at least, announcing to you our intentions, with the hope that such a misunderstanding will never happen again between our two families."

"And by the way, I know where those paintings are," Don Rodolfo inserted. Before Don Carlo could protest Giammarco's death declaration on his nephew, Giammarco had hung up the phone.

Don Carlo Marchese only sat there at the coffee table of his hotel room. He was silently sitting there for several long minutes, staring out of his eighteenth-floor window. His nephew Marco had been kidnapped for his reckless actions, and now he was about to pay for them with his own life. Don Carlo began to weep, his tears dripping onto the glass coffee table next to his empty espresso cup. He had never felt so helpless. The irresponsible actions and murders which his nephew had committed have now come back full circle, and he now had the blood of his over-zealous nephew on his hands.

He knew that his sister and brother-in-law would be devastated upon hearing the kidnapping and probable death of their only son. But there was nothing he could do. He tried several times to contact Marco's cell phone. But there was no answer. He then called his sister in Casalvieri and broke the terrible news.

Later that morning, Don Marchese received a video, showing his nephew tied to a chair, while a masked, hooded executioner beheaded him with a giant sword, 'Al Qaeda' style.

The following day, RAI UNO reported the discovery of a young man's decapitated body at the very bottom of the ancient catacombs of the Roman Colosseum.

His beheaded body had been chopped up and severely mutilated. In the same symbolic method that Vito D'Amore's body was dumped off the historic Ponte Vecchio Bridge in Florence, this young man's body had been butchered and abandoned. It was as though his dead body had been left for the hungry lions of the ancient Roman games, which once preyed on thousands of helpless Christians who were mutilated and murdered over two thousand years ago.

Marco Fontana was now the latest, modern-day Roman to be tortured and killed in the Colosseum.

CHAPTER THIRTY-SEVEN

The taxicab driver was maneuvering around the traffic on the Kennedy Expressway that afternoon last September, as Frank Mercurio was fumbling with his airline tickets in his coat pocket. His Alitalia Flight 731 was departing from Terminal Five at 4:45 pm, and he had his marching orders from Don Carlo. He was to arrive at Rome's Fiumicino Airport at 9:30 am, and then take the Trenitalia Rapido Express train north at 11:30 am for an eight-hour train ride to Bolzano, Italy, changing trains in Milan. It had been a few weeks since Don Carlo's reckless nephew, Marco, was murdered after transporting the Uffizi art collection from Germany to the secured, tenable warehouse in Bolzano. Mercurio was expected to go to the warehouse, check on the contents of the Uffizi crates holding the forty-two paintings, then acquire Fra Lippi's 'Demons of Divine Wrath' art within the collection, to be shipped to Detroit via special air freight.

It came to be known that, amongst these various, forty-two priceless masterpieces that included the works of Raphael, Rembrandt, Donatello, among others, Fra Lippi's 'Demons of Divine Wrath' was the most sought after, most priceless masterpiece within this collection. Because of the Fra Lippi's elusive career as a former Carmelite monk, a fresco painter, and his very adventurous, promiscuous life, this particular painting was virtually unknown and hidden by his artist son, Filipino Lippi in Spoleto, Italy, until well after his son's death.

Filippo Lippi was born into a sizeable low-income family in Florence in 1406. After the death of both his father and mother, the young Filippo was raised by an aunt, then later placed with his brother in the convent of

Carmelite monks at Santa Maria del Carmine. By 1432, Lippi had become well known for the painting of many beautiful frescos among many churches and convents within the Tuscany region. During his time as a Carmelite monk, he fell in love with a cloistered nun and impregnated her. He was forced out of the monastery and was later abducted by the Moors of the Adriatic, and held as a slave for 18 months. It was Lippi's artistic talents that eventually set him free after he painted a portrait of his slave owner. In 1434, Lippi was living in Padua, and it is believed that this is where he painted his most beautiful masterpieces. He later returned to Florence and became a favorite artist of the prominent Medici family, painting many frescos and alter paintings for their many churches and buildings within the region. After he died in Spoleto in 1469, many of his Padua paintings, including the 'Demons of Divine Wrath' masterpiece, were either initially unknown or were hidden by his son. This particular oil painting has been sought after by art collectors and museums worldwide over the last five hundred years, especially after disappearing initially from the Vatican, and then later, the Uffizi Museums after the war.

The Alitalia flight aboard its Boeing 747 was quite turbulent, as Frank Mercurio was gripping the arm of a twelve-year-old boy sitting next to him while gulping down several Crown Royals. The jet finally landed safely at Fiumicino Airport in Rome, an hour behind schedule, and Mercurio had a difficult time going through customs, acquiring his luggage and hailing a taxicab to the Roma Termini. He barely made his 11:30 am train. After the long train ride and changing trains in Milan, Frank finally arrived at Bolzano just after 10:00 pm local time. He then hailed a taxicab and was transported to his luxury suite at the Hotel Eberle on Via Santa Maddalena.

He wasn't in his room more than five minutes before the telephone in his hotel suite rang.

"Hello?"

"Frank? You're in Italy. You're supposed to say 'Pronto,'" Don Carlo joked. It was the first time Marchese had smiled since the violent death of his nephew, Marco.

He had instructed the hotel concierge at the Hotel Eberle to contact him when Mercurio checked in.

"Boss...I'm too tired to follow telephone etiquette right now," the family underboss replied.

He was already stripped down to his boxer shorts and was about to collapse on his bed. It had been a long trip between his turbulent airplane flight and his long, slow 'funeral train' voyage, with its frequent stops towards Milan and eventually, Bolzano. Mercurio was exhausted and barely had enough strength or energy to hold the telephone receiver in his hand.

"Frank, when you're done unpacking, splash some water on your face and try to get over to that warehouse. I have a bad feeling about those paintings crated up and sitting there," the Don said.

"Boss? It's almost ten-thirty. Who is going to take those paintings now?"

"The Giammarco Family is looking for those paintings, and I heard they might already know where they are. They just might be waiting for you to get there and turn off the security system and for the security guards to be relieved before breaking in."

"That ain't going to happen, Boss. Besides, I'm too tired to go anywhere right now. Let me sleep for a few hours, and I will go over there later. Right now, I need to close my eyes."

Don Marchese was a little perturbed with Mercurio's response but knew there was nothing that he could do. The head of the Northside Chicago family was used to having his way and expected his soldiers and especially, his underboss to jump at his command. But Frank Mercurio had been with the family for over forty years, and the Don had too much love and respect for him. He decided to let him get his rest, and hopefully, Mercurio would be able to get out to the warehouse first thing in the morning.

Frank Mercurio got up at 5:30 that morning, and calmly took his time showering and enjoying a continental breakfast of several 'cornetti' and freshly brewed espresso. He had reserved a rental car at Europcar in town, and they didn't open up until 7:00 am. When Mercurio finally arrived at the rental car agency, they didn't have the Volvo SUV that he reserved initially, so Frank got the Audi station wagon instead. It had to be large enough to transport that painting to the air freight company in Milan, and he figured that the station wagon would do. Using his GPS, he drove twenty minutes to the warehouse location, a remote five thousand square foot brick building located on the outskirts of the city.

There was a twenty-four-hour security guard posted on the outside of the entrance of the building, sitting in a small, blue Fiat Cinquecento. An entry security code and a unique key (that he acquired from the security guard) was needed to open up the overhead door, as there was a motion-activated laser system that secured the contents of the spacious warehouse. As Mercurio was given clearance, he took out his codes and entry key as he pulled up to the warehouse and parked in front of the building door.

As he pushed open the overhead door, the warehouse looked dark and eerie. The three wooden crates, stamped with the Nazi eagle symbols and the word "FIRENZE" still imprinted on the outside of each container, were sitting in the middle of the open warehouse space. After turning off the security alarm system, Frank approached the three crates. He then realized that he had neither tools nor a hammer to open the nailed shut wooden crates, so he went to the back of his rental car and looked for a crowbar or some other tool that would assist him in opening them. He found a four-way cross wrench and used the sharp end of it to pry open the nailed down containers.

He had an image of the Fra Lippi painting that he was looking for on his cell phone, and after withdrawing several of the other paintings, found the 'Demons of Divine Wrath' oil painting that he was seeking. It was tightly wrapped and full of dust, with the outside of each wrapping marked with the title and the artist of each oil painting. Mercurio withdrew the Lippi painting, which was wrapped in thick, dark burlap material, and loaded it into the back of his station wagon. After nailing shut the open container, he slowly backed out of the warehouse and closed the warehouse door, initiating the elaborate alarm system.

Conspicuously located two hundred yards away, a man was sitting in a dark Mercedes watching the Marchese henchman. He was wearing a black jacket and a dark woolen hat, and he took off his dark sunglasses before using his sophisticated pair of long-range binoculars.

He intensely began watching Mercurio enter the secured, gated warehouse. He was ordered not to assault or attack Mercurio, but to observe him as he came and gained access to the warehouse building where the paintings were located. He was able to acquire the access codes and wrote down the numbers and symbols from far away.

The stranger then watched him acquire one of the paintings and then load them into his car and leave. When Mercurio left the warehouse and gated complex, the man made a phone call. He was calling his contact to let him know that he had the security access codes.

"Stefano...Ho i codici di accesso."

Mercurio had his orders to drive the painting directly to Milan and bring it to the air freight company in charge of safely flying it back to Detroit for delivery. The long 229-kilometer trip was over three hours. Mercurio only stopped on one occasion to get gas and cigarettes, but otherwise continued to drive straight through to the international air freight company. The JAP Air Forwarding and Freight Company was located on Via Raffaella near the Malpensa Airport in Milan. He had an appointment with Mario Loconte, one of the managers with the air freight company. Mercurio signed a few documents and gave him his credit card, paying the two-thousand-euro fee in advance, which included guaranteed two-day delivery and insurance directly delivered to the Detroit Institute of Art, in care of Mr. John Males, its board chairman.

The travel itinerary for Frank Mercurio was to drop off the car at Europcar in Milan and take a direct flight from Milan back to Chicago. As he was about to return his rental car, he received a cell phone call from Don Carlo Marchese.

Frank initially figured that his boss wanted to verify that the painting had successfully been shipped from Milan, Italy, to its destination in Detroit.

"Ciao, Don Carlo..." Marchese sounded disturbed.

"Frank...did you happen to notice anyone around when you opened the warehouse door and acquired the painting?"

"No, Boss...absolutely not. The only one who knew I was there was the security guard, who handed me the access key before I opened the warehouse door. Why?"

"We just got a phone call from the Bolzano police."

"What happened?"

"Someone beat up the security guard and accessed the warehouse about an hour ago. The security guard was messed up pretty badly and was sent to the hospital, where he later died," Marchese informed Mercurio.

"What happened to the paintings in the warehouse?"

"They're gone. The warehouse is empty. The security cameras and entry codes were accessed and compromised."

Frank Mercurio was in shock. How could have someone acquired those security codes and gained access to that secured warehouse? Between the laser detection alarms and the security cameras, the protection and safekeeping of those Uffizi paintings were state-of-the-art. It seemed impossible for him to comprehend how someone would have been able to access that warehouse.

A black box truck was coming down the Autostrada SS12 that late afternoon near Verona. Stefano Iannucci had been patiently waiting for the truck to arrive along the side of the road near Via Mirandola for almost an hour, as the vehicle pulled up behind Stefano's black Mercedes.

"Che cosa ci avete messo così tanto?" he asked them, wondering why it had taken them so long.

The two men driving the truck were associates of Iannucci's. They were supposed to knock out the security guard, shoot out the security cameras, and then access the warehouse door using the codes Stefano had given them. They had a difficult time disabling the security guard, as they had beaten him up pretty badly to get him to give up the security key. They also had a hard time using the hand lift pallet jack that they had brought along, as it was insufficient in maneuvering those heavy wooden crates and getting them loaded onto the box truck.

"Abbiamo dovuto caricare tutto a mano," one of the men said, stating that they had to load everything up by hand, which took more time than expected.

Stefano shook both of the men's hands and gave them an envelope, which contained five thousand euros in cash.

"I will give you the rest of the money when you help me deliver these crates," Stefano stated in Italian. He then got back into his car and instructed both men to follow him.

He had a discrete location to put the Uffizi art collection in safekeeping until he could finish this transaction with the Pope Emeritus. He had an extraordinary hiding place that he knew he could count on, a secret place where no one would ever suspect or access the location of these paintings.

He got back onto the Autostrada, following the directions of one of the white signs pointing southbound via E35:

Assisi – 401 kilometers.

CHAPTER THIRTY-EIGHT

It was almost eight o'clock on that frigid January morning as I parked my car in the adjacent garage on North Racine and headed to my office at the Sun-Times building. An overnight cold front had invaded the Windy City, as the thermometer had dipped below minus twenty degrees without the windchill. It seemed as though our unusually cold Chicago winters were getting even more frigid with this current polar vortex, as the environmental climate change was now directly affecting our already brutal Chicago winters.

I was a little tired from last evening, not getting a whole lot of sleep after my wonderful dinner date with my new investigative reporting partner. My emotions were all over the board that morning. I was excited, apprehensive, happy, nervous, anxious, and considerably suspicious, all at the same time. I felt like a teenager, a high school sophomore who had just gotten home from the prom at three o'clock in the morning.

And yet, I was a little mistrustful too. Was Veronica attracted to me, or was she just interested in being a part of this investigative story? Did she see an opportunity to be a part of this news investigation? Or was she using it as an excuse to start some sort of relationship? I was perplexed. Judging by that amazing 'good-night kiss' that I unexpectedly received before she boarded the taxicab last evening, made me believe that she, at the very least, was attracted to me. But was she just using me to be a part of this story?

I realized that morning that I was very rusty at all this. It had been a very long time since I was in a serious relationship, and I just didn't know how to read women anymore. Honestly, I was scared to death.

I settled into my office with my extra-wet Starbucks cappuccino and began pounding on my computer keyboard. I started writing new details of this Marchese homicide and trying to remember the new information that Veronica had explained to me about the Uffizi paintings and their connection to the Vatican and the Pope Emeritus. The specifics were a little faded after several glasses of wine last evening, as those luscious, moist red lips of hers tasted like summertime cherries.

Maybe I needed to clarify some of the details that Veronica had so patiently explained to me last evening? Perhaps I needed to make sure I had remembered everything she mentioned correctly? Maybe I needed an excuse to call her?

At that moment, 'Perry White of the Daily Planet' walked into the newsroom. While still trying to defrost, Mike Daudelin lunged for his coffee cup and B-lined it to the kitchen with his coat and green, woolen Michigan State hat still on. It seemed as though the colder it got for my boss during this wintertime cold, the more caffeine his six-foot, five-inch frame demanded first thing in the morning. It seemed unusual to me that Mike's brain could never fully de-crystalize until he was on his third cup of coffee, so I decided to wait for a half-hour or so before walking into his office and announcing my new investigative partnership.

"Good morning Mr. Crawford." Mike was trying to sound pleasant when I eventually knocked on his office door.

"Morning, Chief," as I tried to make myself comfortable and sat on one of his two wooden chairs. I thought about putting my feet on his desk but realized that with all of his strewn papers and clutter, that there was no room for them.

"So…tell me about your date?" Mike was smiling.

"What date?" I was shocked. My assistant editor looked at me and continued to smile.

"Stop playing stupid."

"I don't remember telling you I was on a date," I immediately replied. "And besides, it wasn't a date, Chief. It was an informative business meeting with a fellow reporter, who now, I might add, is going to assist me on this Marchese homicide story."

Mike Daudelin continued to smile, disclosing that famous quirky look on his face.

"Uh-huh."

"Yeah, Chief…Veronica Giancarlo is going to be assisting me with this investigation."

Mike's face started to change.

"You do understand; there is company policy against fellow employees getting romantically involved and dating one another on company time."

The Chief was always very good at rattling off different rules and regulatory policy information, according to the Human Resource Department. I just rolled my eyes in the air.

"Chief…I'm not sleeping with her. I'm only working with her on this story, an investigative story, I might add, that she began and submitted last summer to one of our editors."

I paused for a moment before continuing. "A story that the paper wasn't interested in printing."

Mike Daudelin glared at me for a moment, then took another long gulp of his third cup of coffee.

"I remember talking to Tom and George about that story," the Chief started saying. "They both said it was garbage and that she made a lot of baseless accusations that were a little farfetched. Plus, at that time last summer, there was no room for her story. Other international matters were going on and being reported. There wasn't a lot of interest in those stolen Uffizi paintings," my assistant editor explained.

"Thanks for telling me all of this, Mike. You would have saved me an earful."

"I figured you would eventually find out about it. Everyone else here heard about her being snubbed. Maybe Veronica Giancarlo should stick to cataloging Egyptian artifacts and let go of her floundering journalism career. She's not very good at it," Daudelin observed.

A few more quiet moments while I listened to Mike Daudelin loudly slurp his coffee.

"So, answer my question, Paulie...how was your date?" My boss always insisted on getting all of the juice and mindless gossip upfront.

"Just fine, Chief. Ms. Giancarlo is all business," I curtly replied.

"Uh-huh." He winked his eye and looked at me with that Cheshire cat grin of his as if I had something to hide.

"I can count on both hands how many reporters in this newsroom would give their back teeth for a date with that gorgeous art curator. She has said 'no' to so many

342

guys around here for so long, I was starting to wonder if she liked boys," Mike commented.

"Just for the record, what's your secret?"

"I'm not sure, Chief. Maybe telling her to go 'F' herself' upfront may have done it. I went to the Art Institute of Chicago yesterday to ask for her help, and she initially threw me out of her office," I answered. "Going out last night and assisting me with this news investigation was her idea."

"Really?" Daudelin sounded surprised. "Well, listen, Paulie...I have no problem with you 'pallying up' with Veronica. Just do me two favors..." he requested.

"You write the final draft and...keep it professional. Get it?" Mike loudly demanded.

The Chief believed that Veronica had a difficult time distinguishing her adjectives from her pro-nouns. He probably thought that she lacked the literary compacity to put together complete and readable sentences in the 'King's English.'

I laughed to myself, as I certainly wasn't in the mood to debate him regarding Veronica's writing skills. I was only interested in completing this investigation and writing up this news story. If working with Veronica Giancarlo was going to help me accomplish that, then I was all for it. My ego was never that big or enormous to ask and acquire help from anyone who could assist me in writing a news story.

If anything developed between us, that would be 'frosting on the cake.' As much as I looked forward to working with Veronica, I certainly wasn't going to jump into the 'cold, frigid water headfirst.' And I wasn't going to volunteer any romantic details to 'The Chief.'

I exited his office and went back to my computer, outlining and summarizing some of the particulars Veronica had laid out for me last evening. At that moment, I pulled out my iPhone. I courageously dialed her cell number.

"I was just thinking of you," Veronica answered without even saying 'hello.'

"Good morning. Did I catch you at a bad time?"

"Not at all. I was just preparing for my Renaissance art seminar that I teach on Thursday mornings here at the museum," she explained.

"An art curator, a reporter, and a teacher too? Wow...I'm impressed."

"Don't be," she laughed over the phone.

"I need some help here. Explain to me again the Vatican connection in this Uffizi painting scandal," I asked.

I wanted to make sure I had the details right, and of course, hearing the sound of her voice was an added benefit.

"Okay. Those forty-two paintings were consigned by Pope Pius XI in 1938 to the Uffizi Gallery in Florence during the war. The Vatican was fearful that the Nazi's would possibly, help themselves to the Vatican Museum's paintings if they were ever raided and occupied Rome," she explained.

"But why would the Vatican be fearful of Nazi Germany stealing art in 1938? Weren't the Fascista's or Mussolini's Black Shirt army in bed with the Nazi's back then? Why would they raid the art galleries of their axis allies at the time? Why would Pope Pius be worried about the Nazi's stealing their art in Rome when Hitler and

Mussolini were in a war partnership together?" I asked, remembering some of my world history classes.

"Hitler made it known from the very beginning of the war that he had the ambition to build the world's finest museum in his hometown of Linz, Austria. He planned to call it the *Führermuseum* and hoped to stock it with the greatest works of art from around the world," Veronica said.

"Hitler would do this by obtaining artworks at a drastic discount, borrowing them, and eventually, looting art collections and museums in occupied territories and then hiding them until the war ended. They had started this by 'pirating' some of these artworks from various art museums back in 1936 and went into full-blown art confiscation after the invasion of Poland in September 1939. Pope Pius suspected Hitler of his art theft intentions and was convinced by Mussolini that those valuable art pieces would be safer at the Uffizi in Florence, where the Black Shirt Army was headquartered at the time," Veronica patiently explained.

I felt like I was one of her 'all too interested' art students after listening to her art history lesson. As one of her diligent students, I thought about sending her a shiny red apple.

"But the opposite happened. Correct?"

"Correct," Veronica said. "Those forty-two paintings were traded in November 1943 for one hundred and three Jewish refugees that were hiding in one of the churches in Florence at the time. The Cardinal of Florence, Cardinal Della Croce, thought he was saving them from persecution and figured Rome's Vatican Museum wouldn't miss them when he traded them off. He believed that he was saving their lives in return for those paintings. Himmler promised him that those poor Jewish families would be sent to Switzerland until after the war. They were instead sent over to the death camps of Auschwitz and eventually killed."

"So, the Nazi's got the paintings and the Jewish refugees too. Correct?"

"Yes. They even killed the church's pastor for hiding those Jews in Florence," Giancarlo described.

"Unreal. So now...the Vatican wants these paintings back since being rediscovered in Munich last summer."

"Yep. And the Pope Emeritus has the paperwork and documentation stating that these forty-two paintings rightfully belong to the Vatican Museum. But the Mayor of Munich didn't quite see it that way, and somehow, that cost him his life."

"Wow," I managed to say. "But who would have 'aced' the Mayor of Munich for trading away those paintings? Does the Vatican have a 'hit squad' of killers walking around?" I inquired. "It just doesn't make any sense. Who else would be interested in these paintings?"

"That's a good question. According to my sources, the Uffizi Museum and its board have made it their mission to reacquire those stolen paintings discovered in Munich. There has been a public relations war going on between the Vatican and the Uffizi as to who owns the paintings. In the meantime, those forty-two paintings have disappeared again, and no one seems to know where they are now or who has them."

I thought about what she was explaining, and how this tug-of-war between the Vatican and the Uffizi related to Don Carlo Marchese being found dead at the Blackstone three weeks ago. I wanted to know more information regarding the Pope Emeritus Honorius V, the chairman of the Uffizi Gallery, Rodolfo Giammarco, and how Wolfgang Schmidt was involved in all of this. Being that Schmidt wasn't talking, and the location of these paintings still being missing, I suddenly had an idea.

"Veronica, you said you had connections at the Uffizi Gallery in Florence. Correct?"

"Yes."

"Hmmm. How do you feel about taking a field trip to Italy? Maybe we need to start talking to your connections in Florence?"

I started turning the idea over in my head. The more I thought about it, the more I liked it. I just needed to get my Chief on board with it.

"How's your Italian?" I asked Veronica, knowing it was a stupid question.

"Molto bene'," she laughed.

"Let me call you back," as I abruptly ended the phone call.

At that moment, I quickly walked back into Mike Daudelin's office and tried to interrupt him while he was on the phone call. No sooner did he hang up the telephone that I bombarded him with my travel plans.

"We're going to Italy," I loudly declared.

"What?"

"We're going to Italy," I said again. "We've followed as many leads in Chicago that we possibly can. We need to go to Florence to pursue these investigative clues further," I explained, summarizing the Vatican and Uffizi connection to these missing paintings to Daudelin, who was still looking at me like I had three eyes.

347

"So, you think you're going to get these people to start talking about where these paintings might be? Aren't you stretching this a little too far?"

"No, Chief. Someone 'aced' the Mayor of Munich for a good reason. Going over there and getting some 'face time' with these people might turn up some leads on these missing paintings and how all of this relates to the Marchese murder."

Daudelin sat there for a few long moments, fidgeting with his fancy ballpoint pen, the one where the illumination light inside turns on and off.

"Okay, Paulie. I'll cut you loose so you can take your little field trip to Italy with your art curator pally," he finally acquiesced. "But I want a full-blown story out of both of you, ready for print when you get back. You've got a week."

I was smiling from ear to ear.

"I hope you're not doing this to escape the Chicago cold. It's not very warm in Italy right now, you know," he reminded me.

"Any place is better than here. Thanks, Chief," as I quickly began to leave his office to call back my investigating partner.

"By the way, Paulie, like I said before...keep it professional," he yelled out loudly as I was closing his office door behind me. I was so happy to book these travel plans that I had not heard a single word he had just said.

I sat back at my desk and speed-dialed her number from my iPhone.

"Andiamo," I said as Veronica happily answered the phone. "We're going to Italy. Pack your 'bagagli.'" I said, using my very limited Italian.

"Sono pronta," she laughed, letting me know that she was more than ready.

I was now in the process of pursuing these investigative leads firsthand, and I knew that going to Florence to hunt them down was the only means of getting my arms around this story. With Veronica's help and her 'art world' connections, I was confident that we could make some progress on this Marchese homicide story. Besides, I could not think of a better person I would want to travel to Italy with than my newly appointed news story partner. I couldn't have been more excited.

As I started pursuing the travel applications on my computer, I looked at the temperature outside that was posted on the lower right-hand corner of my desktop: Minus 22 degrees. Real feel: Minus 40 degrees below zero with the windchill.

I smiled to myself as I looked up the airfare prices and ticket availability. I couldn't wait to book these airline tickets and fly out of O'Hare Airport as soon as possible. I spent the rest of the day making the travel and hotel arrangements to Florence, calling Veronica periodically to verify her available dates and times. I couldn't wait to fly out of this cold weather and into Italy to continue investigating this stolen Uffizi Painting Scandal.

It was now 'Arrivederci Chicago.'

CHAPTER THIRTY-NINE

The bumps on the brick-paved road were uncomfortable on that humid August day in Italy, as Stefano drove his white BMW convertible up the long, winding driveway lined with cypress trees. The old, ancient convent was a large, brown stoned building with red clay tiles and antiquated stones that reflected its twelfth-century architecture, sitting at the bottom of a foothill. The convent looked very small from a distance, reflecting the sun from the vast, surrounding vineyard. The holy order of devoted sisters in this ancient convent operated an old granary, in which they baked and sold their bread, along with a small winery with its infinite rows of neatly gardened grapevines.

Upon the wrought ironed gate into the entranceway, the words 'Ave Maria' was carved onto the black iron steel that arched over the entrance. Alongside the door, there was a small, white marble sign engraved into the right, stoned column, saying only 'Convento di San Francesco.'

The convent of this holy order of religious sisters was located approximately twenty kilometers outside of Assisi, amid Umbria's rolling hills and vast domains of wheat fields and ancient rows of grapevines. The vast ninety acres of land has been cultivated and sowed by the Cloistered Sisters of St. Francis for centuries, since the days of Saint Clare, its founder.

As he drove his sports car closer towards the renaissance style convent, the antique structure began to appear larger than life, the way he remembered it as a little boy. Stefano had a special connection to this ancient, old convent, as his aunt was once affiliated with this religious order before passing away several years ago. He had visited the convent several times as a little boy along with his mother and was still in contact with Sister Annunciata, the convent's mother superior.

Iannucci's relationship with his religion was extremely complicated. He was baptized as a Roman Catholic and went to a local parochial school in Naples as a young boy. He fervently believed in the Holy Spirit and its afterlife but chose not to associate its Christian values and commandments to the dreadful, murderous activities of his chosen profession.

He still wore an 18-karat gold crucifix, which was given to him by his aunt as a little boy, and irregularly attended Sunday mass. Stefano lived his life as a paradox of sorts. What he did for a living was strictly business, and according to him, had no relationship to his Christian beliefs. Although Stefano was exceptionally ruthless, he was also religious.

As he parked his white sports car in front of the convent, Stefano put his black sports coat on, which he had folded in the back seat of his car. He was well dressed that day, wearing a sports coat and button-down shirt, which matched his casual slacks and expensive black shoes. The loud noises of the water from the splashing, historical fountain of the old convent was deafening, as the well-dressed contractor approached the front entrance. He rapped the brass door knocker several times on the old wooden door when a small-statured nun abruptly answered.

"Chi sei', per favore?" the older nun inquired, dressed in black and white religious vestments.

"Sono Stefano Iannucci, per visitare Suora Annunciata," he responded.

She kindly asked Stefano to wait by the atrium garden entrance, which faced the beautiful courtyard with its lovely manicured red rose bushes and white blossomed trees. There was a tall statue of Saint Clare overlooking the garden entrance, with several kneelers surrounding the adorned religious structure.

After several long minutes, Sister Annunciata finally appeared. She was wearing black and white ecclesiastical vestments typical of her holy order, and several black rosaries were dangling from the white ropes of her divine uniform.

"Buon Giorno, Stefano," she greeted the handsome assassin, as he bowed to kiss her right hand after giving her a warm hug.

Sister Annunciata was an older nun in her late seventies, who had been with the religious order of the Cloistered Sisters of St. Francis her whole life. She entered the convent at the age of fifteen, along with his aunt, Sister Rosaria, with whom she was extremely close. She remembered Sister Rosaria bringing along her sweet young nephew to several holy masses and religious feast celebrations within the convent many times. Although she was well aware of his dark, covert activities as a prominent 'contractor,' she had always hoped that he would give up his 'murder-for-hire' activities and fully embrace the complete edicts of his Catholic faith. Since the passing of Sister Rosaria several years ago, the Mother Superior assumed the role of Stefano's surrogate relative, as she continuously prayed for the salvation of his soul while willfully accepting his very generous donations.

"How are you, dear Suora," Stefano asked.

"My arthritis had been acting up, along with my back pains," she complained. Her aches and bodily pain probably had much to do with the many years of harvesting the wheat and grapes of their religious convent estate, along with the other sisters.

"I was hoping you would come to visit us soon, as we are very grateful for your donations," she thankfully said to her adopted nephew, acknowledging the one-thousand-euro donation he had made to the sisters in cash last Christmas.

"It is always my pleasure, Suora," he replied as he followed her down the dark hallway into her small, remote office facing the beautiful atrium garden outside of her window. As they both sat down at her office, they made small talk about his family and especially, his old mother in Acerra, whom he still financially supported.

"You do know how much we all pray for you, Stefano. We hope that you may fully embrace our dear Lord's Commandments someday, and abandon your sinful lifestyle," she lectured. Although she was very much against the methods of his immoral, contractual obligations, her holy order, like so many others, enjoyed the generous fruits of his labors.

"Someday, Suora...someday," he dutifully replied. They both sat there quietly and uncomfortably in silence. Mother Superior then inquired about the purpose of his visit.

"I have a special favor to ask, Suora," Stefano began, as he was in dire need of the personal services of Sister Annunciata's convent. "I need to make a special deposit of sorts."

"A deposit?"

"Yes, Suora. I need to place three large containers, valuable wooden crates with unique contents that need to be discretely hidden away from the authorities," he tried to explain.

"Stefano, I hope you understand that we do not wish to participate in your criminal endeavors," she sternly answered.

"Sister Annunciata, please let me explain. These contents are the rediscovered Uffizi paintings that were stolen by the Nazis during the war. They were rediscovered in Munich a few months ago, and I am in the process of delivering these paintings back to the Pope Emeritus and the Vatican Museum," Stefano elaborated.

The Mother Superior looked at Stefano bewildered, not understanding the total circumstances of what and how these priceless Uffizi masterpieces were related to the Vatican. Iannucci then explained to Sister Annunziata the situation and history of those forty-two paintings, and how he was hired to find and return them to Pope Honorius and Rome.

"I'm sorry, Stefano. We do not wish to participate," she firmly said again.

At that moment, Stefano reached into his black suitcoat pocket and withdrew a large white envelope. He then placed it on her somewhat disheveled desk.

"Suora, you know I am always appreciative of any holy masses that you and the other sisters may offer on behalf of my beloved aunt, Sister Rosaria," he requested.

Sister Annunciata opened the envelope, which enclosed a tightly wrapped stack of one-hundred-dollar bills, all in new, unmarked American currency.

"Would five thousand dollars be sufficient?"

The Mother Superior smiled at her surrogate nephew.

"My dear Stefano, you are relentless," as she quickly grabbed the opened white envelope of currency and placed it in her bottom drawer.

"We will pray again for your beloved Zia Rosaria," she gleamed.

Stefano smiled as he began to recite the details of his unique delivery.

"I would like to have the crates delivered and stored in the warehouse behind the granary in the back of the estate where the wine is stored. We will need to cover the crates with bales of hay and other objects so that their location here will be well hidden and discreet."

The Mother Superior nodded her head, silently agreeing to Iannucci's unusual request. He finished giving her the remaining details of this transaction, letting her know of the date and time that he anticipated their delivery. They then both rose from her desk, as Stefano hugged and kissed his surrogate aunt. He then left her office and found his way out of the convent.

Within twenty-four hours, a large, unmarked black truck with the three wooden crates containing the Uffizi paintings came directly from Bolzano, Italy. It arrived at the remotely located convent within the green, roving hills of Umbria early that morning, with Stefano supervising its delivery. Two men with an onboard forklift unloaded the three wooden crates, which still had the word "FIRENZE" and the Nazi swastika stamped on the sides of each container.

Stefano assisted the delivery men in hiding the three gigantic wooden crates, placing several bales of hay around all sides of the stacked boxes in the back of the warehouse, where the large barrels of stored wine was fermenting from the last grape harvest. He then paid the delivery drivers and left strict instructions to Sister

Annunciata that no one was allowed near the secluded area where the three Uffizi crates were hidden. The secluded warehouse was then locked, with only the Mother Superior and Iannucci having the key. Stefano then quietly drove away, returning to his apartment in Naples.

A black Mercedes sedan was parked several hundred yards away from the entrance of the Cloistered Sisters of the Convent of St. Francis. The car had been sitting there for a few hours after following the unmarked semi-truck transporting the three Uffizi crates from Bolzano, Italy, to the isolated convent in the hills of Umbria. A man patiently sitting in the sedan watched the sizeable black truck unload its contents and, eventually, leave the cobblestoned entrance.

He then picked up his cell phone and dialed his boss's telephone number.

CHAPTER FORTY

My body was full of adrenaline as we landed at the Amerigo Vespucci Airport in Florence on that cloudy Thursday morning. The short, turbulent flight from Rome on that small jetliner was enough to make anyone's heart rate beat out of control. My left arm was severely bruised as we disembarked the airplane, the result of Veronica's fingernails digging deep into my forearm during that bumpy flight. I was wondering if she had permanently left a lifetime scar for me to remember her by.

"I'm sorry about your arm," she apologized. "I get very nervous about bumpy airplane rides."

"This is why one's alcohol level should never be below the legal limit when flying Alitalia Airlines," I observed, as our originating flight from Chicago to Rome was just as rough and as jarring as our connecting flight to Florence.

"I don't know about you, but I think I need an alcoholic beverage," she said, as we acquired our luggage from the airport baggage carousel and walked outside of the terminal to hail a taxicab. The weather in Florence on that mid-January day was comfortable, as the outdoor temperature was almost fifty degrees.

"This sure beats Chicago," I said out loud, knowing that the frigid climate there was still below ten degrees.

We took a taxicab to our five-star hotel, the Grand Hotel Baglioni, located on the Piazza Della Unita Italiana in the central part of Florence. The hotel was located in Florence's Duomo neighborhood, a walkable distance away from the shopping districts. The city's natural beauty could be easily enjoyed by our hotel, near the

Boboli Gardens and the Piazzale Michelangelo. The Santa Maria Novella Basilica and the Uffizi Museum and Galleries are located centrally within the other cultural attractions near our hotel as well.

We checked into our rooms, each of us having our suites adjacent from each other down the hall on the fifth floor. The famous hotel was quite old-fashioned but very luxurious on the main piazza of Florence's central city. The views from our hotel room were incredible, as the 'Il Duomo' and Florence's bell tower were a short distance away. We agreed to go upstairs, to freshen up and get comfortable in our suites, then meet at the hotel bar downstairs within the next hour. Being that it was already three o'clock in Italian time, I was hoping we could get into the Uffizi Museum and interview her curator friend before it got too late.

I had changed and was sitting at the spacious, oak-laden bar, drinking my usual Crown Royal on the rocks when Veronica came downstairs.

"Ciao, Paolo," she exclaimed, giving a gentle, wet kiss on the cheek. That was the first time that she had called me anything other than my last name, as she sat down at the bar next to me. Veronica was dressed in a very tight pair of blue dress jeans and a red blouse, which was unbuttoned halfway, strategically exposing just the right amount of cleavage. Her long black, curly hair, which she usually wore in a bun, was flowing nicely across her shoulders, as her distinctive, Creed Acqua Fiorentina fragrance was beginning to sensuously take over the room.

"Are you starting to feel any jetlag?" she asked, as I ordered her a Grey Goose vodka and cranberry.

"Not yet," I replied, noting that it was only eight o'clock in the morning back in Chicago.

I had changed into a casual pair of blue jeans, a white, untucked, button-down shirt, and a black V-neck sweater. I was still feeling the pain of her fingernails on my left forearm, as the black and blue marks from her jet flight nervousness were still quite evident. She asked me to roll up my sleeve, then grasped my left arm and started gently rubbing it, hoping that her soft, magic touch would make the bruises go away.

"I am so, so sorry, Paul. Why didn't you tell me that I was hurting you?" she said after we had both gotten our afternoon drinks, toasting to our safe arrival.

"I was enjoying it. The pain from your death grip was keeping my mind away from the possibility of not surviving our flight to Rome," I diplomatically replied.

We had enjoyed some lengthy discussions on our airline flight from Chicago that day, and we were beginning to get to know each other better. Her parents had immigrated to Chicago from the Tuscany region of Italy before she was born. She was the oldest of three children, growing up with two younger sisters in the Bridgeport neighborhood near 33rd Street and Cominsky Park. She went to grade school at Our Lady of Nativity, and then to the prestigious St. Ignatius High School, where she graduated with high honors. She went on to the University of Michigan, graduating magna cum laude and got a job immediately after getting her master's degree with the Art Institute of Chicago.

Veronica had just celebrated her 45th birthday over the holidays, but she looked at least ten years younger than her age. She was divorced and told me about her very brief marriage twenty years ago to a man she had met while in college. Veronica elaborated on how her cheating husband, who was a Merrill Lynch stockbroker in downtown Chicago, had made time for every other woman on LaSalle Street except for her during their brief marriage. Veronica confided that she had not done a whole lot of dating since her divorce. She explained that she had little time or patience for relationships, especially those with the opposite sex. She had no children and didn't waste a lot of time 'standing in front of the mirror anymore, watching her biological clock tick away.'

"Aren't you lonely?" I inquisitively asked.

"No…not really. I have a few close friends that I get together with now and again. I'm sort of a hermit," she tried to say. "I don't go out very much, other than to visit with my parents and sisters in Bridgeport."

"Well, …you certainly don't look like a hermit."

She was still giggling over that 'Chicago Man-Hater's Club' comment I had made to her during our first tumultuous encounter several days ago at her office. She thought that the way I had stood up to her on that day was admirable, as she had never had that same experience with other men. She didn't directly say it, but I could tell that she wasn't used to being put in her place, which may have looked rather attractive for someone like myself.

"You know, Crawford…I seemed to have been the only one doing most of the talking on our flight over here. You haven't said much about yourself."

I only smiled, realizing that perhaps my resume was nowhere near as impressive as hers.

"What would you like to know?"

"How is it that you managed to stay single all these years? You're a handsome, very successful man. Why isn't there a beautiful woman in your life?" she inquired.

I took a long sip of my Crown Royal and smiled, thinking about the best explanation that I could give her without sounding like a 'mama's boy.'

"I do have a beautiful woman. It's my mother."

Veronica raised her eyebrows, not realizing that I was half-joking.

"I run too fast," I managed to say.

"Come on, Paul. Seriously. You're not playing fair here. I've told you so much about me, and I know so little about you," she observed, twirling the ice cubes in her drink after taking several sips.

"I spend a lot of time looking after my parents, who live alone in Park Ridge," I only explained, trying not to elaborate.

"You're lucky to have them still. How old are they?"

"Mom is 76, and Dad is going on 81."

"You must be very close to them," she observed.

"Of course."

She looked at me, her soft, alluring brown eyes were getting more significant, as I must have said something that appealed to her.

"There is an old Italian saying: Puoi sapere molto d'un uomo nel modo in cui si tratta sua mama," she said in flawless Italian.

I sat there for a few seconds, waiting for her translation.

"You can tell a lot about a man by the way he treats his mother," she complimented.

I only managed to say, 'thank you,' not wanting to elaborate on my parents or especially my relationship with my loving-but-very-overbearing Italian mother.

"So why aren't you married?" she asked.

"I was engaged once to a medical student when I was living in Boston. She broke off our engagement three months before our wedding date," I slowly explained.

"I'm sorry," she apologized. "You must have been devastated."

"I was...for a while. I realized later that she had done me a huge favor. I probably would still be living in Boston, a complete alcoholic, sitting at the bar of 'Cheers.' I would probably be shucking clamshells and living on clam chowder," I joked.

Veronica started laughing. "You would have made a great 'Sam Malone'."

"Probably. But to tell you the truth, I just couldn't imagine my life right now if I wasn't living in Chicago," I observed.

"Chicago is a beautiful city. Maybe you need to start being a better 'ace' reporter and start pushing these city politicians to get the crime rates down," she blurted while taking another sip of her drink.

"I'm doing my best. There is a lot of cleaning up that needs to be done at City Hall. Our next mayor will have his or her hands full."

"I agree."

A few moments of uncomfortable silence, as I twirled the ice cubes of my Crown Royal.

"So, Paul...tell me about her," as she moved closer and put her arm around mine. 'Was she beautiful? Was she smart?" she innocently asked, trying very hard to get personal.

I only looked at her, trying very hard to control the smirk on my face.

"Was she a sassy brunette, like me?" she flirted. I couldn't tell if it was her drink or her jet lag that was making her so damn seductive. There must have been a gleam in my eye when I nodded my head.

"Yes...as a matter of fact, she was a lot like you. I must have a weak spot for beautiful, brilliant, and very educated professional women," I observed.

She laughed and took another long swallow of her alcoholic beverage.

"I would say the man has good taste," smiling while referring to me in the third person. She then ordered another round of drinks for both of us.

"Just stay away from the Italian ones," she jokingly advised.

At that moment, a beautiful blonde with a black leather coat and long black boots entered the hotel bar and called out Veronica's name, as she stood up from her barstool to greet her. They excitedly started talking to each other in Italian, as they continued to hug and kiss each other on both cheeks.

Veronica then turned to introduce me. "This is my friend, Claudia Romanelli, the assistant curator at the Uffizi Museum, the one I was telling you about..." as I got up from my barstool and immediately tried to shake her hand. She instead approached me even closer and kissed me on both cheeks.

"This is Paul Crawford, my reporter colleague from the Chicago Sun-Times," she said, as we both made eye contact.

"Pleased to meet you. Veronica had told me a lot about you," I kindly said.

"Hopefully, she left out all of the bad stuff," she said in flawless English.

Claudia was a shapely, taller blonde, with bright, alluring blue eyes and an attractive smile. She could have easily won first place in any Scarlett Johansson look-a-like contest, as her infectious laugh and bubbly personality seemed addicting.

She sat down next to us at the bar and ordered a Negroni with a lime on the rocks, while Veronica and I were on our third drinks. By then, we were all starting to feel good while Veronica and Claudia were giggling, mixing up their English with Italian phrases that they thought that I didn't understand. With having an Italian mom, I had heard some of their provocative languages before, and I got the impression that they were gossiping about me in another language.

"English, please," I finally reprimanded the two of them, as they continued giggling like schoolgirls.

"I was just telling Veronica that you would make a wonderful boyfriend for her," she confessed while the two of them continued to laugh.

"Thanks," I blushed, "but it's not just up to me."

Veronica looked at me with those warm, alluring brown eyes, and I got the impression that she was starting to like the idea of the two of us as an item. They then continued talking and drinking while I was trying to keep up with their conversations.

"So, Claudia," working very hard to break up their sorority party, "what can you tell us about these missing Uffizi paintings?"

Claudia took another sip of her almost empty Negroni. "There seems to be a lot of people looking for them," she observed.

"As they should be. Those works of art are priceless," Veronica interjected.

"Especially Fra Lippi's painting," Claudia said.

"Do you mean that 'Demons' painting?" I said.

"The 'Demons of Divine Wrath'...yes. That painting alone is worth millions," Claudia reiterated. "The Vatican had been looking hard for that art collection and has hired outside investigators to travel the world to find them," the assistant Uffizi curator said.

"Our board chairman had been looking high and low for them too."

"Do you mean Rodolfo Giammarco?"

"Yes," Claudia said.

"Perhaps we can talk to him? Maybe he can give us some more clues as to what he knows and who has them."

Veronica suddenly looked at me with a distressed look on her face, as if I had said something wrong. Her demeanor had abruptly changed, and she suddenly made me feel very uncomfortable.

"Don Giammarco doesn't speak to the media," Veronica softly explained. Her voice for a second had the same sound and caliber as Marlon Brando, while Claudia nodded her head.

"Don Giammarco?" I said, realizing that his local community prominence went far beyond his Uffizi board chairmanship.

I decided not to push it at that moment. Whoever he was and however he was involved as far as these stolen Uffizi art paintings, it was probably best that I find out whatever I could on my own.

We continued to discuss the Uffizi paintings and our thoughts as to who may have them and where they might be. After some lengthy discussion, I convinced Claudia, too, at least, let us talk to one of the board members so that we had someone official in our investigation that we could use as a source in our story.

We then finished our drinks and talked about getting a bite to eat somewhere. I initially hoped I could have dinner with Veronica that evening. But she thought that it might be a good idea if she went out to eat with Claudia instead. She had said that they had 'some catching up to do.'

I graciously stepped aside, as I kissed both Veronica and Claudia farewell and allowed them to go out and have their time together. I decided to try to begin working on this story.

It was almost ten-clock at night, and I was starting to get very tired. I continued to doze off, trying to get a good Wi-Fi connection while attempting to type on my laptop. I was watching the Italian RAI UNO news program on TV with English sub-titles out of the corner of my eye.

I must have fallen asleep with my computer on my lap until I was abruptly awakened. I looked at the clock...it was 12:05 am.

There was a loud knock on my door.

CHAPTER FORTY-ONE

"I can't sleep."

"What?"

"I can't sleep. Can I come in?"

It was past midnight, and Veronica Giancarlo was standing in front of my hotel door, wearing a pair of black gym shorts and a long, white tee-shirt. She was holding a bottle of red wine and two wine glasses. I couldn't have imagined her looking so sexy as she stood in front of my door in the middle of the night.

"Of course," I eagerly said.

She was barefoot, and she eagerly walked into my room and sat on my bed, holding out what looked like an expensive bottle of red wine.

"Could you open this, my dear? Maybe this wonderful wine will help us both to sleep and overcome this damn jet lag."

"Where did you get the wine?" I ignorantly asked.

"I had room service bring it up from the bar. I had it charged to the Sun-Times, of course."

I started to laugh.

"Veronica? I will have to include all of our partying supplies on my expense report for my editor's review. Not sure he is going to like us having a great time on the paper's expense," I said, my tongue in cheek.

"Oh, Paolo, don't be such a party-pooper! We're on vacation!"

"No, Veronica...we are on assignment. We will need to have a full-blown story written for the paper before the end of the week."

I looked at the bottle of wine more closely while acquiring a cheap corkscrew located in the hotel room's bar drawer.

Toscana Soldera, 2009 it only said, with a very fancy black and gold label. It looked very expensive.

"Veronica?" I started to raise my voice.

"You can call me Ronnie if you like..."

"How much was this bottle of wine?"

"Three hundred euros...I think," as she was smiling, sitting upright on my bed with her legs crossed, still holding the empty wine glasses. She was eagerly waiting for me to fill them up.

I almost dropped the bottle on the floor when she told me the price of that wine. At that point, I don't think I ever had or tasted a three-hundred-euro bottle of wine in my life. She started to laugh as she was observing my shocked expression.

"Are you kidding?"

"Oh, come on, Paolo...we are on the verge of breaking the greatest mob story to hit Chicago since Al Capone and the St. Valentine's Day Massacre. The paper will appreciate the additional investment; trust me," she giggled as I very slowly and very carefully removed the cork from that priceless bottle of wine.

I poured the red contents into both of our wine glasses and made a halfhearted toast.

"Cheers," I sheepishly said. I was suddenly sensing how Adam must have probably felt at the Garden of Eden when Eve was giving him a bite of that forbidden apple.

"Here's to Al Capone," she giggled.

"You do mean Carlo Marchese?" I corrected her.

"What's the difference? You've seen one Chicago wise-guy, you've seen them all," she sarcastically replied, as Veronica took the first sip of that costly wine.

"Hmmm...not bad for three hundred euros," she replied, swirling the wine around in her mouth. I was trying very hard to stay focused on her beautiful brown eyes, and not to let my vision stray towards the other more vivacious parts of her body.

"Veronica...make me a promise," I requested.

"And what would that be?"

"Promise me that you will find me a job sweeping floors at the Art Institute of Chicago when the Sun-Times fires me after this trip."

Veronica started laughing.

"Oh, come on, Paulie! After we finish investigating and writing this news story, every newspaper in the country will be clamoring for the reporting services of the great investigative reporter Paul Crawford," she replied, as she moved closer to me. We both sat there, drinking our wine and watching the RAI UNO news channel, still on the television with its English subtitles. I felt very awkward, as I didn't know what else to say or talk about at that particular moment.

"Where was that 5K Race?" I asked, noticing that her long white tee-shirt was from a local Chicago 5K race benefiting Multiple Sclerosis.

"Lincoln Park...I run this race every year, benefiting MS," she said.

"Really? Right in my back yard," I said. "Where does the race start?"

"Right on West Fullerton near the Lincoln Park Conservatory. Where do you live?" she asked.

"Wrightwood and Southport, near DePaul University."

"Do you run a lot of 5K races," I asked, remembering that she mentioned that she was an active runner along the lakefront during the summer months.

"Only the ones where I think I can win my age group in," she jokingly said.

"Does that happen often?"

"Usually. I ran track and field in high school. When I can run a 5K race under twenty minutes, I'm doing pretty good, and usually can snag a medal or two," Veronica modestly said, trying hard not to brag.

"That's about a six-minute mile, correct?"

"On my best days, yes...it is."

I could tell she was the competitive type, and that she enjoyed beating up her men, both on and off the track.

"How about you, Paul? Do you work out? You look pretty fit and trim."

She wasn't noticing my ever-growing waistline. Since I stopped running a few years ago, my weight was starting to exceed the limits of my five-foot, eleven-inch, moderately stocky frame.

"I used to run years ago until my back and knees started telling to do otherwise. I try to get to the gym three times a week if I can. It depends on how busy I am at work."

She looked at me, waiting for me to elaborate.

"Weights? Cardio? Spinning classes? Hot yoga? What do you do to stay in shape?"

"Cardio, mostly. I bike ride along the lakefront in the summertime and take spinning classes twice a week in the winter, whenever I can," I mentioned.

"Staying in shape is a full-time job," I interjected, as Veronica nodded her head.

"I couldn't agree with you more."

More moments of silence, as we were awkwardly drinking our glasses of that delicious but terribly expensive red wine, compliments of the Chicago Sun-Times.

"How was your dinner with Claudia?" I neglected to ask.

"It was good. We were just exchanging girl-talk. She is having boyfriend problems and is on the verge of breaking up with him."

"Really? Why?" I asked, trying to keep the spirit of the conversation going.

"Too much of a Mama's Boy. Claudia has never been married, and she is looking to tie the knot. She wants to have children and start a family."

"What were your thoughts on that?" I asked.

"I told her that marriage wasn't all that it's cracked up to be," she bluntly replied.

I laughed to myself after she made that statement. I figured that Veronica Giancarlo, a card-carrying, exclusive member of the Chicago Man-Haters Club, would predictably make such a blank, general statement.

"Besides," she mentioned, "Claudia has met someone else through the art gallery that she is interested in seeing. Some handsome, rich guy from Naples named Stefano."

"Stefano?"

"Yes. She told me a little bit about him. She said he pulled up to the Uffizi Galleries last week in a white BMW Sports Car convertible, requesting a tour of the Renaissance art gallery displays. He apparently asked for her number, and he's been calling and texting her ever since."

"Really?"

"Yes, he's asked her out a few times," Veronica mentioned.

A few more moments of silence passed.

"He also mentioned to her that he was very interested in the history of the Uffizi art collection that was discovered in Munich last summer. She thought that he was using that as an excuse to take her out for dinner."

"Interesting," I managed to say, still enjoying our costly glass of wine.

"Don't you think that is unusual? Who was he, and why would he be asking questions about the Uffizi art collection?" I eagerly asked.

"I don't know," Veronica answered. "The art collection discovery in Munich has been in all of the papers. Claudia thinks that he's just a wealthy art collector."

I thought about it for a few moments. I was beginning to wonder how so many art collectors, investors, museum curators, and art dealers were looking for these rediscovered paintings.

"In any case, it looks like her and the 'Mama's Boy' are done."

I laughed, "It certainly sucks to be a Mama's Boy!" I sarcastically exclaimed.

Veronica suddenly came closer and kissed me on the cheek and then whispered very sensuously into my ear.

"Are you a Mama's Boy?" she asked. She began kissing my ear several times while juggling her empty glass of wine.I was trying to momentarily resist her advances, if for no other reason than to be a gentleman and not to take advantage of her. She was sitting on my bed, only wearing a tee-shirt and a pair of shorts. That line of thinking lasted for about five seconds. No sooner did we both put our wine glasses on the floor that Veronica began kissing the corner of my mouth and planting long, wet kisses on my neck. I felt almost embarrassed, staring at the television set with RAI UNO blaring in the Italian language that I did not understand.

"Should I shut off the TV?" I casually mentioned not wanting the kisses to stop.
"I don't care," she whispered in my ear, "I've wanted to kiss you all day, especially when we were sitting on that airplane, while you were bravely allowing me to grab onto you with all of that turbulence."
"Really?"

"Yes. I was so scared, and you were so brave. You weren't afraid at all," she complimented, planting more kisses on my neck and now unbuttoning my shirt.

She was kissing my chest, caressing my gold crucifix, and planting more kisses along my neck. I couldn't control my sexual urges any longer and began to grasp her white tee-shirt and pull it over her head. She then took off her black gym shorts, exposing her black, sheer Victoria Secret bra and matching black thong panties.

I reached over to shut off the light and offered to shut the television off, but for some reason, she still wanted it on. She began to attack me with a barrage of wet, moist, delicious kisses. Her lips still tasted like cherries, as the aroma of her perfume began to hypnotize me, feeling the sweat running down the middle of my back.

She started unzipping my pants and pulled them off, as I was laying in the dark in my underwear, watching her silhouette continue to kiss every part of my body with the light of the television in the background. She was planting wet, passionate kisses up and along my shoulders and stomach. She started holding my gold crucifix, placing more kisses along my shoulders. She then unbuttoned her bra and began pressing her incredible, well-endowed breasts up against my chest. From what I could briefly notice, her dark tan lines stopped where her amazing breasts started. She had rosy, large red nipples, that complimented her size 36 DD breasts very nicely. They were absolutely gorgeous.

I finished taking off her thong panties and began strategically placing my wet kisses up and down her tight, six-pack abdomen and her belly. I then began pressing my mouth against her rosy large nipples and breasts. We both began groaning with excitement as we pulled down the bed comforter and bedsheets and positioned our naked bodies, crunching up against one another as we continued to kiss each other's body. Her warm body felt amazing next to mine, as I continued to place love bites along every part of her shapely, well-toned body.

We continued our lovemaking for what seemed to be hours and hours until our bodies were ravaged with exhaustion that evening. I remember thinking to myself, what a dream come true, to be making incredible love to the most beautiful, most alluring woman on Michigan Avenue here in beautiful Florence, Italy. I could feel her sleeping, as her head, with her dark, flowing hair, was resting up against my chest. We were both falling in and out of romantic consciousness. I was trying very hard to keep my feelings and my thoughts to myself.

We held each other close, staring at the window with the most beautiful view of Florence's famous Il Duomo. I was listening to the bustling morning traffic slowly getting louder with the rising of the early morning sun. I couldn't remember the last time I had felt so emotionally satisfied. It was as though a peaceful feeling had transformed my soul, and it felt amazing.

We were both sound asleep when her cellular phone started ringing. She must have had it in her gym shorts pocket. I looked over at the clock next to the bed.

It was 5:45 am.

She reached over to get her cell phone and then excused herself. Still naked, she walked into the bathroom to take her call, with the door closed and locked.

As she was speaking Italian, the only phase that I initially understood was when she answered her cellphone before closing the bathroom door:

"Buon Giorno Zio..."

CHAPTER FORTY-TWO

John Males, the executive chairman of the Detroit Institute of Art, was nervously pacing his Woodward Avenue office on that autumn day. He was just informed by the armored car company that the priceless masterpiece, 'Demons of Divine Wrath,' had just arrived at Detroit's Metropolitan Airport on JAP Freight Airlines' two-thirty flight that afternoon. The armed security guards were on standby, waiting for the cargo plan to unload this priceless painting and, after going through all the customs 'red-tape', would be transported by two armored cars, and also escorted by several unmarked Detroit Police squad units. The reason for the two armored vehicles, according to the plan, would be to provide one armored car as a 'decoy' in case someone tried to stop and rob the armored car conveying the famous painting.

This financial transaction and the logistics in acquiring this priceless painting from Italy had become nothing less than a nightmare for the art museum executive. After their meeting between Don Licovoli, his attorney Peter Cataldi, and Don Carlo Marchese at Sogni Per Tutti last August in Corktown, what was supposed to be a simple cash transaction has turned out to be nothing short of a complete, total nightmare. Males, thinking he would have no trouble convincing his board to pay the two-million-dollar price tag, had to intensely lobby several board members to cough up a large portion of the funding. When Males was still a half-million dollars short, he then had to approach the Comerica Bank chairman, Mr. Thomas Rodgers, for his help. He convinced the bank executive to begrudgingly make a 'short-term' loan to the art museum to cover the remaining costs of this painting acquisition. Males even had to personally guarantee the loan with his own collateral, hoping that the additional revenues that could be generated by Detroit's most famous museum would be able to cover the new painting's acquisition costs.

Since the utmost discretion had to be exercised as part of this painting deal, he also had a difficult time keeping this art purchase 'under wraps' and away from the media. When the Detroit Free Press somehow got wind of the arrival of Fra Lippi's most famous painting, John Males had to deny the rumor and 'play dumb.' The art director had to make sure that no one, other than a select few, knew of the painting's arrival until after the deal had been finally completed and famous Florentine painting had safely arrived at the Detroit Institute of Arts.

To make matters even worse, Males was frequently updated on the Mafia-Vatican wars that were going on in both Italy and Germany to acquire that elusive Uffizi art collection. He knew about the Giammarco Family's intense desire to acquire back those rediscovered paintings, and the 'tug-of-war' fiasco that was going on between the Vatican Museum and the Uffizi Galleries. He had also heard about some of the casualties that both the Marchese's and the Giammarco's had suffered over this priceless art collection. John Males realized early on that spilled blood was very much a part of the price tag of this famous masterpiece. By this point in time, he was now extremely sorry he had ever gotten involved in this art deal.

But Males also knew of the public relations potential in permanently acquiring Fra Lippi's most famous, most elusive painting masterpiece from

Florence. This painting has always been one of the art world's most treasured, most unique art masterpieces. Since the death of Fra Lippi's artist son, Filipino, and the discovery of this cherished painting in Padua in the sixteenth century, many art collectors and cultural institutions have tried to acquire this valuable painting for their collection.

When it became known that this Vatican acquisition had been consigned to the Uffizi Gallery in 1938, then subsequently stolen by the Nazi's, the cultural art world has been waiting decades for this rare Renaissance masterpiece to resurface. To have this Fra Lippi painting in Detroit's art museum, would be a significant accomplishment for not only Males but the upper echelon of the Motor City's elite class of art lovers as well. The cultural high class of Detroit's most prominent residents would have something significant to celebrate, and John Males would be their artistic icon.

Males's cell phone rang on his desk, as the art executive rushed to answer it.

"Hello?"

"Mr. Males, we just acquired the painting from U.S. Customs, and we have it now loaded on one of our armored trucks. We will be leaving Metro Airport shortly," said Lieutenant Michael Butz. He was a veteran police officer of the Detroit Police Department and was in charge of the safe transportation of the valuable masterpiece.

"Splendid," Males excitedly exclaimed.

He knew the caravan of security patrol cars and armored trucks would take no less than thirty minutes from Metropolitan Airport to the Detroit Institute of Art on Woodward Avenue downtown.

378

He then made a phone call.

"It's on its way," Males said to the party on the other line.

———————————

Don Carlo Marchese and Don Pellegrino Licovoli were having a late afternoon 'cinetta' together at the Bella Giornata Ristorante on Gratiot Avenue on the east side of Detroit. Marchese and his associate had just arrived from Detroit's Metropolitan Airport, and they all insisted on meeting first before going over to the art museum.

They had gotten together for two reasons: To witness the arrival of Fra Lippi's 'Demons of Divine Wrath' painting to the Detroit Institute of Arts and to, most importantly, receive the balance of the sale proceeds due to John Males and the art museum's directors.

One hundred-thousand-dollar deposit had been given to Don Carlo almost a month ago, and after a series of snags and issues in Marchese acquiring the painting, this critical, red-letter day for the art museum was also a big payday for Marchese and Licovoli Families.

The two mob bosses had arranged to split the two-million-dollar proceeds, and both of them were already making toasts to their highly anticipated, 'major art score.'

"Salute," Don Marchese said as he solemnly held up his glass.

"Salute," Don Licovoli replied, as he was hanging up his cell phone. He had just received word from John Males that the Fra Lippi painting had just arrived from the airport and was on its way to the art museum. Everyone at the table held up their wine glasses.

Attorney Peter Cataldi and Caesar Giordano, the Licovoli family consigliere, and Frank Mercurio were sitting with them, enjoying their Chicken Cacciatore, Linguini, and Zuppa di Mare entrées. There had been a tremendous amount of work put into the acquisition of this priceless painting from Munich and Egenhofen, Germany, to Bolzano and Milan, Italy, to finally, the Detroit Institute of Art.

Don Carlo Marchese was very quiet that afternoon. He was very reflective and remorseful, not saying much during their conversation. He was still grieving the loss of his nephew and his sister's only son, Marco. The Chicago Capo was feeling responsible for his nephew's reckless behavior and his tragic, brutal death in Rome.

Don Rodolfo Giammarco, his nemesis, who is also searching for the Uffizi art collection, had also experienced bloodshed. His family suffered the deaths of his nephew and family heir apparent, Mariano, and their long-time street captain, Vito D'Amore. At this moment in time, neither family knew where the other forty-one paintings were.

And of course, Don Carlo, through communications with his cousin, had received word that the Pope Emeritus, had hired a 'professional' to search and find those outstanding Uffizi paintings. Papa Onorio made no mistake in collaborating to those around him that Chicago's Don Carlo Marchese had betrayed him and that the person whom he had hired would stop at nothing to acquire those paintings, and 'seek revenge' in correcting this 'papal embarrassment.'

When Marchese asked Monsignor Iacobelli who this 'professional' was, he only gave him the answer of 'you know who he is' and only referred to him as a 'contractor.'

Don Carlo immediately realized who this contractor could be. He knew that the internationally renowned 'contractor' Stefano Iannucci was the most ruthless and the most callous of all professional killers. Marchese knew that he would stop at nothing to fulfill his contractual obligations, especially to the Pope Emeritus.

"Gianpaolo, you do realize that your Pope Emeritus is completely out of control. You do know this, correct?" Marchese said to his cousin last night over the phone.

"Yes, for a man of his holy stature to enlist the services of a 'professional contractor' for the sole purpose of restoring his abysmal papal reputation is deplorable," Iacobelli agreed.

"Well, Cugino, we have talked about this before. You must do whatever it is you need to do," Don Marchese strongly advised his cousin.

"I believe," Marchese continued, "that your Papa Onorio is no longer a man of God."

"Yes...I believe you are correct," Iacobelli replied. "I pray that God's *divine wrath* will finally find its way to this reckless Pope."

As the afternoon 'cinetta' was concluding, Don Licovoli insisted, as their gracious host, in settling their lunch tab when the waitress brought over the bill. He pulled out several one-hundred-dollar bills and placed it into the billfold.

The five men then left the restaurant on that sunny, September day and climbed into the waiting black, Cadillac limousine. They entered the I-696 expressway and headed directly over to Woodward Avenue and the Detroit Institute of Art. This would be the beginning of a glorious celebration.

Or so they thought.

CHAPTER FORTY-THREE

A PAINTING ARRIVES

It was almost four o'clock in the afternoon, as Don Marchese, Don Licovoli, Peter Cataldi, Frank Mercurio, and Caesar Giordano were patiently waiting with John Males in the executive cafeteria of the art museum. The head of the security unit, Detroit Police Lieutenant Michael Butz, had made the phone call at 2:00 pm that afternoon, informing Males that they were on their way. What should have taken thirty minutes from Metropolitan Airport to transport that painting was taking over two hours, and the caravan of armored cars and security vehicles had still not arrived.

Males continued to look at his watch, pacing the lounge while Marchese and Licovoli were enjoying their third cup of espresso. Cataldi continued to call his legal office for his messages and was returning some phone calls while doing business on his laptop. Mercurio and Giordano were patiently sitting there at the table, making small talk while periodically dozing off from all of their 'cinetta' wine. The six of them were tolerantly waiting for word that the elusive masterpiece had finally arrived downstairs.

At 4:27 pm, John Males answered his cell phone.

"We've arrived, Mr. Males. We are all downstairs with both armored trucks. We are all here," Butz declared.

Males then smiled while excitingly announcing, "It's here...the painting is here."

The six of them casually got up and walked over to the elevator, taking it three floors down to the warehouse basement area of the museum. As they exited the elevator, the two armored trucks were both parked side by side, with six or more unmarked Crown Victoria Fords, black in color, parked around the two security vehicles.

Lieutenant Butz walked directly over to Males, and after introducing everyone, shook each gentleman's hand. They then walked over to the one armored vehicle that had transported the expensive masterpiece and watched the two security guards unload the wooden crate containing the painting and place it in the middle of the museum warehouse where everyone could see.

By that point, thirty or more museum employees had gathered in the basement of the museum warehouse to witness the arrival of this Fra Lippi masterpiece finally.

As the wooden crate was standing upright, Butz handed the crowbar over to John Males, asking him if he would like to do the honors in uncrating the nailed down boards of wood covering the painting.

"This is a great day for the Detroit Institute of Art," he announced as he started to pull off each wooden board with the crowbar. He pulled off several wooden boards, and two of the security guards assisted him in finally pulling out the old, valuable masterpiece, which had been covered with burlap, still displaying several of the Nazi symbols stamped on the wrapping.

Another employee gave Males a sharp cutting knife, and he carefully, cut off the burlap wrapping and pulled off the paper covering, finally disclosing the Fra Lippi masterpiece, for all to see.

There was suddenly, total silence as if the whole room gasped at once.

John Males dropped the knife on the floor and stood there frozen for about ten seconds, as the silence of the museum basement became deafening.

Finally, Don Licovoli loudly proclaimed,

"What the fuck is this?"

The unveiled painting, which was wrapped in burlap, was a painting of a colorful clown, wearing a yellow and red clown outfit, laughing and smiling from ear to ear, and holding up his *middle finger.*

It was serial. It was appalling. For about three whole minutes, everyone in the basement museum was in shock.

"Is this some kind of goddamn joke?" Peter Cataldi loudly yelled.

Don Carlo Marchese gave the dirtiest of looks to his family underboss. His eyes were fuming with anger. He looked as though he was ready to lunge at his family underboss and wrap his hands around his thick, fat, nineteen-and-a-half-inch neck.

"Boss, I swear to God, I personally packed and loaded that painting myself," Frank Mercurio nervously exclaimed.

It turned out that the Fra Lippi masterpiece, which was safely loaded by Frank Mercurio at Malpensa Airport in Milan and signed for and witnessed by the JAP Freight Company, *really did* arrive at Metropolitan Airport in Detroit. When the painting was ready to be unloaded for inspection by the U.S. Customs agents, two of those agents were Salvatore Giancarlo and Reno Mazzara. They were both longtime members of the Giammarco family in Florence and had flown to Detroit nine hours earlier to pull off this switch.

Disguised as U.S Customs Agents, they were able to pass through security through the terminal gates successfully. They then overcame and tied up two of the assigned federal agents before they approached the JAP Freight Jetliner. The two of them were able to board the airplane and switch the Fra Lippi masterpiece with the silly clown painting, which was specifically picked out by Don Giammarco himself. The decoy was stamped with fake swastika symbols to look like authentic burlap wrapping from the outside.

The two disguised federal customs agents then switched the painting on the freight airliner, with the decoy art piece stored in the adjacent motor cart nearby.

While the clown painting was unpacked off of the plane, Mazzara and Giancarlo unloaded the real art piece off the opposite cargo door on the plane's other side. The original masterpiece was then hidden into one of the airport motor carts and found its way to another armored truck waiting nearby. The 'Demons of Divine Wrath' was then immediately transported to Willow Run Airport in nearby Ypsilanti, Michigan, onto a small, private jetliner.

As the armored truck carrying the decoy painting was about to leave, Mazzara handed the armored truck driver an envelope with five-hundred dollars in cash.

"Take your time," he advised the driver, making sure that he took the longest, most traffic-filled, passage route to the museum. The truck driver stretched the half-hour motorcade into over two hours.

By the time the security caravan had arrived at Detroit's museum, the DC-8 jetliner had already taken off and, at that moment, was flying over the Atlantic Ocean.

After two hours in the air, Mazzara called Don Rodolfo Giammarco and proudly announced to his family boss: "Fra Lippi sta ritornando a Firenze."

Fra Lippi is on his way back to Florence.

CHAPTER FORTY-FOUR

It was a warm and balmy fifty-five degrees, the typical climate for the Tuscany region of Italy in January. I walked outside of the Hotel Baglioni for a moment with my morning espresso, enjoying the bright morning sun gleaming brightly into my eyes. It was sweater weather on that early morning, and I was wearing a red sweater over a button-down blue shirt with a pair of dress jeans, which appeared to be sufficient for that time of year.

After our night of intense lovemaking, Veronica was still sound asleep at 7:30 in the morning, so I decided to clean up, shower, and get dressed without waking her. She was probably exhausted. Between the jet lag, the bar beverages, the expensive bottle of wine along with the passionate sex last evening, our bodies, and our livers needed some rest. I left her a note, telling her I would be downstairs in the lobby with my laptop. I was eager for some coffee and some breakfast but decided I would hook up in the hall and set myself up to do get some work done.

I was writing the news story that I needed to finish and made outline notes of some additional information that I needed to acquire before I could continue the story. One of those 'bullet points' was to get some additional information on the Uffizi board of directors chairman, Rodolfo Giammarco. For some unknown reason, Giammarco was not very friendly with the press or the media, and I was curious as to why. I decided to hook up to the hotel Wi-Fi and 'Google' his name. There wasn't much said about him, other than he was the board chairman of the Uffizi Galleries of Florence, and he was the President of Artiste Vineyard and Winery here in Florence, located on the outskirts of the Tuscany Valley. I looked at some other online sources but found very little about him, other than his involvement with the museum and his winery business.

I needed another espresso doppio, so I walked over to the bar in the lobby and ordered another caffe'. Giovanni, the 'barista,' who knew some English, was making my coffee, and he seemed to enjoy making small talk about who I was and where I was from. Since there wasn't anyone else at the bar, I decided to pick his brain.

"So, Giovanni...how long have you lived in 'Firenze'?" I asked.

"Tutta la mia vita...my whole life," Giovanni replied.

"So, you probably know all the big shots who live here, right?"

"Big shots?" he asked, not knowing what I meant.

"You know...big shots...'spacconi,'" I said, remembering the Italian word my mother often used when describing someone who thought they were too big for their egos.

"Oh, si," he replied, while he was brewing my dark roast caffe'.

"Who is Rodolfo Giammarco?" I asked.

The barista's face completely changed, as if to verbally mention his name out loud in public was a cardinal sin. He only shook his head as if he refused to answer my inquiry.

I looked at him at first, not knowing why he refused to acknowledge my question.

"You don't know who he is?"

"No, Signore," he said while putting my white cup with my espresso doppio on the bar.

"Five Euros, Signore Crawford."

I pulled ten euros out of my pocket and gave it Giovanni, telling him to keep the change.

"Grazie, Giovanni."

"Prego, Signore," quickly taking my money from the top of the bar.

I stood there, trying to make eye contact with him, as I wasn't satisfied with his answer.

"Giovanni? Are you 'sicuro'? Are you sure you don't know who he is?"

He looked across the other side of the hotel lobby, making sure that no one else was paying attention to our conversation. Afterward, looking at me straight in the eye, he used his right pinky finger and made an imaginary scar gesture on his right cheek.

Giovanni then shook his head, letting me know by his eye contact that asking questions about Rodolfo Giammarco was not very acceptable, especially at the hotel. I stood there for a moment, holding my espresso caffe' and only said, "Grazie."

Judging from what I could tell, Rodolfo Giammarco was a Florentine gangster who had a tremendous amount of influence and power within the Tuscan region. I spent the next two hours trying to access copies of any local newspapers or documentation regarding any reference to Giammarco. I only then concluded that perhaps, his name and references were censored on the local internet and the Italian 'Google' search engines.

So, I decided to send an email, via my cell phone, to my editor, since it was only three-thirty in the morning Chicago time:

Chief...need information on a local businessman, Rodolfo Giammarco. Send me recent items and news briefs for my investigation. Have some leads. Thanks, *Crawford.*

At that moment, someone had snuck behind me and placed a well-planted kiss on my right ear.

"Good morning, Handsome," as I turned around and gave Veronica a coffee-flavored kiss on her left cheek.

"Good morning. How did you sleep?" as I looked at my watch. It was almost ten o'clock in the morning.

"I nodded right out. I must have been tired," as she sat down next to me on the black leather couch that I was sitting on in the lobby.

Other travelers were checking out of the luxurious hotel, and Veronica situated herself next to me. She made some endearing comments about how beautiful our intimate moments were last night and then inquired if I had a headache from all of the wine we consumed the previous evening.

We then walked over to the atrium restaurant, Ristorante Galileo, which was situated on the west side of the Hotel Baglioni. It was a large, spacious dining room enclosed under a glass roof, with grapevines and grape leaves adorning its exterior. The décor was extraordinarily bright and airy as if we were sitting in an outdoor garden with the Florentine churches and landmarks as its backdrop.

We both ordered Cappuccini and 'colazione,' which included eggs, salsiccia, and toasted panettone bread with strawberry 'marmalata.' We made small talk for almost an hour, getting to know each better when our breakfast entrées arrived.

"So...how did you sleep, Crawford?" she asked.

"I was sound asleep until your cell phone woke me up. Who was it that was calling you at 5:30 in the morning?"

I knew I was out of place for asking, as it was none of my business. But I was curious, wondering what was so secretive that she had to lock herself in the bathroom to take the call.

"Oh...no one important. Just family, making sure I arrived safe," she replied.

"Oh, I see...do you always talk to your family in Italian?" I inquired.

Her face changed as if her eyes were on fire. Her eye contact was directly saying, 'How dare you to ask such intruding questions.'

I could tell she was trying to respectfully, formulate an answer.

"Yes, I have family here in Italy," she replied.

We began eating our breakfast while I was thinking about her response. She looked very uneasy, answering my questions as if she had wished for me to mind my own business. I then remembered the phrase she used when she responded to her cell phone very early this morning.

"Veronica...'Zio' means 'Uncle' in Italian, right?"

"Yes...why?" she slowly replied.

"Well then, that would make sense. You answered the phone 'Zio,' so I figured you were talking to family," I diplomatically observed.

Veronica became very silent for several moments. For a few seconds, she gave me the same dirty look that I had initially received from her at the art museum last week when we had our initial blow-out.

At that moment, I realized that she was definitely hiding something, and there was something significant to that early morning telephone call that she had to take in a locked bathroom from her 'Zio.'

I decided not to push it. But her reaction and her mannerisms by the way she was answering my inquiries made me very suspicious. I started questioning myself and Veronica's intentions, not only as to why she bothered being intimate with me but why she was even involved with me in this story.

What was her angle? Why did she want to be associated with this story so badly? Was she looking for information? Was she after the paintings too? Why was she even bothering to get so involved with this news investigation?

Except for introducing me to her friend, Claudia, and the additional information she had on the theft of the paintings, she didn't bring anything new to this news story.

I was suspicious.

We finished our breakfast, and I brought along my laptop in my backpack when we went to the Uffizi Museum to visit her friend Claudia. We slowly strolled through its hallowed halls, up through the Palazzo Pitti within the medieval structure of the Uffizi building. We must have passed two dozen or more Renaissance paintings that Veronica and I stopped to admire. She was giving me the nickel tour of every masterpiece displayed within its old halls. She was an encyclopedia of information regarding the Renaissance. As we approached the Vasari Corridor, Veronica seemed to know her way around the medieval gallery.

"Aren't you afraid you'll get lost?" I asked her as she walked and navigated her way around Florence's most famous cultural museum as if she were walking through the halls of her old high school.

"Are you kidding? You have no idea how many times I have been here."

"I can tell," I complimented her.

The morning Tuscan sun was brightly illuminating its gigantic corridors, as we walked past the Torre dei Mannelli into a smaller, darkened hallway, where there were several offices located on the left side of the building. Veronica then knocked on the third door to the left.

"Permesso?" she inquired as we entered.

"Si' accomodi," Claudia responded. She was sitting at her desk in a small, dusty room with an old wooden desk and two wooden chairs.

She got up and hugged and kissed the two of us, as we sat down in front of her. They then started gossiping in Italian for about ten minutes or so, until I darted them both a dirty look, in which they converted their conversation to English.

"I was telling Claudia about that wonderful bottle of wine we both enjoyed last night," she explained.

"Indeed. Considering that she put it on the newspaper's tab, I'll probably get fired when we get back," I replied.

Trying to keep the conversation and the purpose of our meeting on task, I pushed Claudia to allow us to interview one of the board members for a source on our news story. She suggested that the only board member that would be around was Dottore Edoardo Giannini, whom she had an appointment with within the next hour.

While we were waiting, I received a text from my editor:

Replied to your e-mail

I then checked out my e-mails on my cell phone and found his reply:

Crawford,
Attached are some recent CNN articles and news briefs on your subject, referred to respectfully as Don Rodolfo Giammarco and his very dangerous, Tuscan crime family, the 'Firenze Mafia.' Please review and take note of the included information.
This guy is the 'Prince of Fucking Darkness,' and has turned 'skull-fucking' into a spectator sport.
Be careful. I am not paying for an Italian funeral.
And don't come back to Chicago in a body bag.
The Chief.

Of course, Mike Daudelin has never resisted the temptation to insert his warped sense of humor while responding to any of my inquiries. I opened up the several news articles and internet attachments which he had found on his uncensored search engines:

There had been several inquiries into the assassination of an Italian magistrate and prosecutor by the name of Giacomo DiFalco, who was killed in front of his family while coming out of a restaurant in Florence back in 2003. Although Giammarco and his crime family were the main suspects in that murder, the current prosecutor was apparently either paid off or too timid to pursue the homicide charges and meet the same fate.

There was another investigation where a local businessman, Michele Selvaggio, was found decapitated in the River Arno in 2007. His sin was that he had gotten over his head in juice loans with the Giammarco's, and Don Rodolfo figured that, with his current outstanding life insurance policies, he was worth more dead than alive. The Italian insurance company investigated the murder but could not prove any direct connection to the 'Firenze Mafia' or his widow. There was a subsequent financial payout made on that life insurance policy, for which Giammarco was suspected in receiving a substantial amount of the five-million-euro proceeds.

According to other information that was researched by my assistant editor, Don Rodolfo runs the Uffizi Board of Directors, like the City of Florence, with an iron fist. He has even gone as far as to get the local internet search engines to censor any malevolent information about him, which is similar to what communist countries do in Cuba and China.

Giammarco and the Uffizi Board of Directors had also publicly called out the Vatican in its demands for the Uffizi painting discovery in Munich last summer. According to the news articles, the Uffizi board reasoned that the art collection was 'gifted' to the Florence museum before the war. The City of Florence then suffered enumerate tragic losses, including the persecution of many of its local Jewish families in relinquishing those forty-two stolen paintings to the Nazi's during World War II.

That afternoon, we interviewed the magistrate judge, Dottore Edoardo Giannini, in Claudia's cramped office, who only reiterated the same information we had already learned regarding the disappearance of those

Uffizi paintings in Munich. He was very vague and didn't seem to want to volunteer a whole lot of new information. We then called and requested an interview with the Chief of Police, Giuseppe Maffei, but he was unavailable to speak with us. He promised to talk to us over the phone before we left Florence, but that interview never happened.

And of course, Claudia and Veronica continued to discourage me from requesting a meeting with Giammarco, as he was very adamant about ever talking to the press or media.

From what I could gather, nobody in Florence wanted to go on record regarding the relentless pursuit of the Uffizi Board of Directors and especially, Giammarco, in trying to recover those stolen paintings. I kept hitting brick walls, no help or assistance from either Claudia or my fellow reporter, Veronica. I was starting to get very discouraged and extremely suspicious regarding the lack of help or support I was getting from either one of them.

After that day, I realized that I was on my own.

CHAPTER FORTY-FIVE

It was eight-thirty in the morning, as I woke up to a cold, empty bed and a throbbing headache. Veronica and I had spent the night together after having an enjoyable dinner at the Trattoria Sabatino on Via Pisana near the hotel. She ordered two expensive bottles of wine, of course, and after the second bottle and a large dessert portion of tiramisu, I was agreeable to anything.

We got back to my hotel suite, and we made love for part of the night until the 'Super Tuscan' red wine we had consumed that evening had finally gotten the best of me. I must have passed out. I came to learn that 'Super Tuscan' was a wine term used to describe some of the red wines from Tuscany that include a mixture of different vineyards, particularly Merlot, Cabernet Sauvignon, and Syrah grapes.

I had gotten up and gone to the bathroom, noticing that the shower had been used, and several wet towels were already on the floor. I realized that Veronica and risen early that morning, showered and made her way out the door without saying a word. I got cleaned up, using whatever towels she had left me, and dressed myself to go out the door.

My first thought was to figure out how to get rid of my terrible hang-over.

Must be the friggin' wine, I thought to myself.

I went downstairs to the bar in the lobby, ready to consume a robust, very forgiving cup of that sweet-smelling Italian java.

"Espresso Doppio," I said to my pal Giovanni, who was the barista on duty. After staying at the Hotel Baglioni for three days straight, he and I were fast becoming good friends.

"How was your sleep, Signore Crawford?"

"Molto bene, Giovanni. How is the weather outside?"

"Un po' freddo," he described, advising me that with the cooler weather, I should probably wear a sweater that morning.

"I see your girlfriend left early," he casually mentioned. I had texted Veronica earlier that morning, but she didn't respond.

"She must-a be very mad with you."

"Why?"

"She come e' downstairs, and some man meet-a with her in the lobby,"

Giovanni's broken English was improving.

"Really."

He placed down a white saucer on the bar countertop and put my double-shot of espresso onto it. I then gave him the usual ten euros.

I was perplexed. Veronica didn't mention that she was meeting anyone that morning, and I didn't know at all where she had gone. She wasn't answering my texts, and I didn't want to come across as an 'over-bearing boyfriend' by blowing up her phone.

I sat there at the bar, very quietly drinking my caffe' with the Italian news channel blaring in the background, with the hustle and bustle of travelers checking out of the hotel.

Giovanni gazed at me for a moment, as I was sitting there in silence. As if he had already read my mind, he simply mentioned:

"Café Donatello"

"What?"

"Café Donatello. It is where all Americans go for breakfast. It is on Via Sante' Monica. You must-a check there."

I looked at him and smiled, throwing down another ten euros on the bar counter.

"Grazie, Giovanni."

I finished my caffe' and went upstairs to grab a sweater. I then darted out of the hotel, noticing that it was indeed, a little 'freddo' outside. I punched in the name of the restaurant on my iPhone GPS, and after walking a few blocks, I found myself right in front of the Café' Donatello.

I counted to ten to myself, wondering what I was going to find inside that restaurant before entering.

As I walked in, within a short distance away from the door, was Veronica, sitting at a table with another man, enjoying breakfast. She hadn't noticed me standing by the entrance door, and I didn't know at first how to respond. My heart was pounding out of my chest, and my hands were starting to sweat.

I had noticed that Veronica was doing very little to assist me in writing and investigating this Uffizi painting story. But after seeing her having breakfast with someone else, and not mentioning anything to me about it, my suspicions were beginning to fly off the charts. This woman had her schedule, and she was doing some investigating on her own.

But why? What was she after? For some crazy reason, I had thought of the possibility that she was 'spying,' trying to gather information about the whereabouts of these paintings on her own. But it made no sense.

At that moment, I just couldn't fit all of the pieces together.

So, I bravely decided to approach the two of them at the table in the restaurant and introduce myself to her friend.

"Buon Giorno," I said, extending my hand out to the gentleman who was having breakfast with my travel companion, news reporter associate, and my part-time sex-partner.

Veronica gazed her eyes up at me, and if looks could kill, my corpse would have been lying face down on Via Sante' Monica.

The man looked at me, somewhat startled. I only started to ramble nervously.

"I texted you earlier, Veronica. I wondered where you went, after leaving my hotel room so early," I loudly said.

At that moment, both of them were raising their eyebrows.

"Gerhard Hildebrandt," the tall, gray-haired man said in a deep, low, baritone voice, shaking my hand. I could tell he had a very thick, German accent as if his English was barely understandable.

"Paul Crawford, Chicago Sun-Times."

"Pleased to meet you," he responded.

"Detective Hildebrandt is with the Munich Police Department," Veronica said, in an almost condescending voice.

"It's a pleasure to meet you, Detective. Mind if I sit down?" as I pulled up a chair from an empty table and made myself comfortable. Veronica had, by now, been giving me a series of dirty looks, which I was finding very easy to ignore. The waitress had approached our table, and I ordered another cup of espresso and a 'cornetti,' deciding to keep my breakfast light and to make myself welcome.

"The detective has been telling me about the Munich investigation and the events that occurred since the discovery of those paintings," Veronica said.

I could tell by the tone of her voice that she was pissed.

"How interesting. How is the investigation into the Mayor's murder coming along?" I asked, remembering that Mayor Kossel of Munich was found murdered at his desk a couple of days after the release of those paintings from Herman Kalkschmidt's apartment.

Detective Hildebrandt went on to brief me on the details of the investigation, including the arrest of Wolfgang Schmidt and his subsequent release on the alleged murder of a Munich socialite, Ingrid Von Stueben. He went on to talk about the discovery of a dead body in the warehouse in Egenhofen, where Schmidt had initially hidden the paintings.

"Mariano Giammarco?" I mentioned his name, whom I had discovered was the nephew of Don Rodolfo Giammarco.

"Yes," he said. His low, baritone voice and thick German accent made it very difficult to understand him.

Veronica sat there silently, while the Detective continued to inform me of the updated details that had occurred in Munich. He made mention of the fact that, regarding Mayor Kossel's death investigation, that he suspected the 'Firenze Mafia,' mainly, Don Giammarco, was involved. But he didn't have any evidence to prove it, and so far, the Mayor's death was an unsolved murder.

As Hildebrandt began discussing his suspicions regarding the Mayor's murder, I noticed Veronica getting very uncomfortable. It was as if she wanted to change the subject.

He continued to discuss some other details, and I pulled out my notepad and started taking down notes, while Veronica continued to sit there, cold and unresponsive.

He then got on to the subject of the Vatican.

"Are you aware of who Stefano Iannucci is?"

"No," I replied. Another dirty look from Veronica.

"He is wanted for murder in several countries and, according to Interpol, is one of the most wanted contract killers in Europe. He is a professional assassin, and we believe he is working for the Vatican is trying to recover those paintings. I've been following him for years."

"Interesting," I responded as I looked over at Veronica. She continued to sit there, expressionless.

After rendering more details regarding the 'Firenze Mafia,' Don Carlo Marchese's crime family connections, and his involvement with his brokering Vatican Museum art pieces, I happened to ask the Detective why he was in Florence.

"I've been trying to get the magistrate to issue a warrant for Giammarco's arrest. We can prove that he had threatened Mayor Kossel only a few days before he was killed. So far, I'm not having any luck."

"Why is that," I asked.

"He's so connected here in Florence, and no one will even talk about him, let alone arrest him and bring him in for questioning."

"He's very insulated indeed," I observed.

Veronica was still very silent.

Detective Hildebrandt seemed to have the whole news story already put together. The only thing he wasn't able to confirm was the whereabouts of the paintings.

"Detective...do you know anything about the 'Demons of Divine Wrath' painting by Fra Lippi?"

Now Veronica had a shocked look on her face, wondering how I knew anything about that painting.

"Yes. Apparently, this painting was separated from the Uffizi art collection last summer. It was probably the most valuable painting of all of the discovered Nazi paintings in that Munich apartment. The Marchese crime family got their hands on this painting, and it was supposed to be sold to some museum in Detroit," the Detective explained.

"I heard that, too," I replied.

"The painting disappeared when it got to the airport, and there are rumors that the Firenze Mafia was involved."

"Meaning that Giammarco probably has it."

"Correct."

"How interesting," I coyly smiled, looking directly at Veronica.

By then, I had finished my caffe' and cornetti, and I could tell I was over-staying my welcome with Veronica, intruding on her breakfast date.

"Well," I said calmly, "I need to get going. I have a lot of typing to do in this story."

I got up from the table and shook the Detective's hand, giving me one of those 'break your fingers' type of handshakes.

I then turned and kissed Veronica on the cheek, which I could tell she didn't appreciate.

"I'll see you back at the hotel, honey," I sarcastically said.

I then excused myself and exited the restaurant. I had a lot of information that I needed to put down on paper, and I wanted to work on this story. I had a sickly feeling in my stomach about Veronica, but I couldn't put my finger on it. A million and one questions were going through my head.

It was as if Veronica had her own program. I had the distinct feeling that she was conducting her investigation as if she were writing and reporting her own version of the stolen Uffizi painting scandal. But was that her motive? Was she really here in Florence as a reporter? Or a private investigator? If she was investigating and gathering information, for whom was she gathering this information for?

I went back to my hotel room and started banging out this story on my laptop. By the time I was finished several hours later, I had over four thousand words to this investigative news article. I read it over to myself several times, making sure that I had chronologically stated all of the facts to this news story investigation.

I then made a long-distance cell phone call to my assistant editor.

"Chief...it's Crawford."

"No," he responded.

"No, what?"

"No...I'm not paying for your funeral," he laughed. I was glad that at least, Daudelin was in a good mood.

"I think I have this story finished. I will email it over to you. Let me know your thoughts," I stated.

Within thirty minutes after emailing the story, Mike Daudelin sent me a text:

Condense it down to 3,000 words, and we'll print it for tomorrow's edition.

Ok. I responded.

Has Veronica Giancarlo been a big help to you?

Yes. I lied.

Realistically, Veronica hadn't done squat, other than introducing me to Claudia Romanelli and Detective Hildebrandt, of which both connections only happened by either accident or coincidence. I had the distinctive urge to cut Veronica out of this story all together, seeing that she hadn't contributed in writing or adding anything to this story at all since we arrived in Florence. But I made a deal with her, and I was not about to 'renege' on my promise. I included her name as a contributing reporter in this news story.

But my suspicions were off the charts, and I knew that Veronica was up to something. She had her own program going on, and she wasn't going to tell me what it was. I texted her several times that afternoon, but she didn't respond. Since finishing this news story, I decided it was time to put our things together and return to the Windy City the next day. I texted Veronica again, emailing her a copy of the itinerary and her return ticket.

I didn't see or hear from Veronica for the rest of the time I was in Florence.

CHAPTER FORTY-SIX

I was completely packed the next morning, and I was about to check out of my hotel suite at the Hotel Baglioni. Carrying my only suitcase, I decided to walk down the hallway and knock on Veronica's door, to see if she was packed and ready to leave.

There was no answer.

I then went downstairs to have my final cup of espresso doppio Firenze style with my favorite barista before checking out.

"Buon Giorno, Signore Crawford," Giovanni proclaimed.

"Buon Giorno, Giovanni. Come' stai?"

"Molto bene...the usual?"

"Yes, please."

The barista quickly assembled and brewed my favorite cup of espresso doppio, neatly poured into a white coffee cup and saucer.

I placed the usual ten euros on the bar.

"I have not seen your girlfriend, Signore. She must-a check out?"

"I don't know, Giovanni. I haven't seen her either."

"Mi dispiace," he said, expressing his regrets.

"Sai come sono le donne," he then translated.

"You know how women are."

"Yes, especially American women," I replied.

408

I then finished my caffe', shaking hands with Giovanni and promising that I would see him again the next time I returned to Florence.

I then walked over to the check-out desk, where Isabella, the concierge, had informed me that Veronica had checked out of the hotel yesterday, leaving no word as to where she was.

Alrighty then.

I decided I wasn't going to worry about it. Veronica had her return ticket information, paid for compliments of the Chicago Sun-Times. She knew she had the flight information and had all of the connecting flight times for her return flight back home. I hailed a taxicab and went directly to the Florence airport, catching a short flight directly to Fiumicino Airport. My connecting flight to Chicago wasn't until 1:15 pm, which would then give me some time to catch up on some emails and get whatever feedback there was on my printed news story that day in the Sun-Times.

I arrived at Leonardo da Vinci-Fiumicino Airport at 11:20 am. I had at least an hour until my connecting flight started boarding. Realizing that it was still too early to contact Chicago, I decided to walk over to the airport coffee shop and get an espresso and a 'cornetti' to go. I figured that this was probably going to be a long, turbulent flight.

I boarded my plane, finding seat 15-E, which was a window seat. I realized that our seats had already been assigned on this flight, so I wondered if Veronica was going to show up and sit at her assigned seat next to mine. Being that she wasn't on the Florence flight to Rome, I figured that maybe, she made her own arrangements back to Chicago.

Just as the stewardess was about to close the boarding door, one would have never guessed who finally came on board. Veronica glared over at me while she put her carryon bags on the overhead bin, and then sat at the seat next to mine.

"Glad you could make it," I sarcastically said.

She first looked at me, not saying a word. She only fidgeted with a book and her magazine and sat there in silence, pretending that I was a stranger.

After the jetliner took off, we were about ten minutes into the flight when I decided I was going to try to make some conversation. That was a foolish idea.

"So, how was your vacation?"

"Go to hell," she replied.

I only smiled, realizing that she was behaving like an immature child.

"Well, that's progress. At least you're talking to me."

"Look," Veronica angrily responded. "This is going to be a very long flight. I would appreciate it if we could just pretend that we don't know each other until we can finally get off this damn airplane and put an end to this miserable trip."

"Miserable trip? Really?" I responded.

"Really."

"Wasn't this supposed to be a business trip? Weren't you supposed to be assisting me in getting information for this story? You instead sneak out of my hotel room early in the morning to have breakfast with some Munich detective without mentioning a word to me about it. Were you not going to share that information with me?"

"You didn't give me a chance. You invited yourself over to the table and totally embarrassed me," she responded.

"'See you back at the hotel, honey.'" She was mimicking me in a voice that didn't even come close to sounding like mine.

"You were sitting there at the table like an idiot. You were acting as though you didn't want me around to assist you in interviewing him for the information on this story. You didn't respond to any of my texts, and you certainly didn't bother letting me know where you were or what you were up to."

I was loudly defending myself, as the other passengers were now starting to take note of our very loud conversation. The stewardess was giving both of us dirty looks.

"You didn't bother coming back to the hotel even to help me write this story, which...by the way, I included your name as the reporter as well," I said in a loud voice.

At that moment, the stewardess came over to our seats.

"Please, you are both disturbing the other passengers. Keep your conversation down."

I waited several minutes until the stewardess was on the other side of the fuselage.

I then said to her in a loud whisper, "Why did you bother even coming? Whatever your program was, it certainly wasn't to help me with the reporting of this story."

"What I do with my personal time is none of your business," she replied.

"But honey…" I started to say.

"Don't call me 'honey,'" she reprimanded me.

"During these last four days, you were acting as though this *whole trip* was your own time, as though you were on vacation. You didn't help me at all," I said in a meager, calm voice.

I was trying very hard to control my temper, knowing that she was on her secret agenda with this trip, and had no intention at all of letting me know what it was.

There were several long minutes of silence, as she only sat there, not saying a word.

"I have family in Florence," she finally said.

"You could have at least told me that. At least respond to my texts. You disappeared, leaving me to wonder where you were and what the hell happened to you," I calmly replied.

"You're not my boyfriend. I owe you nothing."

"Yes…I can see that" I replied. "But you can at least give me some common courtesy and let me know where you are and what you are doing so that I don't worry or wonder what happened to you," I calmly responded.

"You don't make love to someone and then disappear," I curtly said in a very soft whisper.

Veronica was silent. She didn't respond to my comments. I then decided to abandon the subject, as I realized that I wasn't getting anywhere with her. Whatever she was doing and whatever she was up to, she certainly wasn't going to share her secret, covert activities with me.

After an hour or so, there was some strong turbulence on our Boeing 737 jetliner, and Veronica started grasping my forearm again, the same way she had done on our flight into Italy. She was frightened. The turbulence became so bad that even I was starting to wonder if there was cause to worry, as my stomach was beginning to feel nauseous.

When the turbulence finally settled down, we both fell asleep. Her head was resting on my shoulder, and her left hand still grasping my arm for security.

That was the way we spent the last seven hours of our flight back to Chicago. Even when she got up to go to the bathroom, she returned to our seats and continued to grasp my right arm, holding it lovingly, as if to ask for my forgiveness.

I decided to remain silent. I didn't know what else to say. I cared for her, but I was having a difficult time keeping my emotions in check. We had spent three wonderful nights together, making love to each other as though the world was coming to its final, romantic end, right there in Florence. I just couldn't understand how someone could make love to another human being, and then to suddenly ignore them and disappear as though they didn't exist. How does someone turn their emotions on and off like a light switch? I was having trouble with that.

I knew at that moment that I was going to regret not saying anything at all to her for the rest of that flight. I wanted to tell her how I felt. I wanted to say how fantastic our brief time was together, holding each other, laughing, making love, being in each other's company in that beautiful Renaissance City of Florence. I wanted so much to say to her what was in my heart.

But I just couldn't do it. I was so afraid of getting burnt, of being emotionally broken. I just didn't want to experience any more heartbreak.

I probably should have said something. But I didn't say a word. We only sat there, in silence, her left hand grasping my right forearm, and Veronica's head resting on my right shoulder until we landed at Chicago's O'Hare Airport.

The Alitalia 737 jetliner pulled up to Terminal Five Gate E-27 at 2:35 pm, Chicago time. The captain's voice on the loudspeaker welcomed us to Chicago, blaring out the cloudy, dismal winter weather and the cold temperature outside of 12 degrees. When the airplane came to a final halt, everyone got up to grab their belongings from the luggage bins overhead.

Veronica quietly got up, gathering her books and her carryon bag. She then bent over my seat and kissed me on the lips.

"Paul, I'm sorry," she simply said. I could tell that her eyes were welling up with tears.

Before I could even respond, she was in line, disembarking the airplane.

I gathered my bags, and my luggage and dutifully went through U.S. Customs. The whole time, I was looking for her, somewhere in the line, getting her bags, or going through the international terminal. I was looking hard for Veronica. I wanted to talk to her one more time. I would have at least...said something.

Anything.

I was feeling remorseful. At that moment, I wanted to fly back to Florence with her. I truly wanted to see her again. I wanted to be with her, to spend time with her, to make love to her just one more time. But there was no sign of her anywhere at the airport.

During the next few days, I tried calling her, texting her, and leaving her a few messages to call me back. But Veronica Giancarlo never did. After spending the most beautiful four days in Florence together, she just simply disappeared.

I never saw or heard from Veronica again.

CHAPTER FORTY-SEVEN

It was early October, and the cool, fall air was starting to overtake the mild, comfortable evenings in downtown Chicago. The once balmy evenings of the city were beginning to get colder, as light sweaters and jackets were the new modes of attire for the constant bustling nightlife of the Windy City.

Don Carlo Marchese was sitting in the dark in the living room of his Blackstone Hotel suite. It was almost two o'clock in the morning, and the Northside Capo couldn't sleep. The glow of his cigarette was the only thing visible within the stark darkness of his hotel room, as the noise of the Michigan Avenue traffic eighteen floors below continued to keep the mobster company in that early morning hour.

Don Carlo was up as usual. He was a lifelong insomniac, and it was a rare occasion when the Chicago hoodlum had a good night's sleep. He usually didn't retire until ten or eleven o'clock in the evening, and even when he was awakened in the middle of the night, he was often up making his espresso coffee at 5:00 in the morning. Marchese was always sleep-deprived. If he wasn't up from the constant pressure and anxiety that he was enduring, he could not close his eyes and relax, his mind always occupied and stressed from the problems of running his many entrepreneurial ventures.

At that early hour, Marchese was worried. He was agitated and distraught over the Uffizi Painting Scandal and the failed sale transaction of the Fra Lippi painting. He was embarrassed by not only the Giammarco Family and the 'Firenze Mafia,' but by Wolfgang Schmidt as well, who was supposed to oversee the sale of that valuable masterpiece.

He blamed the Chicago-German art dealer. Had Schmidt personally handled the delivery of this painting like he had promised, that precious picture would have arrived safely in Detroit. If Schmidt had been thinking more about the business at hand, instead of his thinking with his 'little head,' this embarrassment would never have happened. The art dealer should have been more concerned about this lucrative painting transaction, rather than spending the night and shacking up with some married socialite in Munich, trusting her with the location of the Uffizi paintings. He then, of course, got caught up in her outrageous murder scandal and was barely able to secure his release from prison.

This painting transaction with the Licovoli Family and the Detroit Institute of Art should have gone smoothly, instead of sending Frank Mercurio to oversee the shipment of the 'Demons of Divine Wrath.' Although Don Carlo loved and trusted Frank Mercurio as his underboss, he knew that Mercurio tended to 'get sloppy' sometimes. Don Carlo surmised that maybe one of Giammarco's henchmen might have followed Mercurio to the warehouse. He had also suspected that perhaps, there could have been others that were tipped off to the location of the art collection as well. In either case, Mercurio's careless actions contributed to the Fra Lippi painting being stolen at Detroit's Metropolitan Airport.

But what he still couldn't figure out was how Giammarco 'hijacked' the Fra Lippi painting. How did he know a hired cargo contractor from Milan was shipping the painting special air freight? How did he manage to know when and where the art was going to arrive in Detroit? Where is the art piece now?

Don Carlo was more than extremely angry. He was mortified. He had never been so ashamed and embarrassed in his whole life. He had to now, make peace with Don Pino Licovoli and refund the one hundred grand deposit to the Detroit Institute of Art. Marchese now also had to convince all the other crime families in New York, Kansas City, Milwaukee, and in Miami, that he and his family were still an upstanding 'family' to do business with.

'Marchese is getting soft' was the new rumor on the streets, and Don Carlo was not happy about the street gossip going around. He not only needed to locate those Uffizi paintings, but he primarily needed to make good on his promise to acquire the famous Fra Lippi painting for the Detroit museum and restore his reputation.

Don Carlo was on his third cigarette at that hour, as his mistress, Caroline Tortorici, was still sleeping in the adjoining bedroom.

"Come back to bed, honey," she moaned softly from the bedroom, stark naked in between the white satin sheets of their king size bed.

"I can't, baby. I've got some business to do."

He needed to make some phone calls, and as usual, he was not about to wait until the morning hours to do so. Don Carlo was never bashful about calling whoever he needed to talk to or interrupt their sleep in the middle of the night.

"Hello?"

"Frank, are you sleeping?"

"Boss…," replied Frank Mercurio, barely coherent, "it's 2:30 in the morning."

Marchese wasn't interested in the time or an apology for waking him up in the middle of the night.

"I will need you to take a few guys and go back to Italy for me," Don Carlo requested.

Frank Mercurio was still rubbing the sleep out of his eyes, as he was trying to comprehend the boss's middle of the night request. The underboss was used to these late-night phone calls from Don Carlo, as everyone within the family knew that he was a suffering, sleepless maniac. Marchese made it a habit of calling him in the middle of the night a couple of times a week. His late-night phone calls, business conversations, and overt requests were cause for Mercurio to doze off in the middle of the day, especially while driving. He had to take many afternoon naps to compensate for his lack of sleep, thanks to Don Marchese.

"What do you have in mind?" Mercurio asked. He was now dressed in a bathrobe and taking his cell phone call downstairs in the kitchen. He didn't want to wake up his always understanding wife, Phyllis, whom he'd been married to for forty-three years.

"We need to find out where those paintings are, and especially, that Fra Lippi painting that never arrived in Detroit," Don Carlo explained.

"I agree, Boss. Where would you like me to start?"

"I had a long conversation with my cousin, Monsignor Iacobelli, earlier today. He has heard that the Pope Emeritus's 'contractor' may have those paintings and that they may be located in Assisi."

Don Marchese and Monsignor Iacobelli were not only first cousins, but they were extremely close, like 'fratelli' or brothers. The two of them were very close in age, less than one year apart, and they went to grammar school together in Casalvieri many years ago. He knew that, no matter what Papa Onorio was plotting, that he could completely trust his cousin.

Don Carlo always believed that Monsignor Iacobelli had his back and that his cousin would take the most exceptional, most discrete care in making sure that any adverse information would be immediately passed on to him. Although he was aware of the Pope Emeritus's desire to take revenge against the Chicago Mafioso, Marchese wasn't worried. He knew that, with all of his security bodyguards and his close relationship with his cousin, that Papa Onorio had little chance to get to him or personally harm him.

It was a fatal assumption that would one day cost Don Carlo Marchese his life.

Iacobelli called the day before to inform the 'capo' that he had overheard a conversation with the former pope, that the hired contractor, Stefano Iannucci, had the Uffizi art collection stashed in a hidden warehouse within the large vineyard of a convent in Assisi. Iannucci was waiting for Papa Onorio to secure the funds with the Vatican Bank, which were needed to pay the contractor for his fees and the sale of the paintings, now over thirty million dollars. This outstanding balance was accruing interest daily.

"Who is this 'contractor'?" Frank asked.

"Stefano Iannucci. Papa Onorio hired him to investigate and acquire the Uffizi paintings. He probably figured that his professional talents and his ability to get the job done at any cost would get him those paintings," Marchese said.

"Iannucci? He's a frigging ruthless animal. That guy would kill his mother, and 'pimp out' his sister for a buck," Mercurio observed.

"I know. What is this damn world coming to that a pope can now hire a contract killer to get whatever it is that he wants? I always knew this Nazi pope was no good! He couldn't pay us for the missing paintings but would rather pay Iannucci to double for them. What an asshole, son-of-a-bitch!" Don Carlo was taking a drag from his cigarette, blowing several smoke circles in the dark.

"I need you and a few guys to go over to this convent in Assisi. You need to let me know if those Uffizi paintings are there. Then I will need you to pay a visit to Giammarco. I'm sure he has the Fra Lippi painting," Marchese requested.

"Okay, boss."

"You will need to leave tomorrow...before someone gets wise and moves those paintings again."

Mercurio had his marching orders in the middle of the night. He went into the family room and turned on the television, now knowing that he would have trouble falling back asleep again. As reruns of "Chicago P.D." and "Bluebloods" were blaring in the background, Frank immediately fell back asleep on his black, leather reclining chair.

"Boss," Frank called Don Carlo as they were loading their bags and luggage into the Europcar rented Fiat in Rome.

"I need the name of the convent in Assisi," he requested.

Frank Mercurio and his two associates, Nicola Alfano and Mario Grana, had just arrived at Rome's Fiumicino Airport and had rented a small Fiat Cinquecento for the one hundred-seventy-five-kilometer trip to Assisi. The trip would take a little more than two hours on the Autostrada, and they still needed to acquire the address and destination of the convent where they were going.

"Frank, my cousin finally called me back last night with the name and the location of the convent. It is the Porziuncola Convent and is located at the Piazza Porziuncola on the outskirts of Assisi."

Don Carlo had received a phone call from his cousin, Monsignor Iacobelli, informing him of the name and the exact location of the convent that was hiding these Uffizi paintings. Marchese had to wait several hours for the information. Even though Iacobelli had informed Marchese that the art pieces had been concealed in a 'convent in Assisi,' the Pope Emeritus did not disclose exactly which convent to his papal secretary. There were several convents with large land estates and vineyards located in the Umbria region, and Iacobelli did not know exactly which one.

Iacobelli waited for Papa Onorio to take his ten-kilometer walk that morning, before going into the Pope Emeritus's office. While Papa Onorio was doing his morning routine, Iacobelli went through the former pontiff's desk and found a card with some recent notes scribbled with the former pope's handwriting. The business card he had seen was for a Sister Marie-Claire Tedeschi, who was the Mother Superior at the Porziuncola Convent.

Presuming that Iacobelli had researched and found the correct location of the abbey, the Monsignor passed the location information on to Marchese, who was now sending his 'associates' to the convent. The three of them were to find the site of the hidden paintings within the abbey, secure their location, and have them sent by freight to the port in Naples, where the three painting containers would be shipped directly to a secured warehouse in New York.

Sister Marie-Claire was in her convent office working that morning. The Mother Superior was an older nun in her late seventies who had been with the order all of her adult life. She was a short, overweight woman who was very old school, always talked with a very condescending tone of voice and was quick-tempered. She was a tough, cranky old nun. The other nuns within her order were very afraid of her and always spoke to her as if they were on pins and needles. She had just attended daily mass with the other nuns in the order and then had breakfast with the fifteen other sisters within their religious order of the Sisters of St. Francis. She was tending to the business at hand when she received a knock on the door.

"Permesso,"

"Vieni," she loudly replied.

Sister Annamaria was a pretty, younger nun in her early thirties. She had requested to see the Mother Superior of the Order of St. Francis that morning, as she had needed to speak with her about an important matter.

"There are three gentlemen here to see you. Something about wanting some information on some paintings," she replied. The younger nun described the three men as older, heavyset men who had come from Chicago to 'acquire some information' on some paintings.

Sister Marie-Claire, knowing that this was an unexpected visit, went into the upper drawer of her desk and grabbed a large knife, and hid it under her black vestments. The old nun was always suspicious of strangers. She then walked out to the convent atrium, where the three men from Chicago were waiting.

"Buon Giorno, gentlemen."

"Sister Marie-Claire," Mercurio extended his hand, trying to greet the Mother Superior, "I'm Frank Mercurio, and these are my associates, Nicola Alfano and Mario Grana. We would like to speak with you about some paintings."

The old Mother Superior seemed to be annoyed with their visit and didn't wish to waste any time with anyone inquiring about any paintings.

"I'm not sure why you are here. We don't have any paintings to sell," she curtly replied.

"No, Sister, we are here for the paintings that are being stored here by Stefano Iannucci," Mercurio slyly replied.

"Paintings from who? We have no such paintings here at our convent. We are not selling any paintings, and we don't have any paintings being stored."

"Sister," Frank tried to be friendly as the other two men looked on. "We know about the paintings being stored here. These are the missing Uffizi paintings. We are here to pick them up."

"I'm sorry, Gentlemen. You have the wrong place. We are the Sisters of St. Francis, and we sell and bottle wine from our vineyards and bread from our granary. We do not sell or store paintings," the old sister was starting to get angry.

"Do you mind if we look around?"

"Yes, I do. You gentlemen must leave immediately," the Mother Superior ordered them to exit the convent.

"Thank you, Sister." Mercurio obediently said.

The three men dutifully left the convent atrium of the Porziuncola Abbey and headed back to their car. As they were leaving, they noticed the old grain silo in the back of the vineyard, within ninety-three acres of rows and rows of grapevines.

"I've got a hunch," Alfano said. He then got behind the wheel of the Fiat Cinquecento and, along with the other two men, drove the rented car towards the back of the vineyard estate, following the white graveled road leading to the end of the Porziuncola Convent. They all exited and approached the old silo structure, which had several padlocks on the entrance door. Alfano took out his Beretta and shot off the latches, allowing the entrance door to the old silo to open easily.

The three men entered the old granary silo. The only thing that they could see were large sectional troughs of grain and hundreds of bales of hay, stacked up along the walls of the silo going up twenty feet high.

"I don't see anything," observed Mercurio. "Are you sure they are here?"

The three men continued to look around the darkened, musty old silo, looking behind the stacked bales of hay and the sectioned off piles of grain.

Suddenly, the silo door was opened. It was Sister Marie-Claire, pointing a .22 caliber revolver gun at the three of them.

"I thought I asked you to leave. Why are you here?"

"Look, Sister, we know you have those paintings. Just tell us where they are, and we will take them off of your hands and leave."

"I've asked before, and I will ask you again. Leave our property now," she loudly said.

Frank Mercurio began to approach her. "Sister, you are not going to fire that gun!"

She continued to point the gun at Mario Grana, as the other two men encircled her in the old silo.

"Take another step, and I will shoot all of you," the mean old nun insisted, as the three men continued to encircle her even closer.

She then pointed the gun directly at Grana and pulled the trigger.

CLICK.

The gun did not go off, as she realized that she had forgotten to load the .22 caliber bullets and that the gun clip was empty. As Grana tried to grab her arm, she pulled out the large knife that she had hidden under her vestments. She managed to deeply stab Mario Grana in the arm as she was trying to overcome them. She kept wielding the knife at the three of them until they overtook her. Mario Grana's ferocious temper was infamous, and the other men knew that they could never control the six-foot, four-inch, 285-pound hoodlum when he became viciously angry. Mario's blood was dripping all over the old nun's vestments as he angrily, tightly gripped her throat with his firm, bloody hands.

It was almost 2:00 on that fall afternoon when Sister Annamaria noticed that the Mother Superior was not in her office. She continued to look for her around the convent estate, asking the other sisters if they had seen her. The young nun continued to look around outside, noticing from a distance that the silo door was open.

She and another nun walked the quarter-mile to the grain silo and entered the already open door.

There was a pool of blood on the archaic, concrete floor of the silo, dripping more blood from the top of the old grain structure.

As they looked up, they saw Sister Marie-Claire's lifeless body hanging by her neck from the rafters of the silo, blood from her badly stabbed and mutilated body continuously dripping onto the bottom floor.

The two nuns continued to scream at the top of their lungs for what seemed like hours as if Satan's demons had invaded the old, dark grain silo of the convent.

As it turned out, the three men had invaded the wrong convent. They had entered the Porziuncola Convent for the Sisters of St. Francis, rather than the Cloistered Sisters of St. Francis winery estate, on the other side of Assisi, where Iannucci was storing the actual paintings.

As the authorities and the local 'polizia' were notified, they became three fugitives on the run, driving quickly back to Casalvieri near Rome so Mario could receive medical attention for his stabbed arm wounds. They hid out there at Marchese's villa for three weeks. They then drove to France, where they inconspicuously flew out of Paris without being detected by the authorities. They never did find those paintings.

In the meantime, Sister Annunciata heard about the murder at the other nearby convent and begged Iannucci to remove the valuable pictures. But he instead hired more security for the cloistered nuns at the convent. He continued to hold the Uffizi paintings, still waiting for Papa Onorio to come up with the thirty million dollars that he promised to pay to take the remaining forty-one artworks out of storage.

The Pope Emeritus knew that Iannucci was holding those Uffizi paintings for ransom...and that they would either be paid for with either someone's money or blood.

CHAPTER FORTY-EIGHT

The breezy gales of November were blowing across the second-floor terrazzo patio, as Rodolfo Giammarco sat at the table that afternoon, staring off at the Il Duomo and the ancient landscape of Florence. Since the sudden death of his beloved nephew, Mariano, last August, the 'Capo of the Firenze Mafia' has not been the same. He had been consistently depressed, unable to sleep or eat much, and was letting his general health steadily decline.

The eighty-one-year Florentine billionaire had utterly lost his will or desire to live. The older man had no other family to look after him here in Italy. His only living sibling was his sister Gianna, who was married and had been living in Chicago for many years. His sister and her daughters were his only living relatives. Other than a few money-hungry distant cousins living in the Tuscany region, he had no other family that he could count on to look after him. He had put all of his hopes and dreams on his beloved nephew, the young boy whom he had raised into a handsome, educated 29-year-old young man. Such a waste of life, to lose such an incredibly vibrant person only for the sake of chasing some insignificant stolen Nazi paintings.

Don Rodolfo now had in his possession, the most valuable Renaissance painting from the forty-two recovered masterpieces from Munich, Fra Lippi's 'Demons of Divine Wrath.' He was able to snag that painting away from the Marchese and Licovoli Families at Detroit's Metropolitan Airport. He successfully hijacked that painting back to Italy, back to Florence in his secured custody.

429

But unfortunately, he wasn't able to acquire the other forty-one paintings. And now, at this point, since the tragic death of his nephew, he no longer cared. In all truthfulness, he didn't want them anymore. He didn't care what happened to those paintings. And now that he possessed the elusive Fra Lippi painting, he didn't want that one anymore either. Every time he looked at that painting, it only reminded him of the terrible, tragic loss he had suffered in trying to recover all of those stolen masterpieces in the death of his beloved Mariano.

Those paintings are possessed, he thought to himself.

He knew who now had those paintings. They were being hidden in a convent in Assisi by a ruthless professional assassin, Stefano Iannucci. He had met him several times before, many years ago. He knew of his callous, merciless means of contractually killing and destroying his victims.

Giammarco was certainly not afraid of Iannucci. He just no longer cared about those paintings anymore, even if they were in his possession. The old Mafioso had heard that Iannucci had the Uffizi art collection, and was working for the Pope Emeritus. He now had those paintings and was waiting for Papa Onorio and the Vatican Bank to come up with the 'ransom money' to acquire those paintings away from Iannucci and brought to the Vatican Museum. Knowing where the art pieces were and who had them, Giammarco could easily have acquired those paintings away from the Vatican and Iannucci.

He recalled a meeting that was arranged by one of his associates two weeks ago in Florence. He was told to meet a young gentleman for dinner that evening to discuss some critical business. He did not know who it was at the time, nor what the meeting was concerning.

As he arrived at the Primamore Trattoria in downtown Florence, he was led to the back-room table where his adversary was sitting.

"Buona Sera, Don Giammarco."

Rodolfo Giammarco recognized immediately who it was and was initially apprehensive about sitting down at the table.

"If I knew that it was you that I was meeting, I would have declined your dinner invitation," the Firenze Capo said.

"I've come here in peace, Don Rodolfo," Stefano Iannucci said. "I wish to sit down with you and break bread with you and discuss the possibility of doing business together."

Don Rodolfo cautiously took off his jacket and sat down at the table with two of his bodyguards standing next to him. He was not about to make this a friendly 'cinetta.'

"What do you want, Iannucci? I have no respect or use for you, and I am not in the mood to be playing any double-crossing games with either you or your Vatican client," he said.

"Don Rodolfo, as I have said, I've come here in peace. Can we not be gentlemen here and sit down and discuss our differences? We both have something that the other wants. Can we not discuss the possibility of doing business together?" Stefano amicably suggested.

"I would much rather gauge out your eyeballs with a steak knife than have dinner with you, Iannucci," Giammarco replied, displaying his total contempt.

Iannucci smiled. "You've done that before," referring to one of Giammarco's victims.

Don Rodolfo then asked his bodyguards to frisk Iannucci, making sure that he did not have a weapon. When they realized that he was not 'carrying,' Don Rodolfo excused them to wait outside for him.

At that moment, the waitress arrived to take their dinner order.

"We will not be having dinner. I will have an espresso doppio, per favore," Giammarco said.

"Same for me also," Stefano replied.

The two men looked at each other in silence for several long moments.

"My sincere condolences on the tragic loss of your beloved nephew, Don Rodolfo. I understand that he was an amazing young man with a bright future ahead of him."

"Grazie, Stefano. I appreciate your sympathy."

More moments of silence.

"I understand that you have the stolen Uffizi paintings," Rodolfo initially said.

"I do indeed. And I understand that you have the Fra Lippi painting," Iannucci volleyed.

"Yes."

"My congratulations on stealing that painting away from Marchese and Licovoli in Detroit last month. I heard how you went about having your men dressed as customs agents in hijacking that painting masterpiece away from the Detroit museum."

"Thank you. I understand that Marchese was not happy about your method of stealing the other paintings away in Bolzano," Giammarco returned the compliment.

A few more moments of silence, as their caffe's arrived at the table.

"So, Don Rodolfo. What are we to do here? I have the forty-one Uffizi art paintings, and you have the most valuable one. Papa Onorio wishes to have all of them together for his Vatican Museum display. He has asked me to approach you about acquiring that painting and keeping the whole art collection together."

The 'Firenze Capo' glared at the young, ambitious assassin for several long minutes, not initially, saying a word.

"My young friend. This has absolutely nothing to do with money. Those paintings, as far as I'm concerned, have always been the Uffizi paintings, gifted to our art gallery by Pope Pius XI in 1938. The Nazis stole them in 1943. We only wish to have what has always been ours," Giammarco patiently explained.

"To make matters worse," he continued, "there was a significant amount of bloodshed paid for by our 'paisani' for those paintings, including the destruction of 103 Jewish refugees during the war. We have more than paid for those paintings in blood."

Iannucci smiled at the old Mafioso. "Don Giammarco, I am not an art collector, nor do I wish to become one. I want the money that was promised me for those paintings which I have contracted for with Papa Onorio."

"How much does he owe you now?"

"Thirty Million Euros, plus interest."

Don Giammarco was silent.

"If you wish to have them, Don Rodolfo, I will sell them to you for twenty million euros in cash. I can have them here tomorrow."

Don Giammarco was again...silent.

"You would then have the total art collection to be returned and displayed at the Uffizi Museum." Iannucci was trying to entice the old man into taking those paintings off of his hands.

"So, you would double-cross the Pope Emeritus?"

"He has had almost three months to come up with the money. So far, he has only made excuses. The Vatican Bank has not been forthcoming with paying the money to acquire those paintings. I believe that the old, senile pope made a deal with me using an empty checkbook."

"Twenty Million Euros?"

"Yes, and you will have them here tomorrow."

The old Mafioso looked at Stefano straight in the eye.

"I have no desire to pay for something that already belongs to me. I will give you five million euros for those paintings and your time. Otherwise, to tell you the truth, I no longer want them."

Iannucci was in shock, as he thought for sure he could make a deal with Giammarco.

"Don Rodolfo, I can sell those paintings to anyone, anywhere in the world and get at least fifteen or twenty million euros for them. I am not going to give them away to you or anyone else at that price," the young assassin explained.

Don Rodolfo then smiled. He quietly finished his espresso and rose from the table, putting his coat back on.

"Then I will keep the Fra Lippi painting, and you can keep the other forty-one paintings at your convent in Assisi. I can assure you, Stefano, that Papa Onorio is a senile, demented older man. He had neither the authority nor the support of the Vatican Curia to make such a deal with you. Unless you can find another buyer, you will be stuck with those paintings for a long, long time."

Stefano Iannucci glared at the old Mafioso, realizing that he was not an easy man to deal with.

"And one other thing, Stefano. Just because I no longer have an interest in those paintings does it mean that I will allow Papa Onorio to have them either," Giammarco stated.

"I no longer want them, and he will not get them either, even if I have to destroy you in the process. I will see to that," Giammarco declared his mandate.

"That Uffizi art collection has been cursed. Too many people have already died for those paintings. When you eventually sell those works of art, Stefano, you will not be around very long either...that I can promise you," Don Rodolfo said.

Stefano Iannucci only sat there, smiling at the older, more respected Mafioso.

He then turned and walked out of the restaurant with his bodyguards.

Don Giammarco was sitting in his comfortable chair on that November afternoon, recalling his meeting with Iannucci and how he successfully was able to push him and his recovered Uffizi paintings aside. The way he was figuring it, there was a terrible curse on those paintings. None of those paintings, and especially the Fra

Lippi painting, was going to bring back is beloved Mariano. He was tired. He was extremely depressed. He no longer had any will left to live.

"Don Rodolfo, please come inside," his butler, Alfredo said to him. "It is time to get dressed for your niece's wedding," he demanded.

That day was the long-awaited day for Don Rodolfo to attend the wedding of his niece from Chicago. He was not in the mood, nor did he have the heart to decline her invitation. He promised his sister that he would attend. He continued to sit there for several long minutes until his butler called him again.

"Don Rodolfo, you must come inside. The wedding ceremony will be starting at the church in an hour."

"Alfredo," the Firenze Capo said, "where is that Fra Lippi painting?"

"It is still in your study, Don Rodolfo."

The older man thought for a few moments. He suddenly decided that neither Fra Lippi's artwork nor any other work of art was going to grip him away from his intense depression. He realized that perhaps, that painting should go to someone who would more appreciate that masterpiece.

Someone who didn't believe in curses.

"Have the painting wrapped up and delivered to the wedding reception this evening," he demanded.

He now knew that his beloved niece would better appreciate this valuable gift of Fra Lippi.

CHAPTER FORTY-NINE

The five inches of fresh, undisturbed snow had accumulated in front of the art store on North Wells Street when Wolfgang Schmidt arrived for work that early morning. It had fallen the night before on March 20th. Even though the calendar said it was the first day of spring, it looked as though the spring weather in Chicago would never come. He struggled to open the front door, as the back of door leading from his store to the alley had been plowed in and buried that morning by the City of Chicago snowplows that evening. Because he didn't have a snowblower, he hoped that the untouched virgin snow in front of his building would be easier to shovel by hand, despite its accumulation.

Schmidt grabbed his primitive red snow shovel and spent the next thirty minutes plowing the front of his store and the adjacent sidewalk by hand. He pushed the snow piles onto North Wells Street with its oncoming traffic, hoping that the small snow mountains in the middle of the street would now be the city's problem. He was grateful to be in somewhat good shape, as he was able to quickly catch his breath after this brief snow plowing exercise, putting his red shovel away in the rear of his upscale, River North establishment.

Wolfgang turned on his espresso machine, making sure there was enough water to render his well-deserved cup of espresso doppio. He went through his mail in the small office located in the back of his art store. It was a very small room, barely large enough to fit an old wooden desk and a chair. He had a dozen or more cameras set up all around the store, and each camera displayed an image onto his fifty-five-inch screen neatly mounted onto the wall of his quaint little office.

It had been eventful several months since the death of his cousin, Herman Kalkschmidt, and the discovery of those Uffizi paintings. He was regretful that he was not able to safely keep and broker those valuable paintings to the art world at large, as Wolfgang knew that he could have made an incredible fortune. But once the word was out that the Uffizi art collection had been rediscovered, it seemed as though the whole world, especially Marchese and the Vatican, was after them.

After the murder of his girlfriend, Ingrid Von Stueben, and his brief imprisonment, he was lucky to have escaped Germany with his freedom and his marriage still intact. He was also grateful to his attorney, Michael Prescott, who was able to secure his unconditional release in Munich after those trumped-up murder charges. Despite his being locked up in a Munich prison for a couple of days, he was able to hide and obvert any information from getting back to his loving wife. She was only told that he was "indisposed for a few days. "

He was also grateful to Prescott for coming down to the Chicago Police Department at the Eighteenth District last January and fending off those detectives in that Marchese murder interrogation last Christmas. He knew absolutely nothing about what Don Carlo Marchese was involved with regarding any of his business affairs at the time of his murder. He was elated that Prescott was able to assist them in answering their questions and to...again, rescue him from any prospective trouble.

Schmidt was feeling extremely lucky. Even though he did not possess the Uffizi paintings, he had dodged several bullets over the last several months, and he was extremely grateful.

He was doing some random paperwork, checking his online bank balances and emails when he heard the jingle of the front door. He presumed it was a customer, as he quickly rose from his desk.

"Good morning, Wolfgang. "

Schmidt immediately recognized the stranger who had walked into his art store.

"Stefan? This is a surprise!"

The stranger who walked into his store was Stefano Iannucci, the "contractor" whom Schmidt had hired to take care of his cousin Hermann in Munich last summer. The two of them shook hands, and Wolfgang immediately escorted Stefano to his espresso bar.

"When did you get into town? " Wolfgang eagerly asked.

"I've been in town for a few days. I came in to celebrate a birthday with a friend of mine at the Chicago Hilton. "

Stefano was wearing a long, black mohair overcoat and a blue sweater over his untucked, white shirt. His dress jeans had the remnants of white snow that he was so unfamiliar with from his native Italy. His black leather cowboy boots looked out of place, soaked in the snow and ice that he must have accumulated walking through the streets of Chicago.

Wolfgang pressed the button on the espresso machine and rendered a freshly brewed, long cup of espresso for his surprise guest. He placed a teaspoon of sugar into the cup, and Stefano happily consumed his coffee, grateful for the delicious taste of the authentic, Italian caffeine.

"Now, this is coffee!" Stefano exclaimed as Schmidt smiled at the delight of his store guest.

The two of them briefly talked and caught up on each other's life events since their last encounter in July. After making small talk, the two of them sat down at the two black leather chairs adjacent to the black marble coffee table next to Wolfgang's elaborate espresso bar.

"So," Wolfgang said as he watched Stefano enjoying his coffee. "To what do I have this pleasure?"

"I have a new client," Iannucci began to explain.

"Really?" Wolfgang answered. "And who would that be?"

"The Pope Emeritus, Wolf. Papa Onorio, your fellow countryman."

Schmidt glazed at the professional assassin, immediately knowing the direction that this conversation was about to go. Wolfgang had heard rumors among the other art collectors within the art world that the Pope Emeritus was genuinely interested in the Uffizi masterpieces that his cousin had been hoarding in his apartment until last summer. There had been a significant amount of interest and media speculation that the expensive, stolen Nazi art pieces had been hidden away again.

Although he had received several interview requests from other media networks and newspapers wishing to acquire more information on exactly how and what painting masterpieces had been discovered in Munich, Wolfgang remained silent. Being accused and falsely arrested on murder charges last August, Schmidt had not engaged or communicated with anyone regarding the Uffizi paintings. After discovering that the Uffizi paintings had been stolen and another person was found dead at the warehouse in Egenhofen, Schmidt has tried to keep a very low profile. For the last several months, Schmidt had been very successful in fending off these Uffizi inquiries.

But he did recall receiving a telephone call from a Monsignor Iacobelli, the Pope Emeritus's papal secretary. He offered a papal audience with Schmidt and wanted to know more information regarding the status of those Uffizi paintings. Like the other inquiries, Schmidt neither answered their phone calls or emails and refused all interviews.

There were several long seconds of silence as if Wolf was too busy reading his mind.

"How does this new client of yours concern me?" he pressed Iannucci.

"I am sure you can guess, Wolf. Papa Onorio has been looking for these Uffizi paintings," Iannucci flatly stated.

"The pope wants them returned to the Vatican Museum where they rightfully belong," Stefano explained.

Wolfgang looked at Iannucci with a confused look on his face.

"Where they rightfully belong?"

"You know the story, Wolf. Some bullshit about 'Papa Pio' placing those Vatican paintings on consignment with the Uffizi before the Nazis stole them during the war. Papa Onorio heard that these forty-two paintings recovered in your cousin's apartment were the same masterpieces consigned by the Vatican over eighty years ago," Stefano recapped.

"Really?" Wolf sarcastically responded.

For a moment, Schmidt was silent, as Stefano continued.

"As you may have heard, Papa Onorio is having a public relations problem. He has been bashed by all the Roman newspapers and the Italian media on his character. They have continued to label him as the 'Nazi Pope' and have accused him of being very anti-Semitic because of his participation as a Nazi soldier during the war."

Iannucci took another sip of his Italian caffe'.

"And how is this my problem?" the art dealer interjected.

The Italian contractor continued. "What better way to score points with the Romans, Wolfgang, then to triumphantly return to the Vatican Museum paintings and masterpieces stolen by the Nazis during World War Two?"

More moments of silence, as the two men studied each other's malicious intents.

"I have the Uffizi art collection, Wolf."

Wolfgang looked at Stefano in shock. "How did you get them?"

"From your friend, Carlo Marchese, whom I had the pleasure of eliminating last Christmas. He apparently decided to get smart with the Pope, who then asked me to get involved."

"I have forty-one of those original Uffizi paintings. But the most priceless one, the 'Demons of Devine Wrath,' is still missing. Don Rodolfo Giammarco has that painting, which he stole from Marchese."

Schmidt sat there quietly for a few moments, studying the face of his one-time colleague sitting at the opposite leather chair across from him at that black marble coffee table.

"That painting was included with the rest of them when they were originally stored at an empty warehouse in Egenhofen last summer. Someone broke into that warehouse and stole all of them, killing two people in the process," Schmidt replied.

The young assassin looked at the German art dealer, with a smirk on his face, silently glaring back at Wolf.

Iannucci only looked at the middle-aged art dealer, expressionless, not saying a word. He only continued to sip his espresso coffee, acting as though he had not heard Wolfgang's reply.

More silence.

"If you have the forty-one other paintings, why haven't you delivered them to the Vatican?"

"I will, Wolf. As soon as the Pope Emeritus comes up with the rest of the money that he owes me for those paintings," he explained.

"But I still have some unfinished business to do on behalf of the Pope."

Wolf gazed at the Iannucci and suddenly put all the pieces together.

"You've been hired by the Vatican, Stefan, so who is now your new victim?"

The hired killer smiled at his new victim.

"You," Iannucci calmly replied.

At that moment, Iannucci pulled out his Beretta pistol, calmly screwed on the silencer, and then pointed it at the art dealer.

At first, Schmidt thought the assassin was joking.

"I don't know why you would want to kill me, Stefan. You now have those paintings. What else do you want from me?"

Stefano Iannucci smiled.

"Pope Emeritus does not like the way you Nazi's treated those Jewish refugees in Florence seventy-six years ago."

"That has nothing to do with me!"

"That has everything to do with you, Wolfgang. Your father was a Nazi sympathizer, and your cousin and your uncle were both Nazis'. Your uncle even signed off on the death of those Jews in Florence, in return for those paintings."

"That's not true!" Wolfgang screamed.

"Believe me, Wolf. It is true," he said.

There were several more moments of silence, as Stefano continued to point his gun at Wolfgang.

"His Holiness has asked for your life in retaliation for the death of those poor Jewish families hiding in that church in Florence. He wishes to avenge the deaths of those poor, 103 Jewish refugees that were persecuted in Auschwitz, thanks to ruthless Nazi soldiers like your uncle and your grandfather."

"That is not true!" Schmidt loudly protested.

443

He started to go into shock as Iannucci looked around the art store.

"I see there are security cameras located throughout your store, Wolfgang. Would you kindly show me where your security system file server is located?" he politely asked.

Wolfgang, now distressed, became extremely frightful and nervous. He considered running over to his office and hitting the security alarm button. Still, he realized that Iannucci was serious enough to put a bullet into him in the process.

The art dealer led Stefano to his back office. With the gun still pointed at him, he instructed Schmidt to shut off the cameras and disconnected the security system. Stefano then grabbed the security disk that was inserted into the computer and put it into his pocket.

"Hmmm...now, let's see Wolf. Where would be a good place here for you to die?" he politely asked the art dealer.

Now Schmidt was fearful of his life. He only stood there, motionless. At that moment, the art dealer had no gun, no object, nothing to defend himself with.

Iannucci then motioned him to go down the stairs to his basement. With the gun still pointed at the art dealer, he instructed him to open his basement safe. He spun the combination dial several times back and forth until it opened. The large, six-foot safe had several envelopes sitting on the safe shelf, four containers of silver coins packaged and rolled neatly inside, and eighteen bundles of one-hundred-dollar bills, stacked in $10,000 denominations.

"If you want to rob me, take the money and go," the art dealer instructed the assassin.

"No, Wolf, it's not going to work that way," Stefano smirked.

He then made the art dealer take out all of the cash contents, including the silver coins, and put them in a large, black bag which coincidently, was already next to the safe.

He then instructed Schmidt to kneel on the floor, with his hands behind his head, in front of the opened safe, as if it were a holy altar.

"You do know the story about Fr. Angelo Gentile, correct?" the assassin innocently asked, pretending to be a history professor rather than a hired killer.

"No."

"He was the pastor who was hiding those Jews in his church in Florence, back in 1943. The Nazis raided his church, 'stole' those forty-two Vatican paintings, and they eventually persecuted 103 Jewish refugees that were hiding, thereby shipping them off to Auschwitz," he coolly explained.

More silence, as Schmidt continued to kneel in front of his open safe, his hand still over his head. It was as though the killer was making the art dealer pray and beg for mercy in front of it.

"Do you know what happened to Father Angelo?" Wolfgang only continued to kneel in silence.

"You Nazi's made him kneel and pray before the church altar, before shooting him in the back of the head."

Wolfgang Schmidt, his body now shaking, tried to protest.

"This has nothing to do with me!" he protested.

"No, Wolf…this has everything to do with you. You're from a family of fucking Nazi's, and your people killed an innocent priest while he prayed to God for mercy."

The art dealer began crying loudly, as the words ', please don't' continued to come out of his mouth between his weeping, howling cries for pity.

The assassin just stood there for a moment, smiling at the whimpering art dealer.

"Pope Emeritus has asked me to avenge the death of Father Angelo Gentile seventy-six years ago. And since you and your family 'stole' those paintings, Papa Onorio believes that you would be the best Nazi candidate to be punished for your war crimes."

Schmidt began crying even louder, as one of the last sounds he would hear would be his killer's continued cursing, calling him a 'Nazi bastard' and condemning him personally for Father Angelo's death.

Stefano Iannucci then pointed the gun point-blank up against the back of the art dealer's head.

"His Holiness sends his regards."

The assassin then coldly pulled the trigger. Blood splattered all over the open safe, as Wolfgang Schmidt's body slumped onto the floor in a pool of blood. As his body was bleeding profusely on the basement floor, Iannucci emptied his gun clip, shooting several more rounds into Wolfgang's already lifeless body.

He then grabbed the black bag with the money and coins and quickly walked upstairs.

Iannucci calmly walked out of the gallery, finding his Mercedes SUV parked several hundred feet away from the art store. As Iannucci pulled away onto the oncoming traffic on North Wells Street, he noticed that no one was walking around the immediate area.

Stefano Iannucci, on that wintry spring day, was able to kill the art dealer in broad daylight that morning unnoticed, as there were no witnesses around as he coolly drove away from the Kunstgeschäft Art Gallery on 524 North Wells Street.

He then put his hands-free cellular phone on speaker while driving on I-94, and then dialed the personal telephone number to his client at the Vatican.

"Hallo" responded a voice in German.

"Es ist jetzt abgeschlossen," Stefano said in broken German.

It is now completed.

CHAPTER FIFTY

Sister Giovanna gently knocked on the door before hearing the Pope acknowledge her request to enter. She had brought him his usual cup of chamomile tea and some freshly baked 'dolce' before retiring after 9:00 pm. It was the usual routine of Pope Emeritus Honorius V. He would usually read the bible, a book, write a memorandum or leave instructions for Monsignor Iacobelli along with a cup of tea before retiring. Sister Giovanna often enjoyed bringing along some biscotti, some freshly baked cake or sweets, or some other goodies that she could put together each evening before bringing up something for him to enjoy before retiring.

"Permesso, Suora," the Pope exclaimed. "You are late," he coldly observed.

"Excuse me, Your Holiness. I didn't mean to interrupt your meeting. I had to go to the other side of the kitchen to get the freshly made 'tiramisu' that I had made this morning. I hope you enjoy this," she exclaimed apologetically.

Monsignor Iacobelli was in the papal apartment, meeting with the Pope Emeritus at the time. They were discussing some Vatican Museum issues before Sister Giovanna knocked on the door.

"Grazie Giovanna," he gratefully replied.

Papa Onorio, despite his severe reaction, was very appreciative of how Sister Giovanna looked after him. She brought him his breakfast, lunch and dinner, three times a day, seven days a week. She made sure that she brought him his usual evening tea to help him fall asleep at nine o'clock every evening. She brought him his medication every morning, watching him take and swallow his blood pressure and cholesterol pills, making sure that he safely swallowed his medicine. She cleaned his papal apartment, picking up and keeping his bedroom clean and tidy each day. She scrubbed his floors and washed his clothes, laying out his papal garments every morning. Sister Giovanna looked after Papa Onorio as if she were a 'wife looking after a husband,' never complaining and always smiling for the Pope Emeritus.

Sister Giovanna was an older nun in her early seventies and had been looking after Pope Emeritus since his papal election in April 2002. She was a Carmelite nun, who was called upon by her order to serve the Pope and his staff at the Vatican faithfully. She was selected explicitly because she was fluent in both German and English. Although some thought of her religious order as glorified 'maids' to the Vatican papal staff, Sister Giovanna enjoyed her job serving Papa Onorio.

As Sister Giovanna entered the papal apartment, she gingerly placed the tray next to the Pope's nightstand and wished him a pleasant evening.

Monsignor Iacobelli walked over to the nightstand, admiring Papa Onorio's late-night 'dolce' before excusing himself.

A small coffee spoon was dropped on the floor, which Iacobelli immediately picked up and put back on the nightstand.

"Buona Sera, Your Holiness," Iacobelli simply said, before leaving the papal apartment.

"Buona Sera, Gianni."

The Pope eagerly changed into his evening attire and, after putting on his bathrobe, laid comfortably upon his bed. He put on his reading glasses as he opened up the bible for his evening prayers and reflection. He was up for a few hours afterward, finishing his tea and cake, until finally falling asleep.

The Vatican guards had noticed that evening that the lights of the apartment for the Pope Emeritus had been turned on at 1:30 am that early morning and were on for the rest of the night. Although they thought this was unusual, they figured that Papa Onorio was having another one of his 'sleepless nights' and was probably up the rest of the evening reading or writing letters of direction to his staff.

But for some strange reason, his bathroom lights were on as well, as one of the guards later noticed. At 2:30 am that early morning, the Vatican guard called the Head of Security, Giovanni Ambrosio, to mention that the Pope Emeritus's lights in his papal apartment were all still on and had never been shut off that early morning. Ambrosio only figured that the old pontiff must have either fell back asleep with the lights on or was up early, which was not uncommon.

"Perhaps His Holiness fell asleep and forgot to shut off the lights. He did look exasperated today," Ambrosio reasoned.

The Swiss Guard apologized again, and they both dismissed the observance. A few more hours passed by until 6:30 am. This was the usual time when Sister Giovanna summoned the Pope for his usual wake up call, with a soft knock on the door.

"Buon Giorno, Your Holiness," she called out softly as she knocked.

There was no answer. Sister Giovanna knocked and summoned the Pope Emeritus again. But there was still no answer. She continuously knocked on his door harder and harder, until finally, acquiring the key to his apartment from under her vestments, and slowly opened the door.

"Your Holiness?" she called, carrying the tray which was holding his morning coffee.

As she entered the bedroom, Papa Onorio was not sleeping in his bed and looked as though he had gotten up to go to the bathroom. The bathroom door was locked and closed, with the bathroom lights still on. She placed the breakfast tray on the nightstand next to the bed and approached the bathroom.

"Your Holiness?" she continued to knock on the bathroom door.

"Are you okay?" No answer.

Sister Giovanna pressed her ear against the bathroom door but could not hear any noises of running water or the flushing of the toilet. She repeatedly continued to knock on the door louder and louder.

At that moment, Sister Giovanna feared the worst. She took out her key and slowly opened the bathroom door.

Thereupon the marble tiled floor laid the Pope Emeritus, half-naked, lying face down. He looked as though he had fallen off the toilet. His mouth was open, and he was not breathing. His eyes were glazed open, his mouth contorted sideways and drenched with saliva and blood. The bathroom smelled like vomit and urine as if the Pope had violently thrown up and choked on his vomit. His face was distorted and ashen as if he had spent the last few minutes of his life fiercely convulsing, choking, vomiting, and gasping for air right there in his bathroom. There was blood on the floor, and his head was bleeding as if he had hit his head hard when he hit the marble tiled floor. She felt his neck and his body. There was no pulse, and the Pope Emeritus felt extremely cold.

Sister Giovanna screamed, immediately realizing that the Pope Emeritus was no longer alive. The sight of him lying face down in the bathroom scared her, and she quickly ran out of the papal apartment to get security and to call Monsignor Iacobelli.

Monsignor Iacobelli arrived at the papal residence several minutes later, along with the Head of Security, Giovanni Ambrosio. The monsignor was vaguely familiar with the Vatican procedure regarding the death of a pope, having experience with Pope John Paul II several years ago. After calming down Sister Giovanna, he sealed off the papal apartment until Cardinal Antonio Mastropieri arrived ten minutes later.

Cardinal Mastropieri was the head of the Apostolic Camera, the 'Camerlengo,' or the Chamberlain to the Holy Catholic Church. His Vatican office was responsible for the administration of the Vatican and the temporal goods of the Holy See during the vacancy created by the death or resignation of a Roman Pontiff. When a pope dies or resigns, the chamberlain is charged with sealing the papal apartments, chairing consultations about the papal funeral, making practical preparations for the conclave to elect the next pope, and chairing a committee of cardinals taking care of the ordinary affairs of the church until a new pope is elected.

Sister Giovanna later observed and commented on the calmness and lack of astonishment in the Monsignor's face, as he quickly summoned everyone away, except for Ambrosio. They both entered the apartment and sealed off the room as Cardinal Mastropieri called out the baptismal name of Pope Honorius V.

"Josef Claus Schroder?" inquired Mastropieri. A moment passed.

"Josef Claus Schroder?" the Cardinal called out again. Another long five seconds passed.

"Josef Claus Schroder?" called the Cardinal for the third and last time, according to papal ritual. The Cardinal then removed the Pope's papal ring, acquired a hammer and immediately crushed and destroyed it. He then turned to Giovanni Ambrosio and gave out orders.

"He must have had a massive heart attack," Mastropieri declared.

"We will need to clean up the Pope," he said, knowing full well that an autopsy, according to Vatican law, would never be performed. A doctor was not called, and no other physical examination was made of the Pope Emeritus's body. Within ninety minutes, a special Vatican undertaker was called upon to remove the old pontiff's body from his papal apartment and to begin the embalming process.

The morning papers all over Rome were proclaiming the sudden death of Pope Emeritus Honorius V. The television reporters and cable vans, with their long antennas and satellite dishes, were beginning to gather in St. Peter's Square, as the official notice and Vatican announcement had needed to be made. It was Holy Week, and the Pope Emeritus passing away on Good Friday, three days before Easter that year seemed like divine intervention, according to the press and media. Crowds were gathering in front of the church, waiting to hear the official word as to the means of the old former pope's sudden death.

Cardinal Antonio Mastropieri was overlooking the gathering crowds and people down below from the papal apartment, as there was a knock on the door.

"Permesso, your Eminence." It was Monsignor Iacobelli.

"Have you prepared a statement?" Mastropieri asked in a loud, annoying voice.

"Yes," as he handed it to the Cardinal.

Mastropieri read the statement and nodded his head.

"I am happy to read that we are assuming his bad heart and cardiac problems as the reason for his sudden passing, is that correct Monsignor?" the Cardinal asked as if looking for concurrence.

"That is correct, Your Eminence."

A shadow of a smile seemed to come over the Monsignor's face as he read the statement for the Cardinal. They both silently paused as they both looked out of the papal window. Iacobelli knew that now, the

Pope Emeritus's plan would soon die with him. His fixation regarding his Vatican Museum duties and especially his obsession with the reacquisition of the stolen Uffizi paintings would finally be put to rest.

It had seemed that the only person in Rome who was interested in reacquiring those once stolen Vatican paintings was the Pope Emeritus himself. Neither the media, the Vatican curators, nor the current Pope, expressed anything other than indifference in the acquisition and rescue of those former Nazi stolen masterpieces. Papa Onorio made this his fascination, and unfortunately, no one else in Rome was interested.

"We have a lot of work to do, Monsignor. We must begin to arrange a funeral for a pope," exclaimed the Cardinal.

"Arrange a press conference for noon today. We will read this statement. Make it very clear to the press that no questions will be answered, and, of course...." he slowly paused, "There will be no autopsy, following Vatican law," he sternly finished.

The monsignor had his marching orders and made the proper arrangements on that rainy, March day to bury Papa Onorio. On 'Pasquetta,' the following Monday after Easter Sunday, Pope Honorius V was laid out in the state. He was dressed in his red, papal vestments, wearing the white, pointed papal hat, with his head resting on a red pillow. His hands were neatly folded, holding a rosary, as his body laid to rest on a long, slanted podium in front of the main altar of St. Peter's Basilica. Hundreds and hundreds of people began filing slowly past his embalmed body, looking almost entirely, as if to be the sleeping shepherd amongst his grieving flock. His funeral mass later that week, was attended by many world dignitaries, celebrated and conducted by the current Pope.

But the grief and the intense mourning that usually are associated with the death of any pope seemed to be missing in this instance. With the death of Pope Emeritus Honorius V, it was as though the Roman Catholic Church and especially the Vatican, had breathed a sigh of relief. No longer was there another conservative, overbearing former pontiff making headaches for the Vatican Church. No longer was there another church head of state, contradicting the current pope in his religious doctrines and policies.

After several hours, which included a formal outside procession of the Pope's body within an enclosed glass casket, his remains were carried into the cave downstairs beneath the grand altar of St. Peter's Basilica. In a white and gray marble tomb, which had already been prepared and opened, his body within the glass casket was placed into the marble encasement. Upon the outside of the tomb read the simple Latin inscription:

Honorivs PP. V

Monsignor Gianpaolo Iacobelli was sitting in the living room of his small, Vatican apartment that early evening after the funeral. He had been very reflective of the papal events of the last several days. He had always suspected that Papa Onorio was behind his cousin's death in Chicago that past December and was mildly content with the final demise of the evil Pope Emeritus. He knew that there was a special place in hell for the Nazi pope, who would go as far as having others murdered to accomplish his agenda. The monsignor was thankful for the divine powers that be, in finally, dictating his ultimate, mortal death.

After almost two decades as both the supreme pontiff and the only pope in six hundred years to resign his position as the head of the Roman Catholic Church, the former Josef Cardinal Schroder of Munich was now at rest. It became quite apparent in the last several years of his life that Papa Onorio was a church leader with defining symptoms of dementia and bipolar disease. This was a dangerous combination, along with his significant papal power and needless obsessions. He was impassioned and fixated in correcting his Vatican legacy.

With the hiring of a professional assassin and his contracting the homicide of Carlo Marchese and Wolfgang Schmidt, the Pope Emeritus was willing to go to any length to fix it. The former pontiff was not of his right mind, and his 'death by natural causes' was probably God's means of stopping him from continuing to commit more of his mortal sins.

Iacobelli got up from his chair and walked over to his bathroom. He then opened up the medicine cabinet and realized that he had not hidden away the small bottle of arsenic, which was still openly displayed on his cabinet shelf. He opened up the poisonous contents and flushed it down the toilet, quietly smiling to himself before destroying the empty container.

He was not about to let the murder of his beloved cousin go unpunished.

CHAPTER FIFTY-ONE

The hot, South American sun was already scorching, as Stefano Iannucci got up early that Sunday morning to turn on the espresso machine and get the sleep out of his eyes. He was staying in an opulent villa in Salinas, Ecuador, and was grateful to his friend, Girolamo Calzante, a colleague who owned this spectacular mansion. He had known him since they were Italian 'Navy Seals' together, allowing him to rent out his vacation home off the ocean. The white, blue stucco tiled structure was over 5,000 square feet, with four bedrooms and a beautiful outdoor pool and patio constructed on the third floor, overlooking the panoramic views of the Pacific Ocean.

Although the seaside town of Salinas settled near the equator on South America's west coast, the temperatures usually straddled between sixty and eighty degrees during May. It was unusual for the famous South American beach town to be so brazenly hot on that spring day, with sweltering temperatures so early in the morning. Stefano walked out onto the rooftop patio and laid down on the lounge chair next to the pool with his eye-opening cup of espresso.

He was contemplating the forthcoming activities of this day, beginning with their four-hour drive to the City of Quito. He had been busy over the last several days, making the arrangements for the shipment of the forty-one Uffizi paintings from Assisi, Italy, where he was storing them, freighted by an unmarked cargo van to Naples, Italy. The priceless shipment was then loaded onto a freight container and shipped to the Guayas Province in Guayaquil, Ecuador, at the Puerto Maritimo. After going through customs (for whom Don Antonio

Copertino had connections), the loaded the paintings were sent to the Museo de Arte Moderno. A special wing had been built and financed by Don Copertino, especially for the arrival and secured display of these forty-one Renaissance Italian paintings.

Don Copertino, through several acquaintances by the Catholic Church, had settled with Stefano Iannucci for the purchase and shipment of these forty-one paintings for the discounted price cash price of twenty million U.S. dollars. Claudia Romanelli had brokered the deal to the Ecuadorian art museum, and her pricey commission of fifty percent was an expensive one.

Stefano was not very agreeable to Romanelli's commission terms. But Romanelli made Iannucci understand that she was risking her own life in brokering this deal to the Archdiocese of Quito and their landmark art museum, hoping that the Uffizi would never find out about her involvement. Stefano Iannucci had realized at the time that this was the price of doing business and unloading these much sought-after Uffizi masterpieces.

Since the death of Pope Emeritus Honorius V almost two months ago, Iannucci was more than happy to sell off these Uffizi paintings at a discounted price to be free of the international pressures of those seeking to locate and acquire these rare masterpieces. He was happy to finally ship the art collection from the convent in Assisi to Ecuador, South America. Continuing to ensure the secret location of these Uffizi paintings continued to be a challenge for Iannucci. He was more than happy to finally be rid of them for the cut-rate sales price of only twenty million dollars.

"Good morning, honey." Claudia's disheveled blonde hair appropriately matched her button-down white shirt, for which she was wearing nothing underneath. She walked over to Stefano and gave him a sensual, wet morning kiss, trying hard not to spill her freshly brewed cappuccino.

"How did you sleep?" asked the Italian assassin.

"Very well, my love," she smiled, winking her eye and making visual reference to their intense lovemaking the night before. They kissed and passionately cuddled each other for several long moments, with only the South American sun as a witness to their pool-side flirting.

"What a gorgeous view!" she exclaimed, enjoying her first morning at the coastal mansion. The villa overlooked the well-placed ocean rocks overseeing the Pacific Ocean, which was very close to the seaside resort town of Salinas. Claudia had arrived yesterday from Florence's Amerigo Vespucci Airport, and after a very bumpy, turbulent six-hour airplane ride, was more than happy to relax last evening at her temporary new digs.

Salinas, Ecuador, is a coastal town on the western tip of Ecuador's Santa Elena province, with its famous beaches and panoramic ocean views. Their rented luxury villa was located on the far side of the popular tourist city and is located four hours away from Quito, the capital city of Ecuador.

Don Antonio Copertino, a very wealthy industrialist and capital investor within the city, was the benefactor who had donated the construction of the new Copertino Renaissance Cultural Art Wing at Quito's Modern Art Museum. He was encouraged to finally fill up the museum addition of his family namesake with the elusive stolen art paintings. The dedication ceremony would be a black-tie event taking place later that Sunday evening at six o'clock, and Stefano and Claudia were invited to be on hand for this historic, special event.

Stefano and Claudia packed up their suitcases that morning. They began their four-hour drive to Quito, eventually checking into the Villa Colonna Quito, a luxury hotel located not very far from the Museo de Arte Moderno. After settling in, Stefano walked downstairs to the lobby of the hotel, as he needed to make an urgent telephone call.

"Cardinal Estaveas, por favor," Stefano requested, as he called the direct line to the Cardinal of Quito. Cardinal Jose Maria Estaveas, was an esteemed and influential Archbishop of Quito and was perhaps, the most powerful cleric in all of South America. His name had been on the shortlist of the last two papal conclaves in Rome and was very well known within Vatican City. Cardinal Estaveas was dominant in assisting in the sale of the Florentine artworks to Quito's Museo de Arte Moderno, with the blessing of the Vatican See.

After the unexpected death, Papa Onorio, Stefano Iannucci was stuck with these priceless paintings and was very interested in selling them on the black market to the highest bidder. Cardinal Estaveas, with the help of Claudia Romanelli and her international art connections at the Uffizi Museum, was able to broker these masterpieces to Don Copertino, with the help of the Cardinal, along with a nominal church donation of $250,000. Iannucci also knew that besides this being the special occasion of the dedication of the grand new museum art wing, that this day was significant for another reason:

Today was payday.

Stefano was apprehensive to finally meet with the Cardinal and Copertino to ultimately collect on the twenty-million-dollar price tag for these priceless Uffizi masterpieces. Copertino had wired one million dollars as a deposit into Iannucci's Swiss bank account but insisted that he acquire the rest of the sale proceeds in cash. Iannucci had an appointment the next day with a banking

460

executive from the Banco Del Pacifico, with whom he had arranged to acquire a safe deposit box specifically for this transaction.

"*Espero conocerte en completer nuestra transaccion,*" Iannucci said in fluent Spanish.

"I look forward to meeting with you and Don Copertino in completing our transaction."

"Indeed," replied the Cardinal. "There will be a small gathering at Don Copertino's villa before the wing dedication ceremony. We will meet there to complete the deal."

The couple arrived at the picturesque, mansion estate of Don Antonio Copertino on that sunny, hot afternoon at four o'clock. The well-manicured gardens complimented the magnificent, beige stucco estate of Ecuador's most notable benefactor. The home looked like it had jumped out of an architectural magazine, with its Spanish style balconies and red, clay-tiled roof. Iannucci had rented a new Mercedes SL 450 Convertible Roadster when he arrived in Ecuador, and slowly pulled his black luxury vehicle around the horseshoe driveway, depositing the car keys to the valet.

Stefano was handsomely dressed in a black, bow-tied tuxedo, and with his slicked black hair, could have passed for a younger version of Sean Connery as James Bond. His beautiful blonde date, Claudia, was wearing a white, sequined dress that was open in the back, exposing her fantastic figure and her incredibly dark tan lines. The two of them made a grand entrance and greeted several guests until a butler personally informed Iannucci that Don Copertino was ready to see him.

Stefano kissed his date on the cheek. "This should only take a minute."

The butler then led him to the west side of the estate to the private office of Don Copertino, where both he and Cardinal Estaveas were waiting.

"It is a pleasure to meet you finally," exclaimed Don Antonio, as Stefano Iannucci formally kissed the affluent industrialist on both cheeks. He then grasped the hand of Cardinal Estaveas, genuflected, and then kissed his ring. They both gave him a warm greeting.

"You and Signorina Romanelli have made the dreams of our family, and the dreams of this great City of Quito come true," said Copertino. He then walked over to his elaborate bar towards the west side of his office and poured three fingers of Louis XVI Cognac into three crystal glass tumblers. He then offered his respective guests each a glass before making his toast.

"To the success of our new renaissance art wing. May this new addition be the beginning of new cultural development for our beloved City of Quito. May this historic day be the start of a new era of artistic and cultural success for not only Quito but all of South America," proposed Don Antonio.

"Salute," as the three new friends enjoyed their first toast together. Both the Cardinal and Don Copertino began to talk about the features of their new cultural art wing for more than twenty minutes, almost completely ignoring the reason for Stefano Iannucci's private visit excitedly.

"Oh, Signor Stefano, I almost forgot!" as Copertino embarrassingly walked behind his desk, opened the doors of his credenza, and grasped something inside. For some reason, Iannucci automatically put his right hand onto his left breast pocket, where he always stored his loaded Beretta M9 Semi-Automatic 9mm pistol. It was a terrible habit, as he had learned to trust no one, no matter how friendly their appearance.

Copertino then pulled out a large, black suitcase, which he placed on top of his desk and opened it up for Iannucci's inspection. There, in neatly stacked dominations of $10,000, were nineteen hundred bundles of new, crisp $100-dollar bills, tightly wrapped and accordingly arranged within the black, Samsonite suitcase.

"It's all there," Copertino proudly boasted.

Stefano withdrew several stacks of bundled currency and inspected the suitcase contents, knowing that he had neither the time nor the patience to count out all of the U.S. currency carefully. He then smiled at Copertino.

"Very good, gentlemen."

But as he was about to close the suitcase, Cardinal Estaveas stopped him, grasping his wrist.

"Signor Iannucci? There is the matter of a well-deserved donation?"

Without asking for permission, the Cardinal brazenly reached into the suitcase and helped himself to twenty-five stacks of $10,000 cash bundles, first placing them on top of Don Copertino's desk. He then acquired a black leather bag from underneath the desk and filled it with the self-served church donation. Iannucci looked at the Cardinal in shock at first, but then quickly closed the suitcase before anyone else helped themselves to his well-earned proceeds.

"It's been a pleasure doing business, gentlemen," as he quickly grasped the briefcase filled with currency and walked out of Copertino's office without shaking anyone's hand. He then walked over to his date, who was sitting at their table, enjoying a dry martini.

"The transaction is completed, my love."

Claudia smiled, noticing Iannucci tightly grasping the sizeable black suitcase, and was garnering immense attention from the other guests. The pair sat at the table for several minutes throughout the cocktail hour, until Claudia finally suggested;

"Perhaps, we should leave and go back to the hotel, darling. I don't believe you want to be tagging along with your black suitcase full of cash all night long," Claudia said.

Knowing that their abrupt departure and abandonment of the art wing ceremony would look extremely rude to their gracious hosts, the two of them decided to leave anyway and finished their martinis. They then casually walked outside, where the valet had their Mercedes sports car parked nearby.

Still holding the black suitcase, Stefano opened the car door for his date and then casually walked behind the car, opening the trunk with his car keys. He was able to fit the large suitcase into the small trunk of his sports car convertible.

While closing the door of his trunk, he reached again into his left breast coat pocket, making sure that his Beretta revolver was still loaded and ready to use.

Stefano Iannucci was having second thoughts regarding Claudia's commission arrangement.

CHAPTER FIFTY-TWO

The Mercedes SL 450 Convertible Roadster was speeding through the winding streets of Quito, exiting the village and into the countryside at a high rate of speed. Iannucci was driving that convertible roadster like a Grand Prix race car, pushing the accelerator in excess of 90 miles an hour. He was taking each curve of the winding road ahead with more and more speed, as the palm trees seemed to sway with the wind of the speeding sports car. It was the early evening, and the Ecuadorian sunset was beginning to cast a shadow on the roads ahead. Iannucci raced his vehicle as if he was in a hurry.

"Slow down, honey," Claudia said to her boyfriend.

"I want to get back into the hotel as soon as possible. I want to check this briefcase in with hotel security, and the head security manager closes his office at 9:00 pm," the professional assassin explained.

He continued to drive the Mercedes roadster down the highway, then suddenly, took an unexpected exit onto an adjoining gravel road. He continued down that gravel road for several minutes, as the sunset turned to darkness.

"Honey? Where are we going?" Claudia inquired.

"This is a short-cut," Iannucci lied.

After a few more minutes, Iannucci suddenly pulled the vehicle onto the side of the gravel road. At that point, Claudia became very scared and suspicious. She tightly grasped her small purse with her right hand on her lap. Stefano very calmly got out of the car.

"Why are we stopping here," she timidly asked.

"Well, my dear," as Stefano withdrew his Beretta M9 Semi-Automatic 9mm pistol from his tuxedo jacket pocket and pointed it directly at her.

"This is where we will go our separate ways."

Claudia was in shock.

After ordering her out of the car, she strolled across the roadside brush in her black high heels. She was still tightly gripping her purse, holding it with her left hand, and putting her right hand inside. Hidden was a small, loaded .22 caliber pistol.

As her back was turned, Stefano continued to talk, "I'm sorry it has to work out this way."

While her back was still turned toward Stefano, she pleaded, "Perhaps we can work something out, Stefano. It doesn't have to end like this."

"No, my dear. I'm afraid it does. Your commission requirements are a little too steep for me. Besides, now that I've sold the paintings, I don't need you anymore," he politely replied.

"And besides, I would really prefer you out of the way."

At that moment, Claudia withdrew her pistol and quickly turned around. As if she was in a great western movie, withdrew her gun from her purse holster and shot Stefano directly in the stomach, mortally wounding him.

Iannucci, seeing that Claudia had a gun, fired directly back at Claudia, almost simultaneously, shooting her straight in the forehead.

It seemed that Stefano, being that he already had his Beretta aimed at Claudia, had a better line of fire, as he returned a single shot.

Claudia Romanelli was dead before she hit the ground.

As Stefano was bleeding profusely from his stomach wound, he pulled out his handkerchief and placed it tightly over his stomach wound with his left hand. He was in a tremendous amount of pain. He started the Mercedes roadster, backed up, and then continued to drive back onto the road leading into town.

Claudia's lifeless body was left on the side of the gravel road, dead and discarded in the dark. Her pistol was still in her right hand, holding her open purse with her left. In her ultimate greed, she had chosen to cash in on the proceeds of the Uffizi art collection by sleeping with one of Hell's most vicious, most ruthless demons. She was now dead and abandoned alongside a dark, South American road, a hapless victim of the devil's divine wrath.

While his stomach wound was still bleeding, Stefano drove the car and arrived at the parking lot of the Quito luxury hotel ten minutes later. Blood profusely dripping, Stefano maneuvered his hand and began placing pressure on his stomach wound. He awkwardly withdrew his luggage case filled with cash and brought it with him as he cautiously entered the hotel. Droplets of blood were being sprinkled onto the marble hallway as Stefano was walking into the hotel lobby and towards his hotel suite. After taking the elevator to the fifth floor, he managed to open his hotel room door with the room key and place his luggage bag on the floor. He then collapsed on the bed.

It was almost nine o'clock in the evening.

At about eleven o'clock, a tall, gray-haired man entered the Villa Colonna Quito Hotel. He knew which hotel room he was looking for, as the Detective had received a text earlier, informing him that he needed to go to Room 522 on the fifth floor.

As he exited off of the elevator, he noticed a trail of blood droplets, making a path on the carpeting to the room where Iannucci was staying.

He knocked on the door several times, but there was no answer. Using a lock picking device, he was able to enter the luxury suite.

There on the king-size bed was Stefano Iannucci, collapsed in a pool of blood all over his bed. The man walked up to the professional assassin and put his hand on his neck. He was barely breathing, and the blood from his stomach wound was still bleeding profusely. His eyes were barely open.

"Detective," as Iannucci recognized who it was, whispering in a meager voice. The professional assassin was well aware of the Munich detective's efforts to locate him over the years. There had been other questionable murders that have occurred in Munich in the past that the detective wished to question him on.

"So, we finally meet," Detective Hildebrandt said.

"Why are you here?" he whispered.

"I'm here to collect for your partners."

"Partners?" Iannucci barely asked.

"Yes. You have some partners that you need to pay off," Hildebrandt coldly said.

He then grabbed the black suitcase that was on the floor and opened it up on the bedroom dresser, making sure the contents were inside. He visually counted the cash, bundles of one hundred U.S. dollars rolled in $10,000 denominations.

"Okay...this will do," Hildebrandt smiled, closing the suitcase and started heading for the door.

"Wait!" Iannucci garbled in a low voice. "Don't leave me here like this," he begged.

"Really? Seeing that you're a professional assassin, what would you like me to do?" Hildebrandt asked.

"What is that old saying? 'Those who live by the sword, die by the sword?'" he sarcastically smiled.

The Munich detective then walked up to the bed where Iannucci was lying. Pulling out the assassin's Beretta M9 Semi-Automatic 9mm pistol that was still in his tuxedo coat packet, the German detective used his handkerchief and placed the gun in Iannucci's left hand. He then took Stefano's left hand with the gun and pointed it up to the killer's temple, point-blank.

And then, using Stefano Iannucci's index finger, he pulled the trigger with the pistol pointed up against his head.

Blood and bone fragments from his skull were suddenly splattered up against the wall and on the room carpeting next to the king-size bed. His flesh, brain matter, bone tissue, and blood was splashed everywhere and was gushing onto the bedroom floor.

Making sure there was no splattered blood on his clean suitcoat and tie, the Munich detective quickly exited the hotel suite, closing the locked door behind him. As he calmly walked out of the hotel with the suitcase full of cash, he entered his rented car and exited the Quito hotel parking lot. As he was driving on the expressway towards the airport, he pulled out his cell phone and texted a congratulatory, one-word message to his partner in German:

Glückwunsch.

CHAPTER FIFTY-THREE

It had been over a year since I had wrapped up my news investigation into the homicide of Don Carlo Marchese and his Vatican killers. As it had turned out, after the death of Pope Emeritus Honorius V and the murder of Wolfgang Schmidt, the stolen Uffizi paintings somehow ended up in a remote part of the world. My subsequent news articles and Sun-Times investigation caused quite a stir nationally and around the art world. I had tied the Vatican to the Marchese murder and inferred that the instigator of these deaths was linked into the Pope Emeritus himself.

Because 'Papa Onorio' was now dead, and Wolfgang Schmidt and Carlo Marchese were no longer around, it was very easy for Monsignor Iacobelli, the papal secretary, to deny any plausible connection between their pursuit of the Uffizi paintings, their underworld dealings with the Marchese Family, and probable 'murder-for-hire' in Marchese's and Schmidt's homicides.

Without any hard proof or evidence connecting the Vatican directly with these murders, it ended up as a 'sensationalized' news story on CNN and RAI UNO television. Realizing that we could no longer make any more accusations without being sued and acquiring the reputation of the 'National Enquirer,' my editor, Mike Daudelin, and I decided to put the story to bed and move on.

It had been later publicized that forty-one of the paintings were now on display at the Quito Art Gallery in Ecuador, South America, as they were 'brokered' for the discounted price of twenty million dollars, per a CNN news story. As the story was breaking, the Archdiocese of

Quito was already covering their tracks. They produced a 'legitimate' bill of sale for the forty-one paintings, saying that an 'anonymous art dealer' had legally acquired and sold the paintings. Considering that the Uffizi art collection was appraised at close to two hundred million dollars, the people of Quito, Ecuador, got quite a bargain for their cultural museum.

When the word was out that the Uffizi art collection was on display in Quito, the board of directors of the Uffizi Museum only rendered a statement of good wishes to Don Copertino and his new art wing. The board members believed that all of those recovered paintings and masterpieces had a 'curse' about them and were no longer interested in pursuing their recovery.

I had also heard later on that there was a gruesome double murder in Quito immediately after their museum dedication, and that one of the victims was Veronica's girlfriend, Claudia Romanelli. She had been found dead on the side of an abandoned road. Her companion, who turned out to be her boyfriend and professional killer, Stefano Iannucci, was also found murdered in their Quito hotel room. The 'anonymous art dealer,' I came to figure out, was Claudia's boyfriend, Iannucci. He was working for the Vatican and the Pope Emeritus in reacquiring those missing paintings and brokered them to the Archdiocese of Quito when Pope Honorius V suddenly passed away shortly before.

The authorities, using their limited forensics and the ballistics from Iannucci's Beretta, closed the case as a 'murder-suicide.'

After all of my excitement in Florence and not hearing from Veronica anymore, I went back to my relaxed surroundings in my comfortable townhouse in Lincoln Park, continuing to take care of my parents in Park Ridge. With my father's prolonged Parkinson's illness, he passed away a month ago at the age of 81 years old, so I had been a little depressed and unhappy since then.

We had a beautiful funeral mass for him at St. Paul of the Cross in Park Ridge, and I gave a nice eulogy for him at his service. My mother has been so lost without him, and I had been trying to look after her daily, which was becoming a full-time job.

I had been back at work for over two weeks now, and I was sitting back at my desk working on some political city hall investigation into the City of Chicago building department when 'The Chief' called me into his office.

"Paulie...Loyola University has put out a press release, requesting some news coverage at an artwork unveiling going on in Lake Forest this weekend. I was wondering if you might be available to cover it?"

"Really? Come on, Chief. I've seen enough expensive art pieces in enough museums to last a lifetime. I'm not sure I want to look at another art painting," I replied.

"Listen, Paulie. You're our resident art expert now, and besides...it's at some high-class, swanky mansion up on Sheridan Road off of the lake somewhere. You might enjoy it. I'm sure the food and the booze will be top-shelf. All the local politicians and big-shots will be there."

That's all I needed—another cultural artworld story. Since becoming somewhat of an 'art expert' after the Uffizi story, the 'Chief' decided to send me up to Lake Forest to do the story on this 'new art painting' donation by one of the local millionaires.

This painting was a Renaissance work of art that had been missing for an extended period of time, and

Loyola University requested some news coverage at its unveiling that Saturday. We were told that the 'painting' was a well sought-after masterpiece that would be donated to the Loyola Museum of Art in Chicago by a wealthy North Shore couple.

I refused at first, telling Daudelin that I just wasn't in the mood. But after some begging from 'The Chief,' I consented. He insisted that I go since he had no one else to send to cover the story. He probably figured that it would take 'my mind off of things.'

I was given the address of this event and its location. It was a newly built, opulent mansion located on the far north side of Sheridan Road, just off of Lake Michigan. It was a few blocks adjacent to the Lake Forest Cemetery and was considered to be one of the most exclusive sections of the North Shore suburb.

The couple hosting the party, Gary and Daniella Halsted, had newly purchased and developed the property six months ago, and all of the local city politicians and various other community socialites were invited to this Lake Forest social event. I looked them up on the internet, only to find out that Gary Halsted was classified as an 'international venture capitalist,' with investments located mainly in Europe.

His wife, Daniella, sounded like the usual North Shore trophy wife, who probably spent the majority of her time working out at the East Bank Club and doing 'high-teas' at the Drake Hotel downtown. They were a local, new money, power couple trying to fit into the community, and hosting this local garden party on the occasion of donating one of these exclusive masterpieces was their way of trying to fit into the upper class, Lake Forest community.

On Friday, I made a phone call to one of my connections at the North Shore Country Club in Glenview, a man by the name of John Markle, asking for any information on the unknown couple. He was on the board of directors of that exclusive club on the North Shore, and anyone trying to fit into the community and wishing to 'hob-nob' with all of the affluent couples applied for admission into their club.

He had told me that the Halsted's had recently applied for membership there, paying the one hundred and seventy-five-thousand-dollar initiation fee to join their exclusive group. The private Glenview club was very selective as to who they allowed joining their association. There was a long waiting list and an extensive interview process that was involved, including prospective member applicants hosting such opulent dinners and parties as a means of gaining the favor of its country club members.

That afternoon, I pulled my car around the horseshoe driveway of the Lake Forest mansion and handed my keys over to one of the valets. I was hoping he would park and hide my older SUV somewhere in between the Bentley's, the Maserati's, and upscale Rolls Royce's parked down the street from the mansion.

It was the middle of June, and the summer weather that Saturday afternoon could not have been more perfect for a back-yard garden party. The three-acre back yard faced up against a large bluff off of Lake Michigan, with three dozen or more steps leading down to the beach and the well landscaped, pictured rocks down below. There were approximately one hundred and fifty white chairs set up in front of a large stage with the scenic lake as its backdrop.

The masterpiece painting, which was covered up by a black, velvet cloth, was set up in the stage's center, along with several trustees from the Loyola Museum of

475

Art seated alongside the painting. Everyone was well dressed in suits and cocktail dresses, while the black-tie servants were serving appetizers and drinks to all of the guests. I was glad that I was astute enough to wear my suit and tie to this event.

As I acquired an appetizer and scotch-on-the rocks, I ran into my Channel Eight news reporter buddy. I kind of figured he would be here as well.

"Hey, Paulie."

"What's up, Chaz…nice spread here."

"Oh, yes. Beautiful place," Chaz Rizzo observed, as he was introducing me to his lovely, much younger date, Elisa. We made some small talk as I was staring at his young, blonde 'arm-piece' while she wasn't looking.

She was dressed in a very low cut, very tight white cocktail dress, and seemed to be walking very cautiously. Chaz's date was probably worried about her 'deli-style' breasts popping out of her incredibly tight Armani dress. I began wondering where Chaz had met his newest flavor of the month, whether it was on Snap Chat or Craig's List.

"It's amazing what these new money couples will do to fit in," he casually mentioned, as I asked him to point out our gracious North Shore hosts.

Gary Halsted, a tall, gray-haired, older man in his sixties, was socializing with several of his garden party guests, while his young, red-haired wife was on the other side of the party talking to another couple. I couldn't get a good look at her, but judging from her stance and her body type from a distance, she seemed to look very familiar. But she was standing too far away.

At that moment, everyone was asked to sit down, as the garden party program was about to begin. Several trustees from the Loyola Art Museum were introduced, and each made a very gracious speech about how excited they were to receive this donated Renaissance masterpiece from the Halsted Family.

The Loyola University Museum of Art, which had opened in the fall of 2005, is a local Chicago museum with mounting exhibits ranging from the spiritual art masterpieces to the various periods of the Italian and French Renaissance, located at the Water Tower Campus on North Michigan Ave.

Then finally, the Halsted's were introduced as they both came on stage to make the presentation. Gary Halsted had an intense, pronounced German accent, as if he was still struggling with the English language, as he made a complimentary speech on how excited both he and his wife were to donate this exclusive painting, which was a 'family heirloom' to the Loyola Art Museum.

And then, he passed the microphone over to his young, red-headed wife. I continued to study her while she was talking, as her face, her voice and her mannerisms were unmistakable.

I almost fell off of my chair, as I immediately recognized who she was:

It was Veronica Giancarlo.

I could tell that she had 'some work done,' as her face and skin looked significantly smoother and less aged. With all of her cosmetic surgeries and probable Botox injections, she looked like a young twenty-something from thirty feet away.

I had heard that she had left her full-time job as the assistant art curator at the Art Institute of Chicago

477

and was no longer a freelance writer with the newspaper. But truth be told, I had not been motivated or interested in following up on her whereabouts since our trip to Florence. She must have recently gotten married. But why the new identity? And who was this Gary Halsted guy?

I continued to study the two of them standing up there, looking like Ozzie and Harriet Nelson, making their extensive presentation of their 'family heirloom painting' being donated to the Loyola University Art Museum.

All of a sudden, it hit me like a ton of bricks.

Sitting on that white, wooden chair at that garden party in Lake Forest, I had finally put all of the puzzle pieces together that Saturday afternoon.

I realized that 'Gary Halsted' was the alias identity for Detective **Lieutenant Gerhard Hildebrandt** of the Munich Police Department. I was sure of it. I remembered him now, as his low, deep baritone voice and German accent was unmistakable. He was now living in Lake Forest with his new, lovely, now red-haired, and cosmetically improved wife, Veronica.

I came to realize that day, that Veronica Daniella Giancarlo-Halsted was related to the Giammarco Family and was the niece to Don Rodolfo Giammarco. It was her 'Zio Rodolfo' that she was talking to that early morning in our Florence hotel room. I researched and found out later that Veronica had a continued relationship with her uncle and had a close affiliation with the 'Firenze Mafia.'

The Giammarco Family, in its quest to acquire back those paintings, were only able to obtain the Fra Lippi painting at the Detroit airport, interrupting the sale transaction between Marchese and Licovoli Families and the Detroit Institute of Art.

I had investigated and discovered that Don Marchese, as revenge against Don Giammarco, returned to Italy to try to retrieve those Uffizi paintings again, only killing a Franciscan nun in Assisi instead.

Veronica must have hooked up with Detective Hildebrandt after our encounter at the Ristorante Donatello that morning in Florence. Together, they figured out who had the Uffizi paintings. That was probably why Veronica went out with Claudia the first night we were in Florence. She convinced Claudia to start dating the professional assassin, Stefano Iannucci.

They both figured out that he had the Uffizi paintings all along. She knew that getting close to Iannucci would lead all of them to the location and eventual sale of that elusive art collection. They eventually figured out that Iannucci had the paintings hidden at that Franciscan convent in Assisi. They must have known that the professional assassin was working on behalf of the Vatican.

When the Pope Emeritus was found dead, and when Giammarco no longer wanted the paintings, Claudia probably convinced Iannucci to sell those paintings to the Quito Art Gallery in Ecuador. It was perhaps Veronica Giancarlo, who most likely arranged for the whole transaction.

I realized in my investigation that it was Iannucci, the hired assassin for the Vatican, along with another associate, who had killed Don Carlo Marchese at the Blackstone Hotel. His murder was a revenge killing by the Pope Emeritus for betraying and double-crossing him on the sale of those Uffizi paintings.

The hired assassin also went on to kill Wolfgang Schmidt for acquiring those paintings, and for being from a long line of Nazi's responsible for stealing priceless art. Schmidt's murder was another means of the Pope Emeritus cleansing himself from being a 'Nazi,' by murdering a Nazi descendant who was indirectly responsible for the wartime Nazi art thefts.

When the Quito transaction was completed, Claudia informed Hildebrandt, hoping he would eliminate the professional assassin, and the three of them, Hildebrandt, Claudia and Veronica could split the proceeds. They were all in on this together.

But after, when the professional assassin and his girlfriend Claudia were both found shot dead in Quito, the large briefcase with the cash proceeds from the sale of the paintings went missing. It must have been Hildebrandt who was plotting with Veronica to acquire the cash proceeds all along. Veronica and Hildebrandt received the almost nineteen million dollars and eventually, got married in Florence, with Don Rodolfo Giammarco's blessing.

I figured out that she had her personal agenda during our Florence trip together, and I was spot-on. She planned to assist the Firenze Mafia, Don Giammarco, Hildebrandt, and Claudia in finding those paintings.

While I was repeatedly saying the "F" word under my breath, it was now time to unveil the prospective Renaissance masterpiece. They introduced it as an 'elusive' masterpiece that was painted by a famous artist from Florence at the time of his painting this valuable work of art.

I couldn't believe it. I suddenly broke into a cold sweat, immediately suspecting which picture was about to be revealed.

It had been rumored that the Detroit airport heist of this painting was the work of the Firenze Mafia. Don Giammarco realized, after the death of his beloved nephew, that if he couldn't have the Uffizi art collection, he was not about to let the Vatican and the Pope Emeritus have it either.

I later discovered that Veronica received this painting as a wedding gift from her uncle when the two were married in Florence over a year ago. Don Giammarco must have allowed her and her new husband to have the 'jinxed' painting and to keep the almost nineteen million-dollar proceeds from the sale of the art collection to Quito. This was Giammarco's ransom reward to Hildebrandt, for finally killing off Iannucci.

But Veronica must have later been informed of the Uffizi art collection's 'curse,' which was probably part of her motivation for donating this elusive artwork to Loyola.

My heart dropped down to my stomach, as the black velvet cover was pulled off, and this 'elusive painting' was finally unveiled:

It was the "Demons of Divine Wrath."

After the presentation and resounding applause from all of the garden party guests, the waiters were passing out champagne flutes, filled with expensive Dom Perignon. Then the party host, "Daniella Halsted," made a special toast on the new art display at the Loyola Art Museum.

"Our congratulations to Loyola, and the addition of this new masterpiece to their extensive art collection. May it be enjoyed by all Loyola students and the Chicagoland community," she said.

For some unknown reason, I saved the contents of my champaign flute glass. While 'Ozzie and Fucking Harriet' were standing in front of the podium stage, smiling and comingling with the other guests, I stepped up to the platform and approached the Fra Lippi painting.

I stared at that Renaissance masterpiece for several long minutes. The painted figures of Saint Michael the Archangel slaying all the emerging demons and devils from hell seemed to be such complete, vulgar hypocrisy.

With the circumstance of where and how this painting was acquired and what so many 'demons' have done to acquire this painting, I was disgusted. That unveiled painting was the product of an incredible amount of bloodshed and greed.

Standing there, I realized how many people were violently murdered with the discovery of those Uffizi paintings. Ever since their incredible finding in that old man's musty apartment in Munich, it repulsed me to realize all of the blood that was spilled on behalf of this priceless Fra Lippi masterpiece.

I glanced at Veronica and her new husband, and the sight of them revolted me. I became sickened and disgusted. At that moment, I decided to do something that I had never done before in public:

I decided to call them out.

As I approached the microphone, I noticed that Veronica immediately recognized me and looked as though she was about to go into a very mild state of shock.

"Ladies and Gentlemen, could I have your attention, please," as I made sure the microphone was on.

"My name is Paul Crawford, and I'm a reporter for the Chicago Sun-Times," I started my speech.

"I would like to congratulate Mr. and Mrs. Gary Halsted, alias Gerhard Hildebrandt of the Munich Police Department and his lovely wife, Veronica Daniella Giancarlo, the beautiful niece of the infamous mafioso, Rodolfo Giammarco. As many of you may have heard, that crime family is the notorious 'Firenze Mafia' from Florence Italy," I loudly said over the microphone.

Veronica's eyes were now bulging out of her eye sockets.

"There is some recent history associated with this painting. This elusive Fra Lippi masterpiece was part of the rediscovered Uffizi art collection in Munich two years ago. A lot of people have since died for this painting. There were Jews in Florence during the Second World War, whose lives were traded for forty-one other paintings just like this one. There has been a considerable amount of bloodshed spilled between Chicago's Marchese Family, the Vatican's victims, and the Firenze Mafia, of which, I suspect, Mrs. Halsted is very much a part of," I announced.

"These two very lovely con-artists have caused or spilled a significant amount of blood for their beautiful mansion here on the lakefront and this donated painting to Loyola. These two international villains now wish to be esteemed members of your community," I loudly continued.

"My sincerest congratulations to the 'Halsted's,' on assisting the underworld in eluting the authorities in the theft of this and other paintings in Europe, South America, and here in the United States. They have now settled amongst all of you affluent residents here in Lake

483

Forest. I'm sure that these two criminal frauds will be an excellent addition to your town,"

I finally said with a smile as I held up my champaign glass.

I looked over to Chaz Rizzo, who was smiling from ear to ear. I then finished my champaign while looking over at their direction. I could tell that the 'Halsted's' were utterly paralyzed and in a total state of disbelief. The silence from the two hundred or more garden party guests was deafening as everyone's eyes were now suddenly fixated on me. I then threw my empty champaign glass out towards the water of Lake Michigan.

Looking over at the two of them straight in the eyes, I coolly said over the microphone, an old phrase that I had learned from my Italian mother when I was growing up a long time ago:

"Non credere a tutto quello che senti, e solo la metà di quello che vedi."

I then translated, "Don't believe anything you hear and only half of what you see."

"Congratulazione," I smiled.

And then, I calmly walked away.